The White Huntress of Africa

Rolf Ackermann

The White Huntress of Africa

Biographic Novel about the legendary Margarete Trappe
on her farm Momella at the Kilimanjaro

Bibliographic information of the German Library:
The German Library catalogues this publication in the German National Bibliography; detailed bibliographic information can be found on the Internet website: http://dnb.ddb.de.

© 2021 Belletris-Verlag, Frankfurt am Main

This book was previously released by Knaur Taschenbuch in 2006 in German language under the title: „Die weiße Jägerin". Copyright of the first edition 2005 Droemersche Verlagsanstalt Th. Knaur Nachf. GmbH & Co. KG, Munich.

Belletris-Verlag
Tamara Pirschalawa
Oswaltstraße 7
60439 Frankfurt
www.belletris-verlag.de

Translation: Bettina Blandin
Editing, setting and cover design: Tamara Pirschalawa
Cover picture: Rudolf Hellgrewe – Brockhaus Kleines Konversations-Lexikon (5. Auflage 1911), source: www.zeno.org – Zenodot Verlagsgesellschaft mbH.

ISBN: 978-3-940808-24-0

Chapter 1

„When elephants fight, it is the grass that suffers "

Julius Nyerere
(former Tanzanian President)

The last sun rays made *Ol Doinyo le Engai* radiate with sublime beauty and set the East African steppes to Caspar David Friedrich's pastel colours. The country was vast, beautiful, and ever so peaceful. Small creeks were winding through the vast expanse like matt glossy asps with blue striped backs. Mountains with magic names surrounded the lowlands. The volcano, worshipped by the Maasai people as „Mountain of God", was reaching up to the evening sky like a natural alter constructed by powerful hands. On the horizon, enormous cumulus clouds gathered to form an approaching thunderstorm, like mountains made of light and shadow. Hundreds of thousands of zebras, wildebeests and antelopes remained tense with expectation at the riverside.

Engai, the Maasai's God, let an incandescent ball of lightning roll over the land up to *his* mountain, as if he wanted to point out its perfect beauty. The sound of the clap coming along with it echoed along the sides of the volcano. All the animals were awestruck. The children under the acacia tree standing in the middle of the Maasai steppe huddled closer together. They looked anxiously at the older man sitting in front of them, his back turned towards the tree.
„These are the signs of our God *Engai*," said Masiani ole Chieni. Dwelling on prestige, the older adult with the sheared head looked at the group of children sitting on the ground, not daring to look in their elder's eyes. Their *Laibon*, the most estimated elder, had only one eye since birth. The children were not the only ones to be frightened of its gaze.

Suddenly, the tranquil meeting under the tree was interrupted by a scream from the nearby Manyatta. A cry which carried death: painful, quite short but cruel.

The children stared at the cottages of the nearest Manyatta. They knew that Nasira, the youngest wife of the warrior Mojo ole Chieni was expecting a baby. The children quickly jumped to their feet and started running.

Masiani ole Chieni took a deep breath. He was the tribal elder and thus their *Laibon*, spiritual leader, fortune teller, ritual expert, and healer. Despite the scream, he kept sitting motionlessly under the acacia. Nasira, the woman who had just yelled, was his daughter-in-law, his son Mojo's wife. Nevertheless, the older man stayed seated and did not pay any attention to the audible excitement. Instead, he stared fixedly at some faraway point in the sky, where clouds were sinisterly announcing an upcoming storm. His eye had a strange glare.

„Olasera ingumok, the richly coloured one, spoke to me from far away,“ murmured the old man. He bowed reverently to something he thought to see in some strange constellation of clouds and colours in the sky and replied: „Engai tajapaki tooinaipuko inono – God, surround me with your protection!“ Next, he went to the cottages. His son Mojo met him halfway.

„Father, Nasira, the most beautiful and awed of my wives, gave me a son before embarking the peaceful path to *Engai*.“

„I know, my son. I know! The colourful one talked to me. He just showed up in the sky in a touch of light pink similar to the colour of a young flamingo, and had a bald eagle speed down from the sky to bring a message to us. Mojo, go and summon the elders together. You should also join us, as you will, later on take over my role as *Laibon* providing wisdom and advice to the people of our tribe. We need to confer because *Engai* sent us signs which, because of our minds being as small as ants, we cannot understand and therefore have to interpret."

Half an hour later, the Maasai tribes' elders came together on a hill near the river. The moon hid anxiously behind a frighteningly colossal rain cloud which hovered over the mountain Ol Doinyo le Engai. Gusts of wind wrenched at the capes of the gathered men.
One of the elders predicted, „This storm brings evil along with it," and resumed, „The wind is in a state of turmoil, the sky's clouds distort into grimaces and the animals down along the riverside are bleating and roaring as loud and fearfully as they usually do before getting together for the big migration to the lush pastures in the North of the country. But the time to migrate has not yet come. Hence, I know that big happenings will occur, may they be positive or catastrophic. Let's carry out an *Engidong*, so that our ancestors may enlighten us to interpret Engai correctly."
The men unrolled a dry cow skin on the ground and dug out of small leather bags some river stones which had become ground smoothed over the years.
The *Laibon* Masiani ole Chieni murmured mystical words while he let the stones roll over the cow skin time and again. He counted them, assessed their colour nuances until after more than one hour late, he left them in a constellation that seemed meaningful to him. Next, he predicted: „Today's death of Nasira, my son Mojo's wife and the child having come to life from her grave will will spawn a new *Laibon* for the tribe of the Matapato-Maasai."
„That is how it should be," the men commented on the elder's words unanimously.
„However, I also see a terrifying white shadow with eyes made of glass and silky, dark hair scurrying over the land and the Maasai tribe. The shadow will keep on accompanying our new-born *Laibon*

forever, just like the day always follows the night and will talk to him in a language of words sounding strange to me."

The men murmured again, „That is how it should be."

„But fear will keep dwelling in my old heart from now on, as I also see a huge iron snake whose black tongue is spitting fire and smoke. It will spread pain, distress, and discord over the planes, hills, and mountains, over the cattle breeding Maasai people."

Once again, the men mumbled, „That is how it should be." The prophecies of their *Laibon* alarmed them. They did not understand the meaning of the prophecy, but they felt that it boded no good whatsoever for the future of their tribe. All at once there were lightnings in the night. The deafening sound of the thunder rolling between the mountains filled the plane. And then, triggered by a powerful gust of wind, it happened: The animals which had been resting on the grassy fields along the river started moving. Hundreds of thousands of black wildebeests, zebras, and antelopes bleated in fear of the night, the roaring thunderstorm and the lightning staccato. The earth began to tremble, clouds of dust hid the stars, and Africa quaked as the enormous herds galloped away.

„The big animal migration has started," one of the Maasai elders shouted against the storm. Masiani ole Chieni, their *Laibon,* remained standing beside a rock and stared into the darkness. He could not see anything, only hear it. However, he sensed what was occurring in the valley below. „No," he screamed against the wind. „They don't migrate. They are escaping! They are leaving this place because they feel that something sinister will happen . . ."

Chapter 2

Around midnight, the slender woman sat at her desk surveying the letter lying in front of her. Her hair was artistically plaited with glass beads. It was sticky and hot in the cramped four-room apartment in Potsdamer Straße near the Botanical Gardens of Berlin.

The unbearable summer heat had been descending on the city for weeks. It almost didn't cool down during the night. Two silver framed steel engravings hung on the wall next to the desk. The larger one showed a seemingly gentle Arabic man in a white caftan, holding a golden decorated curved dagger in his hand. The other picture showed a palm-fringed palace with several sailing ships anchoring in the harbour in front of the castle.

The woman at the desk was barely older than forty. Nevertheless, the gentle face with Arabic facial features, accentuated by small dimples, already showed wrinkles of grief. Tears ran down her cheeks. She pulled a cloth out of the sleeve of her dress and dabbed the tears away. Then she took some deep breaths. This letter addressed to the German emperor would decide her future. It would be her last attempt to influence the seemingly inevitable destiny. Was she going to succeed? Or would the emperor Wilhelm I view her request as audacious and brash or even as arrogant? Thus, nothing she expected from the German emperor was daring. All she asked for was justice. It was German law. She reread the letter:

Berlin, June 14th, 1884

To His Majesty, Emperor Wilhelm I

– by courier –

As your noble Majesty will undoubtedly have gained knowledge about in the meantime, I reverently addressed my concern to his Excellency the German Reich Chancellor, Fürst Otto von Bismarck-Schönhausen. His Excellency, the German Reichskanzler, unfortunately, rejected my subservient request for an audience and to support the claims I raise against the Sultan of Zanzibar. Supported by the hope for justice, I will take the liberty to beg your Majesty, as emperor and supreme commander of the army of the German Reich, imploringly to appreciate my case.

May your Excellency, motivated by your natural kindness, allow me to begin with some personal lines before getting to the rather judicial aspects, related to the law of succession, of my subsequent statements. Just as the day may neither exist nor be explained without the night, good without evil nor passion without pain, my ordeal cannot be understood without previous knowledge regarding the power of love.

The beautiful but also painful experience taught me that love is not an ideal but a longing. It was this very longing which led me – by the hand of my beloved – leave my distant homeland and come to Germany where I became a most humble citizen of the German Reich and a confessed Christian.

However, love is also ecstasy, rapture and often means repeal and ignorance of the social rules. Such a love made me and my late husband and kind father of our children, may God be merciful to his soft soul, do what the providence made us do. For God is my witness that our actions arose from limitless purity and innocence. This love could only be fulfilled by renouncing my former faith as a Muslim and becoming a devout Christian, to be a worthy wife for my husband and mother for our children, also educated in the Christian faith. Thus, the yoke of punishment and injustice that burdens me and my children seems humiliating and its cruelty intolerable to me. God already snatched our beloved husband and father away from me and the children. His punishment turns out to be a never-ending martyrdom, the Sultan's refusal to grant me the legal rights to the hereditary title, increases the suffering in my soul, caused by the fear of poverty, to unbearable heights. Nevertheless, I have a breath of hope that with the help of Your Majesty, justice will be brought to me, and my inheritance claim will be certified, and be it only to assure an unclouded, happy future for my children.

Your Majesty will discover from the attached inventory of my late siblings (and their fortunes) which I am to inherit by law, that an amount of 400,000 to 500,000 Reichsmark is not presumptuous at all.

In this helplessness and despair of mine, I mercifully crave the support of Your Majesty, as in my former homeland Zanzibar, only a law represented by imposing warships is considered as convincing. My previous attempts to have justice done to my legitimate claims against my half-brother, Sayyid Barghash ibn Sa'id, sovereign and Sultan of Oman and Zanzibar, failed miserably. I reverently request Your Excellency to grant protection to my three children and me during my next journey to East Africa through a German warship to assert my claim against the Sultan of Zanzibar vehemently.

Sustained by the hope of a mother to secure her children's future and in the firm belief in the justice and benevolence of Your Excellency the German emperor, I remain in humble expectation of your highly estimated reply

Your loyal subject,
Sayyida Salima bint Sa'id bin Ahmad Al Bu-Sa'id
Princess Salme of Oman and Zanzibar,
Mother of Antonie, Rudolph-Said and Rosalie,
widowed Emily Ruete.

*

The men at the entrance door were nervous. The Chancellor of the German Reich, Prince Otto von Bismarck, was expecting them for an audience. That very morning, he had given a passionate speech in the Reichstag about the commitment of the German Reich in Africa. This speech, the five men had witnessed from the stands, had caused trouble and rioting in the hall.

Lost in thoughts, Otto von Bismarck was standing in front of an oversized map of Africa. As the delegation stepped in, he turned around and approached a small slim man with nickel spectacles. „Doctor Peters, it's a pleasure to meet you again. How are you? What about your ambitious Africa plans?"
„May I express my great respect, Excellency! Your speech was inspiring!" the narrow-chested man in the black frock welcomed him. „I want to thank you so much for having granted us this audience today! Regarding Africa, everything is happening according to plan, Mr. Reichskanzler. We have begun the founding of the ‚Gesellschaft für Kolonisation' (Association for Colonisation), and hope to have it registered at the Commercial Registry in Berlin by October this year at the very latest. As things currently stand, we will probably set out on an expedition to East Africa no later than October. May I first introduce some of my partners and fellow campaigners to your Excellency? You certainly already know Chamberlain and landowner Earl Joachim von Pfeil und Klein-Ellguth."
The Reich Chancellor smiled jovially. „Of course, Earl von Pfeil is well-known to me! Some years ago, I read his informative descriptions of South Africa with great interest," he replied and looked respectfully at the handsome man with an exceptionally huge forehead.
„The gentleman on my left is Dr Karl Jühlke, a lawyer by profession. It is a great honour for me to present Kommerzialrat Dr Becker to you. You certainly know his private bank, which declared their willingness to finance our undertakings in East Africa. And Your Excellency will have noticed the young age of this man who nevertheless is unusually skilled: Dr Alfred Zehe from Silesia. His family

12

owns an estate near Sagan. The young man is an excellent geographer, and his profound knowledge will undoubtedly make a decisive contribution to the success of our expedition."

Prince Bismarck shook hands with the five men. He remained for a short time in front of the young geographer Alfred Zehe and looked into the eyes of the tall man, saying, „As you know from my speech to the Reichstag, dear Dr Peters, opportunities are quite good for men like you now. We need courageous German undertakers who are willing to take a risk and found commercial establishments autonomously overseas. For Germany, East Africa is not only an exciting objective in the economic plan. I want to be quite open: What interests me about Africa, gentlemen, are the English and the French! The English are well underway to controlling the complete East African trade from Zanzibar, as well as the sea routes to India and Arabia. The maritime domination of the British is beginning to take on frightening dimensions. And if we do not succeed in opposing the superiority of the British naval forces, we have to find other ways for the German Reich to also get a slice of the African cake."

The Reich Chancellor abruptly turned away from the map of Africa and looked at Dr Carl Peters, who stared at the plan with glancing eyes.

„Gentlemen, let's avoid any ambiguity: Whatever you intend to do in Zanzibar and on the East African mainland, you do as private individuals, as German traders. You are acting with autonomy! I know that land acquisition in East Africa it is straightforward. You can get a document with some nigger's crosses on it in exchange of some shotguns and glass beads. But whatever you do, keep in mind that you are not to cause a lasting disruption to the current amicable relationship with the Sultan of Zanzibar, with the English and French as well. Starting an argument with the Sultan will offend the English and French."

The Reich Chancellor Prince Otto von Bismarck pulled out his pocket watch demonstratively. It was just before noon.

„Gentlemen, please comprehend that I have to end our conversation. I still have some other appointments which, to be honest, also are related to Africa unfortunately. It is quite strange. The world seems to orbit exclusively around Africa . . ."

After three hours on a train, the young Earl Alfred Zehe changed in Hansdorf, Lower Silesia, on to another train heading for Sagan. He was very stirred-up. After the enthusiastic feeling caused by the private audience with the Reich Chancellor Prince Otto von Bismarck at the Reichtstag, his euphoria gave way to an oppressive air. As the capital of the eponymous principality appeared on the horizon, he noticed that he had sweaty palms. He was afraid, afraid indeed, afraid – of his father!

By chance, a locomotive to Glogau stood on the sidetrack in front of the brickwork building of Sagan station. He could have reached Buchwald station near the paternal manor in some minutes' traveling time. He decided, however, to get off the train in Sagan. He griped to a coachman, „To the guesthouse Walfisch", and boarded one of the waiting cabbies.

Some minutes later, the carriage turned after the barracks of the Podielsky 5th field artillery regiment, shining dark red in the afternoon sun, onto Bahnhofstraße. Instead of going directly to the pub, he strolled down to the Bober riverside and sat on a bank below the Kaiser-Wilhelm bridge. He felt miserable, and his head was aching. Several young couples walked along the riverbank. They stared perplexed at the young man in the black frock coat and the cylinder as he scratched the outline of Africa into the sand with his mirror-polished shoes.

*

At the same time, the Reich Chancellor Prince Otto von Bismarck entered again the room on the first floor of the Reichstag building in which he had received Dr Carl Peters earlier that afternoon. Two gentlemen, in marine officer uniforms were awaiting him. Both men were standing in front of the map of Africa. When the Reich Chancellor approached, they turned to face him.

14

„Vice-Admiral von Caprivi, I am pleased that you honoured my request for a personal conversation so quickly."
The man aged about fifty with a bushy white moustache saluted Prince von Bismarck nonchalantly and tucked his peaked cap under the arm.
„Mr. Reich Chancellor, may I introduce you to Captain Herbig, one of our most talented officers for delicate military missions; he has been an active Officer for the military Intelligence of the Admiralty for quite some time and has already gained experience in German Southwest Africa. He is the right man for your issue."
Prince Bismarck reached his hand out to the man dressed in the white marine uniform. He unconsciously noticed the officer's firm handshake and self-confident look. Slowly, he strolled to the African map on the wall.
„Gentlemen, I had a short conversation with D. Carl Peters and some of his business partners at noon. I would like to speak most frankly: Peters is a dangerous fool! Nevertheless, I think that Peters and his associates might be very helpful to us soon, with their megalomaniac ideas without even being aware of it. But I don't want to anticipate you, Admiral. I had asked you to gather valuable information about Dr Peters, as until now, I only know that he seemingly wants to incorporate the whole of Africa into the German Reich. Who is Peters? Is he just megalomaniacal?"
„May I suggest, Mr. Reich Chancellor, not to underestimate megalomaniacal people. Even less when they succeed in raising enthusiasm for their projects amongst other men, who are at least as megalomaniacal as they themselves are. Mr. Herbig informed himself and also called upon our intelligence to find out what Peters really wants. Please, Captain Herbig, go ahead."

Bismarck listened very intently to Herbig's precise explanations. Dr Peters seemed to have been impressed by the idea of German colonisation in Africa for a very long time. His passionate commitment finally led to the foundation of the „Deutsche Gesellschaft für Kolonisation" he had reported to Bismarck about during the audience.

A quarter of an hour later, Captain Herbig closed his file and looked expectantly at Prince Bismarck.

„Your dossier is excellent, brilliant, Captain Herbig!" murmured Prince Bismarck. „It is first-class work! Knowledge is power, as the saying goes, and I think we should use our knowledge very carefully." Bismarck turned around and approached the two officers. He smoothed his moustache thoughtfully with his left hand, then stopped abruptly at the big table and pointed to the second file the intelligence officer had brought along.

„Is this your dossier about the princess, what was her name?"

„Princess Salme of Oman and Zanzibar respectively Emily Ruete," the secret service agent came to the aid of his Reich Chancellor.

„This woman, this mysterious princess, has really got admirable moral courage. First, she writes me a soul-stirring letter. As soon as she gets my answer that I, unfortunately, do not see any possibility to help her, she begs her Majesty, the German emperor, personally! She asks for neither legal assistance nor financial support. No, she sends a messenger to the emperor and asks for a battleship! She wants a warship! It is incredible! An Arabic-African princess asks her Majesty the German emperor for a battleship so she might frighten her brother, the Sultan of Zanzibar, to make him pay out a fortune to her!"

The Reich Chancellor approached the map of Africa again, tapped with his index finger on an island in front of the East African mainland, and said quietly: „Zanzibar, gentlemen! For some weeks, everything in this house suddenly revolves around Zanzibar. The English would like to change it to a protectorate. The French are vying for the favour of the Sultan of Zanzibar. Furthermore, Dr Carl Peters, with his colonial association, wants to make the Sultan sell tracts of his lands on the African mainland to him. To top it all, there is this princess who asserts that part of Zanzibar belongs to her. All these happenings are simply absurd, aren't they Captain Herbig?"

„Your Excellency, the fact of the matter is: After having both the English foreign office, and the English war ministry, review the case of the princess mentioned above, thoroughly, they concluded that

Princess Salme of Oman and Zanzibar's claims against the Sultan of Zanzibar are barely legally justifiable."

Prince Bismarck gave the secret service agent a questioning look. „So, how do you judge the legal situation?"

„Well, Mr. Reich Chancellor, being nevertheless the Sultan of Oman and Zanzibar's bodily daughter, the princess, might, in principle, have some considerable hereditary titles. Yet the fact is that due to her hurried flight from Zanzibar and her conversion from Islam to Christianity, it is outside of her former country's law. Thus, she should not expect more than the Sultan's benevolence. Unless . . ."

„Unless what?" Bismarck seemed to be irritated.

„Well, Vice-Admiral von Caprivi had an idea. To be honest, it seems brilliant to me."

The Reich Chancellor's nervously shifted his focus between the two officers.

„What kind of an idea is it, Admiral von Caprivi?" he asked.

The Admiral coughed slightly and pulled some documents out of the file. „Following the Islamic law, the applicable Zanzibar legislation, a woman cannot claim any power at all resulting from a hereditary title. But: The princess has a son of legal age named Rudolph-Said. His father is a German citizen – and an officer of the German Reich as he completed the military academy in Bensberg near Cologne. His mother, thus the princess, is the Sultan's sister."

Bismarck interrupted the Vice-Admiral. „You are not talking seriously, Admiral? What you have in mind, my dear Caprivi, would be a coup d'état! The most crazy one ever!"

The Reich Chancellor started to walk restlessly up and down the room. „I recapitulate: You want to make this German son of our princess, this German officer with Zanzibar blood, a Sultan and her a Sultan's mother – and thus practically found a German-Zanzibarian dynasty? Is this correct?"

„Yes your Excellency, I would consider that!"

„Admiral, your intentions are laudable, but this is insane! This leads to war with the English and the French at the same time in fact! The idea is just absurd!"

The Reich Chancellor kept quiet for a long time, shook his head slightly, then talked as low as if he were afraid some stranger might hear what he said: „No gentlemen, we cannot proceed this way. However, I have a vague idea of how it might work . . .“

After more than one hour of heated debating, the Reich Chancellor signalled that he had come to a decision.
„Dear Caprivi, kindly inform me about the availability of a German warship for a journey to Zanzibar with this princess – and how many additional warships would be available to accompany it. Captain Herbig, please get ready for departure. You are assigned to leave with immediate effect. Your trip to Zanzibar and East Africa is a state secret! You travel officially as a private person. I expect your detailed report about the defensive capacity of Zanzibar in three months’ time at the very latest. I want to know how this island is secured and every single detail about how the towns on the African mainland, belonging to the sultanate, are equipped militarily speaking. I also want to have a good idea about how many armed forces and ships the English and French might be able to gather in the East African area in a rush. And now, gentlemen, I apologise for having to reflect.“

*

At the same time, Alfred Zehe covered the few kilometres from Sagan to the manor in a cab. He was a bit drunk. He came from a heavy drinking session with a couple of friends he had met in the „Walfisch”. The sun was low on the horizon over the hills and birch woods of the Bober meadows. However, the romantic atmosphere of this June evening could not distract one from the small size and the few grains on the wheat ears. The scorching summer threatened to destroy the whole harvest. The son of the manor was already aware that the harvest year 1884 would again be a bad one. Behind the little village Deutsch-Machen, a few kilometres away from Sagan, the road wound up the flat hills through oak groves and vast meadows.

In the cab, he could hear the sound of cheerful people's laughter coming from the garden of the tavern „Prinz von Eugen" near the road not far from the domestic manor. The owner of the tavern, Otto Gringmuth, waved to him.

„Good evening, your excellency! Did you have a good time in Berlin? I don't want to worry you, but I think your mother is not well. The doctor came by at full gallop two hours ago . . ."

As soon as the wooden church tower of the Petersdorf Augustinuskirche came into sight, the coachman slowed down and turned to the right behind a forest. Petersdorf manor was situated almost 100 metres from the road, hidden under majestic chestnut and oak trees. The property consisted of the central white house with the classicistic portal at the right side of the access road, the estate manager's residential building on the opposite side and the storehouses, horse stables and cattle sheds built in the direction of the meadows, followed by the servants' quarters in some distance. The cab stopped in front of the two-story building. Three dogs came along, wagging their tales and welcoming the young squire. It was only at the last moment when Alfred Zehe noticed his father sitting in the evening twilight in front of the fountain under the trees, smoking a pipe.

„Good evening," he said and approached his father.

„You are late! The train passed four hours ago!" was all Karl Zehe said. The lean man with sparse hair stared at the fields behind the estate stretching as far as the eye could see.

„I had something to take care of in Sagan," Alfred Zehe lied. He had the impression that his father was quite pensative.

„Your mother is not well," Karl Zehe murmured and stuck a wood shaving in the pipe embers. „The doctor has been with her for hours, but he cannot do a lot against her pain. At her age, childbirth is very risky."

„But it is much too early for confinement," Alfred Zehe answered and sat down on the stony spring fringe beside his father.

„The child should only come into the world in seven weeks. God will fix it. But for now, tell me about Berlin." His father's words almost sounded like an order.

„I met Dr Peters there, father."

„Peters? Who is he?"

„It was you, father, who introduced me to him to me in March at the Conservative Club in Berlin, at the conference about the colonisation in Africa."

„I see, this man whom newspapers start to quote, who delivers excellent speeches about the colonisation! I remember. What dealings do you have with him?"

„I contacted Dr Peters two months ago as I had read that he was looking for young geographers as scientific companions for his expeditions in Africa."

„You want to go away from here, leave Petersdorf manor, leave your Silesian homeland?" Karl Zehe spoke very calmly.

„Yes, father. Don't misunderstand . . ." Alfred Zehe wanted to explain his reasons to him. However, his father interrupted him.

„Africa is supposed to be very beautiful, with excellent hunting opportunities. And they say that there are plenty of fertile lands. It is the right decision indeed to go to Africa. You are a brilliant young man. Sending you to the university was one of the best decisions I made in my life. I don't know what you intend to do in Africa, but it is good to go. Go with God's blessing, my son. A young man like you has a better future anywhere else than in this country, on this farm. Everything is dying here. The Sagan duke's rent collector came along at noon and set a time limit for me. The noblemen are bloodsuckers. They blithely disregard whether the harvest is good or bad. If you cannot pay the rent, they take your last savings away from you. No, my son, there is no future for you and your sisters Frieda and Tine on this manor, which was already farmed by my great-grandfather."

Karl Zehe took several deep breaths. Suddenly he laid his arm around his son, stayed silent for some minutes, and then abruptly rose.

„Furthermore, I know very well that you would never be a good landlord. You love nature and faraway countries. You are very sensitive and freedom-loving. To manage a manor, one must be a mas-

ter: strict, rigid, and severe. Even to oneself. But you are not of this nature and you will never be. Perhaps that is a good thing."
The Nobleman walked around the fountain thoughtfully.
„Let me know tomorrow when you are leaving and how I might help you. I might also go to Africa one day. And then we will go hunting together . . ."
All at once, a yell interrupted the silence. The men both looked in a panic to the window of the main house's second floor, where the mother was in birth pains. They simultaneously rushed to the house.
„Martha!" Karl Zehe, the lord of the manor, shouted: „Martha . . . !"

Chapter 3

Never before had Alfred Zehe felt as happy and pleased as he did on this November day. His life had taken such a decisive turn during the last months that he still could not believe it, sometimes he even had the feeling that he was living in a fairy tale of the 1001 nights.

The man aged twenty-three sat on the deck of a small dhow with a khaki lateen sail, sliding out of the Port of Zanzibar into the Indian Ocean. A muscular Arab with a bald head and a wide garment stood at the rudder of the ship. The sail was being reaped by a black African with an impressive biceps, wearing a loincloth.

The ship rapidly gathered pace on the open sea and slid past the lighthouse of the coral island Chumbe. Soon, the sultan's palace on the hill and the Arabic fortress were no more than silhouettes. In his hands, he held a letter from his father which had arrived by mail steamer from Germany at Zanzibar a few hours ago! The very first letter he had received ever since he had left his homeland three months ago. It was a strange but wonderful feeling to read from the beloved ones at home, being amid the Indian Ocean. With tears of joy in his eyes, he scrolled through the letter in the striking handwriting of his father and re-read the penultimate page:

. . . Your mother finally recovered quite well from the very exhausting birth of your new-born sister Margarete. Unfortunately, this years' October is very cold and rainy, so that your mother cannot take the baby carriage into the garden very often. This year 1884 has brought us some unusual weather capers. First, a never-ending heat, leading to another lousy harvest. And now the autumn spoiled by rain. The nanny has to take care of little Margarete in the house, and I can tell you that it is quite an exhausting task. The young worm is full of vim and vigour! She cries around the clock and only stops when being breastfed. In the beginning, we thought she was sick and had pain. However, the doctor said it is just a cute, very healthy child full of vitality.

Well, dear Alfred, although I am a little sad God gave us a girl again (you now have three sisters, dear Alfred), I am nevertheless proud of small Margarete crying so loud and vigorously. She is gradually getting beautiful dark hair! And I presume she will be charming later on. As long as she is in good health . . .

The young geographer grabbed a glass of port wine and dreamily closed his eyes. As smooth as a dhow in the waves of the Indian Ocean, his thoughts went back to the happenings of the last months. He remembered his father's surprising willingness to support his Africa plans. He had even given him money before his departure so he could purchase proper tropical equipment and new hunting rifles. On August 3rd, after lots of pain, Mother had given birth to a healthy daughter. Although his father was happy about the uncomplicated childbirth, he did not conceal the fact that he would have preferred a late-born son. For now, he had three daughters: Tine, Frieda, and little Margarete. Alfred Zehe reached for a notepad. The slight monsoon wind made the sail flap and blew through his hair. He appreciated the eternalise blowing winds on Zanzibar. *Kuzi* and *Khazkazi* were the names the indigenous people had given to these airstreams, blowing alternately from northwest or southwest and making the ships drift between India, Arabia and the East African coast throughout the centuries, contributing a lot, in that way, to Zanzibar's wealth. „*Ninataka Bira na chakula,*" he shouted to the young African at the sail who thereupon brought him a beer and the prepared picnic. He was proud of his ability to communicate a little bit in Swahili after such a short time. „*Asante,*" he thanked the boy, bit into a delicious mango fruit with pleasure and began to write a letter to his parents in Petersdorf.

Zanzibar, November 5th, 1884

Dear Father, dear Mother,
I can imagine the great excitement this letter with all its beautiful and exotic stamps from Africa, will cause in the empires post office

of Sagan. Soon, when I leave this island to go forth on an expedition upon the African mainland, you will probably not hear from me for a long time. Should you write back, please be aware that your letters take a long time to reach me. In very urgent cases, you may send a telegram to the German consulate in Zanzibar, to the attention of Reichskonsul Gerhard Rohlfs. By the way, his spouse was on the same ship. The sea voyage from Genoa across the Mediterranean Sea to Egypt was terrific.

In Alexandria, a man got on who has kept us preoccupied ever since. He is a retired Captain who was dishonourably discharged from the German Navy some weeks ago. The reason is unknown to me. But somehow, it has to do with the fact that he was in German South West Africa a while ago. He is now traveling to East Africa at the order of German bankers to investigate lucrative trade opportunities. This is very interesting for Dr Peters. The name of the retired Captain is Jürgen Herbig; he is quite a grumpy person. I don't appreciate him a lot as he behaves arrogantly and has many prejudices about English and French.

The train journey to Suez was quite comfortable indeed as the train starts directly at the harbour, so no problem having our luggage reloaded. However, I can tell you that the railcars were just awful! We were eight people sitting in one compartment – with all this hand luggage! When we arrived in Suez, the local Consul was already awaiting us. Mr. Rohlfs had arranged it because of his wife. By the way, she is a brilliant lady and is traveling alone to Zanzibar on our ship. As she told us, her husband is still onboard a German Marine ship in South Africa. He should, however, come to Zanzibar shortly after our arrival. We had no problems at all reloading our boxes on board the steamboat of the British P.a.O.-line.
This ocean steamer was very comfortable, indeed! I had a very cosy cabin of my own and enjoyed the journey to Aden very much! I was incredibly impressed by the onboard life. Passionate things happen all day long on such a ship, and one meets people that have travel-

led a great deal. You know that at 6:00 a.m., a steward is already serving tea in bed. One has lots of time to rest and enjoy the start of the day. They serve breakfast at 8:00 a.m., a real social event amongst English, as it consists of a complete meal of warm food.

We can still enjoy the splendid backdrop of the Red Sea coasts and can read for a while before lunch. It only consists of cold dishes with lots of salad and fruit, but it's very tasty and benefitted my stomach, which was quite strained from the long journey. The peaceful afternoon is interrupted at 4:00 p.m. by teatime, this is followed by the main meal, the dinner. During the first days, I felt very out of place. I was not accustomed to and had indeed not expected to dress up for dinner as if going to the Berlin opera. The few ladies onboard must have brought along huge boxes full of dresses, as every time I see them at either breakfast, lunch, teatime, or dinner they are always in different attire. English men are not better. In the morning, they already walk around in strange, multicoloured checkered light suits. They somehow appear to be elegant clowns! In the evening, everyone appears in full regalia.

It got increasingly warmer after two days at sea. Passing Sinai, we reached the infamous city of Aden. It is so incredibly hot there that all the ladies refused to disembark as they feared to get a heat stroke. I did, nevertheless. First, I was frightened by the indescribable chaos of the crowd in the harbour and the town, where thousands of half-naked negroes and Arabs dressed in fluttering gowns rushed around. During the two hours of our tour through Aden in a hackney carriage, we got the opportunity to have a look at the fascinating water reservoir. They harvest water in huge recipients and then channel it with tubes through the town. The city itself is not situated at the seaside but in a cirque where it gets so hot that I understand why they also call Aden „the hell".

I got even more excited when after one week, passing Lamu, we reached Mombasa. Africa! I assure you I could already feel and smell Africa a long time before we saw Mombasa appear on the horizon. Here amongst the tremendous equatorial heat, the humidity le-

vel is very high. The air is filled with fascinating scents, as if in a greenhouse. One transpires without even moving. We eventually reached Zanzibar, accompanied by dolphins and beautiful blue „flying fishes" doing huge jumps out of the water, looking like giant prehistorical birds with magnificent wings, flying long distances above the waters. The city of Zanzibar seems cosy and metropolitan and has eighty thousand inhabitants, among those five thousand Indians and five thousand Arabs. The remaining population consists of Swahilis and people of mixed origins. Our first walk through the town made us believe we were in some Oriental tale.

The traders in the dark shacks, as well as the women and children squatting in the background, were all Indians; it was teeming with black and lighter shades, all clothed in the long white shirts of the Swahili people. The brown girls flocking to us have curiously plaited hair, although it is quite short.

The city is built on a flat tongue of land and the last sandy tip is called Ras Shangani. The Sultan's palace overtowers the huddle of houses in the North: a square building, surrounded by porticos, faces the part of the road where the merchant ships lie at anchor. A high tower rises over the palace roof and a highly visible clock displays the Arabic time. Outbuildings and the harem connect to the right. A free space stretches from the palace to the sea, where the red Sultan's flag flies on a high mast during the day. It is brought down slowly and solemnly at 6:00 p.m. amidst the sound of a Goan orchestra, cannon shot sounds and the whole palace is illuminated with bright electrical light until 11:00 p.m. when the Sultan is present. Another lamp on a wireframe burns just as long, more than thirty metres high, standing to the left, which during the day serves to announce the arrival of the ships through flag signalisation. When the Sultan dwells in Zanzibar, the military band plays during the evening in front of the palace.

The most exciting things happen daily. Time and again, I meet interesting people from all over the world. The acquaintance of the German Consul, Mr. Rohlfs, is beneficial in this regard. I somehow feel that he does not appreciate Mr. Peters and the other gentlemen of the Deutsche Gesellschaft für Kolonisation a lot. Dr Peters is a very nationalistic thinking man who, I have come to believe, is ready to do anything to achieve his goal and I literally mean everything! It is, however, not up to me to judge his choice of tools.

For the time being, we are all living in a hotel with the promising name Grand Hôtel de l'Afrique Centrale, as there is a significant lack of houses with European standards. It is not as bad. And the meals are tasty. Despite all these exciting events, I feel a little home-sick for Petersdorf today. I think of you often and ask myself, what my little sister Margarete might look like at present.

Speaking of meals! We are all invited to attend a celebration tomor-row by the Sultan of Zanzibar. I will report more on this later on. In the meantime, I remain with you and my three sisters in thoughts. A very tender kiss to little Margarete!

With love, yours, Alfred

*

Unlike his wife Lonny, Gerhard Rohlfs did not appreciate festivities such as this reception by the sultan due to his arrival as the first German Consul in Zanzibar a bit.

„I don't like Dr Peters at all, Lonny! He speaks so disparagingly to the locals that I was about to discipline him. He is a member of the master race, one of the worst kind. And I don't know what to think about Captain Herbig either."

„Well, Gerhard," his wife tried to appease him, „you are taking all this way too seriously. They are businessmen searching for fortune here in Africa. Besides, there are some very nice men among them. The young earl von Pfeil is always very charming and gallant and this geographer from Silesia is a kind and well-educated young man."

„I'm not talking about them. But some suspicious individuals surround Peters. Believe me, Lonnie, they will cause us lots of trouble!"

„But it would insult the sultan if you did not invite even one of the Germans who are present here, Gerhard. You can't do this!"

Consul Gerhard Rohlfs was aware of it. However, he suspected that his assessment was correct. As the sultan had put hackney carriages at their disposal, the „German Armada", as Dr Carl Peters had instantly named the long carriage convoy and thus caused surprise not only to the German Consul, crossed the city. After 90 minutes of journey, the carriage convoy reached Chuini, the country house of Sultan Sayyid Barghash ibn Sa'id, whose carriage drawn by eight horses was already in the driveway. Twelve mounted guards in red uniforms were waiting in front of the carriage with the noble black Arabic horses and another twelve behind it. The simple, bright red flag of the sultanate of Zanzibar blew along the side of the main entry beside the flag of the German Empire. Minions of the Sovereign of Zanzibar guided the German guests directly into a hall, excessively decorated with mirrors and chandeliers. Lonny Rohlfs was very impressed.

„Look at this, Gerhard! Most beautiful French porcelain, those countless golden and silver bowls! He must be rich, this Sultan . . ."

„Rich?" whispered Gerhard Rohlfs. „No, he is the guardian of an incredible treasure, of a value which cannot adequately be measured by numbers!"

The festivities turned out to be a never-ending lunch. Mountains of roast goose, duck, foie gras, chicken, beef filet and ox tongue with beans as well as vegetable and pastry made most of the German guests groan. Some guests finally retired to the bathhouses of the sultan's palace. There, they recovered in the cold marble rooms from the straining meal. A small group of men assembled on the roof terrace, which offered a sublime view of the Indian Ocean. Among these the American Consul Cheney, the Belgian Consul van der Elst, the British General Consul Sir John Kirk. Also, Dr Peters and Captain Herbig, with his eternalise grumpy expression, had taken place on the damask cushions of the balcony. Gerhard Rohlfs, dressed in a white uniform, noticed this to his great annoyance.

Alfred Zehe was sitting next to the Captain, who was conversing animatedly with Anthimos, the twenty-year-old son of the Greek businessman Koundouriotis, who had been working in Paris up to now and come to Zanzibar to continue traveling on to Bombay from here. Alfred Zehe had gotten to know the Greek family at the reception of the French in Zanzibar and immediately got on well with Anthimos, who was almost the same age as him.

Some moments later, Sultan Barghash arrived and took seat in an armchair, escorted by two guards. The overweight man with a mischievous look and infallible signs of progressing elephantiasis wore a white garment under the black caftan, beaded with gold plated bands. The loose clothing hid his bulging stomach. His turban sat lopsidedly on his head. On the small finger of his right hand, he wore a gold diamond ring. The gem was of hazelnut size.

Consul Gerhard Rohlfs got up. To the amazement of those around him, he began his speech in fluent Arabic: „Your Excellency! In the name of the German emperor, Wilhelm I, and his imperial Chancellor Prince Otto von Bismarck, but also in the name of all present German subjects of his Majesty the German emperor, I thank you for the honour of being guests of the Sultan of Zanzibar at this successful celebration . . .“

Sultan Barghash did not hide his surprise about the German with the round eyeglass lenses speaking such good Arabic. He smiled benevolently at the somehow unhealthy-looking man from Germany. The English had forwarded information about Mr. Rohlfs to him through diplomatic channels, which left no doubt in his mind that this German Consul was a smart man fond of traveling and had excellent knowledge about Africa. In Europe, the son of a doctor had made a name for himself as an explorer, archaeologist, and writer. However, he was no diplomat. It was a complete mystery to him as well as the English, why the German emperor sent such an undiplomatic man to Zanzibar. Due to its excellent position in the Indian Ocean, the Europeans conceived the sultanate of Zanzibar as the ideal stepping-stone to the interior of the African continent. The sultan of Zanzibar had always known it.

„They all want Zanzibar," his father had reminded him during his lifetime and advised him to continuously seek friendship with all European powers, not only with the English. „You have to take the English with a pinch of salt," Sultan Barghash remembered the words of his late father, „they smile at you, help you to fight their own enemy – and secretly support the second enemy at your back." His father had advised him, and this knowledge had enabled him to strengthen his authority as the third Sultan of this island.

However, the German Consul's surprising appearance alarmed him as well as the English. Until now, the German Reich had shown almost no interest in Zanzibar. Apart from this unpleasant story about his sister, Princess Salme who made these crazy inheritance claims, there had never been any problems with the Germans. Over the course of the last few months, almost every ship had brought Germans to Zanzibar. Most of them were adventurers, ivory hunters, and merchants. But now the arrival of this German Consul Rohlfs, with such short notice and heralded by the German Reichs-Chancellor himself. Sultan Barghash said to himself, „no, . . ." with Gerhard Rohlfs closing words in his subconsciousness, „no, this is no coincidence!"

*

Dr Carl Peters, president of the Deutsche Gesellschaft für Kolonisation, believed it was pure coincidence when retired Captain Jürgen Herbig came onboard the ship to Zanzibar some weeks ago in Alexandria.

After a few days aboard the ship that the officer was traveling to Africa at the behest of a consortium of German investors and bankers to investigate the trade opportunities. As soon as he learned about this, he couldn't get the retired Captain of his mind. The outlook was not good for the finances of the Deutsche Gesellschaft für

Kolonisation. Captain Herbig and all the other members of the expedition had taken up lodgings at the Grand Hôtel de l'Afrique Centrale. Peters met the reportedly dishonourably discharged Captain of the German marines again two days after the reception at the Sultan's, around noon in the Hotel Foyer. It seemed to be a pure coincidence.

„Good morning, Captain," Dr Peters greeted his compatriot, who was wearing an elegant white suit, „Your outfit indicates that you have a promising plan!"

„No, my dear Dr Peters, I don't have a plan, I have already brought it to fruition!" Captain Herbig answered. „I had an audience with the Sultan. Unfortunately, it was not a very pleasant one!"

„Was the avaricious Arab in a bad mood today?" Carl Peters asked laughingly.

Jürgen Herbig pretended to be very peeved. „This silly prince charming is barely more than a vassal of London, a minion of the French," he answered in a brusque manner. „He is refusing to give me any authorization or letters of reference for an expedition into the interior of Africa. I am allowed to visit the coastal towns, but nothing else."

„The English are behind this," answered Dr Carl Peters and eventually saw his chance. „Why not just sit on the hotel terrace together, have a drink and share a meal, Captain?"

„I agree," Jürgen Herbig answered and triumphed in silence for having bated Peters on the very first occasion.

Both men went to the hotel garden and sat down at a table with an ocean view. Dr Peters determinedly came back to the issue.

„You, dear Captain, have the permission of the Sultan to visit the coastal towns. I have all the required reference letters allowing me to travel to the interior of the country – in fact, along both caravan routes up to the Kilimanjaro! Why not combine our interests?"

Carl Peters stared expectantly at the former marine officer. Jürgen Herbig knew what to say. He was aware that the president of this colonisation company was in desperate need of money. He answered in a seemingly reluctant manner: „I'm afraid my dear Dr Peters, I don't have any choice. Would you care to explain how you imagine putting this into practice? You should be aware of this: my customers have significant resources. They would not be content with a few enterprise shares of your limited partnership. They want power!"

„Captain, this is not an issue! You see, we are just starting our productive entrepreneurial activities in Africa. Partners are always welcome, be it investors, which means silent partners or active fellow combatants. Because . . ."

Jürgen Herbig interrupted his counterpart.

„I assume that my customers are exclusively interested in a silent partnership. A certain political thoughtfulness has to be applied; do you understand Dr Peters? These men are in highly exposed positions which do not let private interests in commercial establishments overseas appear as politically convenient."

Dr. Carl Peters felt he had to appease his conversation partner. „Of course, I understand, Captain. You can rely on my silence!"

After one hour, the men said goodbye. The very moment when the retired Captain Jürgen Herbig, a marine officer with a special mission of the German Reich Chancellor, left the hotel, he could see, from the corner of his eyes, Dr Carl Peters grinning almost triumphantly.

The president of the Deutsche Gesellschaft für Kolonisation, Carl Peters, was indeed delighted about the course of this conversation. He was now aware of not only having an additional capital of 100.000 Reichsmark at his disposal, but also excellent new political contacts to members of the government with the German Reich. On this hot November day, Dr Carl Peters told himself that his dream of the colonisation in Africa was beginning to come true . . .

*

On November 10th, the first day of their African expedition, Alfred Zehe already sensed how quick such dreams could turn to nightmares. Together with Dr Peters, Graf von Pfeil and Dr Jühlke, accompanied by thirty-six porters, six personal servants and two interpreters, he had crossed from Zanzibar to the African mainland. The landing with the three dhows near the small coastal town of Sadani almost turned into a total catastrophe. The sailing ships were utterly overloaded with the expedition equipment and could not reach the banks in the shallow coastal waters of the estuary areas of the river Wami. They had to anchor approximately one km away from the beach. The porters refused to carry more than one hundred boxes through the water up to the shore. They knew about the sharks in the Indian Ocean. The Africans only dragged the expedition equipment through the deep sea up to the beach once Carl Peters took out his gun, had one of the porters stand at the bow of a dhow, pointed the muzzle of the gun at his chest and threatened to shoot him down if the load was not on the shore before evening. It had happened three weeks ago.

Alfred Zehe had been ever so euphoric on that first evening beside the campfire in front of his tent, the romantic outdoor atmosphere of the Indian Ocean had fascinated him. But his excitement diminished every day that followed. All of them had difficulties withstanding the baking heat. The refreshing winds decreased only a few kilometres inland from the coast. Even the porters suffered from the extremely high humidity and the myriads of mosquitoes plaguing them at night. With great hardships, they eventually reached the valley of Mukondwa near the village of Kilossa, where the eponymous river flows into the river Mkata. They had learned in Zanzibar that the south-east heading valley was considered the gateway to the Usagara highland. When following the river, one reached the old caravan route to Tabora, on which slaves from the interior of Africa were still displaced to the coast and further to Arabia and Persia.

After almost one week's walk, they reached the villages Useguha, Ukami, and Unguu. During the negotiations with the local chiefs, Dr Carl Peters began to show his true colours. The happenings of November 19th, which ended with raising the German flag for the first time over an East African village, now emerged again after three weeks.

That evening, Alfred Zehe sat in his tent near a village in the Usagara mountains, some fifty kilometres from the Indian Ocean and more than eight thousand kilometres from his native town of Petersdorf. Dr Peters and the others were already asleep. Only the kerosene lamp in the tent gave light to the German son of a landowner while he wrote the second letter to his parents in Petersdorf.

Dear Father, venerated Mother!

Something hideous happened today! We are now in the Usagara mountains, in the interior of Africa. The local sultan offered us two very young women from the village, actually still girls. Suddenly I heard Dr Peters yelling loud and furiously. He dragged one of the half-naked girls out of his tent. He piled up three empty beer cases under a tree in front of the camp and, with a gun in his hand, forced the girl to climb up on the beer cases. Then he tied a rope around the neck of the girl, who was frightened to death, threw the other end over a branch, tensed the string, and yelled at her: „Knock the cases over, come on you black whore, knock the boxes over!" As the young girl refused to do so, she cried, and yelled, he approached her and shouted in her face: „As soon as I have a say about the laws and orders, stubborn young nigger whores such as yourself will just be hung!" Later on, the girl went back crying with Dr Peters to his tent, and I felt ashamed!

I would like to get away from these men. They don't need a geographer. They are not interested in the land. They cheat the people out of their property. Yes, that's what they want: to steal property! This is not what I imagined my work in Africa to be. And East Africa is ever so beautiful. It is a paradise on earth, with much space to live and endless freedom. I love this untouched, vast, splendid Africa and will try to find my luck – alone! Please don't bother. I will forge ahead. However, I do not yet know how to get it done.

Your son Alfred

During the afternoon of the following day, Alfred Zehe shuddered when he thought of what was to come. While he crossed the poor village behind the others, keeping the guns demonstratively in the crooks of their arms, he caught himself thinking that he wanted to leave, go back to Zanzibar, back to Germany – no matter where, just away from Dr Peters and his ruthless business partners! He hated these men, their brutality and greed, their inhuman behaviour! As an employee of the colonial society, he was powerless and helpless. On this day of the year 1884, he sat stony-faced under the huge baobab tree in the Usagara mountains. From there, he watched disgusted as the arduous negotiations with the Sultan of the village concluded. Dr Peters had called it the „takeover and civilisation of a Negro empire,“ and what was to be followed by a takeover ceremony.

Sultan Muinin Sagara, a middle-aged man with a warm smile on his harmonious face and surrounded by a simple but graceful aura, sat on a carved ebony armchair, dressed in a colourful cape. He was the sovereign of twenty-three thousand people throughout the valleys and plateaus of the Usagara mountains. His son stood behind him, Dr Peters at his right, Graf von Pfeil and Dr Jühlke at his left.

„Tell the Sultan, that in our country it is a custom to conclude a contract between two powerful rulers with a special drink,“ Carl Peters barked at the Zanzibarian interpreter Ramassan, grabbed a bottle of rum, took a small sip and handed it over to the Sultan. The African ruler nodded at the interpreter, put the bottle to his mouth, and took a long pull. The high-proof alcohol brought tears to his eyes. Dr Peters smiled diabolically, reached again for the container, and took another tiny sip. He handed the bottle back to the Sultan, who now obviously was keen on the drink and, with a smile, drank twice laughing. Dr Peters got up, grabbed a paper roll, and tried to look very dignified while starting to read in German the document written by himself:

„Sultan Muinin Sagara, sole and the absolute ruler throughout Usagara and Dr Carl Peters as representative of the Deutsche Gesellschaft für Kolonisation, herby enter into an eternal treaty of friend-

ship. Sultan Muinin Sagara receives several gifts; further future rewards will follow; this puts him under the protection of the Deutsche Gesellschaft für Kolonisation resp. its representatives. The Sultan, in exchange, due to his absolute and unlimited authority, cedes the sole and exclusive right to bring colonisation throughout Usagara to Dr Carl Peters.

Dr Carl Peters promises to make use of this right. For this purpose, Sultan Muinin Sagara cedes the sole and exclusive power of complete and unlimited exploitation throughout Usagara to Dr Carl Peters. Furthermore, the Sultan cedes any right, which, following the concept of the German constitutional law, make up the epitome of governmental sovereignty. Among those: the sole and unlimited right to exploit mines, rivers, forests, the right to impose customs, levy taxes, to set up own justice and administration and the right to establish an armed force.

In return, the title Muinin Sagara remains hereditarily in the Sultan's family. The Sultan's acquis under private law is recognised and guaranteed by Dr Peters, the representatives of the Deutsche Gesellschaft für Kolonisation will receive instructions on how to help to enhance it. The Deutsche Gesellschaft für Kolonisation will apply all resources to make sure that no more slaves will be displaced from the territory of Sultan Muinin Sagara.

This contract is executed today, December 4th, 1884, in front of the people of Usagara by consultation of several valid witnesses, by Muinin Sagara, sole and unlimited overlord throughout Usagara and Dr Carl Peters through signature and initials from both sides in a quite legally binding form."

The Sultan was drunk. He had hit the bottle of rum several times while Dr Peters read his pamphlet. His first attempt to get up failed miserably. His son standing behind him, had to support him. His wide-open mouth grinning, he reeled towards Dr Peters, who stood in front of a transport box converted in desk, demonstratively signed the contract, and showed to the Sultan where on the contract he had to press his thumb coloured with black ink. The Sultan found this ceremony funny. Again and again, he pressed his black thumb on the paper and giggled. Once the others had signed as witnesses, the representatives of the Deutsche Gesellschaft für Kolonisation proudly went to a provisionally erected flagpole in the center of the village square. With a loud „three cheers for his Majesty the German emperor“, they raised the German flag, pointed their guns, and fired a spread of bullets in to the peacefully setting Arabic night. The Sultan ducked frightened and stared full of fear at the white men.

„Now the Moors know what they have to be prepared for if ever they intend not to comply with this contract,“ Dr Carl Peters laconically commented on the Africans’ fear of the gun noise. He stared derogatorily at the Sultan: „Hey, you nigger prince! If you did not get it yet: From now on, you are a compliant subject of the German emperor . . . !“

Addressing Graf von Pfeil, Carl Peters recapitulated: „I presume we acquired approximately one hundred and forty thousand square kilometres of best African land during the last three weeks. It is good land, ideal for German colonialists who will make a paradise out of this nigger kingdom!“

„I did not imagine that our dream would come true so quickly . . .“ Graf von Pfeil answered and stared spellbound at the flag of the German Reich, outlined against the early African evening sky.

Chapter 4

At midnight, Gerhard Rohlfs stood on the terrace of his house and stared out at the open seas in front of Zanzibar. He felt very troubled. He had conceived his position in Zanzibar as a challenge in order to extend friendly relations between the German Reich and its bordering European countries through the discovery and the exploitation of economic opportunities within Africa. Reality, however, looked quite different. He soon became aware of the fact that his competences in Zanzibar were subject to orders from Berlin, and his tasks were mainly of a frighteningly banal administrative nature. He had no say in his own decisions. His day to day consisted of attending boring receptions. Months had gone by, and one lunch, dinner, and picnic followed the other, becoming increasingly unbearable due to dull landside or boat excursions. Once again, a big party was coming up: the eighty-eighth birthday of His Majesty the German emperor, Wilhelm I. It had taken weeks to prepare the festivities. The whole diplomatic corps of Zanzibar was invited. To top it all off, the warship „S.M.S. Gneisenau" of the German marine had come back to Zanzibar two days ago from a trip to the waters near Mombasa and Lamu and was now anchoring outside the harbour.

At eight o'clock in the morning, the „S.M.S. Gneisenau", with all her sails fully raised, had already saluted the flag of Zanzibar with a twenty-one gun salute and hence terrorised the town for a brief moment of time. In the evening, thirty invited guests eventually showed up at the Consul's house. Once Rohlfs had delivered a short speech in honour of the wellbeing of the emperor, the illustrious company almost froze when all the Germans shouted triple cheers on the emperor towards the evening sky and finally sang „Heil dir im Siegerkranz".

The evening had been so seemingly easy-going and merry at first. Still, it was noticeable that the presence of the German battleship off the coast of Zanzibar made the English and French, yet, even more so the Sultan himself uneasy.

Eventually, the Sultan arrived around eight o'clock in the evening. Upon the arrival of his carriage drawn by eight horses and accompanied by his guard of honour, the Sultan's small orchestra played „Wacht am Rhein", which especially encouraged the officers of the „Gneisenau" to cheer for the emperor frenetically.

Sultan Barghash sat down in an armchair under the German flag while Rohlfs as German Consul sat facing him under the Zanzibarian flag. They felt the disharmonies that had been dominating the relationship between Germany and the sultanate Zanzibar for two months.

„Consul Rohlfs," the sultan began the discussion, „I am troubled by having to usurp such a significant celebration as the birthday of the German emperor as an occasion to discuss my worries and fears, regarding the German-Zanzibarian relationship with you. But as you undoubtedly know, German newspapers implied some time ago that the German Reich considers annexing the sultanate of Zanzibar!"

„Oh please, your Excellency!" Gerhard Rohlfs tried to adopt a conciliatory tone. „As a German Consul and as your friend, I assure you: Germany does not intend to challenge the sovereignty of the Sultanate of Zanzibar in any way!"

„My dear Mr. Rohlfs," the English Governor General Sir John Kirk who was also in attendance stepped in, „I have no doubts regarding your personal integrity. You know that, as a person and as a Consul, I appreciate you very much. However, your verbal appeasement attempts and the actions of the German government are worlds apart!"

Sultan Barghash nodded his agreement. He seemed to be very concerned.

„It all started some months ago, when Dr Peters and his business partners, without my knowledge and permission, hoisted the flag of the Deutsche Reich over twelve villages on the mainland, thus considering vast estates as their property. The men did not raise their own company banner, but it is the flag of the German Reich, which now flies over villages that belong to my empire! This equalled a declaration of war, Mr. Rohlfs! When I later sent an expedition force, with the help of my English friends, to put an end to the illegal activities of this Deutsche Gesellschaft für Kolonisation, I was offended by the German emperor. On February 27th of this year, he issued a charter of the German Reich for these estates, annexed through a pack of lies, and when I again protested, he confronted me with an ultimatum: give or take!"

Gerhard Rohlfs cleared his throat embarrassedly.

„Gentleman, The German Reich is bound to protect the interests of its citizens trading abroad. Furthermore: The final act of the Berlin Congo Conference, which was inked on February 26th, 1885, clearly indicates that . . ."

Sir John Kirk interrupted him rudely.

„Peters had already illegally annexed these estates months before the conclusion of the Congo conference! Issuing an imperial charter for these properties is the same as retrospective legalisation of land theft!"

Sultan Barghash became agitated. „The German emperor threatened me with severe consequences, should I not approve this illegal land annexation," and complained, short of breath due to the excitement: „And right now there is a German warship brimming with cannons anchored at the entrance of my port. What a strange birthday greeting from the German emperor!"

The birthday celebration of the German emperor in the German Consul's residence in Zanzibar had ended ingloriously with these words. During the farewell, the sultan brought up the bothersome subject of his half-sister, Princess Salme. He expressed his dismay and his incomprehension about the German government listening to her so much. On this evening, Gerhard Rohlfs, however, did not attach great importance to this remark. He did not know much about the matter of Princess Salme. He secretly asked himself, why did I not know about it? Why was I not informed from Berlin before setting forth to Zanzibar? Everybody talks about this princess, this half-sister of the sultan – I am the only one who is in the dark.

Gerhard Rohlfs was still standing on the terrace of his house at midnight. The situation worried him. He could not help feeling that plans were being forged in Berlin, which he did not know about.

Gerhard Rohlfs pondered, what does Bismarck really want here in Zanzibar, in East Africa?

*

At the same time, retired Captain Jürgen Herbig sat in a seaside oriented cabin of the „S.M.S. Gneisenau" anchoring off Zanzibar, studying charts of East Africa and Zanzibar. His dossier for the Reich Chancellor and the admiralty would be submitted to Berlin by telegraph the next day. He had charted the position of the cities along the East African coast in a meticulous manner. Satisfied, he wrote:

. . . in conclusion, after a three-month journey along the East African coastal region and intensive research on the island of Zanzibar, I consider that the defensive capability of the sultan of Zanzibar is remarkably low. Without any doubt, the weak point is that his ships anchor almost permanently in the harbour, which is surrounded by land on three sides. Thus, they would not be able to take up a combat position in the case of an unexpected attack from the seaside or to escape in the open seas. A surprise attack on Zanzibar and the coastal cities by the German marine seems to be of almost no risk. Taking eventualities into account, I believe that a deployment of six warships of the German navy with a landing force of approximately one thousand marines to be sufficient.

To the Chancellor of the German Reich, your Excellency, Graf Otto von Bismarck, submitting the best wishes for your birthday on April 1st, signed with expressions of the highest esteem

Captain a. D. Jürgen Herbig
Currently S.M.S. Gneisenau
Zanzibar

*

On this April 2nd, Reichskanzler Fürst Otto von Bismarck felt discontented and melancholic. His seventieth birthday the day before was not supposed to have been like this. He had secluded himself in his manor Varzin in Hinterpommern to escape from the legions of congratulators from the political and financial world and the exhausting receptions in the Reich capital. In the privacy and quietness of his beloved manor, he wanted to have time for his wife Johanna and go for long walks in the splendid woods of his feudal estate. At Varzin manor, he wanted nothing but to be in peace.

This peace had been disturbed for one hour. During his morning walk, his estate manager had informed him about the arrival of a courier from Berlin. He plodded angrily across the forest clearing in front of the castle, stepped into his study, and threw two wooden trunks as thick as an arm onto the embers of the oversized chimney, without taking notice of the courier already standing at attention. He walked to his desk in silence.

„If you have good news, you may keep me company for lunch," he growled at the young man in the marine officer uniform and continued joking, „if the news is terrible, you will have to travel back to Berlin with an empty stomach!" Without awaiting any reaction, the Reich chancellor accepted the sealed envelope from the officer and looked at the sender. He immediately recognised Admiral Caprivi's handwriting.

The envelope contained three documents, among those a detailed dossier from Captain Herbig, who was just on a battleship of the German Marine off Zanzibar. After having read the reports, he sat down at his desk. Half an hour later, he finished the letter for Admiral Caprivi with the words:

. . . Based on these circumstances, I handed the courier an urgent message for His Majesty the German emperor and supreme commander of the German Army. In this letter, I recommend the following to His Majesty: Send Sayyida Salima bint Sa'id bin Ahmad Al Bu-Sa'id, called Princess Salme of Oman and Zanzibar, as well as her children to Zanzibar on a warship of the German Marine. At

*least five more battleships, including marines, should accompany
her.*

Signed
Reich Chancellor Fürst Otto von Bismarck
Varzin, April 2nd, 1885

*

In the early afternoon, the courier left the Pomeranian castle Varzin
with the Reich chancellor's letter and arrived in Berlin that same
evening after a long train journey. At almost the same time, Dr Carl
Peters and a dozen men came together in the restaurant „Hiller" Unter den Linden 55. Their purpose was the celebration of the official
registration of the newly established „Deutsch-Ostafrikanische Gesellschaft Carl Peters und Genossen" as limited partnership in the
trade register. Lorenz Adlon, the owner of the restaurant, led the
men to a small saloon. Carl Peters took seat at the top of the festive-
ly decorated table. August Leue, the renominated secretary, sat at his
right. His future task would be the organisation of the relocation of
German emigrants to East Africa. Carl Peters watched proudly as
the flag of the new company was draped on the wall behind him. A
large black cross separated the white flag. Five golden five-pointed
stars on a red field emblazoned the upper left square. „A beautiful
flag," he mumbled. He had eventually arrived at the destination of
his dreams! His successful land acquisitions in East Africa had convinced further bankers. He now had more capital at his disposal.
Furthermore, following the orders of his investors, the dismissed
Marine Captain Herbig had contributed two hundred thousand
Reichsmark to the limited partnership. Content, Carl Peters turned
the pages of the partnership agreement lying in front of him and
skimmed over the statutes. Yes, he had managed it! He had succeeded in obtaining the protection of the German Reich for his estates
in East Africa. If ever conflicts with the sultan of Zanzibar or the
English would arise, he would be able to act knowing that German

warships and German soldiers would defend his interests. Thus, he and only he, had helped Germany to get a colony in East Africa. It was only a matter of time until he, Dr Carl Peters, would travel to Africa as a Reich Commissioner. He would no longer have to face that fat, despotic and arrogant Sultan Barghash of Zanzibar in his khaki expedition clothes. No, he would be received with all military honours and all the respect owed to an ambassador of the German emperor, wearing a gala uniform of the German Reich! He was ever so sure that it would not take long now.

Carl Peters began his speech with a content smile: „Gentlemen, this day today, this August 2nd of the year 1885, fills me with endless pride. I managed to do what so many critics and pessimists thought impossible . . . !" he continued, fishing for compliments. He did not hear one of the present bankers whisper to his neighbour: „He is, if I may say so, barely more than a primitive colonial gangster with a lot of business sense, but not more! And the worst of all is that our emperor and our Reich Chancellor gave so much power to such a megalomaniac man."

*

Karl Zehe said to his wife, Martha: „I consider this Peters to be a very dangerous man." He put away the newspaper showing a photo of the president of the Deutsch-Ostafrikanische Gesellschaft on the cover. Karl Zehe was disappointed. He had hoped to read something about his son Alfred in this article also, but that was not the case. He looked thoughtfully at the newspaper's date. August 3rd! He had been without news from his son for more than four months.

Alfred had just hinted in his last letter that he might separate from Dr Peters and maybe try his luck as an ivory hunter. The doings of Dr Peters he had read about in this letter seemed alarming. This man seemed to behave like a despot in Africa. The newspapers did not mention it, quite the contrary. It was all about colonisation. He had a feeling as if Germany had fallen into a real colonial frenzy. Karl Zehe worried about the whereabouts of his son. His secret hope had been that a short congratulatory telegram due to the occasion of Alfred's sister Margarete's birthday, would arrive and with it a sign of life from his son. However, this hope was disappointed. The one-year-old girl, dressed in her birthday dress, crawled around the trunk of a huge oak tree and made squealing noises, as a tree frog jumped suddenly up in front of her.

Karl Zehe was proud of little Margarete! She was a very vivid, bright, and joyful child. In the sunlight, she even looked gorgeous. Two red ribbons adorned her dark hair. The brown eyes sparkled with life. From morning till evening, she was full of energy, curious, and had lots of fun discovering the garden. He had to admit that his initial disappointment of having had a girl again had turned into enthusiasm quite some time ago. Margarete was unlike her two older sisters. Tine was very quiet, almost apathetic, and hard to get enthusiastic about something. Frieda loved to play with dolls. They were typical girls. He was sure Margarete would be different. „Let's go inside, Martha," he marbled sadly, as again he had not heard from Alfred, „it starts getting fresh. The little one might get a cold. Maybe Alfred is just sitting somewhere in Africa and writing a letter to us . . ."

*

At the same time, Lonny Rohlfs lay in bed already – more than eight thousand kilometres away from Petersdorf – when her husband entered the bedroom. „It will be war, Lonny!" he said, through tight lips shocked. In his hands, he held a telegram from the war ministry in Berlin he had received a few minutes ago. His hands were shaking while he read out:

„Based on the increasing escalation between the sultanate of Zanzibar and the German Reich, His Majesty the German emperor as the supreme commander of the German army considers indispensable that women and children have to leave the island of Zanzibar as well as the coastal cities Dar es Salam, Tanga, and Bagamoyo as

Signed
War Minister von Schellendorf
Berlin, on August 3rd, 1885."

*

Sayyida Salima bint Sa'id bin Ahmad Al Bu-Sa'id, Princess of Oman and Zanzibar, widowed Emily Ruete, could still not believe it! Her heart beat so loud that she thought, the First Officer standing beside her might hear it. She carefully leaned over the ship's rail and looked down on the bow. The „Adler" of the East African squadron of the German marine made swell waves as it gained momentum. A strong South-West monsoon blew over the deck.

At last! She had been awaiting her return to Zanzibar for more than twenty years! Her memories, pictures from the past came back to life. With every further nautical mile, they became more plastic and melted together with the starlit sky to form a dream image. There was her happy childhood as a princess in the palace and on her father's manors and her mother's profound love. In blissful years, she had become a pretty young woman – until the day when Allah's providence had a young man with an extraordinary development of the heart move in a nearby house. It did not take long until her heart united with the empathic German businessman who lived on Zanzibar as a representative of a Hamburg-based trading company. And as she could only live her love to him by renouncing her faith as a Muslim, she had left her homeland and beloved family to find happiness together in the distance. Tears streamed down her face while she remembered these occurrences. She suddenly felt melancholy – but also fear. Could she come back to her former homeland forever? I left Zanzibar as a good Muslim and a princess, she thought. I now return as a bad Christian and half German, with my children Rosalie, Antonie – and with Rudolph-Said, the eldest who, with the help of

German warships, might soon be the new Sultan of Zanzibar and make me a Sultan's mother . . .

*

Sultan Barghash rushed up the stairs of his palace tower in panic, followed by the chief commander of his guard of honour and Sir John Matthews, his English military advisor. He remained on the terrace of the observation tower, his face showing utter horror. He looked to the open seas where the silhouettes of six German warships stood out in the morning sun. The „S.M.S. Gneisenau", having anchored near Zanzibar for weeks, had unnoticeably changed her position by hundreds of metres overnight and now lay pointedly near and alongside the harbour. The cannons of the German warship pointed at the Sultan's ships lying in port and at the palace.

„These German bastards! They want war! They want Zanzibar!" the Sultan yelled and stared at his English military advisor. Sir Matthew kept silent. He scanned the horizon with binoculars and watched the German battleships. He lit a cigarillo and blew the smoke in a remarkably calm way into the morning breeze. Sultan Barghash was still staring at him with a pale face.

„That's impressive! The complete East African squadron of the German marine is visiting, Your Excellency! A magnificent sight! But I somehow fear, honourable Sultan, that this German Armada has not come for lunch! They want Zanzibar and probably more . . ."

The Englishman looked at the speechless Sultan with an ironic smile.

„I would say, your Excellency, we are not really in a position to disapprove this cold fleet call! Honourable Sultan Barghash, we have no chance against this. The only thing we can do is negotiate!"

It was late in the evening of August 13th, 1885. German battleships anchored off Zanzibar within visual range. Their canons were demonstratively pointing at the island. Six hours later, the German commodore Paschen, Admiral Knorr, the British Governor General

Sir John Kirk, the English military advisor General Matthews and Sultan Barghash met in the palace. The atmosphere was frosty. The sultan was afraid. Both English seemed to be exceptionally calm.

„Gentlemen," Commodore Paschen opened talks, „in the name of his majesty, the German emperor, King of Prussia and supreme commander of the German army, Wilhelm I, may I express my regrets, that his Excellency, the Sultan of Zanzibar, vigorously refuses to approve the demands of a German subject on the sultanate of Zanzibar! Mrs. Emily Ruete is on board one of our ships – you certainly know her better as princess Princess Salme of Oman and Zanzibar."

Sultan Barghash's eyes flew wide open with surprise. But before he was able to express his indignation, the German commodore continued his unswerving speech.

„In our opinion, the hereditary titles of the princess to the Zanzibarian sultanate are legal. The German Reich has the mission to protect her and help her to enforce the claims."

„She fled Zanzibar, married a Christian, and even accepted the Christian faith," Sultan Barghash complained. „According to the applicable Zanzibarian law, she renounced and lost any claims." His eyes sparkled maliciously.

„That may well be. But she is now a citizen of the German Reich. Thus the German law applies to her!"

Admiral Knorr noticed how upset the sultan was. The English officers, however, restrained themselves. He knew that there had been consultations between London and Berlin a week ago and that the Berlin Federal Foreign Office had advised both officers to stay neutral in this conflict regarding the princess and so to say support the German claims for the lands on the African mainland.

Admiral Knorr cleverly exploited the sultan's helplessness.

„Should your Excellency, however, decide to acknowledge unrestrictedly the German claims for the lands on the East African mainland, His Majesty would consider forgoing a further support of the requirements of princess Salme – and recognise the sovereignty of the sultanate of Zanzibar as well as the interests of the English on Zanzibar in the form of a friendship and trade treaty!"

Sir John Kirk smiled secretly. What a smart move the Germans had made, he thought. They conceal their interests on the African mainland behind the right of the German Reich, legitimate under public international law, to guarantee the protection to German subjects, even abroad. Sir John Kirk was hardly surprised, to hear the German commodoure adding after a short interruption: „Therefore we ask with all due respect Your Excellency, the Sultan of Zanzibar, to henceforth acknowledge the territories of the Deutsch-Ostafrikanische Gesellschaft of Dr Carl Peters, stated as protectorates of the German Reich in the charter of His Majesty, the German emperor."
Sultan Barghash swallowed. His face turned red. He fumbled nervously with his diamond ring. Searching for assistance, he looked to Sir John Kirk and General Matthews. But both English officers showed that they could not help him by decently shrugging their shoulders.

*

Surrounded by German warships, Sultan Barghash had seen no other option than to recognise the German possessions and agree to the admiral's proposal.
The reaction to the quasi-capitulation of the Sultan of Zanzibar, a telegram from the German Reich Chancellor, Fürst Otto von Bismarck, was forwarded from Berlin without any comment to the commanding ship of the German Marine's East-Africa squadron, to the attention of Admiral Knorr:

The success will do! We will not claim what the sultan is not willing to do for his sister, as we are mainly content. The friendship with the sultan must be looked after, and Mrs. Ruete has to be brought back to Europe . . .

Signed
Reich Chancellor Fürst Otto von Bismarck
Currently at Schloss Varzin

Around noon, Admiral Knorr went aboard the tender „Adler“, and sought out Emily Ruete, Princess Salme of Osman und Zanzibar, and her three children. Admiral Knorr did not really feel comfortable in his own skin. The Reich Chancellor's approach seemed cynical and inhuman to him. Hence, it was difficult for him to tell the princess that upon highest orders from Berlin, she had to return to Germany. It was even more tragic to let her know that the sultan, her half-brother, continued to refuse to recognise her inheritance claim and that she had no chance to get financial support from the German Reich besides a donation of five thousand Reichsmark granted by the German emperor.

The monsoon blew gently over the bridge of the German warship. The admiral stared at the open seas thoughtfully. Seeing the questioning facial expression of the seemingly helpless sultan, once the most powerful man of East Africa and now barely more than a lackey of the European superpowers, and the face of the desperately weeping Arabic princess Salme and her kids in his minds' eye, he quietly mumbled: „The Moor has done his duty, the Moor may go.“

Next, he looked melancholically at the banner of the German Reich. „A cheer for his Majesty, the emperor! Long live German East Africa . . .“ he whispered cynically.

CHAPTER 5

(20 years later)

Call!

According to the circumstances, any risk from the city Dar es Salam through the current ongoing disturbances may not be visible. Nevertheless, sending the Kaiserliche Schutztruppe (Imperial Protection Force) to the southern districts, which was necessary for military objects, generated concern among the population of Dar es Salam and the wish to facilitate weapons training to able-bodied inhabitants arose.
The imperial governor thus agreed to the formation of a voluntary civil guard.
All European male inhabitants of Dar es Salam, who volunteer to join the civil guard, are asked to be at the yard of the Askari barracks at five o'clock on Tuesday 22ⁿᵈ of this month. Those who belong, as an officer or reserve non-commissioned officers or Landwehr, to the German Reichsheer or the Marine are asked to bring along their military documentation.

Dar es Salam, August 20ᵗʰ, 1905
The Kaiserliche Bezirksamt

Alarmed, Alfred Zehe paced up and down the veranda, holding in his hands the letter from the Kaiserliche Bezirksamt, which was almost a general mobilisation. He had been living in Africa for twenty years! And now: war! He spent some moments remembering the times when, together with Dr Peters, he had stepped on African ground for the first time not far from here. Twenty years! He could not believe how quickly time had gone by. It had been a very nice and peaceful time. And now this mobilisation! It somehow seemed frightening to him that precisely two decades ago, German warships had made clear to the sultan of Zanzibar, who was the new boss of German East Africa. „This dream of German East Africa did not last long, Africa is burning," he mumbled. He sensed that troubled times were ahead. Sweat flowed in torrents down his forehead. It was a mystery to him how his Greek friend and partner Anthimos could stand living at the seaside. Alfred preferred the inland himself, the plains at more than one thousand metres of altitude near Moshi and Arusha, the magnificent mountains of Pare and Usambara where he had bought some land many years ago and built a farmhouse near Wilhelmstal. From there, he spent months on ivory safaris in the Serengeti, along the river Rufiji or sometimes even as far South as the Zambesi.

On this August afternoon, he wondered whether he was again going to see his home, his farm in the near future. He grabbed a glass of Gin from the table and began to write a letter to his sister Margarete:

Dar es Salam, August 20th, 1905

My beloved birthday child!

Of course, I know, dear Margarete, that your birthday was on August 3rd! I did not forget it. More than anything, I remembered how much you were longing for this day as you now are twenty-one years old and of full age. Eventually, you may do as you please!

I am actually with my friend Anthimos in his house at the seaside. He sends you his warmest greetings! When I showed him your picture the other day, this old charmer said that he regretted being so old. Otherwise, he would court you! Today is not a lovely day. They are forming a militia because of the uprisings which broke out three weeks ago. But don't worry! That's due to nothing more but some Africans who went crazy and are running with spears, bows, and arrows around quite far from here. Our troops will undoubtedly get this quickly under control!

In any case, you will come to see me here, as we agreed. By the way, here is a useful hint: There is an office of the Deutsch-Ostafrikanische Gesellschaft in Berlin. They advise Germans who want to go to Africa. Talk directly to the retired Captain August Leue. He is the secretary of the association, has been here for a long time (also with the Kaiserliche Schutztruppe), and knows East Africa very well. Talk to him and give him my best regards if you please. He might be able to tell you who could provide you Swahili lessons. You would benefit a lot.

Don't be mad at me if I stop writing for today. The mail steamer of the German East Africa line will leave tomorrow morning. I have to finish the letter and have it delivered directly to the port now. I will get back to you soon with more information. Please give my regards to my sisters Tine and Frieda and a big hug to Mother.

Your loving brother
Alfred

PS: You might not want to talk to your mother about your Africa plans yet. She has been worrying too much about you all since father died!

*

Mojo ole Chieni felt tired and hungry. His throat was as dry and as rough as the lake Mandusi which had turned to a white shimmering salt desert with thousands of animal skeletons at its centre in the last years. Almost dehydrated elephants, buffaloes, wildebeests, and antelopes had stepped on the deceptive salt, hoping to find water somewhere at the centre of the lake. They had sunk up to their waste and got stuck. Bleating day and night, fidgeting and fighting for their life, they eventually died with their jaws wide open and their eyes distorted by insanity. An odour of decomposition had settled on the land for months. One could smell death. It had only been a time of abundance for vultures, marabous, and hyaenas. However, when the hyaenas suddenly left the land, the council of elders decided to send for help.

It had started many years ago, at a time when his son Kinai was six summers old. It was the year the prophecy of his father Masiani, the *Laibon*, had been fulfilled. News had spread through the Maasai land just like bushfire, driven by summer winds, that somewhere east, a powerful black creature crept on iron pathways through the area, emitting black breath to the sky just like a terrifying monster. This thing wound along steppes and hills and made such awful sounds that even elephants panicked, running towards the horizon. And it was said that when this thing ran out of breath, hideous white men sprang out of its belly.

No doubt! It was the „Iron Snake"! The prophecy of his father, the *Laibon* Masiani ole Chieni, had been fulfilled! The destruction had begun. Suddenly the big herds of cattle of the Maasai died. Dehydrated and thin, they perished by the thousands and thousands. The wealth of the Maasai people had turned to dust in just a few months, and the children cried out so loud and miserably for milk that their mothers plugged their ears with clay in order not to go crazy. There only seemed to be water and hope for life left on the mountain Meru, where the white people lived.

Two days later, Mojo ole Chieni knew that the story was true. A wide fertile valley with a beautiful river lay right in front of him in the morning shadow of the powerful Meru. The banana plants on the fields were bearing fruits, and women sold fruit, vegetables, and sugar cane wayside. All the people were well-nourished. He met men from other Maasai tribes everywhere. A big white house with thick walls and a tall tower in the center sat enthroned on a nearby hill.

There was a bustling activity in the valley below. Waarusha men, young Wameru men, but also many Maasai people went back and forth, carrying construction material across the river. Three white men with leather boots and strange helmets on their heads directed the workers. Mojo ole Chieni was pleased to see other Maasai and hurried quickly to them. Before he could greet his tribal brothers, he was shouted at loudly by one of the white men who held a hippo skin whip in his hand. He yelled: „Hey, you! Come here!" Mojo sensed the hate in the words of the white man. He looked with questioning eyes at the other Maasai. They indicated him by hand signals to approach the white man.

„Carry me to the other side of the river," the Muzungu barked at him. Mojo wanted to reply that he was not going to do it, but the looks of the other Maasai men made him feel insecure. He approached the white man, reluctantly. The pot-bellied man had an ashen face and an evil eye. Mojo was afraid.

The white man grabbed his sleeve and pulled him to the riverside. Even before Mojo was aware, he sat piggyback on his back and clasped his throat with his left arm. „Go ahead, take me to the other side, you stinky warrior," he yelled.

Just some metres further, the water came up to Mojo's knees. Suddenly he felt the painful hit of the White man's whip on his left thigh. „Mind what you are doing, you stupid nigger, I am getting wet," he yelled and started striking another whiplash. Mojo froze. His eyes flashed. Full of hatred, he grabbed behind him, as quick as lightning hurled the white man in the water and lifted his cane abruptly to let the knob of fist-size whiz down on the man's head. Right in the stroke, he heard the horrified cries of his tribesmen. He looked shoreside and saw all the Maasai men running away. The white man in the water in front of him shouted in panic. Mojo released him, hurried through the water towards the shore, and ran after the other Maasai.

Lieutenant Georg Küster was beside himself with rage. He was afraid, too. An officer had reported about a Maasai who had thrown one of Lieutenant Küster's officers into the water, hit him several times with a billet, and almost killed him. The incident had confirmed to the commander of the German Fort of Arusha that the Maji-Maji Rebellion had reached this region. The riots had affected the South of German Africa so far. Such respectless behaviour from a Maasai and the following escape of more than three hundred indigenous auxiliaries was a severe incident. One thing was clear, indeed. The German Fort in Arusha, the so-called Boma, was extremely well fortified, a German and a Maxim machine gun were available on the two towers. Especially the Maxim, with its six hundred shots per minute, was a high performer. It was not called the „devil's toothbrush" for nothing.

The personal situation however really alarmed him. Only three German officers and approximately thirty Askaris were under arms to protect the few Germans and Boer, but Palestinian colonisation had also settled on the Meru on the land of the Deutsch-Ostafrikanische Gesellschaft. However, if more than three hundred Maasai refugees joined forces with other rebels such as Waarusha and Wameru warriors to attack them, the situation would be critical.

On the other hand, the understaffing of the Fort did not allow the pursuit of the evaders into the mountains.

Major Schleinitz, commander of the Kaiserliche Schutztruppe in German East Africa, and Governor Graf von Goetzen, who were both staying in Dar es Salam, could only be informed with a major expenditure of time. Reinforcements for the deployment, if any, would not arrive before eight days. The pending birthday of the Empress with its festivities to which all German settlers and a top-level delegation from Dar es Salam had been invited, made the situation even more dramatic and required an immediate response.

„We have to prevent the fugitives from assembling, arming, joining other tribes and attacking us," he said to Officer Weinertz, who stood soaking wet in front of him. „Contact the superintendent of these Maasai workers immediately and tell him that I guarantee to forgo any punishment if the evaders surrender, show remorse and resume work."

The officer had hardly left the room when Lieutenant Küster murmured: „I have to make an example! Otherwise, we will be overrun by legions of armed niggers."

At noon of the following day, it was announced that the supervisor had succeeded in having the refugees volunteer to return to work at the German fort. During the late afternoon, thirty armed Askaris of the Kaiserliche Schutztruppe formed an honour guard on the path leading from the valley to the fortress. As the last sun rays shone on the Meru, the bevy of Maasai dressed in red cloaks moved silently towards the fort, preceded by Mojo ole Chieni.

Without any guilty feelings, he approached the white walls of the German Boma. When the Maasai were only fifty metres away from the two watchtowers built at the right and left side of the entrance gate, the fatal sound of the machine guns tore through the silence. Men were yelling. Blood was trickling on the road. Eventually, a deathly silence fell over the valley and the German Boma, commanded by first Lieutenant Georg Küster whom the African population had given the nickname of *Bwana Fisi* – „hyena man".

*

The Maji-Maji rebellion spread like wildfire throughout German East Africa. What had begun in the summer of 1905 in the region of the river Rufiji under the command of the magician Ngamea, escalated in very short time and turned into a civil war. Thousands upon thousands of Africans armed with billets, lances, bows, and arrows went marauding through the Southern provinces. They were not afraid of bullets. They lived with confidence that thanks to the magic miracle water of the Maji-Maji, any projectile would bounce off them.

On August 1st, a German police department under Sergeant Hoenicke was worn down by one thousand five hundred Wamatumbi warriors. Two weeks later, Benedictine Bishop Cassian Spiess, as well as two fellow brothers and two sisters, were killed. The very next day, rebels slew the German settler Hopfer, a wild crowd attacked the Liwale army post, poisoned arrows killed Sergeant Faubel and a German merchant. Underestimating the situation, Governor Boetzen had written on August 20th in the imperial district office of Dar es Salam, „. . . a rebellion can be observed approaching daily in the cloud of smoke caused by the burning of the fields on the

other side of the harbour . . .“ The leaders of the Kaiserliche Schutztruppe suddenly recognised: German East Africa was on fire. And
the victims, without exception, were Germans!

*

On October 16th, Alfred Zehe and his friend Anthimos sat on the terrace. The ivory hunter and geographer wore the uniform of the German protection guard. As a conscript, he had completed his military
service in the Prussian army and was now drafted as a reserve officer. His gun model 98 was lent up against the balustrade of the
porch, and he checked his M/89 revolver in his hand.
„Anthimos, do you think this is only a regional revolt, or is it more
than that?“
The Greek with the long scarf on his right cheek took a deep breath
before answering: „This is war, Alfred! And it was just a matter of
time before it would happen. The way most of the Germans treat the
black people here, this could not end well.“
„I think the hut tax was a huge mistake,“ Alfred Zehe answered.
His friend interrupted him. “All of the German Reich’s colonial political policies in Africa are a mistake,“ he said. „I read somewhere
that your emperor Wilhelm dreams of providing all Germans with a
place in the sun. How is this being realized? You grab the hippo
whip and turn Africans into black Prussians! You don’t come to
Africa as guests, but as racist occupiers! It will not work, Alfred.
Look what happens. The is a civil war in the German southwest
where the Herero and Nama defy your yoke. If my information is
correct, the Germans are bringing thousands of soldiers into the
country because they cannot deal with their subjects. It’s also erupt-
ing here. The Africans are sick of the German yoke! They’re defend-
ing themselves. And they’re doing it their way: with bows and arrows and plenty of hatred. My dear friend, the only advice I can give
you is the following: If you are about to go into battle today, you
better get some of this Maji-Maji, the wizard’s wonder-water, to
make yourself bullet-proof.“

Two hours later, the reserve non-commissioned officer Alfred Zehe from Sagan in Silesia marched to the beat of Prussian marches through Dar es Salam. The expedition corps, under the leadership of Major Johannes, consisted of the 8th and 13th company, each one hundred and fifty men strong, and a division of one hundred men as well as seventy-three irregulars, mostly settlers, armed with breech-loading rifles. In Kilwa, more troops were to join them.

German settlers shouting cheers lined the street „Unter den Akazien". They had left their manors and fled to the capital of the reserve. The soldiers walked through Bismarckstraße and, alongside Wilhelmsufer, passing the statue of emperor Kaiser Wilhelm II, arriving at the Paradeplatz, where governor von Goetzen gave a speech in Swahili and German.

„Soldiers! Our young colony is going through a hard and critical time. I had you assemble because I wanted to see you again. Once you are at war, follow your leaders and do well as capable soldiers do. I wish that every one of you returns healthy. Farewell, Askaris!

Na kwa moyo wangu napenda ninyi wote kurudi wazima. Kwaheri Askaris . . . !"

Alfred Zehe had a strange gut feeling. He knew that punitive expeditions such as this one were cruel. The German military in Africa had a preference for the „scorched earth" tactic. It would be the same this time.

He could not stop turning the words of his Greek friend over in his head: „If you are about to go into battle today, you better get some of this Maji-Maji, the wizard's wonder-water, to make you bullet-proof . . ."

Together with his comrades of the 8th company, he sang the last verse of the protection troups song: *„ Tret' ich die letzte Reise, die große Fahrt einst an; auf, singt mir diese Weise statt Trauerliedern dann; dass meinem Jägerohre dort vor dem Himmeltore es kling' wie ein Halali: Heia, heia, Safari!"*

„ When I once will start the last journey, the great journey; go ahead, sing to me this way instead of mourning songs, so that there, in front of the sky gates, it sounds like a tally-to to my hunter's ears: Hey, hey, safari!*"*

*

Margarete Zehe was nervous. She stared unsatisfied in the mirror. She did not like herself on this day. Her shoulder-length dark brown hair seemed to be too greasy, her eyebrows as always appeared a little bit bushy, and she found her cheekbones too protrudant. She knew that she was pretty, tall, and slim with a deep look in her dark eyes. Many young men courted her. However, she was unhappy with herself most of the time, just like today. And it was such an important day.

Again and again, she tried to braid her hair and pin it with a hair clip, but she did not succeed. She threw the silver hairclip angrily on to the chest of drawers, grabbed her winter coat, and rushed to the door. She heard her mother shouting from the kitchen, „Where do you want to go at this time, my girl?"

„I am going for a walk," she answered and let the door bang behind her. Bahnhofstraße was very busy. Snow covered the streets. Despite the icy January cold, people seemed to be quite wild, all intoxicated by the festivities of Kaiser Wilhelm II's Birthday Honours. The cavalry division of the 5th Field Artillery Regiment of Podbielski, stationed in Sagan, had been on a torch parade on horseback through the town the evening before, dressed in their parade uniforms. The drummers with the white gloves with their kettle drums provided the rhythm for the soldiers, following them in the light of the torches. The spectacle had been magnificent but also appealingly sinister.

The very same morning, a splendid military parade had taken place on Kornmarkt, and even the royal district administrator had assisted, dressed in his staff uniform.

The highlight of all the festivities, however, as it was every year on the emperor's birthday, was the 5th regiment's Officers' Ball in the officers' mess in Bahnhofstraße. It was the main social event of the garrison town anyway. Everyone who was anyone would attend. And she had been invited for the first time in her life!

It was not the only reason why Margarete was nervous. This evening would decide her future, either way! She felt that the day had come; *he* would propose to her.

With large eyes, she looked up to the emblems of the Reich, the Prussian Eagle and the imperial crown on the facade of the district court. She wondered why these emblems fascinated her in an almost mystical way. They meant more than just a symbol of the monarchy to her. She felt the same way about the omnipresent emblems on the doors and facades of the ducal purveyors to the court. They were symbols of wealth, glamour, and glory – of a life which had been no more than a dream for some time since she had to sell Gut Petersdorf after the death of her father and moved to a confined four-room apartment in Bahnhofstraße 15.

She had been suffering so much ever since! It had been six long years since her father had died. She still missed him. No-one could replace him. He used to know, to feel that she had two souls, that she was torn between her mood swings, sometimes sad, melancholic, and then again ever so agile and full of vitality. He understood because he, too, carried those opposing forces.

She had been his „princess"! She knew very well that he had devoted all the resources at his disposal to keep the beautiful, almost pompous manor Petersdorf. He had taken on debts, mortgaged family jewels, and sold several hectares of land through the years, just to provide a carefree life for his children at the manor. The manorial estate, which once had more than one thousand seven hundred hectares of land, had become a barely productive farm. The manor was bankrupt when he faded away, careworn without vital force. Once he died, mother gave up on everything and moved with her, Tine and Frieda into this awfully narrow flat.

It was not only the narrowness of the flat which discomforted her. Margarete suffered enormously from the social relegation, had complexes and feelings of guilt. She had fallen into severe depression because of the lack of means and any social contact. She became mournful and no longer laughed. Her skin became fallow. At some point, she had begun to escape this deep sense of poverty by walking through Sagan and going everywhere the sight of wealth was evident, where ducal emblems on the facades signalised a life in abundance. Throughout the years, she had created an imaginary path of illusion and dreams passing mansions, churches, monasteries, and crossing parks. She had learned that the night was her best intimate friend.

She especially loved to tiptoe through the Ludwigsgarten of the ducal castle at nighttime. There, she sank into reveries and imagined herself in the lordly times of Graf Peter von Kurland and two of his four daughters, the famous duchess Wilhelmine von Sagan or her sister Dorothea von Dino. Thinking about the beautiful Wilhelmine particularly inspired her fantasies and visions. She had read all the available books about Wilhelmine, absorbing all facts and stories. Margarete believed that some kind of spiritual kinship connected her with the duchess.

Returning from these visions to her real-life in Sagan had become more and more unpleasant during the last months. This reality had three names: Georg, Graf von Rantzow – and Ulrich.

Georg was the son of an estate owner in the small village Deutsch-Machen, not far from Gut Petersdorf. He was a nice guy, not very smart, however affectionate, had funny knock knees, and an exceptional feeling for horses. He loved them. She knew it. But she also knew that she should not love him if she wanted to go to Africa. That was the reason why she had avoided him deliberately over the last months and told him clearly that she expected more from her future than a life on a medium-sized manor in Selesia.

Things looked quite differently concerning Graf von Rantzelow. The Major, more than forty years old, had been a friend of her late father. Everybody in Sagan knew that he had a wealthy but also ugly and nasty wife, and seven children – with three wives, this also was known to everybody in Sagan. The duke was of small stature, had a bald patch, and it was beyond all question that he was very educated and charming. He was a real gentleman. Her internal voice told her that she could only conceive him as a friend. Then there was Ulrich Trappe, a twenty-three-year-old Lieutenant of the mounted division of the 5th field artillery regiment of Podbielski, stationed in Glogau. She had only known him six months ago. His short military haircut and the quite square chin did not make him look handsome nor somehow attractive. He only looked impressive in his parade uniform. As an officer, he was used to requesting, conducting, and speaking, very loudly most of the time. He did not like any contradiction and had difficulty listening. What unquestionably distinguished him was his determination. He knew very well what he wanted. He wanted her!

Margarete did not love him. However, she could imagine that her sympathy might increase once they spent more time and lived their shared passion for horses and hunting together. She believed he was the only one who could make her burning desire to go to Africa come true!

This dream began seven years ago, on the day her father had given her a beautiful art nouveau luxury edition of *Brehms Tierleben* with gilded edges for her sixteenth birthday. The images of elephants, lions and leopards, endless savannas, and impenetrable ancient forests, of martial black warriors and thundering waterfalls, fascinated her. She spent days and nights sitting in the haystacks above the horse stables with this book on her lap and dreamed of the Black Continent. She did not know what her view of the images made her long for, but it was such a strong feeling! Father had shared her childish enthusiasm and said: „Princess, when you have grown-up, we will go to Africa together to see your brother Alfred and hunt together on the Kilimanjaro!"

When Margarete returned to reality from her daydreams on this late afternoon of January 27th, 1907 in the park of the ducal estate and walked home alongside the river Bober, she was sure about what she would answer to Ulrich at the officers' ball that evening once he proposed to her. She had chosen the words she would utter, learned them by heart – and decided that nothing would keep her from doing

that. Ulrich's family had money. He was an officer so that he could ask for a transfer to the protection troops in German East Africa.
Margarete continued along her way with confidence and whispered the words she had memorised: „Yes, Ulrich, I also love you. And if your love is honest, marry me and let us go to Africa together . . .“

*

For Emily Ruete, it was one of these awful, cloudy, and foggy February days in Berlin, which made her suffer immensely from depression. There were only a few things that could give her courage to face life after the traumatic happenings in Zanzibar more than twenty years ago. Ever since, she followed the incidents in her former homeland from the far away Germany where she had to return unavoidably and with few resources. During the last months, she had observed the internal political disputes about the African colonisation in the German Reich with undistinguished malicious glee. German South-West Africa had been bathed in blood by war for a long time. In German East Africa, which once had belonged to the sultanate of Zanzibar, the bloody Maji-Maji-rebellion shook the colonial image in Berlin. Germany's colonial adventure in Africa turned out to be a fierce slaughter – and an internal political disaster!
Emily Ruete glanced at the clock. She was awaiting a language student for Swahili, a young woman who wanted to go to East Africa with her husband. This lady had been assigned to her by the administration of the Deutsch-Afrikanische Gesellschaft. The young woman had a most unusual request. As she lived somewhere in Silesia far away from Berlin, she had asked for several hours of lessons per day over four weeks. She would live with relatives during this time.
She could not stand these Germans, those settlers who wanted to establish themselves somewhere on the African land near the Kilimanjaro, leave Germany because they did not find work. But she needed money urgently. This student was probably another German with this wrong conviction, which could be read some time ago in one of the numerous German colonial newspapers „. . . The tribal people

are ignorant – we have to educate them; they are lazy – we have to teach them how to work; they are dirty – we must wash them; they are sick, with all kinds of ailments – we must heal them; they are wild, cruel and superstitious – we have to appease and enlighten them. Altogether: they are big children in need of education and direction!" Well, many of these German colonialists who came to her to learn Arabic or Swahili had this conviction. She hated these sickening settlers and emigrants!

A few moments later, someone knocked at the flat door. Emily Ruete opened. A young, slim woman with long dark hair stood in front of her.

„*Jambo*, Mrs. Zehe?" she welcomed the woman, knowing that this Swahili phrase of civility completely unsettled most of her students at the first moment.

But the young woman reacted completely unexpectedly: „*Jambo*, Mama Ruete!" she answered fluently.

Emily Ruete was surprised. „Welcome, Mrs. Zehe. I am astonished! You already speak Swahili!"

„Not so well, Mrs. Ruete," Margarete Zehe answered and smiled. „My brother has been living in East Africa for a long time. In his letters, he taught me some Swahili over the years."

Emily Ruete looked her new student in the eyes. She intuitively felt that this young woman was different than all her former students.

„*Karibu* . . . ," she welcomed Margarete Zehe and let her step in.

Chapter 6

Africa! Finally! The coast of German East Africa appeared on the horizon out of the spray of the troubled Indian Ocean in the morning mist. Dar es Salam – the „House of Peace" shimmered in the first sunlight like a pearl, encrusted by lush tropical vegetation. What a beautiful name for a city, „House of Peace," Margarete Trappe thought. She stood at the bow of the Ocean Steamer of the German East Africa Line and took a deep breath. The German Mastiff Cäsar, her favourite dog, had laid down beside her. Tell, the pointer, rambled around the deck.

In fractions of seconds, last month's tension gave way to overwhelming joy; a new, unknown feeling of happiness. Tears of joy rolled down her cheeks. Her lifelong dream was over there, close enough to reach out and touch: Africa! Many years had gone by since the images of Africa in *Brehms Tierleben* had triggered this dream. And she had to cruelly endure long months since she attended the regiments ball in Sagan with Ulrich Trappe for the first time: that evening when she had decided to choose the man who now stood beside her on the ship.

„Ulrich, this is the happiest moment of my life . . . !" Her voice trembled, her eyes were sparkling. Her long hair whipped in the morning breeze.

„I do hope, princess, that we will find our happiness here."

The voice of the retired Lieutenant Ulrich Trappe seemed to be more worried than happy. As if he wanted to pull his wife back from her euphoria to reality, he added pathetically: „We have to find our happiness here! We have to! I – we gave up everything in Germany!"

Margarete Trappe glanced at her husband from the corner of her eyes. There it was again, this strange, reproachful tone! Ulrich seemed to have completely changed since they had boarded in Naples. He seemed to be very serious, was taciturn, and showed almost no emotion. She could not detect any joyful anticipation! He had never mentioned it during the two weeks on board. However, she felt that he was questioning his decision to give up his officer's career and go as a settler to German East Africa with every nautical mile that brought them further away from Europe and brought East Africa nearer. But there would have been no other option. On July 17th, they got married in the protestant Gnadenkirche (Church of Mercy) in Sagan and were surprised to get the notification that his requirement of transfer to the Kaiserliche Schutztruppen in East Africa could be satisfied; a transfer, however, would only take place in five years. Five years! She had not been prepared to accept this. More cruel, lonely years in Sagan? No!

The preparations for the journey to East Africa had already been in full progress. The war ministry had informed them about the suppression of the Maji-Maji rebellion in German East Africa and assured that the Country was safe now. Thus, they had spent a lot of money buying tropical tents, hunting guns, saddles, tropical clothing, and all kinds of equipment for Africa at Trippelskirch & Co. in Berlin, the only German shop for tropical equipment. They had already booked the ship tickets, the price of seven hundred and fifty Reichsmark per person for the first-class passage from Naples to Dar es Salam had already been paid. The negotiations with August Lehe from the Deutsch-Ostafrikanische Gesellschaft about acquiring land at the mountain Meru were also almost concluded when the message arrived that Ulrich had to wait for five years. She had rejected that entirely.

She could not imagine turning back.

Moreover, she absolutely wanted to search for her brother's grave. Alfred had been killed in action near Neru during a fight with rebelling Africans and only been provisionally buried by his mates. The grief had almost killed her. Alfred had gone to Africa twenty years ago. For many years, they had been corresponding, sending letters time and again and promising to meet soon in Africa. ‚Soon' had turned to endless years. And now that everything was prepared, she should wait another five years? Definitely not!

Now more than ever! She wanted to go to Africa, also to provide an honourable grave for Alfred. For this reason, she had forced Ulrich to choose either to quit the military service and go with her as settlers to Africa – or to follow her in five years. „If you love me, you join me – now!" she had stated. He had done it. For love, as he had assured.

However, during the last weeks on board, she had felt that he regretted this decision. Maybe he was frightened about his audacity and now feared the consequences. It tormented him, but he probably did not dare talk about it. His officer's conceit did not allow him any margin for any alleged weaknesses or joy. One thing was clear: he already mourned his past, especially his career as an officer.

At the pier of Dar es Salam, the marching band played a melody for the arriving people. The governor of the colony, Freiherr Albrecht von Rechenberg, stood on the gangplank and welcomed each German personally. August Lehe from the Deutsch-Ostafrikanische Gesellschaft was also waiting for them. They had met him twice in Berlin during the negotiations about the land acquisition. He was a very straight and brave man. There was no doubt he knew East Africa exceptionally well. During the ship's journey, Ulrich had read a book about the colonisation ability of German East Africa, written by Leue, and had been very impressed by him ever since.

A tall, quite haggard man with a southern air who, even from a distance, seemed to be very dynamic stood beside Leue. She had never seen this man before; however, she already knew a lot about him and instantly anticipated that he was the Greek Anthimos, her brother Alfred's closest friend and business partner. A wide-brimmed leather hat engulfed his face in shadow. He was sunburnt, wore khaki-coloured trousers, a wide white shirt, and strikingly dirty leather boots reaching up to his knees.

„*Bonjour, Karibu* – welcome in East Africa, Margarete! I may call my best friend's sister Margarete, right?"

The Greek did not say more. His gentle voice with a strange tremolo and French accent gave her goose pimples on the back. He took off his hat and reached his hand out to her. Only now she saw the scar on the right side of his face her brother had mentioned. A leopard had attacked Anthimos a long time ago. Confused, she looked at him. There was an uncertain melancholy in his dark eyes. His handshake was firm. He radiated self-assurance and, at the same time, wonderful tranquility. Even before she could answer, she was interrupted by August Leue.

„Not East Africa! It is German East Africa, German . . ., Mr. Koundouriotis! We are in German East Africa!" Addressing the Trappes, he said, „Welcome, my dear lady, Lieutenant – on your future homeland!"

The way August Leue looked at the Greek and how he accentuated „German East Africa" made Margarete Trappe notice immediately that these men did not like each other. Ulrich seemed to have noticed how much Anthimos fascinated her. In officer manner, he briefly and abruptly straightened his upper body, signalising a vigilance posture in front of the former Captain Leue – and nodded in the direction of Anthimos Koundouriotis. With outright contempt in his eyes, he looked at Anthimos' boots and said rather smugly: „As I do not see any dust grain far and wide, I presume you just come from the wilderness and did not have time to take a bath, Mr. Koundouriotis, right? But my wife and I appreciate indeed that you receive us personally, in German East Africa."

Margarete Trappe could not explain to herself why her husband and August Lehe spoke in such a disrespectful way to Anthimos. Her eyes jumped back and forth between both men. Next to Anthimos in his casual attire, Ulrich and August Leue looked like fops in their white, freshly pressed tropical suits. They looked grumpy; he had a pleasant smile. Alfred once wrote that Anthimos was like a brother to him, had mentioned time and again what kind of a tolerant, generous, and warm-hearted man he was and how much he appreciated his education and humility. August Leue's words tore her from her thoughtfulness.

„I presume you are tired and fatigued by the journey. You will, of course, be my guests at my house during your stay in Dar es Salam. My servants will take care of your luggage and the freight."

„We brought a horse along," Margarete Trappe pointed out, „a thoroughbred Arabian stallion! He has been standing below deck for two weeks and needs to be moved urgently before being fed. Otherwise, there would be a considerable risk of colic!"

August Leue embarrassedly cleared this throat.

„A horse? Hm, this is kind of difficult. I don't have stables near my house. But I inevitably could . . ."

„I can take care of the horse," Anthimos Koundouriotis interrupted him, „I love horses. And there is a place in my stable. When you and your husband leave for the inland in a week, the stallion will be bursting with strength. I might show you the beautiful beaches in the South of Dar es Salam during a ride. The Arabian horse will like it here! They are desert animals. They love the heat and the freedom – like we Greeks do . . ."

*

On the day of their departure from von Dar es Salam the heat seemed almost unbearable to Margarete. The Indian Ocean shimmered in the blazing noon heat. She felt tired but also full of energy and enthusiasm. The night before, she and Anthimos had gone on horseback to an African village outside the city boundaries. Anthimos had told her that the natives held a Ngoma during harvest moon nights and offered them to join him as it was a fascinating spectacle. Ulrich having considerable reservations, spoke about the end of the Maji-Maji-rebellion; however, one should not trust the Africans. But she had insisted on not only seeing the part of Dar es Salam along the two splendid promenades, the German administration buildings, the tennis, golf, and soccer courts. She wanted to see how the Africans lived. Anthimos had ensured that there would not be any problems. Eventually, they set off late that night in the southern direction towards a village near the beach.

The *Ngoma*-drummer, a gigantic, bald Negro sat on the earth in the centre of a big, dense circle of people, surrounded by high blazing campfires. His heavy beats on the drum, a hollowed tree trunk with a stretched skin on it, engendered strange rhythms and sounds, sometimes loud, sometimes scarcely audible. Male and female dancers moved in the rapture and change of the rhythms, individually, paired or in rows, without touching each other, sometimes slowly, sometimes quickly, always with predatory suppleness. The spectators sang and clapped their hands, laughed, and drank *Pombe*, an intoxicating drink made of coconut palm juice. The full moon was above the village, and the night wind whispered through the palm trees. For the first time since her arrival, Margarete felt like she was being transported into another world.

There was, however, another feeling which initially scared her as she sensed it any time she approached Anthimos, stood beside him, or looked at him. She did not know why it occurred, nor did she want to explore it. It just happened! And it was stunning. She just knew: Her soul became wonderfully calm when she was near him. She felt safe and protected. It was a feeling she knew from her childhood when she hid in the haystack above Gut Petersdorf when melancholic thoughts troubled her soul – but nobody had ever been there to help her. At present, Anthimos was here!

On the ride back to Dar es Salam she suddenly saw the shine of a huge fire. Ulrich again had reservations to ride there and check what was happening. Still, the Greek swiped away Ulrich's fears by saying, „The night only scares the ignorant . . .“

Down by the sea, only a few metres from the shore, two fires were burning on rafts, surrounded by men and women in Indian clothing. Two corpses lay on the wooden rafts. They had watched the spooky burial ceremony from a respectful distance, observed silently how the blazing flames consumed the dead bodies, and the low-tide stream led the rafts gently floating into the open seas.

During the few remaining hours of last night, she had slept badly. Only the cool ocean breeze of the early morning and the smooth light of dawn blurred the images of the dancing Africans, the colourful Indians, the drifting corpses, and of Anthimos.

A scarcely audible, very reassuring „*Hodi! Kahawa tayari*“ of a servant on the other side of her room doors awakened Margarete from last hour's deep sleep. She slowly drew the mosquito net over the bed to the side and looked out of the window on the turquoise, peacefully seeming Indian Ocean. She was happy! She was amazed by this custom of a domestic serving a cup of coffee and some pastry in her room early in the morning. Everything here surprised her.

Some hours later, she and Ulrich left Dar es Salam to the north in the direction of Tanga. Anthimos Koundouriotis had already said good-bye the previous evening. He wanted to travel to the South of the country at the end of October to hunt elephants. He had promised to visit her on the Meru when he returned, which would only be at the beginning of the rainy season.

Just a few kilometres behind Dar es Salam the road started winding snake-like through dense mangrove bushes and palm groves. The hills ascending parallelly to the coast in North-East direction were densely wooded. Trickles, creeks, and rivers splattered downhill through the valleys. Gigantic ebony trees up to thirty metres of height, entwined by lianas, rose over idyllic valleys. All over the place, small African villages with reddish loam houses were hidden in palm groves.

After several days of a journey in bullock carts, they reached the coastal town of Tanga. Margarete Trappe felt faint and exhausted. Nevertheless, she was happy. She already imagined herself in this dream world she had only been reading of so far: in *Brehms Tierleben* – and in her brother Alfred's letters.

The one hundred and thirty kilometres of train journey with the Usambara-rail from Tanga to the inlands as far as the terminus took almost five hours. Shortly before their arrival, when the stinking and puffing train creaked up the final slopes of the Usambara mountains, the air humidity already decreased noticeably, and the outside temperature became more comfortable. It was only then when August Leue informed her that they would join a settlers' convoy of German Russians in Mombo:

„Why German Russians?" Ulrich Trappe wondered. Despite the cooling airstream, his kaki suit was soaked with sweat.

„Oh, they are wretched creatures, about fifty in number, some come from the Rhenish-Hesse Palatinate region, most of them from Swabia," August Leue answered. „Their ancestors followed an invitation

of Katharina II at the end of the last century, the German Princess on the Tsar throne. The settlers were to colonise the almost deserted areas around the Wolga, the Black Sea, and the Caucasus. The purpose was to help the open South flanks of the Russian Empire. Tsar Alexander II decided in 1871 to revoke the privileges of the German colonisation. They were equated to ordinary Russian farmers and had from there on to submit to their laws and duties. From 1874 on, the colonists' sons had to do military service in the tsarist army for the first time. The school lessons had to be held in Russian language under the reign of Alexander III; business affairs could also only be done in Russian. The German colonisation left any right to self-government in their villages. Hundreds of thousands emigrated to America. And some of them now try their luck in Africa."
„On what will these people live?" asked Margarete Trappe.
„They are poor, without exception. None of them have money to lease big estates from us. Some were granted support from the German Reich. But they learned to work hard. Those who are willing to work hard for a life in paradise will find fulfilment here in German East Africa."

*

The German settlement Wilhelmsthal was situated in Mombo, a shabby dump at the foot of the mountains. The railway station in the centre of the hilly landscape consisted of a tiny rubble building. An arrayed German railway official with a handlebar moustache, dressed in a spotless white uniform, bossed the black porters around.
Ulrich and Margarete Trappe kept silent, confused. After Dar es Salam with its promenades and the cosy town of Tanga, this Africa oppressed them. The euphoria of the last hours turned into silent dismay, given the sadness of this village.
However, the gate to paradise was just some hours behind this soulless space. The over two thousand metres high mountains of the Usambara range shone in the light of the early afternoon. The landscape was green and hilly and of incredible beauty. Strange, en-

chanting smells filled the air. Exotic plants, bushes, and magnificent flowers lined the oxcart path. As soon as the convoy of bearers comprised of several hundreds of Africans and dozens of mules left the last hills behind them, a wide, seamingly endless plain opened, ending in the mist of the horizon. Stunned, Margarete Trappe kept silent.

„Do you see it?" August Leue asked and pointed North West.

„What should I see?" she asked and protected her eyes with her hand to look against the setting sun at the other end of the world. She saw the land, vastness, and incredible gigantic cloud formations that loomed at the end of the plain like oversized cotton pads.

„Over there, amid the cumulus clouds! The Kilimanjaro – it does not always appear as beautiful: snowcapped, majestic . . ."

She saw it. There it was! She saw something so sublime and perfect that she did not want to believe it was a mountain.

They pitched their first camp aside a forest near a river in a nameless plane. But there was a wonderful scent of grass, flowers, and heavy, fertile earth, just like soil shortly after plowing. Margarete could see the Kilimanjaro through the light crowns of the acacias. The evening sun tinted both its summits in light pink. Everything around her was so smooth; the sounds dimmed, the odours intense. Far away, a zebra herd wandered through the steppe. She had never heard what she was listening to now. The scents seemed alien to her. Her perceptive faculty was overpowered by what she saw. As she found no words for her sensations and felt she had to be alone, she sat down on a hill above the river, away from the camp, and cried. Margarete felt that for the first time in years, they were not tears of desperation but of joy. The gun lay beside her on the grass. She did not feel like she needed it here. But suddenly, he stood in front of her, barely 30 metres away: he was tall, terribly tall. Oh my God, how beautiful he is, she thought. And so perfect and powerful. She could not explain to herself how something as tall could move so silently. She had not heard anything.

He looked in her direction. Without moving, her eyes wandered across the grass tilting towards her in the evening wind. The wind

74

was against her! That was good. He could not sense her; however, he tried to. He saw her, she saw him. His trunk lifted between the splendid tusks, curved and soaked up the odours of the evening. But nothing bothered him, so he carried on in slow motion, to the reeds on the riverside where he clasped the tips of the plants, tore them off and made them disappear in his small mouth under the tusks with relish. His huge ears clapped against his body. The only sound which drowned the murmur of the river was the crushing.

„Margarete! Are you crazy?"

Ulrich's scream pulled her out of her thoughts. He stood a few steps behind her, his rifle in his hand. The bull elephant whirled his head around. She could not discern his eyes, but she imagined what she would see in them. Her eyes jumped to Ulrich, back to the elephant and again to Ulrich.

The elephant put up its ears. Ulrich raised his rifle in position. The bull did not waste time with warnings. He came rushing through the bushes, with his head defiantly raised, the trunk and ears directed forward. He was fast, dreadfully fast.

She did not know the elephants' body language. However, she instinctively felt that this grey hulk wanted to kill them. A shot was fired. Unconsciously she realized the dry sound of the light calibre weapon. Ulrich preferred the light calibres for shooting. Perfect for gazelles and antelopes, but not for elephants.

„No . . . !" she yelled. Another shot was fired. The projectile ripped a piece of skin as big as a fist out of the animal's head over the right eye. But the elephant crossed the bushes. His look was painful. She jumped up, grabbed her big-bore gun, yanked it up: notch – bead sight – pause – slightly above and between the eyes, as she had read in the hunting books about Africa. Aiming beyond the gun barrel, she faced him directly. The bull had ridiculously small eyes. The skin between them formed jagged square ornaments made of wrinkles. Up close, he looked very ugly, he was furious and massive and only a few metres away from her.

The strong recoil pulled her backward. The elephant bull threw his head back as if an imaginary, powerful fist stopped him. For some moments, his front legs lifted off the ground. Tons of skin, flesh, and bones fell to its knees. The tusks bore into the red earth. Next, he fell to the side, inanimately, pitifully clumsy, and without any dignity. He was lying so near to her that Margarete could smell him. In death he looked even larger, but she was not afraid. She also did not shiver. She felt upset instead. She was sad. Slowly she turned around and looked at Ulrich. Margarete noticed that he was panicked. And he became aware that she disdained him . . .

During a two weeks' walk through the steppe along the river Pangani, the mountains had been on the horizon in front of her all the time. Now they came sharply into focus. The Pare mountains in the East disappeared. The land was gently sloping. The mood was quite galled. After the incident with the elephant, Ulrich and Margarete had avoided each other. The atmosphere between her and Hauptmann Leue had also been very oppressed. Without saying it out loud, he seemed to make her responsible and blame her for the elephant incident. She had left the camp against his instructions. She endeavoured to explain Ulrich's intervention and show understanding for it rationally. Nevertheless, Leue's permanent presumptuousness and paternalism triggered her bad mood. Eventually, the situation escalated when Leue made a point of her, as the only white woman, being carried by four Africans in a kind of sedan char, instead of walking. She could not stand being in this swinging thing overcast with mosquito nets for more than five minutes. She had put on her tall boots, taken the rifle, and walked in front of the column together with the African trackers. Hauptmann Leue was horrified about this.

The very day they reached their destination, the mount Meru massif after a fourteen hours' walk, something strange happened. Ulrich and the others had joined them in the meantime. The camp was situated on an elevation with a beautiful view of the Maasai steppe behind them, glowing golden in the evening light. To mark the occasion, Ulrich had opened a bottle of red wine. August Leue was satisfied. The journey had gone well, except for the incident with the elephant. They had barely seen lions or other predators, nor natives. Although the African porters talked about the Maasai being around, they did not see them. She had only spotted one, a young man with wondrously plated, ochre-coloured hair and with white symbols painted on his legs. He suddenly appeared in front of her, supporting himself on a long lance, one leg bent, and its sole put against the other leg. He stood there like a stork, one-legged, motionless, funny to watch, and had fixed her silently. He was a handsome man, tall, haggard, muscular, with a striking profile and concise facial features. As soon as she had taken off her hat and put on her sunglasses, he had disappeared in the bushes as quick as lightning.

The dull rumble of leopards had been heard three times at night and had only alarmed Margarete Trappe because Leue had told her that leopards had a preference for dogs. From that time on, Cäsar and Tell were allowed to sleep in her tent, reluctantly accepted by Ulrich. Apart from that, nothing had happened, and the mood was accordingly tranquil that evening.

„What a wonderful country! I already feel very much at home here. It is so wide and beautiful, almost deserted, and everything is ever so peaceful.“

„I presume that our troupes made it clear to the blacks who the new masters of this land are,“ August Leue started showing off again. She already knew his opinion concerning this topic. She had read in the German newspapers that the Maji-Maji rebellion had been quashed by brutal force by the protection troops, but she was disgusted by the details August Leue told her. He was a militarist of the worst kind, a power seeker. She thought for a moment that this might be the reason why he got along so well with Ulrich.

„The blacks are lazy, awkward, and refuse to work,“ Ulrich started to approve Leue's theories. He held his glass of red wine in his hand. The rifle hung behind him in the tent.

„This will be one of the problems you will permanently have to deal with here,“ August Leue continued. „There is enough land, wonderful, fertile land. However, it will be difficult to find trusty workers

for your farm. The niggers are hard to motivate to come to work regularly."
„The niggers are just not civilised people," Ulrich Trappe pondered.
„Without the help of the white man, they would still be in the same
place as they had been a thousand years ago. But I do not think I
would have a problem with this. I will be able to accomplish what I
was able to accomplish with my recruits with these savages. The magic formula is discipline. And it always works."
Margarete Trappe kept silent. She knew Ulrich's banalities ever so
well. The sad fact was his firm belief in what he said. She tried to
change the topic.
„So how much land would we need to run a productive farm?"
„Well, this depends, of course, on your financial resources. There is
very fertile land which is suitable for planters, especially in the
Usambara and Pare mountains. If you intend to raise cattle, which
seems to be your intention, you could get your own land for little
money. But you also need funds to buy cattle and pay your workers.
It requires a certain sum. You will probably need twenty thousand to
thirty thousand rupees, approximately thirty thousand Reichsmark,
to build a farmhouse, a Boma which is a fenced terrain for the cattle,
and servants as well as equipment."
„We are somewhat toying with the idea not only to raise cattle but
also grow plants. What are the chances we might be successful and,
in particular, the possibilities to sell our products?" Ulrich Trappe
asked.
„This is an excellent idea. For one thing, you will be self-sufficient,
have your small vegetable plants on your farm, have fruit, own poul-
try, pigs, and the income from the cattle breeding. On the other side,
you are protected against the imponderables of nature. The rinder-
pest was almost eliminated since the last big scourge eight years
ago, and the foot-and-mouth disease occurs very rarely. But you
might live dry years with low rainfall. As a planter, you have a side-
line."
August Leue stopped abruptly. His look turned away from Ulrich
Trappe into the darkness. They suddenly stood right before them in

the light of the campfire. It was difficult to see how many they were. The night was surrounding them. Their red capes gave them a night-marish aura. The spearheads reflected the fire. They silently stared first at the two white men, then fixed Margarete Trappe.

„Maasai . . . ,“ August Leue hissed. „They are warriors, many war-riors. A great many!“ He squinted anxiously at his rife, lying beside his chair.

Ulrich Trappe got nervous. „What do they want? Are they hostile?“ he whispered. Welding beads appeared on his forehead. He did not dare to put down his wine glass. His eyes assessed the warriors, who were only twenty steps away. They were all slender and wiry. One of the *Moran* murmured some words to the other warriors. A barely audible „*Aaayaaa*“ gave a hint of consent for the presumable leader.

„What do they say?“

Ulrich Trappe saw how the warriors were still staring at his wife

„I barely understand their language,“ August Leue answered quietly. „It is about an Iron-Snake and eyes of glass.“

„Why are they staring at my wife in this way?“ Ulrich Trappe asked.

„I don't know!“

„Are they dangerous?“

August Leue's terse response was, „Maasai men are always danger-ous.“

„Are they not afraid of our rifles?“

„The Maasai people are not scared of anything. They are fearless. Absolutely fearless.“

The leader of the Maasai suddenly left the group and walked confi-dently towards the three white men. His spear was taller than his head by several hand breadths. A dagger dangled at his right hip. He fixed Margarete Trappe almost hypnotically and seemed to ignore the two men. He stopped at the table. Margarete noticed that she for-got to breathe. Her temples throbbed. The wind blew her long hair over her face. However, she did not dare to lift her hand or even move.

The Maasai leaned forward and slowly grabbed her sunglasses, which lay on the table in front of him. He cautiously took the frame in his hand and was intrigued. He took one more step forward in the direction of Margarete Trappe. His left hand reached for her silky hair, palpated it carefully, touched her temples, leaned forward even more, pursed his lips, and blew into her hair until it moved in his breath.

„Jeyo!" he whispered. Then he turned to the other warriors, held her sunglasses in their direction, and murmured some incomprehensible words. An „Aaayaaa," came from the Morani.

„Jeyo!" The leader said more, stared at Margarete Trappe as if hypnotised by her, and nodded his head slightly. Next, he dropped the glasses, turned, and walked away. Some seconds later, the warriors had disappeared into the darkness.

„What the hell was that?"

Ulrich Trappe jumped up from his chair, hurried to the tent, and grabbed the rifle. His eyes were full of panic. He was drenched in sweat; his shirt was dripping wet. He loaded like a flash, fired a shot into the air, repeated, fired, repeated.

Margarete Trappe perceived the fear in her husband's eyes. August Leue still sat on his chair without moving. She wondered why she was not really afraid.

„These bastards are the most sinister and dangerous people in East Africa," August Leue whispered.

He reached for the wine and took a swig from the bottle. „Everybody is afraid of them: the niggers, the Indian, Arabs – and me also. They are unpredictable, very warlike, and incredibly brave!"

„They did not seem to want to cause any harm," Margarete Trappe's tension diminished. „He looked deep in my eyes, the whole time, his gaze was steady. But he was smiling a little bit."

Ulrich Trappe became exited. „Why did our guards not interfere?" He ran to and fro hysterically. „Askari! Ahmadou!" he yelled at the leader of the camp guards. The square-shouldered African with the shoulder-length pigtail slinked along and, with hanging shoulders, stopped in front of him.

„What did these Maasai shitheads want?" Ulrich Trappe shouted at him.

„Bwana,“ the Askari stammered, „the Maasai only came to have a look! They did not want to harm us. They wanted to see *Jeyo!*“

„Damned, don't talk so stupidly! Who is *Jeyo*? What does that mean? Speak out, you lousy bastard!“

„In the Maasai language, *Jeyo* means mother.“

Ulrich Trappe fell silent abruptly. His eyes moved questioning from August Leue to his wife.

„Leave him! The Askaris are also afraid,“ August Leue interfered. „Whatever this *Jeyo* means, I don't know either. But I know one thing for sure: These Maasai are very dangerous and battle-tested.“

„Why doesn't our Kaiserliche Schutztruppe do anything about these savages? Why do they not shoot down those sons of bitches if they do not observe any law?“

Margarete Trappe looked horrified at her husband. Ulrich's hate frightened her.

„Who should do that? Who should fight against the Maasai?“ August Leue murmured and stared into the fire. „There are hundreds of thousands out there in the steppes. They are semi-nomads. Freedom means everything to them. Today they are here, and tomorrow they are there. If you shoot one of them, hundreds will come to take revenge! If you shoot hundreds, thousands will come. The English military tried some years ago in Kedong Valley, not far from Nairobi, to crush the Maasai once and for all. They call his region ‚Blood Valley' ever since. Because the Maasai destroyed the English troops down to the last man.

As I already said: These people are absolutely fearless. You should watch them killing a lion. Then you would understand me. Every Maasai man has to kill a lion by himself only with his spear, to be nominated a warrior, a *Moran*. Believe me. Such a young warrior approaches a lion with his head up high until the lion feels so cornered that it attacks, has to attack. Lions don't have any natural enemies. Besides elephants, nothing would challenge them like this. The lion has no other choice than to prove its supremacy. It has to attack! The Maasai does not back off one millimetre, not even one single millimetre! When the lion starts to jump the last few metres, the *Moran* gets on his knees, rams the end of the spear into the ground, holds it angled in front of him – and lets the lion jump right into the spear."

Margarete Trappe listened fascinated by August Leue's stories. She felt kind of a strange fascination for this seemingly ever so brave and also warlike Maasai tribe.

August Leue got up. He was tired and went to his tent. On the way, he mentioned: „The lions are said to leave the land when they see a Maasai spearhead on the horizon, they are that afraid of the masters of the East African steppes. And just to be honest: I feel the same. But what worries me most is: What the hell did the warrior mean by *Jeyo* . . . ?"

The Maasai people were omnipresent the next day. At the first dawn twilight, two warriors stood on a hill many hundred steps away from the camp. They just stood there, dead still, like statues, shimmering reddish-brown in the first light just like the strange termite hills in the plains. They stayed there when camp was broke, the mules packed, and the fires extinguished. They still stood there as the column of hundreds of porters went on their way towards the mountains.

As soon as the two Maasai-*Morani* where out of sight in the dust whirls generated by the morning wind, four more Maasai stood on another chain of hills above a dry riverbed. Their red capes fluttered in the wind. They also just stood there, seemingly uninterested, and bored. They were too far away to see their faces, but too near for the German settlers to feel fearless.

Ulrich Trappe was even more nervous than the evening before. He carried a loaded rifle in the crook of his arm and another one over his left shoulder. Time and time again, he looked at the warriors, searched for other Maasai behind the surrounding thornbush, and wandered restlessly through the hill chains in front of the caravan. His wife was riding her horse beside him. Her rifle was in the case fixed to the saddle. She seemed to be totally relaxed. Ulrich watched Margarete out of the corner of his eyes. Her face had taken on a tanned look from the last two weeks. Margarete wore linen breeches with leather trim and a light khaki shirt. Her slim, well-proportioned body was seducing as she sat so upright and self-confident in the saddle. Her hair was plaited into a braid and hung over one shoulder on her breast. She just looked desirable. Her calmness and strength attracted Ulrich, fascinated him, increased his lust. However, he felt that strange distance between them as he had felt it during the last weeks ever since they had arrived in Africa. She was not unapproachable and had not repelled him, but she had an inner strength that intimidated him.

He had also been aware of how Margarete admired this Greek and sometimes even stared at him openly. But no matter how much he kept an eye on Anthimos, searching for alleged signals of his interest in Margarete, the Greek had always shown up as an honourable man – and free spirit. He was a man of excellent education and best manners. Despite his dressing down and jovial behaviour, he had perfectly mastered the etiquette at the evening festivities in Dar es Salam. He had always kept an absolutely correct distance to Margarete. Ulrich was impressed by what he had heard and knew about him. Anthimos Koundouriotis was said to be one of the best big-game hunters in East Africa. Due to his father's diplomatic career, he had seen a lot of the world and came from well-to-do circles. Nobody knew whether he who was already forty years old had ever been married. It was also a mystery why he was not married. But everybody affirmed that his behaviour towards the white women in Dar es Salam was correct. No doubt, the Greek was a gentleman, an aging gentleman.

And Margarete was a Lady. A gorgeous and young lady.

That was Ulrich's very problem. She was too strong for him! As strong that he dared not physical closeness to her. Why was she never afraid? Why had she not panicked when the elephant attacked her? Why did her wrist not tremble when she shot her first rhinoceros? She had let the attacking animal approach so much that the African rifle porters and trackers were about to run away in panic. No, she had allowed the colossal animal to come near and waited until it lowered the powerful horn for the fatal attack. Only then, had she pulled the trigger and shot the bullet so precisely into the neck that the hulk broke down instantly. Rifle porters, cooks, servants, and porters: all Africans admired her. He also did, very much indeed. But he did not dare to show this admiration or even his lust. He was afraid of being rejected by her.

The land rose continually. The caravan only advanced slowly. It separated near a village called Leganga. The German-Russian settlers remained there. They would settle down right here, at the Western slopes of the Meru, run their small agricultural farms, or work as craftsmen.

Margarete and Ulrich Trappe moved on, along the South-Eastern foot of the Meru. The mountain itself was out of sight, and clouds covered it. Wafts of mist pervaded the dense forests. August Leue had gotten two horses in Leganga and accompanied them on the ride in the region they had been offered land in.

They did not see the Maasai people who were still omnipresent. They all felt it just like everybody sensed that people were watching them from everywhere in the mountains and the forests which were becoming lusher.

The climb became harder in the afternoon. The horses had difficulties with the stony ground. Shreds of clouds hid the Meru. The fog was caught by the dense bushes. The atmosphere was spooky. The roaring of a waterfall resounded from some canyon parallel to their route.

All the sudden, there was neither the rustling nor the murmur of a creek, nor the sound of the breeze nor of the birds. The conglomerate of fog and shreds of clouds hanging low on the mountain was so dense that August Leue decided to tie together the porters with cords so that no one would get lost – or take the opportunity to get away with the precious cargo.

Margarete Trappe was worried. She hated the fog. The atmosphere up in the mountain made her nervous for the first time. There were elephants and buffaloes everywhere. She had not seen any during the last hours, but there were spoors and manure everywhere. Some of the big piles of dung where still fuming. She intuitively felt that this impenetrable mountain forest was dangerous. If ever they were to meet some buffalo or elephant or even a lion, the time for reacting would be extremely short, the possibility to aim a shot almost nil.

She walked highly concentrated beside her horse, holding a shotgun in her right hand. A rifle porter followed her closely, more due to fear than a sense of duty. The large-bore rifle hung loaded and unlocked over his shoulder. The proximity of the rifle porter was very unpleasant to her. A loaded and unlocked weapon always made her nervous. The fog had wholly soaked her clothes. Strands of her hair covered her face. Her boots were soaked. A blister on her right heel hurt. Ulrich led his horse right in front of her. He held a pistol in his hand. She noticed by the abrupt side movements of his head that he was extremely tense.

The first scream came from higher up to the right out of the bushes, very nearby, only a few paces away. It was the most horrifying scream Margarete had heard in all her life: shrill, guttural, aggressive. Next, the screams echoed throughout the whole forest. Everywhere.

She swirled her head. Her horse shied and tore her to the ground by the bridles. Dull pain in her knee made her scream. Her rifle hit a rock. The rifle porter behind her also screamed, without even knowing why. Ulrich threw himself on the ground and shot randomly into the fog. Porters shouted further ahead, where August Leue was supposed to be. Chests crashed down. There was chaos, panic, and horror everywhere around them, in the trees, bushes, fog, above, in front of and beside her. Trees swayed, branches ripped through the air. The forest was in revolt.

Next, she saw the face, the black and white mask with the long hair, saw the nightmare rush towards her, she rolled to the side, and grabbed the rifle.

The face was about to make the jump, arms wide open. The creature behind the face loomed massive, and the eyes, evil and bloodshot, made her blood freeze in her veins. She lifted the gun and shot. The recoil made the gun stock hit her in the stomach. The pain made her scream. When she pulled the trigger, she noticed too late that the face wanted to rush past her. Then horror fell on her, as she saw that it was dead.

„Margarete . . . ! Margarete!" Ulrich Trappe stumbled through the thicket, still shooting left and right into the fog, without noticing that he was out of bullets, he fell, got up, fell again, and threw himself over his wife with his last effort. Only her head could still be seen. Her body was covered by an animal, almost as tall as she was, with a huge tail and long white hair on the shoulders and in the face. Half of the head was shot away.

Margarete Trappe's face was white like snow. She was sobbing and trembling with fear. Blood from the blasted head of the dead Colobus monkey dropped on her cheeks. She stared at the monkey's eyes and noticed that it must have been a stunning animal.

*

Where the dozens of hills and canyons arising from the valley united in one large crest, the mountain cleared to a woodless high plateau, interspersed by massive granite rocks. The world was soundless. The ocean of clouds and fog in the valleys below opened, and the first single trees popped up, next whole forests and eventually paradise on earth appeared.

„We will stay here . . . ," Margarete Trappe whispered. Her husband stood next to her and grabbed her hand. Their gazes went down to a vast clearing, surrounded by dominant trees at the foot of a mountain. A small lake was amid the clearing, fed by a creek winding out of forests through the meadows. Elephants romped about in the mud of the bank. A heard of buffaloes, zebras, gazelles, and antelopes were grazing in the verdant pastures.

All the sudden, as if God were not satisfied with his work of all this magnificent wonder of the African nature, the clouds and fog banks dispersed, and first, a small hill popped up behind the lake and then more slopes and tiny clearings. The seemingly endless yellow-brown and golden Maasai steppe lay behind the hills.

Margarete Trappe took a deep breath. She felt her husband's hand in hers. It was a wonderful feeling.

„Look, Ulrich, over there," she started chattering delightedly and pointed to the Kilimanjaro. „And there!" She swirled around. Behind them, between verdant meadows and a bastion of forests and bushes, were small and big lakes, draped like marbles on an evergreen floor of moss. Flamingos stalked through the lake scenery. Hippos opened their mouths wide and grunted pleasantly at the sun.

„It is the most beautiful thing I have ever seen," Ulrich Trappe murmured. His eyes glazed. She looked at him from the side. She had never seen tears of joy in his eyes before. Never before she had felt so familiarly close to him. It seemed to her that it might be love.

„There!"

Again, she pointed at a new miracle, a very high, massive, picturesque mountain. An even higher peak grew up into the sky, into the clouds. The African rifle porter suddenly stood beside them.

„This is Meru, and the mountain behind is Tululusiek, the gatekeeper to Meru. And in Maasai language, the clearance down there where the buffaloes and gazelles are grazing is called *Ngongongare* – The Eye of the Water."

Chapter 7

The older men with the wrinkled faces and tiny eyes sat in a valley of the Meru massif, which the Maasai people called *Ngare Nanyuki*. The men looked quite harmless. However, the purpose of their meeting was to talk about killing.

Kinai ole Chieni, the youngest of all present, was the first to take the floor: „The prophecy of our *Laibon* Masiani ole Chieni, my fathers' father, having the same blood as me in his veins, has been fulfilled! Finally, what *Engai*, God of all Maasai people told him through an angel one night a long time ago has come to pass – that something terrifying would come over the Maasai tribe like the night over the plain!"

The men, more than twenty men, chiefs and elders of the Wareru, Waarusha, and Wachagga, but also Maasai agreed.

„*Aaayaaa* . . ." The big fire in the centre illuminated their faces. Their eyes sparkled. They listened spellbound to the words of the young Maasai's whose fate was known to all of them.

„The iron snake our *Laibon* predicted is creeping hissing and fuming and stinking through our land.

It is winding from the big water in the South up the mountains to Mombo, in the hills called Usambara. And it will soon come here, to the Meru. The iron snake spits fire and smoke, and Wazungu, who steal our land, force our men to do slave work and hang them with ropes if they refuse, ooze out of its belly. And if they don't have enough ropes and trees to hang them by their throat, they mow them down with machine guns: as they did to my father, Mojo ole Chieni, the son of *Laibon* Masiani. You all heard how he was killed many years ago by the Germans' in front of the Arusha *Boma* . . ."

„Aaayaaa . . ."

„According to the will of my tribe, my life should be devoted to the task of a Laibon. And you all know that from the date of my father's death, I dedicated my life to the revenge. Hate will be alive in me until my death!"

„Aaayaaa . . . !“

„And as this corresponds to *Engai's* will, I am sitting here today in front of you as *Moran,* as a warrior with the wisdom of many years.“

„What are you expecting from us?“ a Wameru asked. Kinai stared into the fire and continued talking calmly.

„We all know that the iron snake, the railway as the *Wazungu* call this thing, changed our life. Because the white men came with it. And it brought ruin along!“

„Aaayaaa . . . ,“ the old men and elders echoed into the African night.

„Tell us what you want from us,“ a Waarusha required. Kinai got up and looked around the fire, looked right into the eyes of every man, one at a time.

„Many things have happened since our last meeting. More and more white settlers arrive. They occupy more and more land. They already took away the most fertile fields at the Meru from the Wameru. They are pushing our Maasai tribe further to the steppe, where there is no water. They want to pen us in reservations, just like cattle. Two German settlers are building a house and are fencing the whole mountain In Ngongongare, land which has belonged to the Maasai ever since. Not far from there, a man, a former soldier, is constructing a *Boma,* which is almost as big and impregnable as the *Boma* of the German soldiers in Arusha. They are building a village with a house where they pay homage to their God in Leganga. A village with many houses the *Wazungu* call Leudorf. The more of them arrive, the more soldiers follow to protect them. If we don't put a stop to them, they will soon steal the air we breathe!“

„How shall we fight the *Wazungu,* Kinai?“ a Wameru interrupted the Maasai. „And why should we just listen to you, Maasai people? The Maasai tribe is stealing our cattle, and they steal the Waarusha and other tribes' cattle also. You only want us to fight the *Wazungu* because they are stealing more of the land than you, but you cannot defeat them alone! They have guns and canons; they talk with wires. After having done it, even more soldiers come. They are strong, powerful, unbeatable! Spears against canons: that would be the defeat of our tribe . . ."

„This is true!" Kinai answered the Wameru chief. „The white men are powerful. It is also true that we, the Maasai people, cannot chase them away alone. Therefore, we have to turn their weakness into our strength – and: We all have to join, fight them together! Because they think that a Maasai breeding cattle will never fight again with a Meru cultivating fields, a Chagga will never fight together with the Waarusha people. They shall continue to think this way! And they shall go on living under the impression that their canons protect them. But we will go where their canons cannot get, into the marshes and the mountains. We have to fight when they sleep; we have to kill when they lay down ill; we must hit their most vulnerable points."

„All this sounds good, Kinai ole Chieni," a Waarusha interrupted him. „However, you feel hate against the white men deep inside yourself because they killed your father. You only need our help to accomplish your revenge!"

„Yes," Kinai admitted, „I swore everlasting revenge for the death of my father, and the other Maasai people killed in front of the Arusha *Boma*. It is true. But I also say that we have only one chance to chase the white men off: We must make life as hard as possible for them using our own resources. We know every dust particle, each cavern, and each mountain path. Therefore, we have to fight together without the *Wazungu* knowing who is fighting them. This is what I have to say with hate in my heart. But your wisdom will decide . . ."

When Kinai ole Chieni left the secret meeting at Ngare Nanyuki late in the night, he was delighted. After a long palaver, the chiefs and elders of the other tribes had agreed to his plan. They were also ready to start the silent, invisible battle against the white men quickly. However, he had not told the chiefs this strange thing about the white woman, about *Jeyo*, who, together with her husband, started building houses at Ngongongare. They had a long consultation with all Maasai elders. However, they had not found out *Jeyo's* relationship to the prophecy of their *Laibon*. It was only clear that this woman was what Masiani ole Chieni had predicted more than twenty years ago: that a terrifying white shadow with eyes of glass and silky dark hair would come over the Maasai land. Yes, it was this woman! However, Masiani ole Chieni had also stated that this shadow would follow a new Maasai *Laibon* forever as a shadow. He had called her „*Jeyo* – mother." And they did not understand it.

*

„There is something in the wind! When the people in the village are no longer dancing and laughing, there is something shady afoot!"
Pastor Martin Schachschneider from the Leipzig mission at Nkoaranga station, on the Meru slopes, could not escape the feeling that something unhealthy had been brewing for some time, something he could not explain. How he would have loved to wholeheartedly be happy about the new church bell the Christian Brothers from Dortmund had donated to the Leudorf church. He would have preferred to think about the construction of the mission hospital and the mission school, which numbered already twenty children, as the village of Leudorf kept growing. New settlers kept arriving and built forges, grocers, taverns, and even a grain mill. But in his black community, strange rumours had been going around for weeks. Since last night, he knew that a great disaster had started in this splendid corner of German East Africa.
In the middle of the night, a scream from his brother Arthur Schindler's room had shaken him out of his sleep. Dressed in his nightgown, he had rushed up the stairs of the mission building and into the rooms of his fellow believer. In the pale candlelight, he held in his hand, he saw Arthur Schindler standing at the headboard of his bed, pointing horrified at the bed. Only when he looked closer, he noticed the snake lying coiled at the foot end of the bed. It was a puff adder, more than one metre long and as thick as an arm, with a large head and tiny eyes. These snakes are very slow and almost motionless when it is cold. When they get cornered, they coil and emit

strange dull sibilants, mostly followed by the fatal bite. Some months ago, a child from a nearby village had been brought to the mission station, as a puff adder had bitten its leg.

One hour later, the leg looked disgusting, because the puff adder poison does not affect the nerve centre as the poison of a cobra or a mamba would. Still, it decomposes the tissue of the victim: it happens very slowly, is extremely painful, and goes along with horrible external signs. The victim can literally watch how the death keeps creeping up the body, how the skin and the tissue beneath change. At the moment of the black girl's admission, her leg had been almost white, the flesh grey, the muscles almost inanimate. A few hours later, the child died as there was no antidote. The only possible salvation would have been a rapid amputation of the leg.
Such a puff adder had been lying in the bed of Brother Schindler. „Don't you move," Martin Schachschneider shouted at him, knowing that these snakes have poor sight, however, orientated by a thermal sensor perceived the movements of their victims. Next, he had rushed down into his room, fetched the shotgun the German Kaiserliche Schutztruppe had put at his disposal, and shot the snake.
It would have seemed just another one of the usual snake incidents in Africa, if whilst getting the gun, he had not had a sudden brainwave about how this very rigid snake might have gotten up to the first floor of the house. During several years in Nkoaranga, where there were lots of tree snakes, pythons, and mambas, his instincts had been sharpened and told him that this snake could not have crept up the staircase. A mamba or a boomslang – yes, but not a puff adder! With dull thoughts, he had immediately returned to his room at the ground floor, loaded the shotgun again, and checked every corner of the room with the light of the paraffin lamp. And Yes! In his room, under a footstool, was also a coiled puff adder, emitting a deadly hissing. Immediately all the occupants of the mission were carefully awakened, all the doors and windows closed from outside. At first daylight, they started searching, assisted by the locals. They scoured every corner of the mission building, uncovered every bed

carefully, ransacked each wardrobe and poked with sticks through all the wall cracks. Around noon, six dead puff adders lay in the mission's front garden. All the attendees knew that this was no coincidence. No doubt, these snakes had been brought into the house with lethal intentions. But who had done this?

Around noon, Martin Schachschneider sent a messenger to the district office in Arusha and the commander of the Kaiserliche Schutztruppen. He had the feeling that something was going on in the villages of the Waarusha, Wachagga, and Wameru, maybe even of the Maasai people. Ant this was related to the increasing flow of German and Boer settlers. He had only been at the Meru for two years, and his colleague Arthur Schindler had just arrived some weeks ago. However, his African Brother Edward Ittameire, who had been part of the Meru mission since 1905, was in excellent contact with his black brothers, he spoke Swahili as well as Maa and the language of the Wachagga and Wameru tribes. It was his idea to take the nightly incident as a reason to talk with Lieutenant Georg Küster, the commander of the German Kaiserliche Schutztruppe stationed in Arusha. The Lieutenant had immediately come running, together with some Askaris.

The men sat on the terrace of the mission building. It was a cold evening, and the sky was cloudy. A storm was brewing on the horizon of the Maasai steppe. Lieutenant Küster tried to calm the pastor.

„Brother Schachschneider, I do understand your fear. But you know that these snakes represent a real plague here. Only last week I had an almost eight metres long rock python in my office. When the rainy season arrives, and it gets cold, the beasts look for a dry place. That's what it is. Therefore, one should always check the room before going to bed. Well, and the rumours you are talking of . . ."

„Well, Lieutenant Küster," Edward Ittameire interrupted the commander of the protection troupe indignantly, „I am African. I grew up with snakes. Of course, it happens time and again that snakes get into a house. But not six in one night! It is absurd! Somebody brought these highly poisonous and very irritable snakes into the mission to kill us – or to send a message! No lightning-fast mambas which shoo out of the room at the first opportunity to escape, no! Puff adders! Every African knows that these animals don't escape but stay lying because of their slowness – and bite as a last resort. Someone tried to kill us!"

Lieutenant Küster cleared his throat embarrassedly.

„Ever since I have been stationed here in Arusha, which has been quite some years, there were always situations to worry about. The puff adder story is quite strange. We will question your black employees later on. But to be honest, you should not pay much attention to the rumours among the blacks. Rumors always occur. As a soldier, I stick to the facts. And I react to them."

Edward Ittameire, a seemingly feeble man of small stature and strange protruding cheekbones had been born in the South of the country and lived among the Brothers of the Leipziger Mission. He shook his head doubtfully.

„Lieutenant Küster, the people here do not easily forget. Nor do they accept quickly that their life has changed – directed by the *Wazungu*. I think you just underestimate the pride of the Africans. And, Lieutenant, you cannot shoot pride!"

Pastor Martin Schachschneider swallowed embarrassedly. This hint was quite direct. He knew that not for nothing, Lieutenant Küster was called Bwana Fisi by the African population. Years ago, the massacre of almost four hundred Maasai people in front of the Arusha *Boma* had spread the reputation of the Lieutenant as „hyena man" all over the Maasai steppe.

The other regional tribes did not appreciate the Maasai a lot because of the predatory and warlike behaviour. The Waarusha, Wachagga, and Wameru people were therefore not interested in what had happened then. However, the residents of the Meru did not forget such punitive actions of the Germans as those that took place late October 1896. After the cruel killing of his two fellow believers Segebrock and Ovir, on October 20th, 1896, the Germans under Lieutenant Johannes, as an act of revenge, had caused an incredible bloodbath amongst the population. Hired by company commander Johannes and Lieutenant Merker with money and promises, more than ten thousand Chagga warriors, supported by German soldiers, had ransacked the villages of the Waarusha and Wameru, had killed, robbed, raped, and burnt down entire communities. The African population had conceived the confiscation of more than six thousand cattle, goats, and sheep, as the cruellest punishment taking away their livelihood, thus creating dreadful famines. This punitive expedition of the Germans, which took place during a year with a particularly short rain season, had gone down in the history of the local people as the „rain war" – and was never forgotten again. Lieutenant Küster seemed to ignore this totally, as well as the recent events.

„Last week, the child of a German settler family died in Leudorf," Brother Martin Schachschneider tried to bring Lieutenant Küster to his senses. „It first seemed as if the child had eaten some toxic plant. But Brother Edward Ittameire found out that the Wameru people rumour that the child died from the poison extracted from a crocodiles stomach, that it was murdered!"

Lieutenant Küster was astonished. „Poison out of a crocodile stomach? I never heard that before."

„This is a common and fierce method of killing unpleasant people in East Africa," the African missionary answered. „As you probably know, crocodiles swallow their prey entirely. They just gulp their victim down as their jaws and teeth are not made for crushing. According to this, their gastric acid is very caustic. Such a crocodile's stomach acid can dissolve an antelope in one day. There is nothing left, not even a bone. The acid is accordingly lethal for humans when it gets mixed into food. If you swallow this poison, you die a miserable death suffering from a horrible pain. Nothing, absolutely nothing can be done about it!"

„Fantasies!" Lieutenant Küster laughed out loud. „The niggers show a conspicuous connection to mysticism, to spirits and gods. They love to invent horror stories."

„Bizarre things have happened during the last twelve months around the Meru, Lieutenant. Almost every white settler lost cattle, goats, or sheep. Many of them! Either the animals were poisoned, or they were stolen. They found one German immigrant stabbed to death, and two others died under very strange circumstances and with symptoms suggesting that poison was involved. A soldier of the Kaiserliche Schutztruppe died near the Arusha *Boma*. A Boer child disappeared without a trace three weeks ago! No, Lieutenant Küster, these are no mere coincidences. The white settlers are afraid! Something is brewing, slowly but unstoppably!"

Lieutenant Küster became subdued.

„Well, of course, I know about all these incidents, but unlike you, I don't see a revolt against the White Man behind it. These are individual cases."

Edward Ittameire interrupted the commander.

„If the African population learned anything during the last ten years, it is that with spears, they have no chance against German guns. They lost several fights with their conventional arms against a well-trained army. Many of their chiefs where hung. Hundreds of them were whipped. Lieutenant Johannes' punitive actions following the burnt soil tactic lead to famines. They understood these lessons indeed! There is no broad united front here in East Africa, something you would call a national unity. However, the people in the villages and cottages will keep revolting against what they conceive as foreign oppression. The question is, how?"

*

Margarete Trappe was happy. She sat at the make-shift table made of wooden chests. She had returned from the nearby Mayo waterfall only some minutes previously, where she had taken a wonderfully refreshing bath, as naked as God had created her.

The sun was setting slowly behind the hills. The evening was pleasantly lukewarm. A cup of hot tea stood in front of her. She looked at the forest from where she heard the undeniable crackling and breaking sounds of feeding elephants. Yes, it was paradise on earth! Ngongongare, her new home country in Africa, was her own garden of Eden, with all the beautiful animals, flowers, bushes, and trees the creator had provided.

No doubt: Through hard work and steadfast belief, they would make a productive farm out of this still wild, unspoiled gem. The conditions were optimal: The climate up here in the mountains was almost like the one in the German highlands. Malaria only existed in the marshes. There was enough pasture and plenty of water. Almost everything they had planted on their Silesian estate was also thriving magnificently here. Ulrich was amazed by his rose beds. He even planned to grow wine. The first paths led through their farm. Soon, a gravel path to Leudorf would be completed, which would reduce the ride to the local shops and the mission hospital to half an hour. Yes, this was the paradise she had been dreaming of from an early age. After the first very difficult months, characterised by hard work, now the first evenings of relaxation such as this one took place, during which she wanted to take the time to write a detailed letter to Emily Ruete in Berlin.

She opened a wooden chest and fished out a writing pad as well as ink and a feather. She wondered how the Princess of Zanzibar was and began to write:

Ngongongare, July 16th, 1908

Esteemed Emily, dearest friend!

I have such a bad conscience because I have not found the time to write you a letter in so long. You certainly comprehend that since we departed from Dar el Salam for the African inlands nine months ago, I have been overwhelmed by new impressions and experiences. Where should I begin my tale? All this monkey business in my head! I can confirm one thing for sure: I do love this land! I love Africa! Here I am happy!
We found our dream, our paradise! It is a big farm of six thousand hectares at the foot of the Meru, not far from the Kilimanjaro. We leased it from the German government; however, we are bound to make use of it. Only once we can prove that we are farming this place, we will be able to purchase it and buy more land.

With good weather conditions, we can see the mighty Meru behind our current camp, the Kilimanjaro to our right, and the endless Maasai steppe up to the horizon in front of us. In the evening, we can watch how the night changes the land, and the snow-covered top of the Kilimanjaro keeps shining quite some time in the sun, while the steppe is already in the dark. What an indescribably beautiful feeling.

Up here at the altitude of one thousand one hundred metres, it is almost always green, with magnificent jungles, uncanny valleys and many lakes, embedded in between the hills just like pearls. But those are alkaline lakes. The water use is restricted. However, hundreds of thousands of flamingos live there. When they get startled, the land and the sky turn into a blaze of colours of soft purple and white. Oh my God, Emily, if you could see this miracle of nature only once, you would know why I am so happy here. Moreover, there is a fantastically beautiful waterfall nearby, as there are also many beautiful creeks all around.

We first had to find an optimal ground for our camp, the subsequent farmhouse. We discovered a beautiful place above a clearing with a lake the local Maasai call „Ngongongare – the Eye of the Water.“ Isn't this the most beautiful name one can find for his new home in Africa? „The Eye of the Water!“ The sound of this name alone describes this place.

The first weeks in the tent, dear Emily, were very romantic, however, also quite exhausting, as we were always searching for things still packed in cases. And as we expected the first rainy season, we had to speed up the construction of the cottages. The African women carried huge loads of Malamba on their heads, wilted and dried banana leaves. Strings defined the cottages' outlines, a strong stem was put every two metres, the spaces between them were filled by thinner stems, twisted together by lianas. The roof construction is similar. I felt like dancing with joy when I felt the compacted soil of the cottage under my feet for the first time. We had not brought any furniture along. The essential chairs, tables, shelves were carpentered, within short time out of cases and boxes. We went along very well, although at first, we even renounced windows and used curtains instead. Once we had taken curtains, covers, and lots of bits and pieces out of the boxes, we were soon comfortable and therefore began to invite other German settlers living nearby over.

Whatever we do, we must consider dangers we do not know from Germany, for example, the grasshoppers. These evil creatures already haunted us, and they were accompanied by some natural phenomenon that surprised me much more than the grasshoppers did. The grasshoppers are a treat of sorts for the storks; and also for the Africans who dry them in the sun after having pulled their legs and wings out and later on eat them with delight.

Once our temporary farm was in progress, we started thinking about constructing a massive house. After some time searching, we found good clay for the bricks, and the brick factory with all its refinement was running. Ulrich is very skilled when it comes to the house. He likes doing this.

The house was soon plastered, and we moved happily into the first room, that was ready. Really happily, as the rats had thoroughly spoiled the housing in the cottage before so that we even returned remorsefully to our tents. Eventually, we had a solid roof over our heads! A permanent place!

August Leue from the Deutsch-Ostafrikanische Gesellschaft bought a magnificent piece of land not far from here, barely more than one hour's ride, where he is building a seemingly gigantic Boma. To be honest, it seems to me that August Leue, as well as some other Germans we only know superficially, are megalomaniacs! Leue's Boma almost looks like a fortress, with high strong walls and battlements and a tower amid a court where he locks several armed guards in at night. It is for sure the most beautiful estate of the surroundings, situated on the ridge of a hill, with a view over the steppe up to the Kilimanjaro, surrounded by magnificent forests and a nearby roaring mountain torrent which he has begun damming to create a big lake.

Margarete Trappe paused her writing. Her gaze moved to the lowlands. She could not see any details in the dark, but she knew there was a huge tree in the Maasai steppe Anthimos used as an orientation point during his hunting trips. When would he return? Would he return at all?

„The grass does not grow faster if you keep pulling it . . . ," he had said while departing. What had he meant? Did he speak about his feelings for her? Did he love her?

Anthimos! When thinking of him, she felt such a beautiful inner calm. This feeling was unknown to her. It was ever so unlike her sensations for Ulrich, to whom she had developed a very intimate relationship since their arrival. He was very reliable, strove to read every wish from her lips. No doubt, he had strong organisational and manual skills. Hunting did not fascinate him that much. He disliked the improvised living out in the wilderness. Well, after the initial disharmony during the safari to the Meru, they had achieved a viable working relationship and become a good team. They made love from time to time, which was quite complicated because of the primary conditions. There was always some employee, some African nearby. They were seldom alone. Therefore, their sexual contacts were reduced to a minimum, they were very concerned about soundlessness, and it only lasted some minutes.

She caught herself developing intense longings with this thought. No, their mutual affection, their love was not tender. Was it love at all? Her memories of Anthimos covered her thoughts of Ulrich. Anthimos would certainly be . . . ! Margarete was spooked. She shook her head as if she had to get rid of these thoughts. It did not work out well. She again grabbed the quill, but the shadowy outline of Anthimos' face always arose in-between the lines she scribbled on the paper. Confused, she went on writing:

Well, dear Emily! Should I tell you something about our material life? I presume we eat quite well. We always have enough vegetables. Early in the morning – mostly very soon – we have tea or coffee with eggs and cold meat. At noon, we have a meat dish with vegetables and stewed fruit. In the evening – work is finished at six o'clock, and the educated Europeans dress up – we have another meat dish with vegetables and stewed fruit, a dessert, or cheese. Just like in good old Germany.
We owe a lot to the railway, which for the time being, leads up to Mombo. Astonishing things happen all over German East Africa. Civilisation is unstoppable. The arrival of the messenger with the mail from Europe, approximately every two weeks, is always a big event. Besides the letters, we also get the German newspapers (funny for us because of the delayed news) and books from Mittler & Sohn in Berlin. We are definitely not getting fed up!
My heart beats much more for hunting than Ulrich's. It represents a beautiful recreation for me. Whenever the work allows it, we sometimes decide suddenly to go on an extended hunting expedition. So, we go with tents, beds, and porters into the steppe, rich with game. Sometimes I am overwhelmed when I see how many boxes we have to pack if we want to go hunting for some days. I prefer to roam the wilderness alone on horseback. I only take our loyal hunting boy and Gillala, a very reliable Chagga along, and if Ulrich is not with us, we sleep just about anywhere on the floor under some tree, protected by a mosquito net. I whole-heartedly love this kind of life!
Finally, I want to tell you a secret, my dear friend. It is something which makes my heart beat whenever I think of it: I am expecting a child! Our happiness will find another fulfilment sometime in March

next year. I cannot imagine anything more beautiful than seeing children grow up here, in this Garden of Eden in Africa. For our children, as we want to have several, it will be what Gut Petersdorf was for me. And I pray to God that this paradise will remain unchanged for them and us for a long time. This is how I will finish this long letter and send all my closest thoughts to you in Germany. Please don't make me wait long for your reply.

In deep friendship, always thinking of you with affection, yours

Margarete Trappe

Chapter 8

One morning, Anthimos had appeared in front of her tent and shouted in Swahili language, „Hodi – is somebody there?“ He had looked exhausted as he had been hunting for months somewhere down South. After breakfast, he had slept almost two days and nights without interruption. He had stayed for two weeks, just like that. It was the most beautiful weeks she had ever lived on Ngongongare. Ulrich had been seemingly discontented the first days, but as always, Anthimos had behaved like a gentleman and never given him any reason to be jealous.

She had discovered the near surroundings of Ngongongare on horseback and by foot, sometimes together with Ulrich, but mostly alone with Anthimos. They had hiked to the Mayo waterfall at the Ngare-Nanyuki River, watched two mating rhinos in the Ngurdoto crater for hours, giggling like small children, circled one Momella lake after the other and time and again amused themselves as hundreds of thousands of flamingos, stalking through the brackish water rose, shrieking and nattering like purple clouds to the sky, after they had clapped their hands.

Anthimos did not know this Meru land, but he knew Africa. He was one with nature. He moved with accuracy in the wilderness like a duck takes to water, deducted out of the smallest details, read almost invisible traces in the sand, folded blades of grass, smells, and sounds Margarete's ears did not hear, information of enormous importance for life in nature. His eyes detected details in the far distance of which she was not even aware. He would not say: „There is an elephant over there on the horizon,“ but „There is a cow elephant big with young,“ or „The lioness behind the bush has babies – her teats are swollen.“

Every minute and hour she spent with Anthimos was like a book full of miracles opening to her. She began to understand the rules in her paradise, learned to distinguish the paw prints of a leopard from the ones of a cheetah. Anthimos knew everything about this Africa he loved, and of which he said: „Sometimes I seem to understand, seem to know, seem to be part of the whole – an African. But then again, the awareness arises that I don't know anything, that I am a *Muzungu,* a white man with conceit: weak, fragile, ignorant, barely more than tolerated – nothing more.“

One evening when they were sitting at a campfire, he had told them he believed that a revolt against the *Wazungu* was developing among the black population. „You are living here on Maasai land. It is not your land, and it will never be. The Maasai always take back what belongs to them.“ He had not gone any further, not explained what made him believe that nor said what they should do. When Ulrich asked him for his opinion, for advice on how they would best protect themselves, he only replied tersely: „Just imagine, Maasai had come to your land in Germany and begun to build their *Manyattas*! What would you have done?“

That was him: Anthimos never accused, did not seem to have his own opinion on things, his behaviour was neutral indeed. He loved hunting, underlining that neither the shot nor the killing captured him. He was fascinated by stalking, watching the animals, the challenge to get as near as possible to the animals.

„Sometimes I don't pull the trigger when I spot a huge elephant bull. I had the biggest bull ever, his tusks surely weighed one hundred and thirty pounds each, at the Manyara lake. I did not shoot him because, in the very last moment, he looked into my eyes, and I had the impression he wanted to tell me something . . .“

That was Anthimos! A sensitive man with a tough exterior. Liberal, educated, and living in harmony with himself and the world. So, the last two weeks had passed in beautiful unanimity. When they broke camp on this early morning to shoot some meat for dinner, Margarete Trappe once more had this indescribable feeling of closeness, of safety in the presence of Anthimos. She did not know what this feeling meant, how to define it. She only knew it was wonderfully big, beautiful, and unique.

The lioness lay only twenty steps away from her. She could not see the feline predator because the grass was too high, and the animal was crouching. However, she heard the low, dull bronchial grumble. For some moments, she seemed to see the golden yellow ear tips between the withered grass. It is probably the mother, she thought and lifted her gun with caution, without abrupt motions, raised the shaft of the weapon slowly to her shoulder and aimed in the direction where she supposed *Simba* to be. The four baby lions at her feet whimpered and mewed piteously. They were barely older than one week.

„Margarete Trappe, you are just too stupid,“ she murmured. „You know that one does not do that. You don't have to be a hunter to know that where there are lion babies, there is a lion mother . . .“

She had just wanted to shoot some meat for dinner, an antelope, or a gazelle or maybe some guinea fowl. Therefore, Anthimos had only taken the light rifle, and she had brought the shotgun along. However, when she had heard the squeaking from the nearby bush, she could not resist approaching and pulling the four sweet balls of wool with the cute faces from under the bush. Next, she had heard the grumbling. Now she stood there with a despicable shotgun with buck shot in the barrel. Only a few steps away, there was a lioness she would only be able to stop with a single shot if she let her come very close and fired both barrels almost at the same time – if she had enough time left to do so . . . She assessed the ground in front of her. From the corner of her eyes, she squinted to the right and left, but there was nothing. The knee-high grass swayed in the wind.

„Oh no, not that,“ she hissed angrily, „The wind blows from behind! The lioness is scenting you perfectly! She knows everything about you, and you don't know anything about her. You even don't know if it is one lion or several. One thing is sure: twenty steps are cursedly few . . .“

Anthimos' voice brought her back to reality.

„Tire! Toute suite!“

His words sounded calm but at the same time as an order. She was angry; he was gibbering again. Any time he was tense, he mixed French, English, and Greek together. He also spoke Swahili and Maa, the Maasai language. Sometimes he spoke all of them at once.

She did not understand any of these languages. She had not learned more than a few scraps of English up to now.

She did not dare to turn to him.

„What did you say there is? I know that there is an animal out there, a lion! And why are you calling me Sweet? Ulrich would not like that very much," she hissed and kept staring spellbound at the grassy plain in front of her.

„I said *tire*. It is French and means: Shoot! Furthermore, I did not say Sweet, but *suite*," he murmured, and it sounded very affectionate. „But, Sweet is not that bad indeed!"

„What does *suite* mean?"

„Do you mean *sweet* or *suite*?"

„What did you say at the beginning?"

„*Toute suite . . .*"

„And that means what?"

„Immediately!"

„And what am I to do immediately?"

„You have to shoot right now!"

She had to laugh softly. The situation was absurd. A lioness was lying somewhere out there in the grass, and she would most probably attack the very next moment and maybe even kill her. And she was chattering with Anthimos as if they were sitting somewhere on the terrace, having a cup of tea.

The lioness in front of her was still not visible. She felt how the weight of her rifle started to be uncomfortable. Her forearm slightly shivered. Beads of sweat ran down her forehead, under the sunglasses and into her eyes. The ground in front of her became blurry. She slowly detached her left hand and pressed the weapon pressed against her shoulder with only her right arm, the index finger on the trigger. She tried to take the sunglasses off and wipe the sweat out of her eyes.

„If I were you, I would not do that! That would be *très bête*," she heard Anthimos' warning.

„I can't see anything anymore. If I do not see, I cannot shoot the lion when it comes near!"

„You should not shoot the lion, but the *Spitting Cobra* at your right! Don't you move! Stay calm. And don't bother about the lion. I will have an eye on it . . .“

Margarete Trappe froze. Without moving her head, she squinted down right past the eyeglass lenses. There it was, not even a metre away from her, raised, almost half a metre tall. The brownish-red and ugly flat head of the snake kept motionless. The fixed pupils located her. It was so near that Margarete could see the black points under the eyes and in between the honeycomb formed scales. A red spitting cobra. Very beautiful, but lethal.

„What am I supposed to do?“

Her voice trembled. The gun became heavier and heavier. Her pulse raced, the sweat was dripping over her body under her blouse. She thought her head might explode at any time. She knew a spitting cobra was able to spit accurately in the eye over a distance of up to four metres to paralyse the victim. If you did not rinse the eye rapidly, you would go blind. And the bite of the cobra was lethal.

„Shoot, Anthimos, do something,“ she begged. „Do something!“

„I can't! You are standing right in my field of fire! I cannot shoot across your trembling legs, can I? If I make only one single step, the lion will come. If it attacks, you will move, quite certainly. Then you will have quite a problem with the cobra as it will bite you. And next, we will both have a problem with the lioness . . .“

„For heaven's sake, Anthimos, shoot!“

She was shrieking. The shotgun began to tremble in her hand.

„You must pitch your rifle very slowly to the front right and direct it to the cobra. No matter where you hit it. Once you shot, you immediately flop, so you get out of my field of fire.“

She did not believe she would manage it. And from the corner of her eyes, she noticed how the snake's head started to tense to the back, ready to bite, ready to spit. She lowered the barrel of the rifle millimetre for millimetre. Her glance rapidly shifted between the snake, the rifle barrel, and the place in the grass where the lioness was supposed to lie.

„*Prête?*“

„What?“
„Ready . . . ?“
„Yes!“
„Allez . . . !“
She pulled the trigger and immediately flopped to the left. The recoil
pushed the rifle out of her hand. The shotgun flew through the air.
While she fell, she saw that she had shot the head of the cobra away.
She waited for Anthimos' shot. But nothing happened.
„Why don't you shoot?“ she asked, trembling and sobbing. She laid
on the floor, flat, very small, the face in the sand.
„The lioness does not want to attack,“ Anthimos answered calmly.
„She has nothing against me. She only has something against you. I
can see her now. It is a stunning lioness, really *très belle, Simba
mzuri sana, very beautiful.* I don't want to shoot such a beautiful
lioness! She only wants us to move back. She wants her children
back, nothing else. And I think this is okay, isn't it?“
Margarete slightly lifted her head. Her hair covered her face. She
saw Anthimos through her strands of hair, some ten steps beside and
behind her. He looked exceptionally well and masculine and attractive. He stood there, calm, relaxed, self-confident, like a monument,
like a Greed statue.
„Get up on your feet and come to me! But without turning around,“
he ordered, and she felt as if she was a small child, helpless, fragile,
seeking protection. Margarete liked this feeling.
She stood up inch by inch, creeping on all fours, watching him, and
suddenly became aware that single tears were falling on the sand below her. And she felt that she became luckier with every millimetre
approaching him.
It took her minutes, endless awful but ever so beautiful minutes,
crawling on elbows and knees through the grass until she lay in front
of him on the ground. She was shivering all over, doubled up, took
some deep breaths, almost did not dare to look at him as she was
afraid, he might see what she felt in her eyes. His khaki trousers rus-
tled while he bent his knees, put his gun with the stock on the
ground beside her, caressed her hair with his left hand and said with

108

a low voice full of warmth and love, „*Très bien*. You are a great woman. Really *toute sweet*, very sweet! I think that is how I will call you from now on. Yes, that's it: Toute Sweet is a beautiful name for you! I could not remember Margarete anyhow. Nevermind pronouncing it . . .“

Heavy downpours occurred the next morning, and Anthimos decided to depart after the thunderstorm. Ulrich had set off very early with some workers to control the cattle herd down in the plane. They sat under the burlap roof and kept silent. Margarete appreciated the silence a lot.
„Toute Sweet, I think we have to talk about it,“ Anthimos suddenly said and grabbed the cup of tea on the table.
„We have to talk about what?“
„You like me too much. Maybe you have started to love me . . .“
„Why do we have to talk about it?“
Margarete Trappe looked embarrassedly at the slopes of the Meru, which were covered by dense clouds. The rain was pattering on the tent annex. The calming sound made her feel cosy and happy. A butterfly sought protection from the rain under the roof and settled on the teapot. It was almost the size of a hand and had turquoise points on the centre of its wings. She did not want to speak, did not want to talk about it. She had always had difficulties in expressing some things. She was not used to expressing her feelings, and she had caused a lot of harm with words before.
„Toute Sweet, you have something which churns me up internally. It started on the day of your arrival at Dar es Salam. I do not know what it is. I even do not want to think about it. I just want it to be as it is. I only know that it is a beautiful feeling. Things don't always need a name. Nor do feelings. The beauty of a tree, a flower or an animal does not change by giving a name to it. Sometimes the attempt to fix something with words creates problems and misunderstandings. If you say ‚love‘ to a feeling, you will have to dissect this feeling, to define it unequivocally. The question then is why and for what reason. And there, the feeling starts dissolving into fragments.

If you say ‚love', your sensations will clash with social, moral, and ethical norms, if your feelings are about a person you are not allowed to love because she already loves another person or is married. Why does this have to be this way?"

Anthimos had gotten up and turned his back to her. He looked at the sky thoughtfully. Clouds passed over the country, whipped by the wind. A small elephant herd was drawing at the edge of the clearing. „Do you believe that a lion wonders about the beauty of a gazelle before eating it? I don't think so! When I shoot an antelope, I don't feel anything. I shoot it because I am hungry. But from the moment we humans give a name to some cute, cuddly animal, we are barely able to eat it."

Margarete Trappe looked at Anthimos with great admiration. His body outlined against the twilight of the thunderous sky. He was very slim and had large shoulders. His black curly hair shone.

„What has this got to do with me?"

„I love a woman, Toute! Saida is in me, unerasable, forever! When the sun rises, I see Saida in it. And also when the sun sets."

She felt the pain like a pinprick in her heart. She wanted to jump up, run away, hear nothing more. But he kept talking unswervingly.

„I make no secret of feeling very attracted by you, Toute Sweet. There is something I feel for you that I cannot explain. It is a powerful feeling, something huge. But it cannot be brought to life next to Saida. And one more thing, Toute: I am well over 40 years of age, you are very young, gorgeous – and you are married. My life is running backward. Yours hasn't even begun."

„I don't know what makes you think I love you," she answered, hoping it sounded convincing. She did not achieve it. However, she kept trying to convince herself: „I think you are nice, charming, and smart. But I can assess my feelings quite well. I love Ulrich. He is a good, caring husband. We will be delighted here and have children."
While she said it, she knew she was lying. Anthimos looked at her from the side.

„I wanted to tell you this for quite some time, Toute: your brother Alfred had been living for more than ten years with an African woman, he loved her. They had to hide out there on their farm in the Usambara mountains because his German compatriots with their arrogant racism did not show understanding for this kind of relationship. She died while giving birth to their first common child. When this happened, Alfred was on the way here very near the Meru with the protection guard. He heard about it one week later. He shot himself in pain."

Margarete opened her eyes wide. She felt paralysed with horror.

„I thought, Alfred died in a battle against Maji-Maji rebels! Why did you never tell me the truth, for what reason?"

„Because the truth does not change the fact that he is dead. It is cruel enough. For me, also. I loved him very much, just like my brother. No, even more. I think Alfred and I loved each other as much as a man can love a man because one estimates the other. When we met the first time more than twenty years ago at a reception of the Sultan of Zanzibar in honour of the German Consul, we already started speaking about these topics half an hour later."

„But why did you never tell me the truth about Alfred's death?" She trembled. Her voice broke down.

„Otherwise, I would have had to explain all this much earlier to you. The people here, the Germans, refuse to bury somebody in their cemeteries who committed suicide."

„And where is he really buried?"

„At the natives' cemetery in a small village near Arusha, on the other side of the mountain. At the very place where his wife was from and where she was buried with the stillborn child. It is barely more than a pile of stones, but he would have wanted it this way."

It was still raining cats and dogs. The place in front of the tent was submerged with water. Two natives plodded through the mud.

„I will set out now! The land is especially beautiful when it is raining. Did you ever notice that the gazelles jump with joy when it starts raining? They jump in the air right away and give twists, just for joy. I love watching that."

The Greek turned around, lifted the rifle over the shoulder, and lit a cigarette.

„At my next visit, I'll bring Alfred's personal things along. It is not much: some books, drawings, his diary, and some hunting weapons. Alfred carried the most valuable thing he owned inside himself. And he took it away with him."
Margarete felt sad. Not because of Alfred, but for Anthimos.
„When will you come back? Will you come back?"
„I don't know, Toute Sweet! I really don't know. An African proverb says: ‚The grass does not grow faster if you keep pulling it!' Look down there to the Maasai steppe. Do you see the mighty acacia tree on the horizon? It is huge. It always serves me as a landmark during my safaris in the Maasai steppe. It is a strange tree, just like there are many strange things here in Africa – for us, white men. This tree has not had any leaves for many years, looks lifeless. But it is not dead, Toute Sweet! Such a tree can be lifeless for twenty years, and suddenly, even without a drop of rain, it starts flowering in the most beautiful colours, just like that. Nobody knows why. No African would ever arrive at the notion of asking. It just is like it is. Time does not mean anything in Africa. It applies to many things here. One day they come alive. And so will it be: One day, I will come back."
He made one step in her direction, caressed her hair, and looked into her eyes. „Even big game hunters can be afraid, Toute Sweet! I believe feelings are what they fear most."

*

Anthimos was gone. „The wind changed, I think I should depart," was his only explanation of why he had to leave. After breakfast, he had saddled his horse and set off. „*Kwaheri, Lalla Salama* – see you, peace be with you!" That was all he said and left her in deep sadness. He had offered her a feather from a kingfisher: The red, blue, and black feather, with yellow spots and incredibly fluffy downs, stuck in her hair behind her ear.
Ulrich came back shortly before sunset. Margarete could see his grumpy face from a distance. He seemed to be very tired. His

clothes were filthy, the shirt was torn, and the boots gave a hint of the marshes down in the valley. He countered Jessy a few metres from her and slid slowly down from the saddle. Her groom Gillala lead the mare away.

„What happened, Ulrich?" She approached him and wanted to embrace him, but he walked past her with a stern look on his face, went inside, and came back with a bottle of Whisky in his hand.

„We lost six more cows. All six were poisoned and died a miserable death. Not even the hyenas dared to approach the befouled cadavers. Three cows two weeks ago, two last week and now six at a time."

„Where did you find them?"

„All six near the Lokie marshes."

„What do the herd boys say?"

„I gave a whipping to those useless bastards. They deserved it. They announced yesterday the cows had still all been there. But this is not true. The cadavers were so bloated they must have been dead for two days, at least. Oh, these shitheads. The only think of drinking and women. If this goes on, we will be ruined faster than we can even imagine. Eleven cows in two weeks . . ."

Ulrich Trappe took a big sip out of the bottle, lowered the bottle, and drank again. His eyes were reddened.

„Something must happen," Margarete said. She insecurely watched her husband. He had been drinking a lot and regularly lately. In Sagan, he used to carouse during nights in the officers' club with his friends and drink lots of wine. Here in Africa, he did not only drink Whisky, which was not always available and sold in the shops of the Indians in Arusha at horrendous prices. She knew that he made the wife of their cook Msiriri provide him secretly with palm wine and other home-distilled liqueurs. She was worried about it.

For the time being, she was much more concerned about the dead cattle. After the purchase of six thousand hectares of land near Ngongongare, they had bought fifty Zebu cattle from a dealer in Arusha, only a few weeks ago. They had built a temporary animal's *Boma* out of thornbushes very close to their camp. An armed Askari of the Kaiserliche Schutztruppe in the thorn shed slept at night, as the Maasai tried to steal cattle all the time, especially by night. They had been awoken three times by the three agreed warning shots of the Askari and rushed out of the tent dressed in nightgowns, to chase away the Maasai with shots. No blood had been shed until now. However, it was only a matter of time before it would turn to severe confrontations with the predatory Maasai. Two cows had been slain by lions during the driving down in the plains. There were only thirty-seven left.

„I will talk with the chief of the Maasai," she told her husband. „It cannot go on like this. If we cannot solve the problem in another way, we must turn the enemy into a friend. Our farm is furthest away from Arusha. We cannot count on the protection of the German troupes. In case of emergency, help might arrive too late. We are living on the traditional grazing land of the Maasai. We must deal with the Maasai. It is the only way . . ."

On the next morning, right after sunrise, she had Comet saddled. Her plan was not to be thwarted by Ulrich, and she ignored his warnings and fears.

The pitch-black stallion with the small blaze on its face was prancing in place. She had not ridden him for two days. He was bursting with strength, and she felt the intense urge to ride the energetic animal at full gallop over the open land. She loved this horse more than anything. From the first day she had seen Comet at a Buer horse dealer in Arusha, she had doted on him. It was extraordinary, remarkably beautiful, of perfect square stature, had beautiful hindquarters, and a deep chest. He was not gunshy at all and had very hard hooves.

Comet had been sold several times during the previous months, but no owner had been able to ride him. He seemed to hate male riders. Whenever a man approached him, he flared his nostrils and rolled his eyes frighteningly. Ulrich had tried it once. However, when coming near, a swift attack by the horse's forehand made him decide that instead of riding, one should rather shoot him. However, after half an hour in the saddle, she had concluded a pact with the black horse:

If he obeyed, she renounced to the riding crop, the curb bit, and the spurs. It was the only way to ride the stubborn stallion, indeed.

She mounted, stroked gently over the neck of the restlessly snorting horse, and petted it between the prick ears.

„The *Manyatta* of the Maasai chief is somewhere between here and Arusha down in the plain,“ she shouted to Ulrich, who staggered half asleep out of the tent. „I will take the opportunity to ride to Arusha and buy some things.“

That day, Arusha seemed almost to be a big city to her. The weeks in the Ngongongare mountains had sensitised her auditory sense for sounds. A few ox carts were making noise, and the Indians, Arabs, and Africans at the market and in the small shops along were shouting. It did not only stress her but also Comet. The stallion pranced along the shops, his tail high, the neck curbed, and chewed the snaffle bit restlessly. His eyes were wide open. He snorted whenever a person came near. She guessed that she would not be able to attach the horse somewhere and leave it alone. The danger he would break free, tear rains and bridle, and even get hurt in the mouth was too big. However, before riding to the Maasai, she wanted at least to leave some orders at the dealers. She decided in the spur of the moment not to dismount. She caressed Comet's neck calmingly. „Come on, old boy, let's go shopping together!“

Small shops lined the scarce pathways in Arusha, about thirty, barely more than wooden shacks, with small, stonewalled houses with low sun shields between them. She passed the shops, got some fruit and vegetables handed here and there, plugged it in the saddlebags, rode bent under a roof to have a closer look at some clothes, and let Comet nibble pleasurably at a corn sack standing at the roadside. She gave a rupee to the astonished Indian dealer.

Jan de Clerk, a Boer settler, had a cattle farm in Ol Dinyo Sambu. However, he earned more money selling horse bridles and agricultural equipment in his hardware store. When Margarete Trappe rode on the snorting stallion through the wing doors of the store, the black labourer dove in panic for cover behind three protecting flour sacks. Comet was stalling, blew through his nostrils, and stood motionless like a statue in the centre of the store. De Clerk stood behind the counter and looked so astonished at her with his mouth wide open that she laughed out loud.

„The Trappe family in Ngongongare needs three sacks of corn, one bag of cornflower, four shovels, twenty rolls of fencing wire, three twenty-litre buckets, ten litres of paraffin, and fifty candles. When will you deliver the goods?"

„Ugh, yes, Madam . . . ," De Clerk stumbled, „I think I can send you a carriage with the products for tomorrow."

The dealer assessed the stallion. Next, he stared openly at the young woman dressed in bright shorts, a short-sleeved T-Shirt, and a brown hat with a white ribbon.

„A very nice stallion, " he expressed his excitement about the horse. Looking up to Margarete Trappe, he lisped: *„And a very impressive little Lady. "*

It happened only a few steps away from de Clerk's store. Riding Comet, she turned the corner, to a cloth shop of an Indian. A brown, saddled stallion stood right behind the corner – a huge horse. She could not see the owner. The reins were hanging to the ground. The brown horse stood there, opened his eyes wide, and showed the white of its pupils. Filled with hatred, he looked at Comet, widened his nostrils like sails so that the red mucosa was seen – and attacked. Margarete did not have the time to dismount. She only knew that the fight between the two stallions could be awful. She rapidly put her right hand under the saddle channel, grabbed both reins with her left hand, and bent her torso forwards in the very moment comet reared up and hammered his front hoof impetuously down on the brown horse dashing towards him. The stallions' fight went on for almost ten minutes. They faced themselves standing on their hindquarters, attacking with the front hoofs, bucked, neighed, snorted, whirled around to kick out with the rear hoofs. They tried to bite each other in the flanks and necks, drumming with the front hoofs on each other. Next, they fell to their knees attacking with bites again. White foam covered their necks, chests, and bellies. The manes were drenched in sweat. They fought with unrestrained hate.

Margarete feared for her life. Several times she almost fell out of the saddle backwards. The brown stallion bit her in the riding boots, it hurt. His back hoofs went down on Comet's belly only some centimetres from her right leg. She had lost her hat. Her long dark hair whipped through the air due to the abrupt movements of her stallion. The noise of the stallion fight drowned the pleasant quiet of the alleyways of Arusha. Humans – whites, Africans, Indians, and Arabs – came running from everywhere. From the corner of her eyes, she saw two soldiers of the protection guard. Next, the fight ended. Both stallions stood facing each other some centimetres apart, necks bent, and eyes wide open. Their flanks trembled. Margarete Trappe still sat in the saddle. Her T-Shirt soaked with sweat. She was foaming with rage.

„Bravo, Madam!" one of the Boers shouted to her. Some of the white men softly clapped their hands. The Africans, Indians, and Arabs were speechless.

Her fear and tension vented. „Who is the damned idiot who left his hack at large here? Why did nobody help me and take the brown stallion away?"

Her vulgarism appalled the white women in their long dresses. „*Sorry,* Madam," another Boer shouted, „we wagered you would fall from the horse. But you spoiled this wager. Respect, Madam! That was very impressive."

„I am the idiot who left his – how did you name it, Lady? – hack at large!"

The man had turned around the corner of the house and stood only a few steps away from her. He laughed maliciously and seemed very arrogant. His blond hair covered his forehead. He was suntanned and approached her confidently. *„Brown – Major Brown. Nice meeting you, Mrs. . . . ?"*

„Trappe! Margarete Trappe!" she answered. She did not know the man, had never seen him before. But she did not like him.

„Next time, before I get trampled by an English stallion gone wild, I will shoot him,“ she hissed at the man and set off.

The *Manyatta* of the Maasai was situated below a mountain near Engare Olmotonj, almost an hour's ride North-West from Arusha. Passing conical hills and volcanic peaks, she reached about twenty cottages in the early afternoon. There was a strong smell of urine and animals in the air. She knew that the Maasai constructed their conical twigs huts with a mixture of clay and cow dung and even made all the cattle and goats get inside the kraal, protected by thorn hedges or also kept calves and goats in their cottages.
They were already waiting for her. It was one of the fantastic African phenomena: News just spread like thunderstorms. There were no secrets in the infinite widths and valleys of the Maasai steppes. One thinks one is alone, neither sees nor meets a soul for miles. But you can see and hear everything, every step of a human, be it a stranger or a tribesman, is closely monitored. News about whatever is done or not, is spread and brought to the villages of the locals in no time at all.
Six men, five of them with bald heads and wooden maces or long sticks in their hands, squatted near the thorn fence in the shadow of a tree. Two of them played, seemingly disinterested with the white woman on horseback's arrival, the *Engehei game*, for which they dig into the earth two parallel rows of between six to sixteen holes as big as a hand. The players have a certain number of small stones and try via fixed rules to forefeel the moves of the adversary and to earn the highest possible number of stones. The two Maasai were squatting in front of the sand holes. One of them, an older man with a face as furrowed as solidified lava and his head coloured to ochre, had dead eyes and quite big holes in his ears, the lobes hanging like wet leather almost down to his shoulders. Tiny pearl strings dangled from the flaps of the ear skin. A beautiful pearl string decorated his right ankle, the surface of which was as rough and as grey as an elephant's. He was the oldest of the six men. Margarete dismounted her horse.

„Jambo, Mzee," she saluted and looked at the old man. „I came in need of the advice of the old men."

The elder looked up. She could see that he was blind.

„Men sit down when they talk," the old man said. She grabbed the reins and just wanted to get into a squat position when the other, a much younger man with long hair and an unusually distinctive profile said in English: „But you are not a man. You are a woman. A white woman . . ."

Margarete Trappe felt confused. She did not know how to interpret these words, how to react to them. The younger man did not look at her. Instead, he stared at the stone game in front of him on the ground. His beautiful face showed a skin as fine and even of a Greek youth of the antiquity. His cheekbones stood out a little bit. The lips were well-formed. Never before had she seen such a beautiful man with such a fascinating aura.

„Why is your horse less afraid of us than you are?" he asked and looked her right into the eyes.

She felt that she got slight goosebumps on her back. She was confused by the beauty, however also the expression of his eyes. The fascinating self-assurance of this man confused her and even frightened her a little bit. She wondered how he knew about her fear.

As if he could read her thoughts, the old blind man said: „The breath of your horse is as calm as the breeze on a morning after a storm. You, however, are breathing quickly. You are afraid. It is essential for a Maasai-*Moran* to know whether those he faces are afraid . . ."

„I was told the men of the Maasai tribe are absolutely fearless. But I was not told that Maasai men fight against women," she interrupted the old man who promptly reacted.

„Be welcome, sit down with us, and tell us what you want."

She squatted and took her hat off. Without showing any emotion, the younger man looked her into the eyes.

„My land is haunted by men who carry hate in their hearts. They steal and poison my cattle . . ."

„It is not your land!" the handsome man interrupted her. „Ever since the sun rises and sets, it has been the land of the Maasai. And our

God *Engai* gave all the cattle to us, only to us. How could we even help you? How do you want to protect what does not belong to you?" For the first time, she sensed a touch of aggressivity in his eyes.

„The welfare of the Maasai depends on their cattle and goats," she avoided his question. „I am willing to provide you my knowledge and the *Dawa*, the white man's medicine to make the cattle of your tribe healthy and robust," she calmly said, hoping to have found a convincing argument. She had come to know that the Maasai had lost hundreds of thousands of cattle during the awful cattle plague at the end of the last century and that the cattle population had still not recovered from this devastating epidemic. She knew that the cattle plague had been brought to Africa by white settlers.

„You are a very courageous woman. You also seem to be very smart," the young Maasai answered. He turned his gaze away from her, stared out into the distance, and stayed silent a long time. Next, he conferred with the other bald men. Eventually, he got up.

„I, Kinai ole Chieni, declare that we will try to consider whether the omnipotence of our god *Engai* and the strength of our forefathers are appropriate to help you, *Jeyo*, to protect your cattle. We will let you know."

She only returned to Ngongongare after dark. The conversation with the Maasai had lasted a long time, but it had turned out better than she had expected.

Comet was tired from the long ride. He was limping on his rear right leg. A flesh wound on his neck from the stallion fight was attracting flies, which made him nervous. Just before Ngongongare, she startled a family of colobus monkeys high up in the trees. The animals with the black and white faces vociferated their resentment out to the dark. For a short moment, she remembered the incident of her arrival day with the monkeys omnipresent in these mountains. She smiled. Oh my god, the black and white grimace jumping towards her had scared her to death.

Much time had passed ever since. She now loved these beautiful animals with their long silky fur. They were living in the tops of the up to forty metres high giant trees, growing on the Meru slopes. When they quarrelled, the trees wavered. And when they shouted because some leopard crossed the underbrush, she still got goosebumps on her back. The screams were very human, awfully shrill. Still, they belonged to Ngongongare as the nightly rumbling of the leopards, the cries of the bush babies during the night, and the permanent rustling and cracking of the elephants and buffaloes roaming the forests. The sound had long become familiar to her, and none of these were hazardous. During the past months, she had learned that there was only risk in her paradise when it became silent, when nature and animals kept quiet. A paraffin lamp was burning in the main tent. Campfires flickered in front of the farmworkers' cottages situated under trees at the edge of the clearing. Someone sang a song in the language of the Chagga living at the Meru with a low voice. The last evening light gave a romantic ambiance to the camp. She was barely fifty metres away when she distinguished shadows against the light of the paraffin lamp. One of them was obviously Ulrich. Astonished, she looked at the tent and let the horse approach with loose reins. Comet straightened up with joyful anticipation. He smelled the water and snorted loudly. The shadows in the tent remained abruptly. Someone turned the paraffin lamp down.

When she came nearer, she saw a figure rush from the tent in the direction of the nearby forest. She was not sure. However, she believed she had identified a feminine figure.

Two days later, the Maasai suddenly appeared. They stood at the first daylight at some metres distance in front of the tent. They stood stoically still, leaning on their spears and stared at Margarete Trappe, who left the tent with tousled hair.

„Jambo! Habari?" she greeted the men dressed in red garments. The four men only lifted the right hand for some lukewarm greeting and grumbled some incomprehensible words. Gillala, her horse boy, joined.

„*Memsahib*, most of the Maasai don't speak Swahili. They don't talk a lot anyhow, but when they do, they use their language, the Maa one."

A little embarrassed, Margarete Trappe scratched her head. She had not thought of this at all when she talked with the Maasai eldest. Everything had gone so smoothly during the palaver in the Maasai *Manyatta*. She knew that the Maasai raising cattle had permanent problems with their animals, especially with ticks and other parasites. Therefore, she had agreed with the eldest to start vaccinating for free all the new-born calves, if the Maasai in return took care that the cattle at Ngongongare escaped predatory people from Maasai and other tribes. She had also promised to recruit four young men as cattle herders, granting a fixed salary and extras such as medicine and essential foods.

The offer had quickly convinced the eldest. Cattle was their most valuable asset. On the ride back to Ngongongare, she had been triumphing internally as she felt she could from now on continue light-heartedly setting up her farm without any fears – with the Maasai as allies.

Not being able to communicate with the cattle herders in front of her complicated her plan. She just wanted to discuss with Gillala where she might get an interpreter from when the Maasai she had been talking to in English appeared at the edge of the forest. He was the handsome one, the one within she believed she had detected a touch of shrewdness or even aggression in his eyes, and who had surprised her a lot by calling her „*Jeyo*". Kinai ole Chieni came nearer. He stopped some paces away from her. He wore a red and blue-checked garment. His long, red-coloured hair flew over his shoulders. He smiled slightly, but again something in his eyes alarmed her.

„*Jeyo*, together with me, these men will protect your cattle and your life. From now on, we will be like shadows of your life . . .“

Chapter 9

(3 years later)

Diffuse moonlight illuminated the room. The silhouette of the African woman popped up in front of the window. She was dainty, but the weapon in her hand gave her all power.

Ulrich Trappe opened his eyes wide. He felt the pressure of the top of the machete against his carotid. His heart was beating. Beads of sweat appeared on his forehead. He did not know what he should do, what he could do. Was she a thieve and only looking for money? Did she belong to those bandits and murderers who had been causing instability in the land near the Meru for more than two years now? Who stole or massacred cattle, slaughtered white women and men, poisoned them, put cadavers, the bowels of their dogs and cats on their doorstep, threw snakes and scorpions into farmhouses? He felt the urge to swallow but did not dare to. Something inside his throat was itching. His breathing sped up. He felt the itching and how his fight against the irritation of the throat made his abdomen cramp. The rising and falling of his chest under the blanket kept accelerating. He broke out in cold sweat. The bed was wet. He shivered. The throat irritation became unbearable. He thought it would make him choke, felt his legs and arms begin to tremble and the pressure of the blade against his throat increased.

Next, he could no longer control the cough. His body refused to obey his mind. The muscles tensed, ready to burst. He jumped up, hit the weapon with one arm, felt how the blade, led by a strong hand, penetrated his throat.

„Nooo!" The blood suffocated his gargling death cry.

He thrashed around in a panic, out of bed, fell over a footstool, his head banged against a hard object. His hands reached to his throat. There was blood everywhere: it was warm, sticky, and viscous. His mouth was also full of blood. He tried in vain to call for help. He looked horrified down at his body. The nightgown was red, all over. Disgusting glibbery intestines hung out of his body. He grabbed for the revolver on the bedside table, felt the metal of the Remington, could feel the drum and the grip.

He kicked the woman with the *Panga* with all his strength, striking her lower abdomen and saw her bang against the wardrobe. Next, he pulled the trigger. Shots whipped through the room.

„Ulrich, for heaven's sake, Ulrich! Wake up, Ulrich!"

Margarete Trappe stood horrified over her husband lying on the floor. She convulsed in pain as he had kicked her in the abdomen. The shots had barely missed her.

He opened his eyes wide in panic and full of hate and lashed out. He stroke his wife's forehead with his fist and shot the black servant behind her in the thigh.

The next day, they sat on the small veranda in front of their house and stared over the hills, like they used to do whenever they did not know what to say. A child was cheering behind the house. Dogs were barking.

Their babysitter Karimbe came around the edge of the house. In his arms, he carried „Bubel," as they used to call their only two week old son Ulrich, wrapped in a beautiful, gaily coloured Maasai blanket. The baby was sleeping. Karimbe had cute little Ursula traipsing beside him, holding his other hand. Her hair was blowing in the wind. She was tanned and looked more than barely two years old.

The November sun shone through the clouds. It was a beautiful day; however, the mood was very tense.

„I really can't believe it. Emperor Wilhelm almost provoked a war because of such a stupid desert state," Margarete Trappe pondered. At the same moment, she regretted her remark, knowing that Ulrich would seize with both hands any opportunity to move away from the main issue. His prompt answer was barely more than what he used to say: „That's the Frenchmen's fault. And the English's also! Let me tell you this: it would have been an excellent opportunity for the German Reich to adjust the power structures in Europe. The English still do not understand who has the final say now. And the French pursue such imperialistic policies in Africa that it is time for us to stop them."

„My grandfather died in the last war against France, that is enough for me," she provoked him and pointedly grabbed the newspapers. The previous edition of the *Deutsch-Ostafrikanische Rundschau*, published in Dar es Salam, had been brought from Arusha that afternoon. The flow of information had improved a lot since the coastal towns Dar es Salam and Bagamoyo had become pulsating centres of the German colony. German mail steamers guaranteed a regular supply of German newspapers. Newspapers were even printed in the country at present. *Der Pflanzer*, a guidebook for tropical agriculture, appeared twice a week; the *Usambara-Post* and the *Küstenbote vom Norden* were published weekly in Tanga; the *Amtliche Anzeigen für den Bezirk Moschi* appeared at irregular intervals.

She turned the pages of the *Deutsch-Ostafrikanische Rundschau*, it reported extensively on the ongoing conflict between Germany and France.

Germany had conceived the penetration of the Moroccan inlands by the French for pacification purposes of civil unrest as a violation of the Algeciras agreement of 1906 and a threat of the German economic and political positions in North Africa, so that on July 1st the gunboat „Panther" was sent to Agadir. England and Russia had immediately reacted by beginning preparations for war.

The sending of the gunboat „Panther" by emperor Wilhelm II. And Reich Chancellor Theobald von Bethmann-Hollweg had been meant as a menacing gesture of foreign-policy to implement the claim. It suddenly took on domestic proportions, when the emperor was increasingly reproached for cowardice by France and England, as well as in the inner leadership circle as in the public circle. Voices asking for a preventive war became louder.

Out of this position of political isolation, the German Reich threatened war to prevent a loss of face.

The threat of military conflict had only been diplomatically averted some weeks ago. The compromise included that France had to concede part of the Congo to Germany. In return, Germany had to assign territories in the colonisation Togo and Cameroon to France.

Ulrich Trappe grabbed another newspaper. He was nervous and pretended to read. His wife palpated her head.
„Do you feel pain?“
He looked at the bump on her head. The hematoma over her eyebrow started turning yellow.
„I am fine. You did not hit me right.“
„I am sorry, princess!“
Full of contempt, she looked into his eyes because he had called her princess.
„It was a nightmare, Ulrich. You neither kicked nor hit me in the heat of the moment. You don't have to apologise.“
„I do feel sorry, anyhow. How is Gillala?“
„I had them bring him to the mission station in Nkoaranga. The bullet pierced his left thigh. If the wound does not get inflamed, he will soon be fit again.“
Again, they stared in silence over the hills. Ulrich knew what Margarete was going to say.
„You have changed a lot, Ulrich. You have those nightmares at regular intervals, and you drink too much . . .“
„I am worrying too much about you,“ he lied. „Awful things happen all around us. It has been going on for two years. Last week Bettina Schneider was found. She had been heavily pregnant. These beasts cut her belly open and ripped the child out.“
„Your nightmares have another reason, Ulrich. I am not astonished you see yourself persecuted by night by African women with a Panga in hand. You are having a love affair with our cook's wife,“ she interrupted him, still staring at the hill. „You are also after our hunting boy Saida's daughter. She is barely older than fifteen. You are a lousy spineless pig, Ulrich!“
Embarrassed, he swallowed and tried to conceal the truth.
„You have also changed a lot, princess . . .“
„Do not call me princess, okay? Never again . . .“

„So your famous big game huntsman Anthimos, the significant philosopher and gentleman from Greece, is the only one to be allowed to do so?“

„He has a good character and style and decency. You don't!“

„Pah! You are spending weeks riding through the bushland alone, sleep in the very same tent. The devil only knows what you are doing! And you are blaming me for touching the tits of some stupid nigger girl. They are used to it. They are bitches. They undress for anyone who would give them some rupees!“

Margarete felt so much contempt she could not even look at him. And his tone frightened her.

„Margarete, you have also changed. You are no longer the woman I came to know five years ago in Sagan.“

„I did not change, Ulrich! No, I am the one I always have been but was never allowed to be. I will always be like this now! And concerning Anthimos: We never share a tent when we go hunting. He would never touch me if I did not want it.“

„So, do you want it?“

„Not until now, Ulrich. Not until now! However, your behaviour towards me will define the future. It depends on you, Ulrich! It is only up to you whether this paradise keeps being one − or if it turns into a golden cage amid Africa for us both.“

Within two years, the jewel Ngongongare at the foot of the Meru, Ulrich and Margarete Trappe's new homeland had turned into a model farm. Only the year after the purchase of the first six thousand hectares of land, Ulrich and Margarete Trappe had bought another two thousand two hundred hectares of land named „Momella“, and 1910 another eight thousand hectares of land near Legurucki. They had established their own small empire near the Kilimanjaro under the protection of the Maasai and through hard work. Over one thousand five hundred cattle were grazing in the meadows and thrived. The pig breeding was very profitable. They built stables for their horse breeding on the various farms. From Germany, they imported centrifuges for milk processing and butter production. Every week, they delivered several hundredweights of golden yellow butter to Moshi and the coast of German East Africa. The business relations to the German government's serum station adjacent to Momella were especially profitable. A lot of cattle were required for the production of serum against the still wide-spread cattle plague, and the Trappe family had many.

The conditions were perfect. German East Africa had become a model colony of the German Reich. An average of five hundred German emigrants settled at the Kilimanjaro every year. Managed by the governor Freiherr von Rechenberg, the territory was covered by a perfect Prussian administration net of twenty-one administration districts. German taverns and roadside guesthouses were built along the streets at about a day's journey away. The steamboat „Hermann v. Wissmann" was operating on the Njassa lake, the governmental steamer „Ulanga" cruised on the Rufiji, the „Gustav Meinecke" sailed on the Pangani.

Margarete and Ulrich Trappe's happiness increased on March 19th, 1909, with the birth of their daughter Ursula at the nearby mission station Nkoaranga.

Soon, they had built a solid farmhouse out of rubble with several rooms, a corrugated iron roof, and splendid orchards, vegetable, and flower gardens. There were vines and asparagus beds – and with cypresses, Ulrich planted near the house: for every year in their Garden of Eden he planted a new tree.

There seemed to be nothing that could cloud the paradisiacal life of the young family from Silesia. Everywhere in the Meru surroundings, the cattle raids at the farms assumed alarming proportions. Brutal murders of women, children, and men caused uncertainty among the settlers and almost unsolvable problems to the German Kaiserliche Schutztruppe and police stations. Ulrich and Margarete Trappe's farm, however, kept being spared from any raid. More and more weeks of light-heartedness followed the first years' hardship. Ulrich Trappe committed himself enthusiastically to his gardens and the construction of new paths. Margarete found more and more time to follow her passion, hunting. She did so together with Anthimos. His hunting trips kept taking longer and lead him to very remote regions. The „White Gold of Africa", as the ivory was called, attracted legions of self-declared big-game hunters. The elephant population decreased drastically. As a consequence, the German colonial government in Dar es Salam passed a strict hunting law in the year 1911. Suddenly, Africa was no more the anarchic playground of the *White Hunters*.

Anthimos Koundouriotis had seen elephant herds of up to five thousand animals during his hunting expeditions, had pursued huntable bulls to remote areas no European had ever accessed. Time and again, he had been told stories about fabulous elephant cemeteries by his African trackers and gun porters. They told him that sick or injured elephants had always lied down to die in some hidden places. Mountains of tusks were said to be at these cemeteries – tons of white gold. The Greek had been a sceptical for years and taken the stories for tales – until a coincidence convinced him.

It happened on a spring day of the year 1912, barely six months after the tragic incident at Ngongongare, during which Ulrich Trappe hit his wife after a nightmare. Anthimos Koundouriotis was camping together with Margarete Trappe at the edge of a steppe crossed by the river Ruaha. The Greek knew from previous hunting trips that big elephant herds usually assembled in this region at this time of the year. They had pitched camp near a dip, which, even during the dry season, was always full of water. The morning sun had risen glistening and without any grace, indicating that it would be a scorching day.

Margarete Trappe sat by the campfire and had a cup of tea. After one week's outward journey, she felt tired and battered and was still thinking of her home Ngongongare. For the first time since the birth of her children Ursula and Ulrich, she had gone on an extended hunting trip. Ulrich had been very comprehensive: „You have been a mother for such a long time – go ahead, together with Karimbe, I will watch the children and the farm."

She was worried about this unusual tolerance from Ulrich. After all, Ulrich could not stand Anthimos. Both got out of each other's way whenever possible. Ulrich was jealous. Ulrich was jealous of any other man indeed. Margarete was not aware of why he almost pressured her to go hunting with Anthimos for three weeks. She knew that she could count on Karimbe, their babysitter boy. No, she was not concerned about the children, rather about Ulrich.

Her thoughts were interrupted by the call of Anthimos' tracker: *„Mzee! Mzee! Ndovu, kubwa sana . . .“* The small wrinkled Chagga with his incredibly thin legs came running excitedly. She appreciated when his black servants called Anthimos *„Mzee”*. Everybody did, all the blacks. They respected him. It was not the kind of fearful respect their people at Ngongongare felt for Ulrich. No, these Africans treasured, worshipped Anthimos and made him understand through their reverent title *„Mzee“* that they liked him and took him for a *Bwana kubwa sana*, a respected gentleman.

She also understood why. Anthimos seemed to know and be capable of everything. He was the most perfect person she had ever met. His excellent education fascinated her.

One day as a giant rainbow was over the Maasai steppe and the pasturing wildebeest and zebra herds, he had said: „It looks almost like the description in the Genesis, on the fourth day of the creation. That was when God decided to realise the animals all over the world.“ Next, he had admired the rainbow and the herds for hours and spoken about a book written by some John Milton and titled *Paradise Lost*. It was an ancient book he often read when he was sitting in front of his tent. She did not know why Anthimos knew the Bible so well. At least, he was very critical of the Christian faith. Another time he spoke with so much knowledge about the Quran and Islam that she had wondered for a moment whether he might be a Moslem. His wife had been one; she knew it. But Margarete had not dared to ask Anthimos about it.

He never put his abilities and knowledge in the foreground. She often felt stupid and uneducated in his company. She had never heard about the Greek philosophers he used to quote, could not even remember their names. On every safari, he carried a box of books with beautiful covers, written in diverse languages. His excellent language knowledge sometimes led to her not knowing which language he was speaking at that very moment. He was a universal genius to Margarete: He never lost his way in the wilderness, seemed to know every hill, mountain, or river. In the middle of nowhere, he remembered a small tree, knowing that was the place one had to turn left. „I was here fifteen years ago,“ he then murmured, and she was not sure whether this shrub had already been there fifteen years ago or if it had then been a measly small bush he should not be able to recognise. But he was! He knew what leaves or roots to eat against diarrhea, plucked all kinds of weeds during the ride to the camp, which he turned into a delicious salad to eat with a steak. This man rode like an Indian and knew how to shoe a horse with cold irons with the most basic means or treat wounds with medicinal plants from nature. Anthimos lived the African wilderness with all his senses. He sometimes lifted his rather large nose in the air, like a pointer, inhaled something only he could smell and said: „*Nyati* – many of them and barely more than two kilometres away.”

When they suddenly stood in front of a huge buffalo herd, he shrugged his shoulders nonchalantly and said, laughing: „Just as I expected!“

His laugh was so enchanting! It was maybe the most beautiful detail about him. He was able to laugh out so loud, open and happily, showing his already a little yellow-stained teeth and such an incredible vitality in his eyes that she had often thought he was the happiest person on earth.

He had a childlike mind when having fun, especially when catching scorpions. Every night by the evening campfire, he loved putting thick trunks of wood in the fire and waiting for the brown scorpions living in the dead trees to race away in panic and being able to catch them with his hands. She admired his rapidity and agility as he grabbed, quick as a flash, the scorpions from above, with his index and thumb right behind the head. He rejoiced like a child because the poisonous animals could neither reach his thumb nor the other fingers with their sting, which they could only move forwards. In fact, Anthimos often seemed to be happy.

However, he was not. She did not know why. He carried something dull and heavy deep inside. Once, she had asked him why he sometimes was so sad. He had evaded the question and just said: *„It is my inscrutable Greek soul.“*

He laughed most of the time. Or he babbled away, like a little child. Just like now with the tracker. She did not understand anything of the torrent of words that developed between him and his tracker. Margarete watched Anthimos. His mouth looked very beautiful when he talked Swahili. He always used his strong hands and arms for gestures to communicate, he could not keep them still. Even his eyes were expressive. Eventually, he approached her, very calmly, as if nothing unusual had happened.

„He says that an elephant is approaching death step by step down there in the swamp, and that he has such huge sweeping tusks, that he probably has to climb mountains backwards.“

„What does he mean by that: approaching death step by step?“

„He says there is an elephant cemetery down there.“

„An elephant cemetery? I heard about this story but thought it was nothing more than yarn. What do you think?“

„I believe it, but I don’t know. You sometimes get further with your belief in Africa than with knowledge.“

He did it again, Margarete Trappe thought. Anthimos’ encrypted words sometimes made her shiver. It seemed to her that he knew something he was not ready to tell her. He continued calmly: „Don’t imagine such an elephant cemetery as one huge place somewhere in Africa where all elephants go to die, Toute Sweet. It is quite a fact that every big landscape has such a cemetery.“

„Why should elephants do this, Anthimos?“

„Sick animals, as well as sick people, are usually thirsty. It makes sense that these giants, conscious of their near end, approach water such as a river or a swamp. They can find water anytime and would not die of thirst. On the other hand, no elephant would ever voluntarily enter a marsh he might mire in. You should watch how an elephant checks every path with its tusk before setting its enormous feet. They can sense if the swamp is riskily deep.“

„And you think they would willingly enter the marshes to die?“

„An old African hunter told me once that there are two swamps called Shikanda and Segwe in a jungle near the watershed of the Congo and Zambesi, in the Walunda land. They say thousands of dead elephants are lying there. The surrounding swamps must be impassable. The elephants go there to die. Next, they sink. The crocodiles assure the death watch, they are guardians of an unbelievable ebony treasure.“

„So, you believe this is such a swamp?“

„Let's go there and have a look,“ Anthimos answered and grabbed his rifle.

They walked for almost one hour; the sun beat down on them relentlessly. The site became greener and wetter, and small trickles babbled their way through the meadows. The reeds around them became higher and more impenetrable. Flies flew around them. The two African trackers seemed to be very tense. Then they reached the outer edge of the swamp. Both had already been bogged down and had a hard time moving on. Grass tunnels made by hippos were everywhere.

Suddenly he was standing right in front of them: old and grey, mighty, peaceful, calm, and almost soundless, almost up to the belly in the water, barely thirty metres away. Only his ears moved from time to time. His body language gave a hint of him wanting to die. He had the most beautiful and splendid tusks Margarete Trappe had ever seen.

„At least one hundred and twenty pounds per tooth, this equals almost four thousand Reichsmark,“ she whispered excitedly.

Anthimos looked at her strangely. She was suddenly ashamed of having quoted the value of the ivory.

„Yes,“ Anthimos whispered. „But do you see all those small birds, the oxpeckers on its belly behind the right foreleg?“

„What is it about?“

„He is injured, severely injured. The oxpeckers eat the worms out of the wound. This old gentleman is suffering torture . . .“

„A bullet wound?“

„No, looks more like a spear wound. Some tribes here hunt elephants because of their meat. They stalk from behind and grab the elephant's tail. When he then starts to run around in circles furiously, they hit their spears from the rear side into the open flank until they hit the heart."

„How cruel!"

„No, brave – the hunters!" He kept thinking for a moment. „I will redeem him! If ever he attacked us, we would have no chance here in the swamp. I think he does not like men a lot. I'd better do him a favour."

Anthimos lifted his double rifle. Just fractions of seconds later, a shot resounded through the swamp. The head of the grey giant was torn backward. A deep sigh came through to them. Then the animal fell on its side in the mire. Half an hour later, the elephant had disappeared. Bubbling air pockets arose from the swamp where he had just been standing.

Margarete Trappe exhaled deeply. She was shocked but also happy. Anthimos talked with the two trackers. The smaller one stood in the water almost up to the shoulders.

„Stay here, Toute," Anthimos then said to her. Without awaiting her reply, why she should stay, he went barely thirty steps away from the place where the bull had sunk. He waded through the swamp, holding the rifle over his head. He advanced, centimetre by centimetre, and suddenly mired up to the neck. He swore and stopped. She could not recognise what he was doing.

„What is he doing?" she asked the little tracker in Swahili.

„He apologises for having killed the elephant, Memsahib. He always does . . ."

It took a long time until Anthimos got back out of the swamp. His clothes were filthy. He seemed very severe. At the edge of the swamp, he went silently to a bush and disappeared behind. Some moments later, he came back with a *Kanga* slung around the hips. The colourful ankle-length African cloth made him look like a Maasai. Bashfully, she stared at his muscular torso.

„You also should undress, Toute Sweet. There are millions of parasites in the swamp. Now they are only in your clothes. But if you don't undress soon, they will eat their way millimetre for millimetre in your beautiful smooth skin. Then you will suffer tomorrow."

He turned around while she undressed and wrapped a blanket around her body. The trackers pretended to look also away.

„Anthimos . . ."

„Yes . . ."

„There is something on my left thigh."

„Something black-brown?"

„Yes!"

„One to two centimetres long?"

„Longer!"

„Where on your leg?"

She was about to hiss at him angrily when he laughed out loud. He shook with laughter, and she became outraged.

„Why the hell are you laughing?"

„Thinking it over, Toute Sweet, I would love to be this leech on your thigh . . ."

At this moment, the little tracker stepped at Anthimos' side. She saw how Anthimos became very serious. There was something in his gaze she had never seen before in his eyes. The little tracker volubly talked to Anthimos, who kept silent. She did not understand what it was about.

Suddenly Anthimos took his rifle, loaded it, and pointed the gun barrel right at the face of the small African who did not seem to be afraid.

„Anthimos, are you crazy?" she screamed as she saw that he was about to pull the trigger.

„No, I'm not!" He said it very calmly while looking right into the eyes of the tracker, looked over at the other *Game Tracker,* and spoke in an English and Swahili gibberish: „*Mzee, you better keep your mouth shut for the rest of your life. There is nothing you have seen or heard. Hakuna Ndovu hapa! If you do not, I'll get kali, kali mwingi sana, and I'll shoot you!"*

„Ndio, Mzee!“ That's all the man with the stick legs said. The other African was much too afraid to be able to speak. He shook his head; however, he decided then to nod his head.

„What is happening, Anthimos? Why are you threatening them?“
Anthimos took the rifle down until the barrel pointed next to the feet of the African. He still stared into the eyes of the small man. A shot was released, and dust swirled up at the side of the older man. But the tracker did not even cringe. Instead, he self-assuredly said: *„Ndio, Mzee,“* and went away without any hurry.

„What the hell is going on here?“ she shouted at Anthimos.

„Out there in the swamp, I felt ivory tusks and skeletons everywhere under my feet. There might be hundreds of dead elephants – a treasure!“

„Why did you threaten to shoot them both?“

„Because they guess what I felt under my feet out there in the swamp. These guys are not stupid. They smell that there is an ivory treasure down there. Furthermore, they know me too well.“

„I don't understand this.“

„Those two have been hunting together with me for twenty years. They know I will leave this holy elephant place untouched. The ivory will stay where it is! I told them both that they should never dare to take the tusks out of the swamp and never tell anybody about it. Otherwise, I will shoot them. I am not a grave robber. I love elephants, even if I sometimes kill them.“

In the evening, the atmosphere in the camp was very depressed, however not only because of the incident. Margarete was embarrassed by Anthimos putting her on a chair, slowly sliding the blanket up her leg until he could see the leech. He poured some paraffin on the spot and waited some time until the worm started moving backwards out of the skin. Next, he carefully removed it with his knife and disinfected the small wound.

She felt very uncomfortable sitting in front of him and him kneeling in front of her so she thought he could look into her crotch, a thought which excited her at the same time. These thoughts were embarrassing, but she enjoyed every movement of his hands and shivered as his fingertips advanced millimetre per millimetre on the inner side of her thigh.

She was convinced he could read her thoughts.

Anthimos had not said much during hours, smoked a lot, and drunk more wine than usual. Shortly after the meal, he suddenly said: „I decided to no longer shoot elephants. There has been a hunting law of the German colonial government for some months. One needs to have an extended hunting license now to be allowed to shoot two elephant bulls. It is the beginning of the end of the great freedom here in Africa. I might give up hunting for good!“

„Why that?“

„When I came here together with your brother more than twenty years ago, this land was very unspoiled, beautiful and wild. A great place for people who were searching for freedom. However, your Prussian discipline and order left scars. What you call civilisation is my lack of freedom, which is increasing dramatically. They are building radiotelegraphy stations everywhere. They will soon establish a station with a range of four thousand kilometres in Muansa. Then you will be able to correspond directly by telegraph from Arusha via Cameroon with Berlin.“

„But this is wonderful, Anthimos. I don't understand at all what the downside should be.“

„Toute, there are no economic interests behind those plans but military ones. The Germans in East Africa are still depending on the English sea cable in the Red Sea. In this sense, in London, they hear every word your Kaiserliche Schutztruppen exchange with Berlin. In the case of war, this would be disastrous!“

„How can you imagine we could have a war here. Honestly speaking, I don't understand you.“

„Your emperor is greedy! Greedy for colonisation. People like the former Captain Leue from this Deutsch-Ostafrikanische Gesellschaft are nothing but henchmen of the German power politics. You don't know that the German government is the main shareholder of this corporation, do you? Your emperor controls these supposed private corporations. Believe me; Berlin wants more. They are building up their fleet come hell or high water. They want to become the main Global Power. An African proverb says: ‚When elephants fight, it is the grass beneath them that suffers'. Trust me, Toute Sweet: If war breaks out in Europe, and it will, there will also be war in East Africa. And we will be the grass that suffers . . .“

She was very uncertain after this conversation and left Anthimos alone. He seemed to be very depressed. Around midnight they were still sitting silently at the campfire. Suddenly he got up and went to his tent. She wanted to follow him, to be near him, as she had been very honest to herself some moments before and discovered that she loved Anthimos. She longed to fall asleep in his arms, yearned to wake up in his arms. She could feel that Anthimos wanted it also, but he went to his tent without looking back to her even once.

*

Lieutenant Colonel Freiherr von Schleinitz was raging. The commander-in-chief of the Kaiserliche Schutztruppen in German East Africa paced up and down the balcony of the district office in Dar es Salam. Dressed in their white uniforms, two of his staff officers stood uncertainly beside the balcony door. They were used to their supervisor's choleric behaviour.

„The gentlemen in the Reichskolonialamt in Berlin have taken leave of their senses. They are crazy,“ Freiherr von Schleinitz got up. „As if we had nothing better to do than planning holidays for the German high nobility seniors.“

„When is the hunting party supposed to arrive here?“ one of the staff officers asked.

„His sovereignty and his son wish to honour us with their presence at the beginning of August. We have only four months left to recognise it.“

„Four months is not long,“ the other officer pondered and added: „If they come with the entire court, this will easily be forty to fifty people. And if we count the servants also, we need to arrange quarters and transport for almost one hundred people – apart from the local porters.“

The commander-in-chief stopped pacing the balcony, and thoughtfully watched the waterside promenade. It was strikingly calm for a March Sunday. Very few German families were walking around. His gaze moved to the harbour where a German mail steamer was anchoring. The ship had brought diplomatic mail from Berlin a day ago. Besides an extensive estimate of the Balkan War, there was an interesting file from the war ministry about the newest technological developments in the aeroplane and airship construction and its future perspectives under military aspects. The emperor price for the best airplane motor had been awarded on January 27th. With this file, the military strategists in the war ministry predicted ground-breaking changes in the military strategy, should it be possible to use airships and airplanes for military purposes. As he had suddenly had a vision of an airship soon flying back and forth between Germany and East Africa, he had been captured by this file until the early morning hours. The homeland would not appear so far away then. For some moments, his thoughts went back. He had been living in German Africa for six years. Up to now, it had been a tranquil, interesting service. After the suppression of the Maji-Maji-revolt, his only task had been the continuous establishment of the military and police apparatus. There had been no notable military conflicts during the last years. Small fortresses had been built countrywide. Thanks to the many telegraph stations, the communication was easy, the streets were getting better and better, and the good railway network made the transportation of soldiers much easier. The Kaiserliche Schutztruppe, formed of fourteen companies, now consisted of two staff officers, seventeen Captains, forty-nine first Lieutenants and Lieutenants, forty-two medical officers, sixty Sergeants, diverse fire workers, and altogether approximately two thousand five hundred Askaris. Thus, the security of the colony was ensured without any problem, particularly as the police were also tightly organised.

All over the colony, voluntary corps made up of farmers and former soldiers emerged, making it easier to control the land. Such a corps had been founded in Wilhelmsthal just three weeks ago in Usambara. It bothered him right now, as something had been boiling up during the last two years between Moshi and the Meru region, which had brought along quite severe complaints from Berlin.

There was little understanding in Berlin for the fact that, especially in this region, white farmers were cruelly killed more or less regularly. Only two weeks ago, the number of victims had increased to eighty-five with the murder of the German settler Meyerhold. Without any exception, they were all Germans! Unfortunately, the announced German visitors wanted to go hunting in this very area! That caused a lot of trouble to von Schleinitz as chief commander of the Kaiserliche Schutztruppe. He thoughtfully turned to the two officers at his side on the balcony.

„These murders around the Meru are alarming me. Berlin already makes me sick, as we just can't find out what is really going on there."

„I already expressed my opinion in my last report about the internal security of the colony. A revolt against the foreign domination through the whites is beginning up there in the mountains," Lieutenant Krawitz interfered. „I am sure these murders are being coordinated among the tribes living there. What else could explain that several actions take place simultaneously during one day or one night – in completely different tribal zones."

„But that would be the first time in the last one hundred years, even the history of East Africa, that opposing tribes join forces to take common action," Freiherr von Schleinitz pointed out. „The Wameru, Waarusha, Wachagga – the Maasai even more – are traditionally enemies."

„This might be true," the other officer rose to speak. „Fact is that we don't have a clue about who is behind it. The aggressors hit unexpectedly and disappear without a trace in the dense forests and rugged valleys of the Meru mountains. We have the statement of this murderer who was executed last year in Arusha about a suggested group of blacks, calling themselves *Ujamaa Kali* and having met once at Ngare Nanyuki. However, I think we should not accord any great importance to this. We are fighting up there against an invisible enemy. We do not know him, and it seems that the population supports him – and he also has the advantage of being able to make use of the confusing landscape."

„And this is the area where they want to go on a safari? That's quite a problem!" Lieutenant Krawitz summarise. „Unless . . ."

„Unless what?" his supervisor Freiherr von Schleinitz interrupted him.

„Well, the Trappe family has their farms up there. There is no better hunting ground at the Meru. Whatever might be the reason: Fact is that there has not been a single incident on Margarete and Ulrich Trappe's farms for years. They are living in paradise and get wealthier and wealthier."

„Well, Lieutenant, it is strange, indeed. We have been talking about this phenomenon several times. But I still cannot accept your estimation that this strange Maasai story might play a role. The devil only knows why the Maasai call Margarete Trappe „Jeyo". Nobody could explain it to us until now. Even she cannot, but it is obvious that she enjoys the protection of the Maasai."

„Or the offenders move back to their hiding places on the Trappe's farms after their attacks," the other officer interrupted the conversation. „The Trappe farms are huge. They could easily hide a whole regiment in the virgin forests, canyons, and mountains up there. This gang of murderers would be very stupid to be active near their hiding place."

Lieutenant Colonel von Schleinitz raised his eyes abruptly. He contemplatively run his right middle finger over his lips. He took a deep breath, exhaled audibly, and suddenly spoke with a very low voice: „Never repeat this out loud, Lieutenant! It is an order! From now on, this suspicion will be treated as a military secret – because I think you might be right! And if so, we found a secure hunting area for our distinguished visitor from Bavaria – and maybe soon also a solution for the security problems in the country."

*

Anthimos Koundouriotis was quite sure of having heard human voices. However, he thought the presence of people in this sinkhole improbable. The blacks did not dare to approach because of Gurumico. The few white settlers living on this side of the Meru did neither know where the entrance to the sinkhole was nor did they move too far away from their farms since the whole region had been living in fear of raids. No, he could exclude with absolute certainty the presence of any other human in the Ngurdoto caldera.

He had a hard time finding his way through the dense undergrowth. His right arm was aching as he had to clear every metre through the jungle with his *Panga*. His clothes were sweatsoaked. He became bogged up to the ankles. Mosquitoes were all around. The sun had just sunk behind the edge of the sinkhole. It would be dark in two hours latest. He knew that millions of mosquitoes would leap at him if he would not find an appropriate place to camp and stretch his mosquito net. But there were only such dry places at the other side of the swamp, where he had heard the voices from – or at least thought he had heard them.

It was also where he had seen fragments of Gurumico's paw trace many months ago. At least he suspected that the mark originated from Gurumico. The ground was marshy almost everywhere and made hunting in this caldera ever so tricky and dangerous. Any trace left on this ground was gone barely one hour later. His uncomfortableness increased even more as without marks, he was helpless, had no idea of what was going on around him. Although there were many buffaloes down here, nothing, not a single hand-sized buffalo trace, nor the sharp paired footprints of antelopes nor the enormous tracks of elephant feet revealed him what had happened yesterday or only one hour ago. He might have been here, waylay him up in a tree or behind a bush, and suddenly attack.

Just like then.

With his left hand, he unconsciously fumbled the long scar on his cheek. It was swollen because of the heat and the high air humidity down here in the crater. His tongue went along the scar in his mouth cavity. He was able to sense the spots where the lower canines had entered his jaw – only a few millimetres away from the carotid artery. He took a deep breath as the memories came back and tortured him. Had he not hung his rifle in the tent then but put the weapon ready to fire beside him as any experienced hunter in the wilderness does, Saida would still be alive. Even if he had not seen in the darkness what had happened precisely and had only heard her lethal throat sounds and later his vicious grumble. If he had only had the rifle immediately within reach, he could have fired into the air. He would have fled without any doubt – and Saida, his wife, and everything existing with her giving sense to his life up to then would still live.

If only! If only he had credited the natives, all this would not have happened. He had laughed down the old Wameru who pretended Gurumico was the devil. He even had derided the first time he had heard this awful scram, which sounded as if a man was gasping in agony. The natives had all disappeared in panic in their cottages. „You were an idiot,“ he murmured. He should have been careful at last when after the scream, his Maasai tracker mumbled, „The evil is crossing the steppe and calling you – it wants to kill you.“ The tracker was a very courageous and experienced *Moran*. As a sign of respect to what had screamed so awfully out there in the steppe he had spit backwards over his shoulder – just as the Maasai do when they are afraid, however, cannot say it as a Maasai *Moran* should be fearless.

No, back then at the edge of the Maasai steppe where the ascent to Ngongongare starts, he had not understood the signal, had not taken the people's fear of the unknown being out there in the wilderness seriously.

So, it had happened by night in total darkness, as they were sleeping on the floor beside the fire, pressed together tenderly. The first thing he had heard had been Saida's wheezing, had thought that she was lovingly yearning for him, speaking while dreaming. Next, he had felt this hot breath above his face, this pain as fangs of finger size delved into his throat and face. His lower jaw ground while breaking. He had opened his eyes for only fractions of a second and dimly discerned something big, black with amber eyes. Next, he had passed out.

Saida was dead, and her neck was broken. Her right shoulder showed four hideous, profound wounds. It was obvious that it had tried to drag her away. „It does not kill to eat," the Maasai had said. „It kills because it wants to kill . . ."

Nobody knew what had killed Saida and injured him in such a life-threatening way. An animal, as the Wameru said, as big as a calf and the Maasai told it was as black as a moonless night. The fur was said to be ragged. Its screams had been heard from time to time, mostly in the forests near the Meru, often at the Ngurdoto Crater. And this was the place the tracks had led him to, those strange tracks that none of his trackers had ever seen in East Africa before. There had been the four oval, small front and the big hind footballs which had left marks on the soft ground. But it was no leopard. It could not be. The trace of a big *Chui* would not exceed nine or ten centimetres. Lions had larger paw prints and cheetahs, much narrower ones. This paw print measured seventeen centimetres from the claw to the ball and was as large and long as the hand of a strong man. The depth of the prints and the pressure the grass had been crushed with led to the conclusion that it was an unusually heavy animal with a body length of easily two metres. Nobody in the Meru region had ever seen such an animal. Therefore, the Wameru and the Maasai thought that is could not be an animal. It was Gurumico – the devil.

He had been hunting it for many years. He knew his soul would only find peace once it was dead, Saida would be avenged so that his feeling of guilt would become bearable. Only this, the hate, and the revenge, gave a meaning to his life. He did not know what would come next; he had nothing to lose. He did not care, just like he had not minded dying for a long time – until Toute Sweet had come into his life. Now he was again afraid of dying. However, as long as Gurumico was alive, he could not imagine a life without hate and with love.

The jungle cleared behind the next big tree. There was a ghostly silence in the crater. He heard nothing but the plop-plop of his own feet in the mud. He stopped abruptly, remained immobile. His ears concentrated on noise from the other side of the crater lake. Doves! Yes, doves ascended from the trees over there. Doves were always sitting in the treetops only. They did not have any enemies there. During the last years, he had learned that there were no birds of prey in the caldera. He knew every square centimetre here, every noise, every trickle, and every animal living in the *Ngurdoto*. If ever the doves had ascended at this hour of the day, something must have frightened them. What could it be? There was nothing to be heard but the flapping of the doves flying to the crater edge.

Only shortly before nightfall, he found the tree on the small clearance with the wonderful view over the crater lake. Whenever he came to the crater, he camped here as it was one of the few places, he felt quite secure and had a good field of fire as well. A big rock behind him protected him from being ambushed. The muddy lake with the grassy shore on the other side was in front of him. He was thinking, the moment will come when it steps out in front of his gun. A small reserve of dry wood remaining from his last stay in the crater lay beyond the rock trail. He reached for the dry brushwood to light a fire. Suddenly he heard the voice again. No, not one, it was several voices, at his left in the dense forest, maybe one hundred metres away. He instinctively ducked. His hand grabbed the rifle. Next, he smelled the fire. His gaze went to the treetops, but he could see no smoke. Whoever was making a fire there, prevented the revealing smoke from arising. It was as silent in the crater as it only is when the sun sets, and the scared animals await the darkness. His senses were highly concentrated, the eyes narrowed to observation slits. He fumbled for the spare cartridges in his chest pocket. Next, he crept in the direction of the edge of the forest. The mosquitoes tortured him, but he did not dare to hit them.
The men sat barely more than twenty-five metres away from him under a makeshift leaf canopy between two enormous rocks, eating *Poscho*. He could smell the corn. Eight men were sitting at the fire, and four were standing on guard. The guardians had spears, one also an

old carbine rifle. He could only discern three of the four men at the fire. They were old Wameru. The others were sitting their back turned to him. Two of them were Maasai, with shoulder-length ochre hair, thus *Morani.*

A slight evening breeze blew through the trees. As flat as a snake, he laid on the ground behind a tuft of moss, his chin pressed in the grass. The damp ground smelled very nice. A few centimetres in front of his eyes, a rhinoceros beetle pressed through the grass. His black quinine shell shimmered in metallic blue. Moss residues stuck on its splendid horn. It was so silent around him that he could hear the bug. The wind carried scraps of conversation to him, but he could not understand enough. He carefully turned his head to the side with one ear on the ground. He closed his eyes, stopped breathing, and concentrated on the word fragments coming out of the twilight of the falling night. A young voice spoke in awful Swahili. Anthimos was aware that he knew this voice, even knew it well, but he had no idea where from.

„A *Bwana kubwa sana* will come, very soon. I think it is one of their chiefs from the far-away land. Many other *Wazungu* will come along with him. They will come to her because they want to hunt, right here on our land.“

„What shall we do?“ and old Wameru asked with a quite lifeless voice. The one who talked awful Swahili spat loudly on the ground.

„Whatever we tried up to now was in vain. The *Wazungu* cannot be expelled. Instead of that, more and more soldiers arrive, and the iron snake is winding deeper and deeper into our land. Soon it will reach the big water in the West where *Wazungu* already carried ships.“

„What shall we do?“ the one with the old voice asked again.

„We do what the *Wazungu* do. During the big revolt in the South, they hung all chiefs by the neck till they were dead and then burned all the villages and fields so that the people had no reason to fight for something. Yes, we will kill the chief who will come!“

„And next we burn down their farms and houses and places of worship and *Boma* in Arusha,“ a third one got excited. His dialect revealed that he was a Wachagga.

„Yes, we should – we must do this – on one day, on one night. White Africa should be in flames! And a new green, fertile grass for our cattle and sheep and gooses will grow on their ashes!"
„Ndio, " all the men agreed.
As soon as they had said this, Anthimos was aware that it was true. His rifle porters and their fathers had told him several times, and he never wanted to believe it. But it was true. Those men at the fire were the leaders of what had been blowing like a breeze before an arising storm through the cottages and over the expanses of East Africa. Those over there were *Ujamaa Kali.* They were the responsible ones for the murders, raids, and all the other cruel actions of the last years! The tribes around the Meru had joined. They were fighting against the whites, the Germans!
Ujamaa Kali, Anthimos Koundouriotis thought very hard. That came from the Swahili language. „Ujamaa" stood for „united, joint, together." „Kali" meant „sun." But also „hot" or even „evil." United under the African sun – together against the evil, against the whites, against the German colonial masters, against oppression and heteronomy! Yes, that was probably the meaning of this name.
Suddenly it was dark. Gurumico came with the first star Anthimos could see from the corner of his eye rising over the Ngurdoto crater. The troubled sounding grumble from the depth of its chest came out of the forest behind the men at the fire. Anthimos shivered with fear and tension, mainly with fear. He knew this horrible, guttural, gurgling scream. Yes, it was there. Somewhere uphill, it was roaming the forests. It knows that were fire is, there are humans. It hates humans for some reason, and it kills them.

The Africans at the campfire had stayed silent after the horrifying screams. The moon did not dare to rise. The stars disappeared in fear behind a cloud. The cool evening breeze became breathless, and it turned overwhelmingly hot. The crater seemed to be filled with fear. Twice again, Gurumico grumbled his claim to power over the crater and the forests into the night. Next, he was silent, and the men at the fire were anxious to disappear somewhere in the woods.

Anthimos only got up more than one hour later. He was afraid. Afraid of this being somewhere in the forests who already knew that he was also there. And he was scared of what he had just heard. He properly shivered with fear. If it attacked now, he would only discern Gurumico much too late in the pitch-black night. If he shot, the *Ujamaa Kali* men would know that another person was in the crater. The shot from the heavy elephant rifle would reveal that it was a white man, as only white hunters had such high caliber weapons. They would come back to the crater and search for him, and Anthimos had the most significant problem he had ever had as a hunter. He would, actually, become the hunted one. He would die. He would die either way.

Chapter 10

The one who was just riding up in the early African morning light was an aging prince. He was from the house of the Wittelsbacher. However, he seemed to be a king in Margarete's view.

On horseback, holding the white head up self-confidently in the direction of the early August sun, the reins of the black horse loosely in one hand, trotting on the path towards Momella, the farm of the Trappe family. He was flanked by tanned Kaiserliche Schutztruppe officers in gala uniforms and many honourable men with pale faces. The prince's full beard shimmered as white as the top of the Kilimanjaro on the horizon behind him and was as unkempt as the head of a black wildebeest. He still was far away, but Margarete Trappe believed she could already sense the fascinating aura of this nobleman whose genealogy was as impressive as Wilhelmine von Sangan's one. This woman who had introduced her in her youth years in her homeland to this fantastic magical world. How she had dreamed then, first as a child and later as a young woman, to get access to this world of emperors, kings, counts, and duchesses. After the loss of their manor in Petersdorf and the sad years spent in the small apartment in Sagan, the glamorous life had seemed to be forever out of reach. But today, on her twenty-ninth birthday, Ngongongare was shining in the splendor of exactly this world.

The older man, however, who came riding the way dashingly up to their farm and who did not look as he was already sixty-seven years old, lived in this very world and brought it to her farm in German East Africa. His father had been a king. And his wife, the archduchess Gisela Louise Maria, was none other than the daughter of „Sisi", the former empress Elisabeth von Österreich. It was the son-in-law of Franz Joseph I., the emperor of Austria, who came riding along to hunt together with his son on their farm here at the Meru in German East Africa.

Excited, Margarete Trappe fumbled with her blouse. For the first time after an extended period, she had not dressed in breeches or shorts, but a put on a wide dress. Instead of a short-sleeved shirt, she wore a blouse with frills. The lace-up shoes she had forced her feet in, seemed much too tight to her. Ulrich stood only a few steps away from her in front of the house. He wore a bright tropical suit and a white hat. At some more distance, Anthimos leaned on a tree. He was the only one not to wear a suit.

She thought by herself how glad she was to have him here and stole a glance at Anthimos. Much to Ulrich's displeasure, she had sent him a telegram to Dar es Salam four weeks ago, telling him that they were expecting high-ranking hunting visitors from Germany and would be pleased if he put his excellent local and hunting knowledge at their disposal. She had signed the telegram „Toute Suite."

He had not answered her telegram, but she knew he would come. Yesterday early morning he had appeared at the door, dressed in quite dirty clothes and incredibly hungry. He had asked with his enchanting smile and eyes always reflecting love: „When *Jeyo* signs a telegram Toute Suite, she empirically also means right away – or should this mean Toute Sweet?" Next, he had eaten like a hungry predator and went to sleep. He had only woken up two hours ago.

She felt excessively happy since he had arrived. The evening before, she had sat on the terrace, lost in nostalgic memories for a long time. Margarete had become very melancholic, Ulrich hat felt it and had withdrawn discretely. She spent hours staring alone in the African darkness, listening to the sounds of the night, passed the last years in review – and thought a lot of Anthimos who, as always, did not sleep in the house but under a mosquito net near the seven cypresses. Her life had so astonishingly turned for better that she still believed it was a daydream.

Quite some time ago, Ulrich had started making efforts not to cause concern to her. He rarely drunk and took care of the farm, made new contacts to increase the sales of meat, vegetables, butter, and corn. There seemed to be no more contact between him and black girls or women on the farm since his nightmare. He was tender, tried to be near her, and even during the night gave her the feeling he loved her. The children were in good health; they were ever so proud of them.

The four-year-old Ursula was very pert and pretty. She loved the many farm animals and cheerfully babbled all day long. „Bubel“, as they called Ulrich, who was a little more than two years old, was his father's pride and joy. The little boy was fond of spending his time with his father in the rose gardens; Rolf, who was almost six months old, had been born on March 30th after a very difficult confinement in the Nkoaranga mission hospital. By day and by night, he made no secret that he was going to be a very self-confident child. Whenever he wanted something, he shrilled so persistently that not only Karimbe, the boy in charge of the children, but also all the female servants came running to spoil him. They had been living a happy life, indeed for a time. The three farms evolved like a dream. The number of cattle had increased. First good proceeds were obtained from horse breeding. Fortunately, they had been totally spared from raids. Margarete was sure it was due to the excellent cooperation with the Maasai and had been aware for quite some time that it had caused the envy and suspicion of many white farmers. However, she did not care about rumours and speculations of their farm neighbours. It seemed evident to her that her proposal to vaccinate the Maasai's calves had been brilliant.

Once a month, together with six of her employees, she went on horseback to the Maasai *Manyattas* down in the plain, vaccinated the calves, and treated sick cattle. She had even occasionally brought medicine to sick Maasai or given them money so they could get treatment in the Nkoaranga mission hospital. The Maasai appreciated it a lot, indeed. Therefore, nothing happened on their farm, particularly as four Maasai warriors worked for her as cattle herders. Among those was Kinai, who apparently had much influence on the other Maasai tribes in this region.

The farm went almost perfectly. Since she had started contacting hunters in Germany over her friend Otto Schlosser, the publisher of the monthly journal *Der Tropenpflanzer*, the number of safari requests also increased continually. It seemed that the year 1913 would turn out to be the most successful and beautiful since their arrival six years ago.

The farming operation got almost nuts with the message from the government in Dar es Salam about the presence of the aristocratical hunting party, which was going to visit Ngongongare and Momella for several weeks. Ulrich went wild. He had spent the last weeks only repairing the path which led from Arusha to them. The house and farm employees got new uniforms and working outfits, the outbuildings of the farms were prepared, fences and stables repaired, ox cart batches of food and beverages supplies had arrived. But her guest intended not only intended to go on hunting. As a member of the Kolonialwirtschaftliche Komitee (colonial-economic committee) in Germany, he also wanted to inspect the farm. During the last years, German East Africa had gained greater awareness in the German public and industry. Ngongongare, Legurucki, and Momella, the farms of the Trappe family, were, in the meantime, considered prime examples of the German diligence concerning the civilisation of Africa.

The dream of a „place in the sun", proclaimed by the emperor Wilhelm II engendered in Germany an enormous interest for the Black Continent. The level of media interest in Africa increased due to sensational „expeditions", such as the one of the former Lieutenant Colonel of the Kaiserliche Schutztruppe, Paul Graetz. He had been the first to cross Africa in an automobile between 1902 and 1904. Because of the motor noise, the African population in German East Africa had given him the nickname „Bwana Tucke-Tucke". In the year 1908, gold findings in Senkenke had engendered a real gold rush; the skeletons of giant dinosaurs found in the Tendaguro mountains North-West from Lindi made the scientists turn their attention to German East Africa. The German economy discovered a vast market potential in the colonisation, as well as the possibility to ensure Germany's need for raw material.

The Kolonialwirtschaftliche Komitee constituted in October 1897, which joined the Deutsche Kolonialgesellschaft, was one of the essential institutions pooling political as well as economic interests of and in the colonies. This committee rapidly became an economic factor of power in the German Reich. Well-known industry groups had joined the committee. The members list read like an encyclope-dia of the German aristocracy among which were to be found Lud-wig III, King of Bavaria; Friedrich August, König of Saxony – and Prince Leopold Maximilian of Bavaria, a passionate hunter.

On this August day of the year 1913, the Bavarian prince rode on a black horse to Margarete and Ulrich Trappe's farm Momella. He gazed up to the top of the grey-black Meru, reaching into the cloud-less sky. „Could almost be in the Alps," he murmured and smiled. His sharp glance wandered across the hills below the farm, over the Maasai steppe up to the Kilimanjaro. Farmworkers were standing at both sides of the path and cheered him.

Prinz Leopold wove back. He was astonished about the friendliness of the indigenes. He had come all the way from Tanga by train until the final station. During his short visit to the German fortress, he could not escape the feeling that the population was not kindly dis-posed to him and the other whites. Having been a soldier for a long time, he noticed that soldiers of the Kaiserliche Schutztruppe were all around – exclusively white soldiers, which gave him food for thought. Of course, his friends in the war ministry had informed him about the unpleasant increase of raids on white farms in the Meru re-gion during the last years. A good friend even advised him for secur-ity reasons not to visit that region. He had answered tersely: „I over-came the Seven-Day War against the Prussians, the Battle of Sedan also – I will surely survive a hunting excursion to the savages in Afrika as well."

Prince Leopold Maximilian von Bayern took a deep breath. The air up here in the mountains did him good. Everything around him had a sense of freedom, extent, and uniqueness. This German East Afri-ca was a beautiful land. Dr Richard Hindorf, the farming advisor of the Deutsch-Ostafrikanische Gesellschaft, had said joking in Dar es Salam that the Usambara mountains and the Meru region represen-ted an ideal retirement home. „Almost as in our homeland – only lions instead of gemsboks outside the window." After only two days, he noticed this was not exaggerated. The climate was enjoy-able, the days not too hot, the nights comfortably cool. The air was

incredibly clean, the landscape magnificent. All this did him right as
the last 12 months had been very exhausting, and also saddening.
Leaving the army where he had been carrying out his duty as field
marshal since 1905 had left its toll on him. For some reason, he suddenly felt old and redundant. At the sudden death of his father in December, gloomy thoughts started oppressing him.
Fortunately, due to his exciting tasks at the Kolonialwirtschaftliche
Komitee, he had not much time dwelling on dull thoughts. Furthermore, he enjoyed increasingly to follow his main passion, the big-
game hunting in Africa – together with Konrad.
His thirty-year-old son rode beside and behind him. He had a vivid
conversation with three gentlemen of the Berlin Reichskolonialamt
and with Dr Schnee, the governor of German East Africa. They were
no more far away from Trappes' farmhouse when Prince Leopold
von Bayern discerned the small group of Maasai under a tree near
the house. He had already seen several of these impressing but also
wild-looking men in Arusha. Large-sized and slim as they all were,
they towered the men of the other tribes. Their long hair, the striking
faces, and their spears gave them a very martial look. They were
very handsome people, presenting themselves with exceptional
pride. He looked with curiosity to the group, which looked back,
seemingly disinterested. It was only now he noticed the white man
of approximately fifty years in casual clothing and high suede boots.
He was not far away from the Maasai and looked very relaxed. It is
probably the Greek hunter, he thought. Dr Schnee had talked of this
white hunter in glowing terms, almost glorified him.

Anthimos Koundouriotis was standing in the shadow of the cypresses and felt too tired to be polite. He did not care about this prince
Leopold von Bayern. Unlike Margarete, who had already been totally hyper yesterday, he felt bored by such aristocratic hunting parties
whose members were of an almost unbearable vanity and whose
hunting ambitions could not be brought into accordance with his'.
These dandified saloon shooters usually started getting exasperated
with the heat and the dust in Africa on the very first day. They con-

sidered all the blacks to be barely more than indomitable savages. Usually, they were such bad shooters that they often only wounded the animals but, later on, refused to assist in the sometimes dangerous after-stalking. No, he had not much respect for these arrayed persons.

Anthimos was about to go to the farmhouse when he noticed the Maasai near him. His pupils suddenly froze as those of a feline predator focusing its victim. He saw one of the Maasai only from behind, but he knew he had seen him before: the day before yesterday, in the Ngurdoto crater – together with the other men at the campfire. Yes, it was him; he was sure about it. „Ksss . . . ," he hissed in direction to the Maasai. The man turned around.

„*Jambo, Mzee! Habari gani?*" Anthimos shouted out to him.

„*Mzuri sana, Mzee! Habariako?*" the Maasai greeted back.

When Anthimos Koundouriotis heard his voice, he knew instantly that he was right. For sure, this man had also sat at the campfire of the *Ujamaa Kali*-men the night before yesterday. It was him! *He* had said that an important white man would come and that they wanted to kill him. Suddenly Anthimos Koundouriotis was aware of why this voice had seemed familiar to him that night. This Maasai was one of Margarete's employees. Kinai! Yes, Kinai was his name. He had seen him often on the farm. He got goose pimples on his back as he got aware: This Maasai and the other men hiding behind *Ujamaa Kali*, had obviously one aim. They wanted to kill this man, this prince from Germany, who was just riding up!

*

Kinai ole Chieni was astonished that everything went so smoothly. He had expected the older man, *Bwana Kubwa*, who was arriving to be guarded much better. At his arrival in Arusha, soldiers of the Kaiserliche Schutztruppe had been standing everywhere. The sheer fact that they were exclusively white soldiers proved the importance of this *Bwana Kubwa* from the faraway country. It seemed strange that only a few officers and just nearly a dozen of Askaris were present on *Jeyo's* farm. The old, white-bearded man felt safe there. It had thus been easy to spy out the plans of this hunting party. One of *Jeyo's* trackers was a loyal Wameru whose son had been hung years ago and now was committed to the *Ujamaa Kali*-aims, had provided him with all requested details about the first safari planned for the day after tomorrow. It appeared that the whites wanted to ride first to the nearby Momella lakes to hunt there. He had found out a long time ago that *Jeyo* always made her guests first hunt in the surroundings of the farm to find out their shooting capacities and physical condition. Only once *Jeyo* knew how securely the shooters handled their weapon and the level of exertions they would endure she defined a definite hunting route. The ideal place for the first hunting days were the Momella lakes. The seven small lakes situated in the hills behind Olgedoido and before the big steppe had been named after a famous Maasai chief. There was a lot of game, the hills could be climbed effortlessly, and the vegetation consisting of small bushed ensured an easy food supply for the hunting party.

To get there from *Yeyo's* farm, they would all ride on horseback along the Kinandia swamps and cross the dense forests near the Rishanteni lake. Up there in the steep slopes of the forests, all horsemen would have to dismount and lead their animals uphill. The assault was planned to take place there. The *Ujamaa Kali* fighters could easily hide in the dense undergrowth, shoot the *Bwana Kubwa Sana* from short distance to death, next disappear in the dense undergrowth of the virgin forest to get back in a great arc to the Ngurdoto crater where they would hide.

There was no resistance to be expected from the Askaris and the protection force officers at this place. The slope was so steep, the undergrowth so dense that all horsemen would be busy leading their horses by the reins. It was very probable that chaos would break out, and the horses would panic after this raid. No matter how well the Askaris of the protection force were armed: they would have almost no chance to use their modern weapons or even start a pursuit. The plan was just as perfect as the hiding place in the Ngurdoto crater. In the merely impenetrable virgin forests and swamps of the crater over there, horses could not be used. One could only go on foot. A pursuit was almost impossible, as even if the hunting party consisted of maybe twenty to thirty white shooters and approximately a dozen of black protection force-askaris: They would never dare to enter this crater before getting reinforcement from Arusha. That would take more than a day, so all traces of the *Ujamaa Kali*-fighters would have disappeared off the swampy sinkhole ground. The troops from Arusha would start seeking the assailants in the swamps and forests of the crater. But those would have long been many kilometres away together with other *Ujamaa Kali*-warriors, attacking white farmers at the Meru, kill men, women, and children, burn down farm buildings and fields, the mission station as well as the Arusha *Boma*.

Yes, Kinai ole Chieni thought and looked with eyes full of hatred at the old white man on his horse, as he countered it in front of Margarete Trappe and dismounted clumsily, yes, this plan was perfect. In two days, the bloody revolt of the Maasai, Wachagga, Wameru, and Waarusha against the white invaders would turn the land into a battlefield. The German colonialists had been reacting for years to any resistance from the black population, driven the East African tribes into cruel famine and stolen the land of their grandfathers and great-grandfathers. Now they, the real masters of these mountains, lakes, and plains at the Meru would use this tactic of scorched earth.

Kinai ole Chieni heard the old man with the white beard say to *Jeyo:* „God be with you, my dear lady." Next, he turned away and left the farm together with the other three Maasai-*Morani.*

„Nice meeting you, Your Excellency," Anthimos Koundouriotis murmured when Margarete Trappe introduced the prince to him. He squinted over the shoulder of the white-bearded man. Embarrassedly he cleared this throat and stumbled: „Sorry, hope to see you soon." Next, he went determinedly past the astonished aristocrat and Margarete Trappe, who stared at him confusedly, to the nearby tree where his gun was. He reflexively charged the weapon and disappeared minutes later in the forest nearby the farm where the four Maasai had gone before. He felt that the situation was awkward. When he had left instead of talking with him, this Bavarian prince had looked at him in consternation. Margarete's face had turned as red with shame and embarrassment as the crop of a Marabou. However, when he had noticed how this *Ujamaa Kali*-Maasai had left the farm at the arrival of the German prince, he had felt again that a disaster was approaching.

He had difficulties in finding the footprints of the four Maasai on the rocky ground. Branches whipped his face as he rushed bent over through the undergrowth, searching for footprints, always avoiding making noises. *„Bloody bastards, "* he moaned when he noticed that the four in front of him did not go to the Maasai steppe, as it first seemed, but made a big arc and were moving towards the Ngurdoto-crater. „Now I know where to find you," he said and smiled triumphantly. He decided to take a shortcut he was aware of to get over the crater edge directly to the place where he had seen *Ujamaa Kali*-men at night two days ago. When he reached the crater edge after one hour, he was drenched in sweat and maltreated by the flies. He knew that the Maasai called this spot Leitong. He was sure the *Ujamaa Kali*-fighters would appear here at some point.

He was angry for having misjudged them because as soon as he had reached the crater ground, lying sweating and breathless on his back, he heard the voices of several men, among those of the Maasai Kinai ole Chieni. Thus, the four Maasai and obviously also some other men were already in the crater. Shit, he thought. There were not a lot of bushes at that place of the crater to cover him. It was as bright as day, and he saw no way to creep up to the meeting point without being noticed by them. He loaded his rifle and fumbled for the revolver at his hip. The idea of being discovered made him feel uncomfortable. He wondered if they were numerous over there? Ten? Twenty? Would they be armed? What would they do if they discovered him? They would not engage themselves in a firefight. It would reveal their whereabouts and ruin their plans.

His thoughts tumbled. His gaze scanned the clearance for coverage, in vain. There were over eighty metres of grassland without any bushes or rocks to hide behind between him and the hiding place of the men. He was about to cut bushes to camouflage himself as his view fell on a trace of his own shoe on the still dry ground of the slope. It was a trace of his right leather boot he had left two days ago here in the crater. He froze. On top of his boot print, there was a paw print. It was a huge one, pressed wonderfully clear and sharp in the clay and well preserved as a gypsum cast. Gurumico! It was indeed its paw print! A little longer than his palm, the five balls, as well as the claws, showed over his shoeprint. He had never seen such a perfect print from it before. Yes, Gurumico had been here, had lurked on the same path down from the crater edge on his own prints. The horrifying thing was that the well-preserved print showed that this monster had come along only a few minutes after him.

He suddenly shivered. This beast had been only a few metres away from him, had followed, scented, and observed him. He remembered at once how, two days ago, he had sneaked up to the *Ujamaa Kali* men – and IT had been directly behind him, probably waiting for his chance to attack and kill him. He had for sure only survived this evening because this beast had felt the presence of other humans in the crater. That was why Gurumico had not attacked him from behind! It was by chance, pure coincidence, that he had survived that night.

Anthimos breathed rapidly. His pulse throbbed violently. A strange feeling overcame him. He did not want to believe what he was feeling. But he had to admit he was afraid – panicked! Because this animal, this monster which had already killed his wife, was clearly hunting him. All at once, he got aware that Gurumico wanted to kill him!

Suddenly, Anthimos discovered half a metre away from the paw print, in a bush directly beside one of his boot prints, a small tuft of black hair with a brownish shimmer. Crouching and looking and listening in all directions for suspicious movements or sounds, he approached it. He had never seen such hair before. It was silky, softly gleaming, almost like the hair of the Colobus monkeys. He bent down and smelled it. That was definitely no monkey hair. It was not the strong smell of a primate and different of any animal he had seen or hunted in East Africa up to now. He carefully grabbed them to take them out of the bush. In a flash, he knew that that was it! This hair, together with the well-preserved paw prints, represented the first useful traces of Gurumico. The first definite traces for years! Finally! This hair of HIM still released an odour.

In fractions of a second, an irrepressible hunting instinct emerged in Anthimos. He crouched over the traces. Just like a predator, he scanned with squinted eyes the surroundings, staring on every bush, searching for almost invisible colour shades, for black-brown shades behind hedges or, ducked away in the grassland and the tops of the trees on the other side of the clearance. But there was nothing suspicious, nothing dangerous – besides the *Ujamaa Kali* men! Anthimos grabbed the knife at his belt with his left hand. The flapping of a bird in the nearby gallery forest made him wince. It was only a Toko, one with a yellow horn on the beak. Harmless.

Centimetre by centimetre, he fumbled the blade out of the leather sheath. In his right hand, he held his rifle charged and reloaded on the ground beside him. He gently stuck the blade of the dagger in the clay, stabbed centimetre by centimetre around the paw print in the ground, lifted slowly the pawprint eternalised on the clay, and put it on a moss cushion in the grass beside him. Next, he bent a reed and used it to take the animal hair out of the bush and put the brown-black hair on the clay piece with the paw print.

Perfect, he thought. Gurumico's scent was thus not overlaid by his. Now he had to pack the secured forensics in an odourless manner and make them transportable. His gaze went over to the forest, where the *Ujamaa Kali* men were staying. Their voices could not be well heard against the midday breeze. But they still were there! And they were many. Using his dagger with caution, he cut moss pieces out of the ground, always avoided touching it with his hands, put one piece of moss over the secured traces, and pushed the other carpet of grass under the clay fragment with the paw print. Eventually, he wrapped some woven reed ropes around it. Now he would hunt this beast – merciless, ready to kill. And ready to be killed!

Anthimos took a deep breath and stared as if hypnotised at the opposite forest. He sensed a strange feeling arising, felt as his thoughts were only controlled by the intuitions and mechanism of a hunter.

160

He was aware that at least a dozen Africans, warriors, and elders, were sitting over there in the forest. They were full of hatred – hating the whites who oppressed them, stole their land, and were ready to make their culture and traditions disappear. How should he prevent the planned attack, the murder of the German prince? Should he prevent it? Should he try to inform the protection force? No, he would neither have the time, nor did this correspond to his inner conviction. That would be taking sides – against the Africans and for the whites. He did not want to do this. Deep inside himself, he felt a strong aversion against these German occupants, the soldiers who, starting from Dar es Salam, covered this magnificent free land with a delicate net of Prussian suppression mechanisms and strove for changing Africa into a white colony. No, he did not want to have anything to do with this war. He wanted to live here, peacefully, free, and happily. He liked the Africans, their way of life, their cordiality, kindness, and deep humaneness they felt for all those who were living here in Africa without wanting to change it or its people. Just like him. He even liked a few whites. Not all were the same; not all were colonialists. Margarete was not. But her husband Ulrich was one.

A gentle murmur was heard out of the forest. He got nervous, started thinking hard. It was clear to him that the men over there were going to transform East Africa into a battlefield. Their motives seemed understandable for him. However, he anticipated that their ways and means would entail cruel revenge campaigns. He had to prevent that. But could he prevent it? Could he do it alone? Himself, Anthimos Koundouriotis? He got up abruptly, hid the grass bundle with the paw print and the hair under a bush, took his rifle, and went right to the forest. He made sure to step in a puddle and on a dry branch. The crackling could easily be heard.

Now he saw the men. They were more numerous he had imagined, maybe twenty. Most of them had weapons. Their eyes fixed him in suspense. He approached the group step by step. While approaching, he saw some of the warriors lift their simple guns. The Maasai called Kinai made a few steps towards him. He had a glance of uncertainty, but also hatred. Anthimos walked up to him with a smile on his face.

„*Jambo*, master of the dead elephants,“ the Maasai answered and lifted his arm for an honest greeting.

Anthimos was astonished to be called „master of the dead elephants“ by the Maasai. This *Moran* obviously knew about the incident some time ago when, together with Toute Sweet, he had followed the dying elephant in the South of the land and discovered the elephant cemetery in the marsh. And as it often happened in Africa when people did spectacular things or had special abilities, the local population in no time at all give them a name which from there on clings to them. He was pleased to be called „master of the dead elephants“.

„Sometimes the wind carries good, however also bad news over the land,“ he answered mystically, hoping the Maasai would understand his reference. For a short moment, there was a sparkle in the eyes of the *Moran*.

„You are the *Muzungu* who has been for years in the Ngurdoto crater chasing a demon whose appearance is only known to the souls of the dead,“ the Maasai evaded the allusion. The other warriors and elders stood petrified behind him.

Anthimos lowered the rifle pointedly and stroke with his hand over the deep scar on his face.

„Not only the dead know that Gurumico exists,“ he whispered. „But the living show respect to the dead who continue living deep down in their heart by chasing and killing the demon.“

As he said so, he assumed the Maasai knew very well that Gurumico had cruelly mangled his wife.

The elders in the background agreed, murmuring respectfully on unison „*Ndio.*“ Anthimos felt that these men were not really hostile but even had respect and esteem for him. The Maasai nodded thoughtfully and leaned relaxed on his spear.

„Only the one who crosses the thorn savanna barefoot makes the pain his companion,“ he said past the white man. Anthimos thought hard. Should this be a hidden hint that the men suspected him to know about *Ujamaa Kali*? Did the *Moran* want to point out that he better closed his eyes and did as he had neither seen nor heard anything? Was this a point-blank but well-meant invitation to keep silent? Or was it a threat?

„I know what you are planning to do," he provoked the Africans. „You intend to kill the old man with the white hair who is visiting *Jeyo*! And you also intend to burn down the farms of the *Wazungu* and chase them out of your country. It is what you *Ujamaa Kali* men are planning! I understand your motives. However, I think it would be the wrong way . . ."

The Maasai's eyes narrowed. The other men started taking a threatening posture. An old Meru with little life but much kindness in his eyes coughed slightly and whispered almost without any emotion: „We could kill you!"

„Yes, you could. But you will not do it!"

The older man seemed to smile. His words sounded peaceful: „You are white! You could reveal us to the Askaris of the *Wazungu* . . ."

„I never would."

„Why not? You are a *Muzungu* as well. You belong to their tribe. Although you have black hair, the soles of your feet are as white as the feet of the soldiers whose boots trample our pride."

Anthimos liked the older adult. He sensed that this Meru did not really want to kill. However, he also noticed how the Maasai and the other young warriors behind the older man got indignant.

He counted on the influence of the old man: „When you came out of your mother's womb many years ago, *Mzee*, you also had bright, almost white palms and soles. We all have white soles when we are born. We are all the same at the beginning. Some become black later on, others white, and in faraway countries, people get yellowish skin after birth. But we all have white palms and soles as *Watoto*. We are all humans. We all want to coexist in peace and watch our children run after butterflies instead of going to war."

The Meru picked his flat nose and thought hard. A young man from the same tribe wanted to say something, but the old one made him a signal to keep silent.

„You are brave, and your words are wise. You only take from this our land what you need to live. You love and protect all the rest. What does your wisdom tell you about how to end the oppression through the other white men? They steal the air we breathe and the land on which we live. They kill our young warriors when we revolt. What should we do?“

Anthimos guessed that this older adult was looking for a peaceful way. He respectfully bent his head, went some steps in the direction of the Wameru, and pointed to the leather case with arrows at the hip of one of the young warriors beside him.

„Give me your arrows . . .“

„Why should I? They are poisoned.“

„I am not afraid of poisoned arrows. I am only scared of poisoned words. Give them to me.“

„One?“

„No, all of them!“

The warrior looked unsettled from Anthimos over to the older man who shortly nodded. The young boy grabbed the quiver, took a dozen arrows out of it, and held them to the white man. Anthimos took the arrows, watched the wooden shafts and the iron tops, and handed them over to the old men: „*Mzee*, take the arrows and try to break them!“

The Meru's eyes did not reveal any emotion when he received the twelve arrows. His bony finger, which seemed to be covered with parchment, enclosed the shafts of the arrows. Without letting the white out of his view, he tried to break the arrows with his gouty fingers. He failed.

„I cannot get it done! Those are arrows made of hard acacia wood. Only a young man is strong enough to break these arrows.“

„Give them to this Maasai there whom I know to be called Kinai ole Chieni,“ Anthimos interrupted the efforts of the old man. He reached the arrows to the one Maasai, who worked on the Trappe family's farm and whom he suspected to be the prime mover, one of the *Ujamaa Kali* leaders.

„So, you try to break them. You are young and strong.“

164

The Maasai, obviously confused, took the arrows. But unless all undertaken efforts, he also failed. He seemed to be angry about it and tried thus to break the arrows on his knee. The arm muscles of the Maasai contracted. The wooden shafts bent but did not break.

„It does not work, *Muzungu.* Can you do it?"

„Yes, I can!"

Fixing the Maasai's eyes confidently, Anthimos grabbed the arrows, broke one after the other, and threw hereafter with ostentation arrow by arrow behind him. A murmur went through the group. The older adult smiled.

„This is the way you should fight the whites! Not with power! Not with anger! No, you must be smart to use your wisdom. If you try it with power, your tribes will be destroyed sooner or later. Because the *Wazungu* you want to fight are too strong. They have ships with canons; they will soon have ships crossing the sky, such as kites and vultures, unreachable for you and your spears. Down here, you will confront them with maces and spears. And they will bring death over you down from the sky. They put the power of many horses in their stinky, noisy thing made of metal. This thing is more persistent than any Maasai warrior. You will fly in panic through the steppe, like siafu ants fleeing from the water, until you starve or get caught or slaughtered by the *Wazungu*. And no-one will feel compassion for you, as they will call you murderers one has the right to punish."

The old Meru swallowed, visibly concerned, and scratched his head embarrassedly. The three other Maasai gathered around Kinai ole Chieni, their leader. Anthimos took a deep breath. He was astonished how insistently he had demonstrated the hopeless situation in an armed battle. But he knew that these men would have no chance in a military conflict with the white occupants. The Germans were very well organised and armed to the teeth.

„You are talking like one of these holy men with full beards in the mission station Nkoaranga," the old Meru interrupted his thoughts. „They are always preaching peace; however, they have guns in their houses. They have hatred in their hearts against all those who are not willing to believe in their God. You may be right, but don't tell us how we should not do it. Instead, tell us how we might defend our freedom. How should we defend ourselves, *Mzee*?"

Anthimos addressed the Maasai Kinai ole Chieni, who obviously was still suspicious. Knowing that the Maasai are fond of drinking cattle blood scrambled with milk, he continued: „Violence only produces counterviolence! Be wise! No Maasai kills the cow, which will give milk to his children during years, only because he has a craving for blood for his dairy product or a piece of meat for a festivity!"

„What do you mean by this, mater of the dead elephants?" The Maasai was unmistakably impressed by this comparison.

„It is effortless! User your wisdom, your mind – and take advantage of the white men's arrogance. They think you are stupid and uncivilised niggers. And because they believe so, they consider out of the question that you can learn from them. The power of the *Wazungu* does not only lie in their modern weapons. No, it also comes from their education, their knowledge. Send your children to their mission schools and their universities. Learn their languages, learn to detect their weaknesses, and to turn their strength into your strength. Their power is of the spiritually superior with a machine gun in his hand. Your strength results from the time you have. It should be your narrowest confidant. Believe me: This is the way you will win at some point! Or you will die and leave to your children a life in lack of freedom . . ."

Anthimos turned abruptly away from the *Ujamaa Kali men.* He shouldered his gun pointedly and walked self-confidently towards the place in the crater where he had secured the paw print and the hair of Gurumico. For some moments, he was afraid that one of the warriors might shoot him from behind, but nothing happened. He slowly crossed the clearance. He felt happy.

For the first time in many years, he had the feeling of having given sense to his life.

*

Margarete Trappe was insane with rage. Only the presence of Prinz Leopold von Bayern held her from cursing loudly! When she was angry, outraged, she could explode within fractions of a second out of a totally calm state, start cursing and swearing, usually getting a deep-red face, and frighteningly roll her eyes just like her stallion Comet. Such outbursts of rage were barely more than temperamental outbursts and empirically appeased after some moments. Therefore, the African farm workers had compared her with a *Kiberiti Kali* – a flaring match which extinguishes right away – and chosen this as her nickname. At this very moment, however, it did not seem to be a short temperamental outburst. Saida, the hunting boy, who was busy cleaning the rifles at some steps beside her, noticed the short flash in „Mama's" eyes, saw how she threw back her deep-red face – and decided to get quickly out of the way of Mama *Kiberiti Kali.*

„*Hatarai! – Mama kali, mwingi sana,"* he warned the cook at low voice about the imminent danger. Next, he disappeared behind the nearest tent. The experience he had built up taught him that he better shunned such situations. „Mama" used to throw things when she was furious. She was fond of using her boots; she could take them off her feet in no time at all and turned them into missiles if she had nothing else available. Mama *Kiberiti Kali* was as good in throwing shoes as the boys of his village with throwing stones to kill birds. His head had already been hit twice by a boot from a big distance. The first time when he had unintentionally pointed the gun on her while he was cleaning it – this was something she hated! The second time when, due to big excitement at the attack of a buffalo, he had handed over to her a shotgun, which was totally inadequate for a lethal shot instead of a heavy gun.

Had they not climbed a tree in the very last moment, the angry bull would have killed them. They had merely escalated the tree as she started ranting like fury, calling him an idiot, and hit him several times with her boot. He had to succumb to her and even for three hours. She sat on the branch above him – under them, the angry bull rammed his head against the tree trunk and smashed with his hoofs the guns lying under the tree.

The other two hunting boys had fled on another tree and almost fell down laughing. Three hours later, she suddenly took the boot and threw it at the bull's head. He had gone, rumbling madly. Later on she had told him that she had not been so angry because of the shotgun. The real reason was that he had touched her but with both hands when he tried to help her to climb up rapidly on the tree. „This is something," she then explained, „even the Bwana is not allowed to do in public."

However, everyone who worked for her knew that she was not as mad when she cursed that way. But Saida was not aware of what made her look so angry and frightening. Anthimos Koundouriotis at least thought he knew it. When he saw her, he guessed it had been an error to leave the farm without giving her any explanation, thus compromising her and her aristocratic guests.

Toute Sweet was standing behind a tent. The late afternoon sun shone threw her hair whipping in the wind. Her silhouette stood out seductively against the reddish evening sky. Her hands were pointedly resting on her hips; one leg positioned to the side, her body posture demonstrated her mood unambiguously. Oh my God, how beautiful she is when she is angry, he thought and waved to her. It was meant to be nice, but she turned around and disappeared behind the tent. It made him smile, but he denied it to himself, knowing her reaction much too well. If she did not feel taken seriously in her helpless fury, the situation became dangerous. He had experienced it twice during common hunting trips. Each time she had run furiously, making wild and vehement gesticulation with the hands, cursing towards the nearest gun. She did it in such an angered way that it was not clear to him whether she wanted to shoot him or not. Due to their unmistakable feeling for danger, the hunting boys had, in both cases, rushed hiding behind trees or rocks as if stung by a viper. They only appeared again once Anthimos had succeeded in calming Margarete down by lots of persuading and eventually taking her in his arms. She had been lying in his arms, shivering, and jittering, sniffing her nose at his shirt, wiping with her big, beautiful eyes and her pouty mouth her tears on his sleeve. As he rode towards the tent, he thought that if she was so angry in such moments, she probably was delighted to stay so long in his arms without being ashamed or having to explain it.

Anthimos had a feeling of warmth and tender affection for her, which he had not felt before. He loved her states of anger because it made her show all this irrepressible vital force and the feelings which lay sleeping deep inside her. When she was angry, she showed her true self. And when she ran away at the end of one of her outbursts of rage, unable to speak a word, she was irresistibly beautiful and attractive. Just like now.

However, he had never seen Toute Sweet as indignant and angry as today. He felt exhausted from the long walk in the crater. He did not feel like confronting her. Besides some farmworkers and the children boy, he had met nobody on the farm after his return. Next, he heard the shots and remembered that Toute Sweet always invited her guests to a barbecue once the guns were sighted. He had a horse saddled and went to this barbecue place on the hill near the lake.

He rained the horse right in front of the tent. Roaring laughter out of many men's throats was to be heard from the fireplace near the temporary camp. It seemed that the aristocratic hunting party was in a very great mood. From the corner of his eyes, he saw Msisiri, the cook, and Saida, the hunting boy. They were looking from behind the food tent and rolled their eyes as an unmistakable warning for him.

Margarete turned her back to him and looked at the nearby lake. Thousands of flamingos in panic were flying circles above the lake, and several hippos rummaged through the water near the shore. He wondered why the hippos were so nervous. Without awaiting her anger outbreak, he said in a calm and determined intonation: „Toute, I need your two dogs! I need them tomorrow morning. It will be very dangerous hunting in a very unclear area. It is impossible without dogs. And it is crucial for me!"

She did not turn around. However, he could see from the side that tears were running down her cheeks. He suddenly felt that she was not crying because of him.

„What is wrong?“

She did not answer his question. Instead, she said with a strained voice: „You can get my hunting boys and the tracker, the Maasai and everything else you might need for your chase. You can even take Ulrich along. But what you will never get from me: my dogs and my stallion! If you want my dogs, you have to take me with you also!“

She kept staring at the lake where the hunting party was, merely fifty metres away. He slowly approached her from behind. He would have liked to take her in his arms. But did not dare to do so because of the employees. Suddenly he saw it. His gaze went over her shoulder to the men at the shore of the lake. The agitated hippos were still churning up the water; the screeching flamingos were flying in circles above the lake. Almost all the men of the hunting party were standing a few metres from the shore. Some had rifles. Most of them had a beer bottle in their hands. August Leue, as the Trappe family's direct neighbour and representative of the Deutsche Kolonialgesellschaft, also present, yelled in awful Swahili at a black servant an order for a cold beer: *„Bira moja, baridi sana – haraka!“*

With naked torso and rolled up trousers, Ulrich Trappe waded up to the knees through the water, waving a bottle of whiskey in his right hand. Only two metres away was Konrad, the sun of Prinz Leopold von Bayern. His angular head with the striking receding hairline shone in the sun. He held a golf club in his hands. He was drunk.

„Again, Konrad! Once again! Hit their big ash again,“ Ulrich Trappe yelled and waved his arms around. The sun of the Bavarian prince took a golf ball, fetched it on the shore, swung the club, and hit the ball hard in the direction of the hippos at less than fifty metres distance. He and the other men watched mesmerised the ball. With a loud clip, it hit the water close to a hippo mother with her baby. Frightened, the strong animal reared up in the floods, the ivory front teeth flashing in the evening sun, and submerged dark grunting with the baby. The men standing at the shore applauded.

„Slightly off, Konrad, only slightly off,“ Ulrich Trappe shouted and took a big sip out of the bottle of whiskey.

Margarete Trappe slowly turned to Anthimos. He had never seen her so sad and angry before. „I hate them! I hate them all! And Ulrich is the one I hate most!“ she sobbed. „They all don't have any respect for the creatures in this paradise. They don't respect anything! Especially not the African people!“

Anthimos kept silent. He made one step towards her, took her in his arms, and with one hand, pressed her head tenderly against his chest. She was shivering all over. For the first time since his wife's death, he felt that he was still able to love. It was *her* he wanted to love.

*

The evening went better as expected after the happenings of the late afternoon. Prinz Leopold von Bayern, who had been visiting the German serum station at Ngare Nanyuki and thus not been present at the revelry at the shore lake, seemed to be in a great mood.

The night had come. The camp was illuminated by the starry sky and two campfires. Under a big acacia tree, a festive table was splendidly decorated with candle holders. Dressed in an elegant white uniform as all the officers of the protection force, the prince sat at the top table under an umbrella thorn, having Margarete Trappe on his right. Ulrich, who was facing him, still seemed to be drunk, as well as August Leue.

At the beginning of the festive dinner, the prince had already expressed his enthusiasm for East Africa with a toast on the hosting family Trappe. While the servants, dressed in black, took the last plates away, the prince raised his wine glass and looked at Anthimos Koundouriotis. „Cheers, honourable Mr. Koun. . . , Koun. . .“

„Just call me Anthimos, Your Highness, this is much easier,“ the Greek interrupted the stammering of Leopold von Bayern. He also raised his wine glass.

„I am thrilled, Anthimos, to be accompanied by a hunter of such legendary reputation! I could hardly experience anything better than to be guided during my hunting trip by such a famous and charming lady like Mrs. Trappe and an ever so experienced big-game hunter like you! May I ask you what made you strand in this beautiful East Africa, so far from your homeland?“

„Well, Your Sovereignty, it surely is the love of freedom and the enthusiasm for all the beautiful and wonderful things that all Greeks have, which lead and keep me here.“

He was about to continue speaking when August Leue interrupted him: „However, the Greeks are also said to be fervent patriots, ready to fight and die for the freedom of their fatherland – like once in Sparta!“

Anthimos pricked up his ears. He did not appreciate the undercurrent in the German's wording as he was one of those organised, staccato Prussian militarists, it made him distrustful. Even before he could answer, August Leue kept on teasing.

„I am just asking because the second Balkan War was still raging a few days ago in your homeland, triggered by the invasion of the Bulgarians in Greece and Serbia. Many of your freedom-loving compatriots fought and fell. You did not! I, as a patriot, would instantly rush to my homeland if it needed to be defended!“

Anthimos would have liked to react harshly, he felt provoked, but he decided to avoid a scandal. He calmly answered: „Stranger, tell the Spartans that we behaved as they would wish us to, and are buried here! You certainly know, honourable Mr. Leue, that these words are written on a famous gravestone in Sparta, don't you?“

„Of course, I know about the legendary battle of the glorious Spartans against the Persian.“

„You see, Mr. Leue: The Spartans were already told as boys to fight and, if necessary, to die as a hero. And as you also know, they all died without exception during this battle doomed to failure from the start. However, when I was a child, I was told by my father that dead heroes could neither be fathers nor patriots, thus no more do anything for their country. They are simply dead!“

Margarete Trappe swallowed confusedly. She felt that the mood was about to shift. She looked with questioning, rather begging eyes to Prinz Leopold von Bayern. The aristocrat responded by a sympathetic glance.

„Gentlemen, please! We should not talk about a war on such a peaceful and magnificent evening! Peace is reigning in German East Africa, and we all want to appreciate it, don't we?"
The prince smiled openheartedly at the Greek. Anthimos started to like the nobleman from Bavaria with his small, almost mischievously sparkling eyes and felt relieved. „Your Highness know, I am Greek. More precisely, my family originates from Corfu. It is evident that the Bavarians and the Greeks have something in common."
„What do you mean by that?" the nobleman asked astounded.
„As far as I know, we owe our national colours, white and blue, to a Bavarian."
Prinz Leopold looked up, stunned.
„You mean Otto I, the Prinzensohn of the Bavarian King Ludwig I?"
„Right! He had once been King of Greece. I think he was only seventeen years old when in 1832, he was brought into power in Greece by the European powers. His reign was not that glorious, but that happened a long time ago. Anyhow, we owe him the white-blue colours of Bavaria."
„I wish to express my great respect to you, honourable Anthimos," the Wittelsbacher answered and nodded, impressed, „I would never have expected to find such a literate big-game hunter like you in the wilderness of East Africa. Even less from the island of Corfu. So you certainly know the Villa Archilleion?"
„Of course, I do, Your Highness! My father was not only an intimate friend of General Consul Freiherr von Warsberg to whom the Austrian Emperess Sisi had given the order to build this villa named after the legendary Achilléus of Troy. He also went to school together with Rhousso Rhoussopoulos, the Greek teacher of the Empress Elisabeth of Austria. I even had the great pleasure of meeting Sisi personally."
Margarete Trappe was speechless. She was inspired that Anthimos had come to know personally Sisi, former Empress of Austria, whom she worshipped just as Wilhelmine von Sagan. Anthimos had never told her he was born on Corfu. He had told her next to nothing

about his origin and his past. He did not hide anything. He only had said cryptically in his very own way that „the knowledge about the history sometimes clouds the view on the future."

She stared at Anthimos with her eyes wide open. Unlike all other men who had come dressed in suits, he only wore a wide shirt, khaki trousers, and – as always – his suede boots. As an exception, they were not dirty. Already upon his arrival, she had noticed that the black curly hair in his neck was remarkably long. He was tanned and looked so handsome with his large shoulders and the dark eyes. A little unsettled, she joined in on the conversation.

„As a young girl, I worshipped and adored the Empress Sisi and read all the books I could get. I learned many of her poems by heart." She looked at the others with hopeful eyes. Only Anthimos and the prince showed their interest by smiling at her. The other men at the table looked as if they had nothing useful to add to this conversation.

„Well, my lady," Prinz Leopold rose to speak, „would you delight our tired minds by reciting one of the lovely poems of my mother-in-law?"

Full of expectation and warmth, Anthimos looked at her. Ulrich tried to be chivalrous and babbled: „Oh, yes, princess, please . . . !"

She cast a contemptuous glance at Ulrich, knowing that he hated poems. The smile of the prince, however, showed that he would really be pleased.

„Well, why not. My favourite poem is called ‚My Dream'. It is a very long poem, revealing the empress's dream of being an emperor. It has many verses, and I will probably mass up the right order, but the verses are lovely. It seems a poem for peace to me. But I don't dare to recite it in the presence of Your Highness as it shows the critical look of the empress Sisi on the aristocracy."

Prinz Leopold von Bayern looked at her with vivid, sparkling eyes. The old gentleman smiled at her, almost fatherly, when responding: „Don't worry, dear lady. My mother-in-law's sometimes very critical opinion concerning the military and life at court is well-known. I learned to live with it. I kindly ask you to let us listen to this poem!"

174

Margarete Trappe was very excited. Never in her life, she had been asked to recite a poem. Never ever! And now it was the son-in-law of Sisi, the former empress of Austria, who requested it personally! He could not know how much she adored and envied Sisi and had secretly played the role of the Austrian empress at Gut Petersdorf, believing that she resembled her a lot. In fact, she had spent hours in front of the mirror, holding a picture of the young empress in one hand, time and again combing her own dark hair as Sisi had it. Without any doubt: The young empress looked somehow alike her. Even very alike, she believed.

Sisi also had loved the country life, had been unconventional and freedom-loving, had adored her father – just like her, Margarete Trappe! Her heart was beating.

She was about to get up as Prinz Leopold, sitting at her left, stood up and moved her chair to the back. She thought the shame would make her sink into the earth and felt that she was shivering. She crossed her arms behind her body, raised her torso self-confidently, moved her hair back over her shoulder, and spoke to the starry sky:

„Mein Traum

Ich war heut' Nacht ein Kaiser,
doch freilich nur im Traum,
dazu noch ein so weiser,
wie's solchen gibt wohl kaum.

Es war seit früh'ster Jugend
Entsagung stets mein Los;
ich lebte streng der Tugend,
nur im Familienschoß. "

„In my dream I was an emperor tonight
but, of course, only in a dream
and such a wise one, too,
that there is hardly anyone like him.

It was from my earliest youth
renunciation always my lot;
I lived strictly by virtue
only the bosom of the family."

She lost her voice for some moments. She tried desperately to remember the following verses.

Confused, she gave a little cough and continued with the next verses
that came to her mind.

„Das arme Landvolk schwitzet,
bebaut mühsam sein Feld.
Umsonst! Gleich wird stibitzet
ihm wiederum das Geld.

Kanonen sind sehr teuer,
wir brauchen deren viel,
besonders aber heuer,
wo Ernst wird aus dem Spiel.

Wer weiß! Gäb's keine Fürsten,
gäb' es auch keinen Krieg;
aus wär' das teure Dürsten,
nach Schlachten und nach Sieg. "

„The poor country folk sweat,
labouriously cultivates his field.
In vain! In a moment,
the money is again stolen.

Cannons are very expensive,
we need a lot of them,
and this year even more,
as the game is getting serious.

Who knows! If there were no princes,
there would be no war;
there'd be no more thirsting
for battles and for victory."

Abruptly she came back to reality from her dream. Her questioning gaze went from face to face. Full of expectation, she looked at Anthimos. His eyes showed that he admired her. Ulrich embarrassedly cleared his throat. She noticed that the prince stood up, and his small eyes started having a strange glance.

„Dear lady, would you please excuse my seemingly foolish words. It does not befit to persons of my age and condition to say such – as we say in Bavaria – crazy things. However, dear lady, it is my most passionate desire to let you know with all the feelings of an almost geriatric man that these were the most touching, beautiful, and lovely lines I heard as an old soldier in a long time! Of course, I know this poem and, therefore, can assure you that Sisi would barely have recited it better. I openly acknowledge it!"

Prinz Leopold von Bayern raised his glass, nodded to the men at the table, and leaned his torso in her direction.

„Here's to you, Margarete! May our God and all the Gods of Africa protect you and your family."

*

She was as afraid as her dogs but did not want to admit it. They had already been spending seven hours in the Ngurdoto crater. Anthimos was strikingly silent. It was muggy. Nothing was to be seen beside the heat shimmer above the swamp and some butterflies. For some reason, there were neither animals nor birds. Rain clouds were gathering on the sky above them. She wondered whether she should tell Anthimos that she was panicking. Her gaze went to Kibo, her terrier and to Tell, the pointer. Both followed their tails between their legs.

„The dogs are scared," she whispered. „They have never been scared before!"

„They are afraid because they sense we also are,“ Anthimos admitted and instinctively groped for the safety lever of his gun. His palms were wet. After a moment of reflection, he concluded that this had never been happening to him before.

„What the hell are we hunting, Anthimos?“

Margarete felt that an animal nobody had ever really seen was lurking somewhere out there in the forests and bushes, behind or on the rocks, up in a tree, or ducked in the reed. She knew that Gurumico existed since Anthimos had told her shortly after their departure in the early morning that HE had killed his wife and harmed him seriously. Her black farmworkers had told her some time ago that a big malicious, demon-like animal was supposed to be in the Ngurdoto crater. She had not credited the frightening depictions of the blacks as, in her experience, the Africans tended to exaggerate and quickly mystify natural phenomena they did not understand. But he existed! Anthimos had shown her the incredibly large paw print and the strange black hairs. She had never seen anything similar before. When the dogs sniffed it to begin the scent, her terrier Kibo had crept between her legs. From that moment on, she had been afraid.

„The dogs have to recover, and I am also tired,“ she whispered to Anthimos. His shirt was drenched in sweat, as well as his leather hat.

„In two hours the latest, the sun will go down. Either we go back right now, or we have to spend the night here,“ he said with a loud voice and stopped.

„Why do you speak up?“

„It does not matter anyhow. He knows that we are here. He knows that we are searching for him!“

„Why do you think so?“

„I don't know. But it is better to do so.“

Margarete thought it over. She had told the prince and Ulrich that they would trace an especially huge elephant Anthimos had supposedly seen the day before. During such quest, it could happen that one had to spend the night in the wilderness. They had taken along dry meat, two tins of beans and water, as well as a mosquito net.

„Do you think he will flee?" She hoped he would say yes.

„No! Quite the opposite! The dogs already picked up the scent three times and lost it again three times. It means that he was already in front of us three times. Every time we approach, he makes a big circle, always to the left, and always through the brackish water to avoid leaving traces and scent. He is incredibly smart! I think he is behind us right now . . ."

„What should we do then?"

„Pitch camp, do as if we stopped searching him. I believe he absolutely wants to have me, wants to kill my soul because it belongs to my wife's. He knows he must kill me to get tranquillity. Therefore, I let him come to me for the killing . . ."

They camped in the last daylight on a rock spur and made a big fire with lots of smoke. They also willingly made a lot of noise. The dry meat tasted delicious, but both were not very hungry. The dogs did not want to eat either. The camp was well-situated, protected to two sides, and upwards by rocks. The swamp was in front of them. If he came, he would have to creep up from the left through the forest, under a big tree having fallen out of the slope over a rock, at some five metres of the ground.

„Toute, it is best you sit in the fallen tree. I stay in the camp so you can see me all the time in the glow of the fire. The only way he can come is passing beyond this tree. You have an optimal shooting field and enough hunting light from up there, due to the fire."

The concentrated, determined, and in an absolutely insensitive way, he spoke made it almost sound like an order. She knew he did not mean it this way. She would never have thought of contradicting him. He never made any mistake when he was hunting.

„You want to offer yourself as a bait?"

„No! I don't have to. He already selected me years ago. However, this night we will put an end to this. Either way!"

It was hot and windless; the silence was oppressive. The other animals in the crater appeared to be afraid of the happenings they seemed to anticipate. The dogs staying with Anthimos at the fire also scented his presence while she laboured her way up the steep hill to climb from above on the overturned tree trunk.

He came without a sound and much too early from a direction he should not have been able to choose: from the rock above the camp. It was no growl, not even a real noise, but something made Margarete freeze in the middle of the slope. She looked in panic downwards over her shoulder, clung with one hand on a root, and tried with the other to pull the rifle from her back. But it was already too late.

She did not see it; only heard how her dog Tell died. It was a short, strange rattle, drowned in blood, bubbling, soft – but lethal. Fractions of a second later, she saw through the bushes how the fox-terrier, flew into the nearby shrubbery like catapulted through the air by a powerful paw. He squeaked miserably when hitting the ground.

Next, there was a big black ugly shadow down in the camp at the twilight of the early evening. And a smaller one. A human shadow. It was Anthimos' shadow.

The shadows seemed to be one. Through the bushes, the silhouettes were but a suggestion, and she could only perceive quick movements. Next, the big shadow was above the small one and she knew she had to shoot. There was no time to be afraid of hitting Anthimos. She dropped the root, dragged the gun from her back while sliding on her butt down the slope, repeated, shot almost from the hip, saw in the muzzle flash the big shadow even increase when he reared hit. She screamed and kept screaming because it was an awfully huge being and because she was afraid of it and even more afraid to hit Anthimos with the next shot.

Again, the breaking of the heavy gun sounded through the evening silence. She saw again how he flipped over, turning angrily and full of pain around its axis, showing his ugly head and very long yellow fangs. The subsequent shot missed, and one more.

Next, he let go, breaking down on the forelegs, roaring when the next bullet hit him in the flank. After that, he hobbled to the bushes, and Margarete did not know what she shot with the following three bullets. The sound of the touch-down of the projectiles revealed to her that she had hit twice.

The jungle suddenly seemed to quake. Monkeys were yelling in the tree-tops; hundreds of birds flew up. Something big broke through the undergrowth very near her. She jumped up, rushed away, saw from the corner of her eyes Anthimos jump up and the gun in his hand, skipped over the fox-terrier on the ground in front of her. Branches were whipping her face. She stumbled, a branch ripped her blouse open, making her scream from pain and fear, again saw Anthimos, saw him close, so wonderfully close. Panting and breathless, they both dashed through the thicket, following him.

„I hit him! He is already a little dead,“ she shouted while running.

„Yes, you got him!“

Abruptly she stopped at the forest clearing near the swamp. The clearance was lightened by the moon. A sound came from very near in front of them, a deafening sound – awful, angry, and painful. The ground beyond their feet suddenly seemed to sway.

„He is stuck in the marsh!“

„I can see him right in front of us. I see his fur, twenty paths from here! Shoot! Shoot! Shoot!“

They shot without being able to aim, both at the same time, directing their guns on the grey-black in front, reloaded, shot time and again. Water fountains were whipping up, mire and fur pieces were flying around.

Some moments later it was deathly quiet in the crater. The shadow in front of them got smaller and smaller, sank in the crater lake. Nothing but the bubbling of the swamp could be heard. After that, he was gone.

„*Kufa . . . ,* “ was all Anthimos said.

„Yes, he is dead!,“ she said expiring.

They looked at each other speechless but in a yet everything phrasing way. His glance went from her eyes over the neck to her torso. She only got aware now that her trousers and blouse were ragged, her breasts showed. It did not matter to her.

„Are you free now that he is dead, Anthimos?“

„*Ndio!* “

„Can you love me now?“

Kibo, the fox-terrier, was still alive. His wounds were not so bad. They wrapped him in Anthimos' shirt and laid him beside the fire and kept on softly running their fingers through Kibo's fur for a very long time. Her shredded blouse was still hanging down on her. He sat beside the fire with a naked torso and caressed Kibo tenderly for a long time. Next, they buried Tell under a tree near the swamp with a lovely view over the crater lake and put heavy stones on his grave so that hyenas could not dig him out.

Margarete was very sad. When they fixed the small mosquito net under a tree near the fire, and she noticed that he was secretly sobbing, she felt secure, happy, and united forever in their shared grief about the dog.

The next morning, her memories of the last evening were quite blurred. For a long time, they had been lying on the floor under the mosquito net, very close to each other, lighted and warmed by the fire, guarded by the moon, staring through the veil at the sky and fainted listening to the sounds of the wilderness. However, she had only listened to his breath, waiting for Anthimos to say something or even say nothing at all and just touch her.

He did not do so for a long time. It only happened when she thought that he still could not do *it*, still needed distance, maybe could not show physically what he felt in remembrance of his dead wife and forced herself to understand it. At that moment around midnight, he gently pulled her against him, pressing her head against his chest – so tight as if he were afraid, she might fight back or wanted to run away. However, she did not want to defend herself; she wanted to stay. With him. Forever.

So, she had completely let go and drifted, in gentle thoughts, covered by a soft coat of bliss, yearning with her eyes closed for his tentative contact. They had touched each other all over with their lips, kissed, caressed their bodies so softly and tenderly with their fingertips guided by timelessness and longing as if they had been doing it a thousand times ago. Sometime, with the first chirping of a bird in the dawn, they had made love for the first time. There was nothing but love. Their naked bodies melt together what their souls had been professing them a long time ago, what they now wanted and would no more have been able to stop. Their hands and lips willingly followed the lust and the craving and the longing of melting two bodies and two souls to only one. Together, they slowly sank and drifted and whirled towards and into one another like down feathers in the morning breeze. And everything on and in their bodies was gentle and delicate and perfect.

When the first sunray came under the mosquito net, she opened her eye. At lightning speed, she closed them again, pressed her hands at them just like she had done as a child when she refused to see something or deemed not to be seen.

Her hand fumbled for him. On this morning, nothing was strange to her: his skin, his smell, his breathing in and out. She did not want to wake up! No! She wished to continue breathing him in her dream, imagine his body, live the experience again. She wanted more, everything – she wanted him!

Kibo woke her up by a quiet cheep. She saw the day through the mosquito net and listened to the birds around. Anthimos was lying naked beside her. His body stood out against the twilight of the early day. Lost in thought, she kissed his mouth, and he opened the eyes. She saw the same feelings and desires in his eyes as the night before.

Later on, they sat at the fire, and he showed her a hole as big as his middle finger in his shirt, just below the left armpit.

„You almost shot me to death, Toute Sweet, although I did not do anything to you!"

They kept on laughing childishly about it for a long time, rolled around over the forest soil holding each other tightly and giggling. After that, they broke camp, went on the path leading up to the crater edge. From there, they continued over the high plane to Ngongongare.

Chapter 11

She heard the noise outside the house around midnight. It was pitch black outside. Ulrich was asleep in the next room. Slowly she straightened up in bed and reached for the pistol on the bedside table. Again, she heard a noise, then a soft voice. „Hodi?“ someone called out in Swahili, following the rule in East Africa of never entering a property without first politely asking if you were welcome. Margarete Trappe put on the dressing gown and went to the front door. With the loaded and unlocked pistol in her right hand, she opened the door slightly and looked out in the dark.

„Karibu,“ she called. A shadow emerged from the darkness of the night. It was a tall, slender man. She could tell it was a Maasai by the cloak and spear. He came closer. The paraffin lamp in front of the house illuminated his face. It was Kinai ole Chieni. He looked very distressed.

„What do you want so late at night?“ she asked, slightly incensed, but guessing that there must be a good reason for the Maasai to come to the farm so late.

„*Jeyo*, my eldest wife sings painful songs of death. She says that the new life inside her will kill her. Can you help her?“

„Your wife is expecting a baby?“

„*Ndio, Jeyo!*“

„And the baby won't come?“

„*Ndio*! My eldest wife has already tried four times to give me a son. But they all died inside her! Will you help her?“

„Is she in labour already?“

„Yes, but the baby cannot come because it sees the world the other way round in its mother's womb and does not know where the light of life is . . .“

Margarete Trappe thought about it for a moment. If she interpreted the Maasai's words correctly, the child in the mother's womb was in a breech position. Such complicated births could endanger the life of mother and child, she knew that from the many labours of horses, cows, and pigs she had witnessed as a child on the Petersdorf estate. Here in Africa, she had had to learn to manage these births herself sometimes. For this reason, she had read many books and sought the German Schutztruppen veterinarians' advice in Arusha. She had learned a lot about African natural herbs from the locals. For example, a tea made from the flute acacia tree's bark helped excellently when a cow stopped with the afterbirth. Another tree bark was an excellent laxative. She had also been able to use her broadening range of natural remedies on the horses of the Schutztruppe. She had often saved the lives of cows and calves, mares, and foals. But the birth of a child? She had never done that before. Her own three children had all been born in the mission station. But now, she did not dare to be a midwife herself. On the other hand, it was impossible to call the doctor at the Nkoaranga mission station now, in the middle of the night. And waiting until dawn seemed like playing with death. „Where is she?"

„The men of my *Manyatta* are bringing her on a stretcher. They will be here any moment, *Jeyo*. Will you help her? Will you help me? I don't have a son yet . . ."

Damn Maasai, it briefly flashed through her mind. The Maasai men's attitude towards women was frightening. Not only did they have several wives anyway, often, very young ones. No, the men also mistreated them and, she had already found out, it was not unusual among the Maasai for men from the same family to have sexual intercourse with other men's wives. This Maasai was certainly not thinking about his wife now. He wanted a son! That was all he was thinking about. Because without a son, there was a heavy stain on his honour. That was the only reason he had walked the long way to her through the darkness. She took an angry breath. There was pity, but also contempt in her words.

„I will do it because you work for me. But in fact, I only do it for the woman and child. When the men come, have them bring your wife into the house. I will have hot water prepared."

Four hours later, at first light, the wife of Kinai ole Chieni gave birth in the house of Margarete Trappe on Ngongongare to a strong, heal-

thy, and spirited kicking child – a boy! To save the life of the young
Maasai woman and the child, she had performed the first caesarean
section of her life on a woman in the sweat of her brow. The child
was fine, but the mother was not. She had lost a lot of blood. The
wound, which had only been sewn up in a makeshift fashion, needed
urgent follow-up treatment. She would have to be driven in a cart to
the mission station at daybreak to see the doctors there.
Margarete was dead tired. Her daring and the emergency operation
of several hours had given her a horrible headache. Exhausted but
overjoyed and proud of herself, she went out onto the terrace to have
a cup of coffee. Outside in the courtyard, just a few metres from the
terrace, several dozen Maasai had gathered, to her surprise. Kinai
ole Chieni stood in the front row. Everyone was silent, staring at
her. Kinai stepped towards her.
„*Jeyo*! Yes, it's you. You are *Jeyo*! The prophecy of *Laibon* Masiani
ole Chieni, father of my father and flesh of my flesh, master of the
thoughts of *Engai* and chosen by the ancestors of all the Maasai to
see the things of life before they happen, this prophecy has come
true with this day! For Masiani ole Chieni had once foretold that a
fearsome white shadow would come over the Maasai people, with
eyes of glass and silky dark hair. And this shadow, it was once said,
will follow our new-born *Laibon* like the day always follows the
night, accompanying him for ever and ever, speaking to him in a language whose words sound strange to us."
Margarete Trappe was confused. She understood the Maasai's
words but could only begin to guess the meaning of what Kinai ole
Chieni had said. She remembered how the Maasai had looked at her
sunglasses and her hair with such fascination when she arrived,
many years ago. Even then they had called her *Jeyo*, mother. But she
had never been able to fathom why. What had the Maasai just said?
With eyes of glass? Yes, that undoubtedly meant the sunglasses. But
what did that have to do with this new-born child?
The Maasai interrupted her thoughts.
„Such, *Jeyo*, was the prophecy of our *Laibon*. And this is exactly
how it happened tonight. And so, it shall be, and so it will be from

this day forward. You, *Jeyo*, were and are the white shadow. You have tonight helped my unborn son, who was already on his way to his ancestors, to return to the land of the Maasai. And so, according to our laws, he will one day be the new *Laibon* of our people. And because *Engai*, our God, has given you wisdom this night and imposed upon you the duty of bringing this child into the world, henceforth your soul will be near his and his near yours forever. You, *Jeyo*, are a part of him. And he will always be with you. Therefore, *Jeyo*, we have decided to name this son of mine, the future *Laibon* of our tribe, *El Ngongongare*, the Eye of the Water, in your honour. Live henceforth forever and ever on this Maasai land – on Ngongongare. We and *Laibon*, born today, will always protect you and your children. For you have become the mother of our future tonight."

*

As continuously as Ngongongare, Momella, and Legurucki developed into flourishing farms on Meru, the Trappes' house on Ngongongare quickly advanced to a veritable menagerie: Maxel, the zebra, a dozen mongooses, the cheetah, the baby elephant, the sweet jumping rabbit, and a small monkey – they all belonged to the family, were playmates of the three children and provided a rather turbulent, paradisiacal ambiance. Reedbucks, dikdiks, antelopes, African birds of prey, ostriches, young warthogs, and sometimes even lion cubs were mainly free to roam around the farm, at least during the day.

Five-year-old Ursula loved to look after cheeky Maxel; three-year-old Ulrich loved the cute mongooses that kept all the snakes away from the farm; and one-and-a-half-year-old Rolf, barely able to walk, was already showing his preference for danger and challenges: He was constantly playing with young lions and cheetahs.

And there was Jockel, the monkey. A few months ago, the dogs had once again chased a horde of monkeys that had been scavenging through Ulrich's vegetable gardens. During the chase, a dam had lost the tiny one. Since then, the small, sweet, black-brown Jockel was the children's favourite. Jockel was still a little monkey, but he was all the cheekier for it. And very curious. One of his favourite pastimes was to open parcels and furiously shred the contents if they did not meet his expectations, so if they were not made of chocolate or other sweets.

He had already done that early in the morning of that sunny June day with Margarete's birthday present from the missionaries of Nkoaranga. And as he had been loitering in front of the house for an hour, staring wide-eyed at the many boxes on the terrace, it was to be feared that Jockel would take advantage of an unnoticed moment to pounce on this mountain of most wonderful packages.

Margarete Trappe thought about it. Ulrich would soon return from Arusha with the children. Then her birthday cake and all the presents would be on the terrace table. In any case that was the plan, to celebrate her upcoming thirtieth birthday at least for a while before she went on the long safari with her new hunting guests.

For moments she paused in her thoughts. The fact that she would not celebrate her thirtieth birthday at home on Ngongongare, but somewhere in the African wilderness, actually only made her a little sad for the sake of the children. What Ulrich thought was basically indifferent to her. She herself was looking forward to the upcoming trip. The two youngest children would not really realise her absence anyway. And five-year-old Ursula felt so safe with Karimbe, the children's boy, that she would not suffer from the long absence either. No, she thought, the children won't mind much. Ulrich could not object in any case because the new hunting guests were once again very honourable nobles from Germany. That was good for business, for „fame", as Ulrich had been saying lately. And that was the only thing Ulrich still was really interested in: fame!

Prince Leopold of Bavaria had returned to Germany after his hunting trip to Ngongongare with unimaginable quantities of excellent hunting trophies. He had the mountains of tusks, rhinoceroses, skins, horns, and stuffed animals exhibited in the Wilhelminium in Munich. And he gave Margarete Trappe an almost legendary reputation in Germany's established circles as a „courageous, glorious German huntress in the wilds of Africa". Since then, there had been no end to the enquiries from German noblemen interested in hunting. And all those who came wanted to go hunting with her, not with Ulrich. That was only right for her, for a deep gulf had long since opened up between Ulrich and her. What still connected them were the children, the farm – and the good reputation as a hunting farm in Africa, which Ulrich attached so much importance to, but which she did not care about.

She went on safari because she loved Africa, the life in the wilderness. And because Anthimos accompanied her on the safaris whenever he could. They were wonderful trips they made together whenever he was there. Anthimos came and went to Ngongongare as he was able – and as he wanted. He came often. Ulrich did not prevent it. Since she had found out that he was having an affair with Fatuma, a Somali girl, and had told him, they went their separate ways. Ulrich went the way of solitude. Her path was Anthimos'. Sometimes they rode out into the wilderness for only a few hours, sometimes for many weeks. It was a time of bliss, with nights in the frenzy of love, detached from everything earthly. And with days when their laughter echoed across the vastness of Africa and when even the animals in the wilderness could see and feel how happy Anthimos and she were. They hardly hunted, doing so only for their own meat needs.

„The most beautiful buffalo I ever hunted," she recalled Anthimos saying when they set up camp at Lake Manyara, „had such indescribably wide horns that I could have stretched a hammock between them. I saw it, big, mighty and formidable, across the sights, a magnificent trophy, took aim at its blade, had my index finger on the trigger – and then let it go because it was so incredibly perfect."

Yes, Anthimos was like that. She loved the way he saw African nature with respect, how he moved in it, became one with it – and took her with him. Crazy they both were, yes, wonderfully crazy! At the Ruaha River, in her exuberance, she had wanted to try to pull a hair out of the tail of an elephant, a very young bull – which had only prompted Anthimos to say tersely, „Bring me a hair too, they're supposed to bring good luck." That was all he had said when she had sneaked off. Later, he had doubled over laughing for hours because – after her miserably failed attempt – she had had to sit for most of the day on a very thorny acacia tree, where the angry bull elephant had shooed her and where he had stood dozing in the shade for hours while she almost died of thirst above.

Yes, they were crazy with love and in an indescribable unison of their souls on these safaris. Wherever a river or a waterfall appeared, they tore each other's clothes off with lust-filled looks and jumped naked into the water, where they splashed around like children. Only Anthimos' carelessness when bathing in still waters had once caused disgruntlement. Margarete knew that all kinds of diseases lurked in murky African waters and had asked him not to bathe in these pools for her sake. „I love you," he had responded very seriously, „that is more dangerous to my soul and body than a few measly bacilli in the water. If you go, I'll die. Not physically. But I would waste away, vegetating only as a shell, a bizarre figure made of skin and bones. So why are you so upset about the tiny animals in the water? They won't eat me."

Her gaze went over the terrace, where dozens of boxes were already packed for the safari. There was only room for the gifts from friends and neighbours on the table. But Jockel was so fixated on the gift table that she couldn't have taken her eyes off it for a minute. Then she had a brilliant idea. „Karimbe . . ." she called after the child-boy. The little man hurried over.

„*Ndio*, Mama . . ."

„You killed a cobra behind the house this morning, didn't you?"

„*Ndio! Nyoka, kubwa sana, memsahib*," he confirmed, indicating with his hands that it must have been a huge cobra indeed, almost one and a half metres long. He told her that the dead snake had been hung in the shed to dry so that the skin could be peeled off and used later.

„*Lete Nyoka,* " she advised him and secretly giggled about her plan. She knew Jockel was panic-stricken about snakes.

A little later, all the gift boxes had been cleared away from the terrace. Only one beautiful, red, large package still stood on the table. Jockel was irritated because suddenly, there was no one to be seen far and wide. The dogs were gone too. He reared up on his hind legs, looked incredulously in all directions, let out an excited snapping sound, and ran purposefully up the stone steps to hop onto the table with a giant leap. Margarete Trappe pressed her hand over her mouth. Only with difficulty could she prevent herself from laughing out loud. She stood in the kitchen and, together with Karimbe, peered out from behind the window curtain onto the terrace, where Jockel was already busily tearing down the wrapping paper and opening the cardboard box.

A shrill scream, a huge leap from a standing position: the box fell over with a thud. The dead snake slithered across the tabletop, right at Jockel's feet. The monkey opened its eyes wide, stared in panic at the cobra, let both arms hang down at its sides as if in a fit of shock, and staggered. It opened its mouth wide, screamed once more, shrieking and seemingly close to death, and then fell backwards off the table onto the floor, stiff as a stuffed animal. There it lay as if unconscious until Margarete Trappe and Karimbe came out of the door and, writhing with laughter, put the dead snake back.

Enraged, Jockel jumped up, yanked his fangs wide open threateningly, and rushed from the terrace across the meadow into the nearby bushes. „He'll never open a package again," Margarete Trappe pressed out with a laugh.

Karimbe slapped his thighs in glee and showed his white teeth. Finally, Margarete went back into the house, sat down at the desk in a good mood and finished the letter to the princess, her good friend in Berlin.

Most honoured lady! Dearest friend!

I can hardly convey to you in words how much this news of your imminent coming has filled me with joy. When I will be back from my next, very long safari, sometime at the end of August, I will think about what little things you could bring me from our German home-land when you join us in Africa in October. It certainly won't be very much. Because as I already wrote, we are doing very well here on Meru. We keep hearing the most wondrous things from our friends and those who stayed at home. They think we are starving here in Africa, living in deprivation, and confronted with infirmity and death day after day.

Oh, how laughable! We hardly lack anything. In our little paradise in Africa, life is more like the land of milk and honey, like the bibli-cal Garden of Eden (as I wrote to you in my last letter, an „Adam" named Anthimos is also already there . . .). What, I often ask myself, what more than such a fulfilled, contented, happy life in this African paradise is imaginable in the wildest dreams? I have everything: three healthy, happy children; a small but very romantic house with a view of Mount Kilimanjaro; beautiful, fertile land stretching from my farmhouse on the mountains to the horizon; a husband who is a good father to the children – and a man who loves me and whom I love!

As I already mentioned, my new hunting guests are aristocrats. They are still very young, however perfect gentlemen, very charming and fun-loving. We will certainly spend some fascinating and also funny weeks together, especially as we will visit a region I do not yet know. The Maasai people say that Engai (their God) created this landscape to show humanity what marvellous things he can form if the humans are willing to live in peace and harmony with all beings created by God. I am very much looking forward to this journey be-cause it must be an incredibly fertile landscape with huge animal herds.

But now, dear Emily and dear Princess, I must end my letter. There is still much to arrange for the safari. And tonight, we will celebrate my thirtieth birthday in advance. For on the day of the birthday I will be in the Ngorongoro Crater – thinking of you!

In impatient anticipation of your visit to us in Africa, I send you heartfelt hugs and a thousand thoughts from Ngongongare to Berlin. My thoughts are always with you.

Margarete Trappe

Ngongongare, June 26th, 1914

*

On Sunday, June 28th, at around nine in the morning, Margarete Trappe left Ngongongare with her new guests from Germany in a hunting party consisting of more than thirty porters, trackers, servants, two ox carts, and eight horses. The sun peeked out from behind the Kibo peak of Kilimanjaro. Dew lay over the mountain meadows below Meru. The land smelled fresh and fertile; the air was filled with wonderful exotic smells. The African porters sang a happy song, Margarete whistled a tune to herself, and her stallion Comet pranced jauntily down the stony paths into the plain, north-eastwards past Meru. No sooner had they left Engare Nanyuki behind them in the early afternoon than the hilly terrain opened up. In front of them lay a vast plain, from which the more than two-thousand-metre-high volcanoes of Ketumbene and Longido, black and threatening, but long-extinct, stood out as signposts to the north, towards Lake Manyara. Margarete Trappe was very relaxed. The three men next to her were chatting boisterously with each other. One, a very likeable-looking young man with a prominent chin and very sharply drawn nostrils, radiated a refreshing light-heartedness with his open laugh.

Lothar Siegfried Freiherr von Richthofen, she knew, was in fact only twenty years old. At the end of the planned safari, in September, he would come of age. But young as he was, he already looked imposingly masculine. She had already noticed his excellent manners on the farm. The fact that he was a native of Wroclaw and thus, like her, also from Silesia, and that he had gone to grammar school in Wroclaw, had connected them from the start and filled their conversation with a certain ease. Moreover, he was an excellent horseman, which pleased her. His garrison, the dragoon regiment No. 4 von Bredow, was stationed not far from Sagan, in Lüben near Liegnitz. As far as she knew, he was currently attending a war school near Danzig.

Out of the corner of her eye, she looked at the scion riding diagonally in front of her, one of Alfred Baron von Richthofen's four. A handsome, attractive young man, she thought and felt ashamed the exact moment as she realised that her interest in the tall, dapper, slender fellow was of a rather peculiar, to her inexplicable nature. Margarete Trappe, she thought secretly, you are crazy. Then she forced herself to think of Anthimos, who, they had discussed a few weeks ago, would join them at the Ngorongoro Crater in about ten days. But somehow, she did not manage to detach her thoughts from Baron von Richthofen, who was by now riding almost beside her. Subconsciously, she listened to the men's conversation. They were talking about politics, but she didn't quite understand what it was all about. The young Baron von Richthofen seemed to be very well informed: „The Balkan alliance between Serbia, Bulgaria, Greece, and Montenegro will cause us a lot of trouble, believe me!“

„I agree with you, Siegfried,“ said one of the others. „This is nothing but a front against our Three Emperors' Agreement with Austria-Hungary and Russia. If the Austrians continue to expand like this in the Balkans and put the stamp of their Austro-Hungarian monarchy even more brutally on the faces of their southern neighbours, there will be unrest at some point. The Slavs are rebellious people. They dream of independence, I'm sure of it!“

„I think it will be the Serbs who revolt,“ intervened the man riding in front of the young Freiherr von Richthofen. „The Serbs have been dreaming of a Greater Serbian Empire for ages. What this Austrian heir to the throne, this Franz Ferdinand, has in mind for the southern Slavs, the Serbs won't like. I can smell it, people!“

The young man, who had spoken in accented Berlin dialect, parried his horse until Margarete Trappe had caught up with him and smiled

at her. „Excuse me, dear Mrs. Trappe. That's the way it is with such young officers from His Majesty's war schools: They always have to talk about politics and war. That's the only thing we learn there!“
„I'm not entirely unfamiliar with it, young man,“ Margarete Trappe replied with a smile. „My husband is also a veteran officer, although now only a Lieutenant in reserve. Many of our friends and neighbours, especially in Leganga and with the Schutztruppe in Arusha, have a very keen interest in political events in Germany and Europe. There are often heated discussions about politics. I am truly used to this philosophising! But I am also, to be honest, very glad that we are so far away from these things here in East Africa. Besides, gentlemen, for the next six weeks, we are far away from any civilisation. Where we ride, there is not a telegraph station in sight. What do we care about the petty squabbles in Europe and the Balkans? So, gentlemen, and now enough of the serious topics! We have wonderful weeks ahead of us in peaceful German East Africa.“

*

At about the same time, around nine o'clock in the morning, when Margarete Trappe, Lothar Siegfried Freiherr von Richthofen and the other aristocratic hunting guests from Germany had left Ngongongare on horseback on that 28th June, six men had also set off separately, ready to kill for the freedom of their people. It was a cloudless day: a beautiful, sunny Sunday morning – the feast day of Saint Vidov. The men carried their weapons hidden under their clothes: four pistols and six mini bombs. Not much, but enough to kill two people they had chosen as hated representatives of a repressive state, to revive their liberation struggle with a sensational assassination. All six men carried cyanide powder. Alive, they did not want to fall into the hands of the guards of their chosen victims.

One of the six assassins, a small, curly-headed man with a sparse moustache and strangely deep eyes, was very nervous when he arrived at the „Schillerecke“ at around eleven o'clock in the morning.

The other five were positioned along the road for a greater distance. Everywhere people were standing and cheering.

Then everything happened very quickly, faster than expected. He hardly had time to think. Suddenly he saw the white-clad, veiled lady with the wide-brimmed hat. Right next to her, he sat, the man with the green, feather-adorned hat of a General. The woman smiled very nicely, and he tugged at his upper lip beard. Both were hardly more than five metres away. He had not thought he could get so close to them. The proximity to the victims irritated him. He could look into their eyes, and he didn't like that. At first, he wanted to throw the bomb, but the many people around him pushed and shoved and constricted him too much. He became extremely nervous, no longer knew exactly what he was doing, only acted reflexively and not quite convinced that what he was doing was right.

Hectically he fumbled for the pistol. The people in front of, next to, and behind him were too close around him. He was not able to take up an ideal shooting position. He fired almost blindly at them. Shots barked out. The recoil of the 9 mm Browning automatic pistol jerked his arm up. The woman with the beautiful hat suddenly had a large red spot on her dress above the wide belt at the level of her navel. She sank with her face between the knees of the man next to her, and it looked as if she was dead. A thin stream of blood spurted from the man's mouth. There was only a small hole where the 9 mm projectile had entered his throat. People screamed; panic broke out.

*

The first ten days were arduous but wonderful. Margarete Trappe could not remember ever having had such charming, polite, and completely uncomplicated hunting guests. And because the daily rides through the steppes, past extinct volcanoes, lakes, and through wide dry rivers towards the Ngorongoro Crater were so entertaining and characterised by nice chats, her hunting guests had initially shown little interest in hunting but much enthusiasm for the romantic life in the tented camp. It was always set up early in the afternoon. The young men then shot venison for dinner near the camp, after which they showed their preference for dry red wine as early as sunset, laughed, joked, enjoyed themselves, and chatted until late into the night or listened to the stories of their „white huntress" who was adored by everyone.

It was a very comfortable and happy safari. And the closer they got to the dense forests on the southern slopes of Ngorongoro Crater, the more Margarete Trappe looked forward to the arrival of Anthimos, who knew the crater and had already enthusiastically raved to her about what he called „the Noah's Ark of Africa".

The day they rode across the plateau between Lake Manyara and Lake Eyasi, past the slopes of Mount Oldeani and into a fairytale-like mountain forest, she sensed how appropriate this description was. Giant trees, enchanted by metre-thick root strands, thick lianas, and orchids gave the high forest a ghostly, fairytale-like atmosphere. House-high euphorbias and pillar trees overgrown with moss lichen stood on the steep slopes. The further they rode uphill, the thicker the fog became. High up in the mountains, where fog and clouds merged to form a sheer impenetrable imaginary wall, they had to dismount and lead the horses by the reins up the steep slopes. The ground was wet and slippery; clothes were dripping, it was difficult for people and animals to breathe.

„I guess we'll soon be in heaven," Lothar Siegfried von Richthofen joked curtly and asked uncertainly: „Are you sure, Margarete, that we're on the right track? You can't see your hand in front of your eyes. I think we are a good two thousand metres up. The air is getting thinner and thinner!"

„Somewhere up here must be the crater rim. And from there, I was told, you can ride down into the crater. At least in the dry season."

„Dry season is probably a gross exaggeration," one of the men groaned. „I swallow a litre of water with every breath; that's how high the humidity is here!"

They thought they had reached the crater rim after hours of arduous climbing. But they saw nothing. Mist and clouds enveloped them. Even mightier giant trees with wide-spreading crowns blocked their view of the sky. Above them was only green, a firmament of leaves and branches. It was only around noon, and yet it seemed to be slowly getting dark. The ancient forest seemed lifeless. Then suddenly, the Garden of Eden lay before them. Margarete Trappe paused, gazed in disbelief at the miracle, stared spellbound at the glistening light that suddenly enveloped them. Gusts of wind swept through the forest. The giant trees groaned. Wisps of mist flitted past them and seemed to disappear, as if pulled down by a ghostly hand, behind the clearing lying in the diffuse light. It became light through the fog. Suddenly the sun was there, with its warming rays, absorbing the mist and revealing a view of something they all did not want to believe existed in the world.

„Unbelievable . . ., we are in heaven, we are in paradise . . . the Noah's Ark of Africa," they pressed out in unison and stared down, more than a thousand metres deep, at a vast crater framed by the horizon, with tiny, small and large lakes, with rivers and rivulets, interwoven with majesty, beauty, and uniqueness.

They set up camp down in the crater by a lake that no one knew what it was called, and in fact, no one wanted to know what name it had. It was simply beautiful, nestled in gallery forests of palms and giant evergreen trees. Hippos frolicked in the fresh water.

Everywhere there were lions, big, magnificent, and black-maned with paws bigger than a man's hand. Cheetahs dozed under the umbrella acacias, and wild dogs rampaged in packs. An elephant herd of more than five hundred trotted by; rhinos grazed not far from their camp. Many antelopes and even more gazelles stood on the grassy plains; herds of zebras made the earth shake in their wild gallops; they could not count the wildebeests. They ran out of words to describe what they saw on that very first evening in front of the campfire and under the starry sky of paradise.

That evening they drank a lot and were silent.

Margarete Trappe's joy was great when a cloud of dust, whirled up by thermal winds into a sandstorm in the midday light, signalised the arrival of Anthimos. Her heart beat faster. At last! Here he was coming. Finally, someone she could tell and make feel how much she loved this land, this crater, this life. She stared out at the shimmering grassy expanse, a shadow emerging from its mirage lakes and moving towards her.

She froze inside. The one coming, on a horse, looked rushed, in a great hurry – and in a paradise where time was meaningless. Suddenly she was afraid. Intuitively, she sensed that something threatening was approaching with the plume of dust from the onrushing Anthimos. No sooner had he parried his sweaty horse and taken her in his arms than Anthimos blurted out: „On the day of your departure, anarchists in Sarajevo shot the Austrian heir to the throne, Franz Ferdinand, and his wife, the Duchess Sophie von Hohenlohe. Everywhere in Europe, they are talking about war!"

The next day they had broken camp. They were now riding at a trot and gallop for the tenth day in a row. During the nights, without pitching tents, they had simply slept on the ground by the fire. Not to give themselves a rest but to the completely exhausted horses. They had instructed the two oxcart drivers to follow as quickly as possible, along with the equipment and the employees.

They were all silent, exhausted, dusty, and hungry, giving in to their dull thoughts, each to his own, hoping to reach Arusha or even the farm that evening. Two horses were lame. They had had to shoot one with a badly swollen leg two days ago. Since then, Anthimos had been riding Comet with Margarete Trappe. The stallion kept stumbling under the load. Both kept silent about their fears. Only when Meru took on precise contours on the horizon did Margarete Trappe clear her throat and say to him: „You knew that these *Ujamaa Kali* men wanted to kill Prince Leopold?"

„Yes, I did."

„And you stopped them from doing it . . ."

„No, I didn't stop them. I tried to explain to them that it would be their downfall. They themselves decided not to do it. How do you know about that?"

„Kinai, the Maasai, confided it to me. Why didn't you tell me right then?"

„Because it was something between me and the Africans, the men *of Ujamaa Kali*.“

„You always want to stay out of everything that doesn't affect you personally, don't you?“

„Yes.“

„You are an egoist, Anthimos! You don't care about other people, not at all.“

„Not if they mean something to me.“

„But there aren't many you cared about or care about.“

„That's true.“

„And if there should be war in Europe now? Whose side will you be on then, Anthimos? You can't always be thinking of your own life.“

„Do you remember, Toute, when I once said that when elephants fight, the grass suffers?“

„Yes . . .“

„I didn't think it would happen so quickly.“

„What?“

„Toute, if there is war in Europe, there will be war here. Far away from here, in Vienna, Berlin, Moscow, London, and Paris, the elephants are fighting – and down here we'll be the grass that suffers. But I have nothing to do with these goddamn wars in Europe, Toute! I just want to live my life in peace!“

„I want that too, Anthimos. Everyone wants that. But for that, you sometimes have to take a stand, be ready to fight for something, be ready to defend it!“

„You mean fight for the homeland, for ideals or something . . . ?“

„Yes!“

„My father died for the homeland, for Greece – in the war. My brother too. Your brother and my best friend, Alfred, too. I, Toute Sweet, have already paid enough bloody tribute to the ideals of this world!“

„I cannot understand your attitude, Anthimos. If there is war, I stand by my homeland. And that is Germany. That's where I was born. My mother and my sisters Tine and Frieda live there. And German East Africa is part of that homeland!“

200

„I'm afraid I see it differently, Toute! I fight for nothing but my freedom – and for the freedom of those people who are dear to me. But I have nothing to do with the war of the nations. You will see: The confused alliance policy of the rulers in Europe suddenly forces friends to fight against friends and peoples against neighbouring peoples. And I won't take part in that!"

On July 28th, 1914, four weeks after the shooting of the Austrian heir to the throne and his wife by the nationalist Gavrilo Princip in Sarajevo, Margarete Trappe, Anthimos Koundouriotis, and the hunting party of Lothar Siegfried Freiherr von Richthofen reached Ngongongare.
On this day, Austria-Hungary declared war on Serbia, triggering a chain reaction resulting from the alliance policy of major European powers.
On August 3rd, 1914, Margarete Trappe's thirtieth birthday, seven years after her arrival on the African continent, Germany declared war on its neighbour France, followed by England's declaration of war on Germany. Another three days later, Austria-Hungary officially declared war on Russia.
In just a few days, the outbreak of the First World War plunged Europe into disaster. Dark clouds gathered over Margarete Trappe's paradise in faraway German East Africa.

Chapter 12

Millions of delicate yellow butterflies fluttered up on their first flight into the vastness of East Africa on this wonderful August day near the Momella Lakes. Tululusiek Rock, the „gatekeeper to Meru", was enchanted by the afternoon sun. The land was soft and gentle and somehow very silent. Nature seemed to hold its breath.

It would really have been a beautiful day to celebrate her thirtieth birthday, Margarete Trappe thought. She regretted very much that she had not been able to spend her birthday in the Ngorongoro Crater together with the hunting party and Anthimos, as she had actually scheduled. But even here, on Ngongongare, it would have been nice, together with the children, if these dramatic events had not intervened.

No, there was nothing to celebrate that day. She was sad. And lonely.

Lost in thoughts, she stood on the terrace of her small farmhouse and looked at the Kilimanjaro. Its two tops, the Kibo and the Mawenzi, looked dusted with icing sugar and shone as bright and majestic as they had rarely done. At this very moment, she was not aware of the beauty of the snow-covered highest African mountain. For the first time since she had seen the Kilimanjaro seven years ago, she wondered why the Maasai called it the „Mountain of the Evil Spirit". Most German settlers considered such things and the Africans' beliefs in their Gods as a mystic frippery. The many years in East Africa had told her not to do so. She was convinced that if she wanted to live in peace in Africa, she would have to respect Africa's gods also.

Ominous premonitions came over her. Her thoughts did not really go to the two mountain peaks but wandered on to what lay on the other side of „Kili". Over there on the horizon, barely more than thirty kilometres as the crow flies and only two to three days' ride away from Ngongongare, lay the English colony of British East Africa – enemy territory!

For on this August 3rd, 1914, England had officially entered the war after Germany's declaration of war against Belgium. This meant that within hours the war had moved from far-away Europe very close to Ngongongare. Since the dispatch rider of the Schutztruppe from Arusha had brought the news of England's entry into the war half an hour ago, only a steppe separated enemies who until a few days ago had been neighbours and friends.

Ulrich stepped onto the terrace. Without asking her, he had decided to volunteer for the Schutztruppe. She saw in his eyes that he was looking forward to being a soldier again.

„You'll see, Margarete, the war won't last long! They'll work it out diplomatically. These are the usual threatening gestures. And even if the French and the English think they have to get involved in a war with Germany, they'll soon realise who they're dealing with."

„When will you leave?" she interrupted him. She was no more interested in his views.

„I ride to Arusha in the morning, where all the volunteers are to assemble by noon."

„You know you don't have to, Ulrich?"

„It is my duty, Margarete. It is to defend our fatherland, our colony. I will not wait to be called. I am an officer in the German army."

„You're a reserve officer."

„But I will ride. Tomorrow."

„You're leaving me and the children alone here on the farm?"

„Margarete, please! You must understand that. It's about the honour and the fatherland duties of an officer. Besides, you are well protected here by our Askaris and the Maasai. I can't do anything for our country here on our farm."

„Then ride, Ulrich! Ride if the honour of an officer means more to you than the safety of your own family! But try to come back alive and not crippled. Try it for your children."

Margarete Trappe looked at her husband contemptuously. In a split second, she realised that she despised him, if not hated him. Perhaps she had always hated him? No, not really hated. But she had despised many of his traits but had always repressed this. She had needed him to give her own life a new meaning and to realise her dream. Only with Ulrich had she been able to escape the dreariness of her poor existence in Sagan. With him, she had succeeded, and for that, she was very grateful to him. She had always been ready to turn this gratitude into love, but he only loved himself. He could not love others. While she had learned to show and live her feelings here in Africa, Ulrich had developed into a power-hungry, uncaring, and often obnoxious person.

The way he stood in front of her now, stocky, small, with an almost shaved head, very large ears, and a thin upper lip beard, she felt for the first time that he was almost ugly and an unsympathetic person. Wordlessly, she turned and walked down the slope to a rock near the stream.

Only a few moments later, Anthimos came after her. He sat down on the ground behind her.

„Will you stay there? Will you at least stay with me?“

She did not look at him because she already knew the answer.

„No, Toute, I will leave tomorrow. I am riding to Dar es Salam and will try to get to Zanzibar as soon as possible.“

„Please stay, Anthimos! Please! I love you. And you love me. Let's wait here together until the war is over. It won't last long. I'm going to separate from Ulrich. Then we can be together forever. There will be good, beautiful times for us.“

„The good times will not come, Toute Sweet. They were already here! I'm afraid of what's happening now. Germany is at war with half the world. They're insane! Nobody knows how this will develop. I am Greek. And already in the Balkan wars, we Greeks got involved in things we really didn't want to have anything to do with. If war breaks out here in East Africa, the Germans won't trust me. And neither will the English. In war, impartial people, people who love peace, are quickly turned into collaborators. There is only one rule: friend or foe.“

„You exaggerate, Anthimos! Why are you so fatalistic?“

„Call it what you like, Toute: Intuition, premonition – devil knows what. But I often feel like the weaver birds here in Africa. They like to build their nests in the reeds along the rivers, always one or two metres above the water level. They know that hyenas and other predators can't get to the nests that way. They let the crocodiles protect them, so to speak. But if you watch carefully, you can see that they sometimes rebuild their nests, sometimes high, sometimes low above the water level. They do it on purpose, Toute! They already know when they build their nests, half a year before the rainy season, how high the level of the river will rise after the big rains! So, they build their nests so high that their young won't be washed away by the flood. They know, Toute Sweet, just like that. That's one of the very big secrets in Africa. How do they know? Nature here teaches you to follow your intuitions, your instincts. And my instincts tell me there's going to be a war here soon."

He slid closer to her and embraced her with both arms. She rested her head on his shoulders.

„Come with me, Toute Sweet! Let your husband go to this pointless war. He loves playing war. Take your children, pack the most necessary things and come with me to Zanzibar. From there, in a few days, we will be on a ship in some part of the world where there will be no war. This is our last chance. Believe me . . ."

„I can't, Anthimos. I can't just leave the farm. I don't want to, either. This is my world, my home. This is where my children were born. And here I have experienced the most beautiful and happiest moments of my life – with you. I can't!"

„You won't understand, Toute Sweet. But I'm going to leave. I'm leaving this country because I believe that this paradise will soon become a battlefield. I'm leaving even though I love you. But I will always let you know where I am. Come to me whenever you want."

Shortly after sunrise, Anthimos had ridden away. She did not know if she would ever see him again. Only with his look had he been able to tell her how much he loved her. Her husband Ulrich had also risen early, stalked around the terrace suspiciously and with unmistakable hatred for Anthimos in his eyes. He, too, would leave. But she knew from him that she didn't really want to see him again.

Ulrich had watched mockingly as Anthimos had given her his heavy elephant rifle and the shirt with the bullet hole. „Take the gun, Toute Sweet," he had said quietly, handing her his favourite rifle, a gift from his father. „I'll never hunt again. Because it will never be the same here. You'll need this rifle soon, I'm sure. The shirt will remind you – of that night with Gurumico!"

It was only later when Ulrich and Anthimos were gone and she had decided not to cry any more, that she had discovered Anthimos' letter hidden in her shirt:

Beloved Toute Sweet,

I have found a name for you. Words for what has happened and will always be between us are lacking. It doesn't need words either. I will go, you will stay. Will we ever see each other again? Is something so „big", as we have always called it, doomed to fail because we have let things take their course, because we thought it would always remain as it is: sheltered, as if in a cocoon; untouchable, innocent, and honest?

Eventually, it happened. We did not part; life is tearing us apart. Nobody can ever take away from me what I bear inside. This time with you to which I owe all these experiences and thoughts about you have become irreplaceable. They are in my heart. You are living in me, silently, wordless – but incredibly strong. I will keep on thinking of you time and again and try to smile.

Before I ride off, I want to reveal to you a thought I had when I saw you for the first time in Dar es Salam seven years ago. I saw you coming down the gangplank and immediately knew: This wife was born twenty years too late . . .

Anthimos
Ngongongare, Africa, August 4th, 1914

Two men left Ngongongare on horseback in the early morning of August 4th. Both also left Margarete Trappe. Anthimos Koundouriotis dashed towards Mombo to continue by train from there to Dar es Salam. He rode away because he was looking for peace and was fleeing the war. With every step of his horse, he wondered if he should return because he loved this woman.

The other trotted smiling towards Arusha because he was looking for war. Absorbed in his self-important, patriotic thoughts of what would now come his way as a reserve officer in the Schutztruppe in German East Africa, he forgot to think of his wife and children.

For Margarete Trappe, it was the saddest day of her life. Of both men, she did not know if she would ever see them again. One was the father of her three children, the other she loved. What she had left were the children – and fear. Panic fear. How dramatically things had developed in just a few weeks! Until recently, she had thought she was in a paradise on earth, had determined her own life, had been the mistress of a wonderful country. Her thoughts and actions were closely connected with the children, a little with Ulrich and a lot with Anthimos. When she thought about her future, it consisted of her children and Anthimos – here in Africa.

Suddenly she realised that it was no longer she herself who would determine her life, her future. In view of the critical situation, the district office and the military command in Arusha had given instructions to prepare for the immediate outbreak of war in the colony. English troops, it was said, were already making preparations in neighbouring British East Africa for an advance on German East Africa. Since it was to be assumed that the locals would use the possible turmoil of war to revolt against the German colonial power, it was recommended that the security measures on the farms be strengthened and that only workers who were considered loyal be used for farm operations. In addition, soldiers, mostly members of the volunteer militia, would be assigned to protect remote farms.

What would happen from then on, Margarete Trappe realised with horror that evening, ultimately depended on two very different men: One, Kaiser Wilhelm II, was sitting in faraway Berlin, developing plans with his Generals to gain power over Europe and the rest of the world. The other she had met in person in January.

*

Lieutenant Colonel Paul von Lettow-Vorbeck, commander of the Schutztruppen in German East Africa, was sitting in the Dar es Salam district office on this morning of August 5th, nervously stroking his militarily short-cropped hair. The situation worried him. The news situation had been very confusing in the last few days. As late as August 2nd, the word from Berlin had been that there was no danger of war in the colony. However, another announced cable with additional information had not arrived in Dar es Salam. This morning, at 04:45, the radio message about the official declaration of war had finally arrived. An hour later, there had been an emergency meeting at the district office with the staff of the protection force and the governor. Since then, events had been unfolding at a rapid pace.

He himself did not really see the multi-front war at home as a cause for concern. The strength of the German army and its allies would quickly force the English, Russians, and French to the negotiating table. But here in East Africa, things were escalating. The afternoon briefing had confirmed that the English in neighbouring British East Africa had been making preparations to attack German East Africa for days. All British warships cruising in the Indian Ocean were anchored in Mombasa. In the border area, especially in the Kilimanjaro region, strong British units were marching. Now, with the official declaration of war, it was only a matter of time before the first fighting could take place.

But differences of opinion had arisen between the general staff of the Schutztruppe with him as commander and Governor Dr Heinrich Schnee about the right tactics. The governor wanted to avoid a battle for the coastal towns, primarily Dar es Salam, Bagamoyo, and Tanga, and advised that the mass of the forces be assembled west of Dar es Salam. Dr Schnee did not want the local population and Africans deployed as auxiliary soldiers and porters to become involved in direct fighting between the Europeans. „This would only shake the colonial rule inside the colony, and the Africans would see a chance to revolt against the Germans," the governor, that short, puny man with the moustache and the big ears, had blathered. He didn't like this Dr Schnee. He was too aboriginal-friendly for him, but he had to get along with him because as governor, he was entitled to such directives from the Imperial Colonial Office. „That, too, civilians in the war," Lettow-Vorbeck was furious and paced angrily through his office on the second floor of the district office.

He himself thought it was tactically far wiser not to wait for an attack but to attack the British beforehand, penetrating as far as Uganda if possible. The Uganda Railway, which ran from Mombasa to Nairobi and on to Lake Victoria across British East Africa, was the aorta of the British colony. And it was the most important supply axis for the troops. If German troops attacked there, the enemy would be forced to use a large part of his troops to secure the seven-hundred-kilometre railway. Of course, there were risks involved in this plan. German East Africa's protection force currently consisted of just two hundred and sixteen whites and a little over two thousand five hundred native Askaris, plus the police force of forty-five whites and a little over two thousand Askaris. The armament was not exactly staggering. Artillery was almost non-existent. But the last thing the English would expect was such an attack by the Germans. But Dr Schnee could not be convinced of that. So, it was more or less a case of waiting and making preparations for defence. And he hated that.

He thought hard. Since he had taken over from his predecessor, Colonel Freiherr von Schleinitz, in December last year, he had not had much time to strengthen and better equip the Schutztruppen. But it could only be advantageous for his career. Where there was war, laurel wreaths were distributed. His experience in bush and guerrilla warfare from German Southwest, where he had served on the staff of General von Trotha, he suspected, he would certainly soon be able to put to use here. Service in German Southwest was unquestionably a plus in the expected fighting. And he would also be able to contribute knowledge from his service as commander of the 2nd Sea Battalion in Wilhelmshaven. For the British would certainly use their navy in the fight for East Africa.

One question arose, however: could the Schutztruppe in German East Africa, with its small forces, significantly damage the enemy, really inflict considerable losses on them in terms of personnel or war materiel, and thus prevent larger contingents of troops from Europe from intervening?

The governor Dr Schnee did not even want to consider such tactical aspects, but he was convinced that the fight in the colonisation would only make sense this way.

Thoughtfully, he looked at the map of East Africa lying on his desk. This huge German colony was, in fact, almost impossible to defend. Almost twice the size of Germany in terms of area, with a total of over four thousand kilometres of borders, there were now just six thousand whites, including women and children, living in this country. The black population was estimated at eight million. How was this country to be defended? The long coastline was completely unprotected. British East Africa lay to the north, Belgian Congo to the west, English Rhodesia to the southwest, and Portuguese East Africa to the south. One was surrounded by enemies. The English troops were vastly superior to them. Their superiority made resistance seem futile at first examination.

But where was the English weak point? And where could the few German forces be deployed most efficiently? His gaze was fixed on a point east of Kilimanjaro. The former border negotiations between Germany and England in the framework of the so-called Helgoland Treaty had made the border there run through a sharp bend around Kilimanjaro, which meant that the highest mountain had finally belonged to German East Africa. This had ultimately earned the mountain the name „Kaiser-Wilhelm-Spitze".

He bent over the map, staring spellbound at a small place called Taveta, southeast of Kilimanjaro, in English territory. He quickly realised that one of the few roads from German East Africa led into

English territory. The Uganda Railway, the Achilles' heel of the English, was hardly more than eighty kilometres away. Up there, in that region, lived very reliable, highly motivated German Schutztruppen officers. These men knew what they were fighting for: their farms! Well-trained Askari companies were available in nearby Moshi and Arusha. Satisfied, he grinned and tapped the map several times. „Yes, that's where it will be!"

Suddenly he remembered an evening in January when he had been the guest of a German farming couple up there on Meru. The lovely and charming young woman enjoyed an almost legendary reputation as a hunter in German East Africa. An impressive woman. Her very patriotic husband, the retired Lieutenant Ulrich Trappe, had rather tearfully quoted a poem by Goethe that evening:

Feiger Gedanken bängliches Schwanken,
weibisches Klagen, ängstliches Zagen,
wendet kein Elend, macht dich nicht frei.
Allen Gewalten zum Trutz sich erhalten,
nimmer sich beugen, kräftig sich zeigen,
rufet die Arme der Götter herbei.

Cowardly thoughts, anxious wavering,
Female lamentation, fearful trembling,
Will not avert misery, nor set thee free.
To stand firm against all forces,
Never bow down, never show yourself strong,
Summon the arms of the Gods.

„Well," said Lieutenant Colonel Paul von Lettow-Vorbeck, smiling smugly to himself and tapping the map again and again on the small town of Taveta. „Let's call in the gods, then. There are enough of them in this damned Africa."

*

The African gods were unanimous: they were not favourably disposed towards the *Wazungu*, the white men of East Africa, from the first day of the war. The white man's war was not their war, not the war of the African people they watched over. And so, the gods did not distinguish between English and Germans but made them all pay a gruesome toll of blood for their dream of wanting to own Africa.

On August 4th, 1914, just a week after Britain entered the war in Europe, English warships shelled the radio tower at Dar es Salam. On August 15th, German troops captured Taveta, chosen by Lieutenant Colonel Paul von Lettow-Vorbeck, in a bloody battle and made the region around Mount Kilimanjaro the centre of their fight against the British troops. From there, German commando units advanced far into English territory, attacking English outposts in guerrilla-style and destroying supply depots. The battle of David against Goliath sent the entire German colony into a state of euphoria. The cruiser „S.M.S. Königsberg" destroyed the English cruiser „Pegasus" off Zanzibar on September 20th, and four days later, Captain Wintgens devastatingly defeated the Belgians at Lake Kivu. The entire German colony rejoiced.

The first major advance by the English against the vastly outnumbered German troops came three months after the war began. On November 2nd, two English cruisers landed off Tanga, along with one English and eight Indian regiments and several special forces under the command of Major General Aitken. One thousand Germans armed with only twenty-one machine guns and light rifles faced the overpowering landing corps. Nevertheless, it was a humiliation for the British. Only two days later, on November 4th, the British retreated in crushing defeat. Lieutenant Colonel Paul von Lettow-Vorbeck became a hero among the German settlers, the „Lion of Africa". But the gods of Africa had made time and suffering their agents of fulfilment and had agreed to use far more perfidious ways and means to make it clear to the Wazungu that this was not the white man's country.

*

Margarete Trappe had expected everything, but not this. Since the outbreak of the war, she had lived in constant fear, had nightmares, hardly ate, and felt crushed by the worries and hardships that had characterised her life for more than a year. The First World War had turned the whole of Europe into a battlefield. Her life on Ngongongare was also dominated by it. It had been a disastrous year.

Ulrich had been taken prisoner by the British during one of the first missions in the Kilimanjaro region. He had remained unharmed. However, she did not know in which English prisoner-of-war camp he was. Without him, the hard struggle for the farm's existence now rested solely on her shoulders.

Anthimos had been arrested on the coast by German soldiers on suspicion of espionage ten days after leaving Ngongongare and deported to Greece a few weeks later. What had really happened and where he was now, she did not know either. An officer friend of hers at the general staff in Dar es Salam had only told her in confidence that Anthimos had tried to get to Zanzibar secretly at night by boat. Because he had previously been in the deployment area of the German troops north of Dar es Salaam and most of the English navy was gathered in Zanzibar, the German military leadership had assumed that he, as a Greek, could betray information about the German troops to the English. This had made Margarete very thoughtful. What had happened struck her as highly cynical and absurd: she loved Anthimos, he loved her. She was a German – and now he, who wanted to stay out of all wars, was sitting in a German prisoner of war camp on suspicion of espionage.

To make matters worse, soon after the outbreak of the war, the German military administration had withdrawn all the farmworkers fit for war and forcibly recruited them. Most served as porters, a few as auxiliary soldiers. Margarete was left with only Kinai and three other Maasai. And a few unskilled labourers, very young Waarusha, useless characters who were not capable of supervising the cattle herds. Animals were constantly stolen or even slaughtered on the pastures. Poaching on their land had taken on dramatic dimensions.

The fields could no longer be cultivated and were already going wild. Basic foodstuffs were becoming scarce, not only on her farm but in the whole country.

As if all this was not misfortune enough, there had been a series of horrific events on the farm. One of her cattle herders, while watering the cattle at Lake Tululusia, had been seized by a water python, easily eight metres long, and dragged down into the lake. His body did not turn up until two weeks later. The man's death was one thing, the Africans' interpretation quite another. Margarete had noted with concern that afterwards all the farmworkers spoke of an evil omen, a curse that lay over the farm. Less than three weeks later, Siafu ants had killed three calves. Billions of these small, inconspicuous, red and black ants had invaded the barn during the night and eaten the leashed animals alive to the bone. Their black farmworkers also interpreted this as a curse. After all, swarms of locusts had descended on the farm three months ago. Within two hours, the ravenous animals had destroyed their vegetable and fruit plantations and with them a year's supply.

Increasingly, she began to believe that there was a curse on the farm – on her life in Africa. The fact that she was completely on her own, that there was not even a strong shoulder to cry on, overwhelmed her. She felt emaciated, exhausted – and lonely.

Her sister Tine from Germany had visited her a few days before the outbreak of the war and wanted to stay for two months. Since the war outbreak, she had to live with her because a return to her homeland, to Sagan, to her mother and Frieda, was not possible. The British naval blockade off the East African coast had turned paradise into a prison. Tine suffered greatly. Life in Africa, moreover in the war, ate her up physically and mentally. Homesickness and fear for her mother and sister increasingly began to break her will to live. Tine helped as much as she could, took great care of the three children, but they were both completely overwhelmed. They could only do the most necessary things, ensure survival.

The physical strain and the permanent fears left unmistakable marks on Margarete. Deep circles under her eyes documented the lack of sleep. Her once beautiful, shiny hair was dull and unkempt. Worst of all, however, were these recurring symptoms of paralysis.

Four months ago, she had been bitten on the face by a tree snake while in bed at night. She had survived the bite of the semi-poisonous reptile after three days with a high fever because the snake had only slightly scratched her skin with its poisonous fangs below her right eye. Since then, however, she has had signs of paralysis in her face. The right cheek sometimes hung limply without feeling and seemingly without any blood circulation. The damage to the nerves had also caused her right shoulder to hang slightly forward. She was not in pain, but she felt pathetic, as she looked now. Her courage to face life was sinking with each passing day. And now this too!

No sooner had the young Wameru, who worked with her as a herd boy, come running breathlessly to the cattle boma shouting „*Jeyo, Jeyo* – come quickly, your *Watoto* are dying,“ than she was already on the horse and dashing at a stretched gallop to the farm.

„The children! Dear God, please, please, spare my children,“ she cried against the wind with tears in her eyes. Jessy stretched under her saddle as never before. The mare seemed to fly over the stony meadows up to the house. And yet Margarete Trappe thought there was no end to the road to Ngongongare. Helpless and full of mortal fear, Tine stood on the terrace when she arrived. All three children were very close to death. The symptoms were the same in all of them: their eyes were horribly twisted, their pupils wide and fixed, and they were writhing in violent convulsions. They whimpered, fevered. Their pulses were fluttering and could hardly be felt. The frighteningly pale Rolf looked pitiful. Ursula was crying but seemed to have the most life in her still. Ulrich was breathing frighteningly fast.

„They have been poisoned,“ she yelled at her sister Tine, „send for the medical officer in Arusha!“

Her thoughts were racing. It would take hours for a doctor to come – if at all. The children would not make it. All the symptoms suggested that they had been poisoned with a nightshade preparation. She had seen similar signs of poisoning in some of her foals until she found out that one of the pastures for heifer foals had such an extremely poisonous nightshade growing on it. None of the foals had survived the poisoning.

Her eyes rushed around the room. She did not find what she was looking for. She dashed into the kitchen. There were three glasses on the table. Two of them were still a little full of milk. Her head flew around. Karimbe, the child-boy, was standing behind her, Tine right next to him. The African showed honest fear for the children.

„Who gave the milk to the children?“

„The new cattle herder, that young Waarusha, Memsahib.“

„Where is he?“

„I don't know. He will have gone to his hut. It is already late in the day.“

„*Lete Dawa*, fetch me the green bottle from the stable, the one with the emetic for the cattle,“ she cried. Then she ran back to the children. They were breathing more and more shallowly. Rolf, the youngest, was the first to vomit. The overdose of the horrible-smelling emetic took effect within minutes. He coughed up the greenish-brown contents of his stomach, gagged and retched. Ursula vomited a few minutes later. Ulrich shortly afterwards. There was a terrible smell in the room. Tine stood trembling beside the bed where they had laid all three children side by side. The paraffin lamps illuminated the room only sparsely. Margarete Trappe was glad of this. She didn't want her employees to see her crying.

Suddenly Karimbe rushed in.

„*Memsahib*, the Askari is dying!“

She looked at the children. Her breathing had become calmer. The convulsions seemed to be subsiding. Margarete was reassured. She rushed off, behind the house, where one of the Maasai night watchmen was writhing in pain on the floor.

„What has he been drinking?“ she asked the other two Maasai Askaris. They looked alarmingly disinterested.

„*Chai* tea . . .“

„Nothing else?“

„He put milk in the tea like you do, *Jeyo* . . .“

Margarete shuddered at the rising suspicion: the Waarusha employee had brought the milk from the stable, had given it to the children. He had tried to poison her children, and the Maasai had just happened to drink from the same milk.

She also gave the Askari an overdose of the emetic. He was already spitting while drinking. She made him take another big gulp. Then she went back into the house. The children were asleep. They were alive, breathing more deeply. The pulse was more stable, but she didn't know if this was just a short-term reaction to the emetic. Only tomorrow would she know for sure.

Margarete called Karimbe. The children boy came running.

„Get this young Waarusha here and tell him that because he is the youngest and fastest, he should take this letter immediately to Arusha to the police post there. Tell him to run for the lives of my children, tell him that!"

Then she hurried to her writing secretary and hastily scribbled a few lines on a piece of paper:

To the officer on duty at Arusha police station:

The bearer of this letter, a young Waarusha who has been working with me on Ngongongare as a cattle guard for a few days, has tried to poison my children and one of my Askaris. Please imprison him! My children are deathly ill. As soon as they are better, may God help them, I will come to Arusha and file a complaint against the man.

Margarete Trappe – Ngongongare

Ursula, Ulrich, Rolf, and the Maasai survived.

Two days later, she sent her three children together with Tine to the mission station Nkoaranga. No sooner had she returned than Kinai had asked to speak to her. The Maasai, whose loyalty was vital to her at the moment, looked very worried: „*Jeyo*, the gods are angry! They don't like the *Wazungu*!"

„What are you implying, Kinai?“

„I see dark clouds that will shroud Kilimanjaro for a long time! My people and I can no longer protect you, *Jeyo*! Our God does not understand what we do when deep in our hearts we hate all other *Wazungu* but protect you. You must know, *Jeyo*, that all over the country, hatred is seething deep in the souls of the people. Here on your farm, too, there are now men, black men, who want to kill you and your children. They are very stupid, these men. They think that the other *Wazungu*, these English, will treat them better. But I know from my fellow tribesmen on the other side of Kilimanjaro, where the English rule, that they are no different. They, too, want to steal our land, want to cram us into reservations. Things are as jumbled as an anthill when an elephant has trampled over it, *Jeyo*. I no longer know who is friend or who is foe. I can't protect you anymore . . .“

After that, Kinai and his three men had left without a word. And Margarete realised that the gods of Africa were no longer in her favour.

What had she done wrong? Or was it not her at all that the gods were angry about? Were they enraged because the *Wazungu* were about to lay waste to this beautiful land, the home of the African peoples? Was it the war of the Europeans, a war that the people of Africa had nothing to do with, that was now bringing about the vengeance of the gods? Was it men like Lieutenant Colonel Paul von Lettow-Vorbeck, was it the German and English Generals, the regents of Europe, who caused *Engai*, the god of the Maasai, to make such a faithful and loyal man as Kinai ole Chieni turn his back to her, *Jeyo*, the mother of their future, as he had once called her?

For the first time in her life, Margarete Trappe suspected that she was caught between two fronts she really wanted nothing to do with. She was now where Anthimos had not wanted to go. That was why he had left the country. His attempt to preserve his freedom had failed. Would she succeed? Would she have enough strength to continue fighting for her paradise in Africa – without Anthimos?

Chapter 13

Until this January 9th of 1916, Margarete Trappe had never heard of the English „wonder weapon". That morning, she saw the first two British planes fly past below the summit of Kilimanjaro – probably to intervene in the fighting south of Kilimanjaro, where most of the German troops had been massed.

„Only an ignorant and a cynic, someone who doesn't care about the suffering of his soldiers and that of the civilian population, can believe that we can win this war," Lieutenant von Lyncker had said to her just a few days ago when they had talked about the increasing importance of aircraft in this war. The commander of the 9th Company, which had been stationed on Momella for some time, made no secret of his personal opinion about the war for German East Africa: „The English Generals have airplanes, dozens of warships, and send armoured cars into the battle for Africa. And what are our commander, the glorious von Lettow-Vorbeck, and his retired officers' club doing? They ride mules or ride bicycles from battle to battle. It's sheer madness! We have absolutely no chance! Our Generals are literally fighting this absurd war on the black skin of Africans! Not to mention us settlers . . ."

Margarete Trappe knew that Lieutenant von Lyncker was right, but she didn't want to hear it. And certainly not believe it. Lyncker and his company were currently her only hope of getting through this war halfway unscathed. For the moment, she felt relatively safe. Since Lyncker was stationed on Momella, there had been no more cattle rustling. In addition, the company was in radio contact with the German troops. So, she always knew what was happening in the country. But she also knew that she and many other German settlers were under an illusion. This war against the overpowering Allied troops could not be won. Allegedly, German East Africa was already surrounded by a hundred thousand Allied soldiers. The British had marched several divisions from their colonies, from Nigeria, India, and now also from South Africa to reinforce them.

This excellently equipped army was opposed by barely twenty German companies. Von Lyncker had told her that each company consisted of only about sixteen white officers, one hundred and sixty black Askari soldiers – and four hundred African porters each. There were no means of transport other than the heads and backs of the forcibly recruited black porters. Their own farm workers had also been conscripted into the force. The armament of the Schutztruppe was downright ridiculous. Two machine guns per company and a few artillery pieces captured from the enemy, that was all the Schutztruppe had to offer.

The colony had been effectively cut off from the rest of the world since the beginning of the war. Radio and telegraph connections to overseas and especially to Germany were almost non-existent. What was happening out in the world, on the battlefields of Europe, the commander of the Schutztruppe did not know. And in the skies over German East Africa, English planes were now circling.

A few days later, when Lieutenant von Lyncker and the 9th Company were already preparing to leave for Moshi, Major Fischer, commander of the troops responsible for the Meru section, rode up to the farm. He gave his order without dismounting from his horse: „Madam, the English troops are trying to advance south of Kilimanjaro. Since we cannot rule out that the English will also attack north of Kilimanjaro, i.e. here near Meru, we must ensure that neither weapons nor supplies can fall into the hands of the enemy. My orders are therefore to bring all cattle and horses and other livestock to a collection camp guarded by the Schutztruppe far away from here!"
Uncomprehendingly, Margarete Trappe gaped at the officer.
„Are you mad? You mean you want me to hand over my one thousand cattle and the fifty or so horses to you just like that?"
„It is an order, madam!"
„From whom does this order come?"
Major Fischer looked up in amazement. Not a single German settler had resisted this order so far. However, he knew from this Marga-

rete Trappe that she by no means put her own interests before those of the Schutztruppe. Only recently, he had learned that Mrs. Trappe had personally offered her stallion Comet, known throughout the region, to Colonel von Lettow-Vorbeck for war service. He had declined with thanks and told her to keep the stallion but to make sure that Comet did not fall into the hands of the English. Fischer was all the more surprised by her resistance. Friendly but firm, Major Fischer replied: „Excuse me, Mrs. Trappe, madam, with all due respect, but we are at war! That is an order. If you resist, I could confiscate your cattle."

Margarete Trappe interrupted him angrily.

„I have asked you before: from whom does this order come? This is not about me resisting. It just seems like a pretty stupid order to me, Major! I have a thousand healthy cattle. Our farm has been supplying the Imperial German Serum Station in Ngare Nanyuki for years. And that is because we have only healthy cattle. Most of my first-class broodmares are in foal. If you cram these cattle and horses with other sick animals now, you are doing yourself a disservice. Leave the animals here. I promise you that I will take care of them."

For one thing, Major Fischer was angry; then again, he did not hide his respect for this moral courage.

„The order is from Colonel von Lettow-Vorbeck, madam. You will understand that I cannot rescind this order on my own. But I gladly agree to bring your suggestion to the attention of the Colonel by radio."

After half an hour, Major Fischer returned. He grinned. The resolute farmer's wife was already standing in the yard waiting for him.

„So, what does the command say?"

„Colonel von Lettow-Vorbeck sends his regards, Madam. He thanks you for your far-sighted assessment and lets it be known that he knows very well that you are in the habit of keeping what you promise. You may keep your cattle and horses until further notice. However . . ."

„However what?"

„The Colonel wants you to promise him personally that the animals will not fall into the hands of the English!“

*

Thomas Nyamweya was lying on a camp bed, delirious with fever. His chest bandage was drenched in blood. Beads of sweat stood on his forehead. His eyes were shining. He was trembling. Again and again, he reared up, pointing with his arm out of the tent to the wide plain below the hill near the small village of Kahe, where the Schutztruppe had entrenched themselves and where the medical tents for the wounded had been pitched.

„I want to see it before I die,“ he moaned, looking at Margarete Trappe like someone who would not live much longer.

She did not understand what he wanted.

„What do you want to see?“ she asked, dabbing the sweat from the severely injured man's black forehead. Pityingly she looked at him. He was a sympathetic man, tall and strong, with features she did not recognise from the natives of German East Africa.

„I know it is out there somewhere, I know it,“ the African gasped. Blood was pouring out of his mouth. It was dark, venous blood, blood from the lungs.

„Get well, soldier, then you will visit it,“ she babbled to reassure him. Her gaze now also went out onto the plain. Night would soon fall – the twenty-first night since she had fled, leaving Ngongongare and the children too. How dramatically things had developed for her in this short time! And actually, only because she had made this promise to Colonel von Lettow-Vorbeck. A promise with fatal consequences, as she had soon discovered, because, after only a few days, strong English troop units under the South African General Smuts and his English Chief of Staff had advanced on German East Africa throughout the Kilimanjaro region. At the same time, an enemy division broke through the German lines near Meru and marched towards Arusha – and thus towards their farm in Ngongongare. From the moment a dispatch rider from the Schutztruppe had delivered the message „the enemy has broken through" to the moment she fled, only a single day had passed. Early in the morning, she had rushed to the mission station Nkoaranga on Comet and said a tearful goodbye to her children and her sister Tine. By noon, she had already rounded up fifty horses and most of the one thousand head of cattle and driven them to the Maasai steppe below Ngongongare. She had only had four African farm workers and a Sergeant seconded by the Schutztruppe at her disposal. The old German with the crippled left arm was a reserve officer who had worked as a handyman on a mission before the war. He was not particularly helpful. The strain of this hasty escape had overwhelmed him.

It had taken almost a week to drive the huge herd first along the Kiwoi River and then further southeast between the Pangani River and the Pare Mountains. With Kilimanjaro always on their left, they had moved forward kilometre by kilometre along the edge of the Maasai steppe. The heat had been unbearable. The dust kicked up by the animals had inflamed their eyes. Several dozen cattle had died in river crossings; some were killed by lions that had invaded the herd at night.

But the worst part of this gruelling herd drive had been that she hadn't known where she was supposed to be riding. German East Africa was in turmoil. The Schutztruppen units had all been detached towards the front. But Margarete had not known where the front was and where the English troops were. It had to be somewhere between Kilimanjaro and the Pare Mountains. The only thing she had thought of was: she wanted to go to Colonel von Lettow-Vorbeck, wanted to get her herds to safety from the enemy and bring them to the commander of the Schutztruppen. She had promised to do so. The reason, however, was not pure patriotism. Rather, she had reasoned, after the war, she would be paid compensation for these cattle and horses by the German government. If she took the herd to the Schutztruppe, part of her property would therefore be secured. But if the animals fell into the hands of the English, she would be as poor as a Silesian church mouse from one day to the next.

It had been pure coincidence that they had finally met a reconnaissance party of the Schutztruppe, led by Captain Walter von Ruckteschell. The Captain, a gifted painter whose portraits and landscape paintings from German East Africa had long since eternalised many a German settler's home, had approached them at a stretched gallop. The plume of dust kicked up by the herd had been visible for miles and had led him to her. The first thing he had said was, „You're kicking up quite a bit of dust, Mrs. Trappe. We saw the dust cloud – but unfortunately, so did the English! Lettow-Vorbeck was already worried about you, by the way."

She had been with the troop for weeks now, far from her farm, cut off from her children. Her nerves were on edge. There was no turning back. The German units had gathered near Mount Reata. The major attack by the English was imminent. She was very pleased that she had met the young Freiherr von Richthofen here again. How she would have liked to have finished the safari with him in the Ngorongoro Crater. That was now almost one and a half years ago. His kind, charming manner helped her a little in the camp to dispel gloomy thoughts for moments. Ever since she had agreed to take care of badly injured soldiers, a thousand thoughts had been tormenting her. For the first time in her life, she had been directly involved in a war. She was at the front! Her little paradise of Ngongongare was unreachably far away. Her children too.

Here in the field hospital, it was all about death or life. This was the intermediate station between life and death. Day after day and night after night, she saw the gruesomely disfigured, crippled, mutilated men in the tents, men, both black and white, torn apart by bullet wounds and shrapnel. The groans and gasps of the wounded no longer allowed her to sleep. The penetrating smell of rotting human flesh, of blood, excrement, and ether clung to her clothes and settled in her mind. It was the smell of war! When she closed her eyes, she could smell death. Open her eyes, and she saw it flitting into the bodies of the wounded soldiers. The unbearable smell of impermanence was omnipresent. So were the vultures and hyenas; and so were the marabous, those ugly, huge wading birds with their vile gaze and glaring red necks. They, the feathered gravediggers of Africa, were suddenly an integral part of her life. There was nothing she could do here, nothing that would help her and her children, and also Tine. She could only wait – and nurse the wounded. And she had time enough to think about how much Anthimos had been right when he wanted to leave this country.

The man in front of her on the bloodstained camp bed groaned again. The punctured lung made peculiar sounds as he took stertorous breaths. She liked this black soldier. By now, she knew he was not from here, not from German East Africa. The day before yesterday, when another small shipment of narcotics had arrived, and the Askari had been pain-free for a few hours, he had told her a little about himself. And he had begun to dictate a letter to his family to her.

Since she had given him another pain-relieving injection a quarter of an hour ago, he seemed to feel better now. He opened his eyes.

„*Jambo, memsahib. Habari* . . . ?“

„*Asante, mzuri sana, mzee.* You seem to be feeling better. Are you still in pain?“

„When I breathe, it sounds like an old hippopotamus when it comes out of the water and puffs its huge nostrils empty. But I'm not as ugly as a hippo.“

She smiled half-heartedly. She would have preferred to cry.

„Shall we finish the letter to your family?“

„I don't know. I'm coming to the end; I can feel it. That is, I don't really feel anything. Something in me is different from before. I think I'll tell you my story today, *Memsahib*! We don't have that much time left. You can write it down later or tell it to other people. Maybe someone will be interested in how Said Nyamweya came here to Kilimanjaro from a tiny village near the Tana River. Then we will finish writing the letter. Who knows what tomorrow will be.“

„Where is this river, this Tana?“ she asked.

„If you were to sail north along the Indian Ocean coast with the south-east trade wind, *Memsahib*, you would come to Mombasa after two or three days. And after four more days to Malindi. And then it's another two days to Lamu. That's where the Tana flows into the sea. It is a very beautiful river. It always has water, even in the dry season. In the interior, about three hours from the sea, lies my village. And that's where my family lives and looks after my mother's grave. When she died, *Memsahib*, everything began for me that now ends here."

„Will you tell me?"

„Yes, I will try."

The African with the blood-encrusted bandage closed his eyes as he began to remember: „My father – God and Allah have mercy on his soul – was a very wise and very unusual man! Believe me, *Memsahib*, he was one of those who are no longer born today! One day his wife was in labour and dying. And because her journey to the ancestors was connected with great pain, my father went to fetch soothing powders from a herb woman in the adjacent village in exchange for empty promises. You must know, Memsahib, that my parents were very poor. Well, that day it happened: Not far from the village, my father saw an oxcart stuck in the mud. One of the white men on the cart had more hair on his face than on his head. My father had never seen that before. Another was so fat that there could be no doubt about his wealth. The third man was very short, had a very funny frame with round glasses on his nose, carried a huge gun, and was very thin, so very poor."

The badly wounded Askari paused. Speaking strained him, but it seemed to make him happy. He obviously did not feel the blood coming out of his mouth again.

„White men, *Memsahib*, had never been seen by most Africans in that time! Of course, my father had heard of the existence of white-faced people before, but it did not interest him. It is true that strange news had rushed from village to village that white men had appeared in the region and had concluded a treaty with a chief called Witu. And it was said that the white men had then raised their flag and declared that the land would now be called Witu Land and henceforth be under the protection of a powerful emperor who ruled far away from Africa. But all this sounded so unbelievable that no one in the village really wanted to believe it. Nor did my father. Until he saw this ox cart."

Blood stifled the next words. He swallowed it.

„Because it kept raining and there was no way to pull the stalled cart out of the mire before nightfall, the whites asked my father if there was a hut where they could spend the night. With this request, *Memsahib*, the *Wazungu* entered my father's life."

Once again, the Askari paused in his narration. Margarete registered in amazement how he very slowly stood up and tried to look past her out of the tent as if he were looking for something out there. Faint, he fell back, breathing very heavily, and continued to speak, this time even more quietly: „So, where was I, *Memsahib*? Oh, that's right: my father moved his wife, who was very close to death, out of the only available hut so that he could give the white guests a dry place to stay. That was the turning point in my life, M*emsahib*. Yes, in my life! Because soon the guests noticed that I was clever and skillful! And because the heavy monsoon rains kept the strangers for three days, they had time enough to find me very nice too. On the day of their departure, they offered my father to take me with them to Dar es Salam, so that they could later take me into their service. Of course, no one in our village knew where this town, this Dar es Salam, was, but these were bad times, and my father certainly only meant well when he agreed. And so, I came to the distant city by the sea to the holy men, to the missionaries, where I first worked as a gardener. I was really very well off there! I was given food twice a day and, moreover, another name. After several weeks of telling me about their Christian God, they poured water over my head and then called me Thomas instead of Said Nyamweya. That was a name, they explained to me, that came from an even holier man than they themselves were, one who had always been very suspicious – just like me."

Margarete Trappe felt fatigue overtake her. She had not slept for three days. But somehow, she suddenly felt very calm. The soldier radiated something she could not explain. Barely audible anymore, he continued to talk. To understand him, she had to move closer to him, hold her ear close to his mouth. Surprised, she registered that the smell of blood and sweat and death suddenly no longer repulsed her.

„I think, *Memsahib*, I stayed with the missionaries for about five years. Actually, they were very nice, though I never felt they really thought of us blacks as their Christian brothers. In any case, they somehow liked me so much that they recommended me to an officer of the German Schutztruppe. He was looking for a boy to clean and tidy his things. Apparently, I did a very good job of tidying up and especially cleaning his boots. Because he treated me pretty well – better than the other officers treated their black boys. At least he only whipped me three times in all that time. Once because I hadn't ironed creases into his uniform. And twice because . . ., because – oh, I don't remember! Anyway, I was soon promoted, which made me the envy of all the other black Askaris. You have to know, the other Askaris didn't like me very much because I wasn't from their country.“

As if his tales had transported him to another, a happier world, the wounded man smiled. „The rest of the story, *Memsahib*, is actually told very quickly. I was just a houseboy, but suddenly I was also a soldier. A German soldier. With a very nice uniform! That seemed very strange to me, because I had never held a rifle in my hand before. But that was the way it was. It didn't bother me much either, because I didn't have a bad life, at least as long as there was peace. Every month I could send money to my village. And twice I visited my family there and could see my son growing up healthy and well cared for.

Everything would have gone on very nicely if this war had not suddenly broken out. A fortnight ago, I came here to Kilimanjaro with my Bwana Lieutenant. On the third day, my Bwana had to go on patrol. I had to come along, of course. It happened on the very first night. The only thing I can remember is that there was a terrible bang in the middle of the night and there was shooting all around our camp. The English had discovered us. And then a bullet hit me.

Just at the moment when I wanted to run away in panic! I only re-member thinking, why are the English shooting at me, a peaceful African bootblack and uniform-ironer! Besides, I come from the country that now belongs to the English. And they were never really my enemies, the English. A bullet hit me in the chest and punctured my lung. And since then, *Memsahib*, I lie here waiting to see this mountain . . .“

Margarete Trappe hoped that Said Nyamweya, the Askari lying there in front of her on the camp bed in the light of a candle, did not see her crying. Never before had the absurdity of this war become so clear to her. The wounded man was now breathing very heavily and closed his eyes. Barely audible, he breathed: „*Memsahib*, it won't work out today with the letter! I am very tired. Write it for me, will you? Write that I am lying in a tent at the foot of a mountain called Kilimanjaro. Write, *Memsahib*, that they say here that there is snow on this mountain, that it is white at the very top, as white as the salt on the little sand islands on the banks of the Tana, where it flows into the great ocean. And please also write that they say the gods of the Africans live up there on that mountain. Write that *Memsahib*, will you?“

The Askari faltered. His hand felt for hers. She felt how cold it was. It was a long time before he could whisper again.

„What is your name, *Memsahib*?“

„Margarete . . .“

„I can't pronounce that!“

„The Maasai call me *Jeyo*.“

„*Jeyo*?“

„It means mother.“

„That's a good name for you. A beautiful name. *Jeyo*! The Maasai will know why they gave you such a beautiful name.“

Again, he was silent for a short time, breathing stertorously. His hand was still on hers.

„You know, *Jeyo*: the only sad thing is that I'm lying here now, and I don't get to see this stupid mountain that everyone is talking about and even fighting over now, and that is supposed to be so beautiful!

Since I've been here, the mountain has gone. It is hiding. You should see it when it is so big and so white and so beautiful. Yes, it's very sad. I have never seen this Kilimanjaro. Never! It's shrouded in clouds, dark clouds. Maybe the gods up there are angry? I don't think they understand why there is war in this beautiful land they watch over . . ."

The next morning, Syed Nyamweya was still alive and feeling a little better. Kilimanjaro was again out of sight. But at the foot of the mountain, in the steppe below, a huge cloud of red dust suddenly built up in the morning light.

„The enemy is coming!" Margarete Trappe subconsciously heard someone saying. For the first time in days, she had fallen deep asleep. She woke up with a jolt. Colonel Paul von Lettow-Vorbeck was standing in front of the medical tent. Never before had she seen him so agitated.

„The English are coming! Do you see that dust cloud over there on the horizon? There are several divisions marching towards us! You must flee, Mrs. Trappe. There will be heavy fighting tomorrow at the latest . . ."

„I'll stay with the troops, Colonel, with the wounded. The wounded need me."

„I'm sorry, madam, but that won't do. The English propaganda has been claiming for some time that women are also fighting in the German Schutztruppe. It won't work. You must leave here."

„What will happen to the wounded?"

The Colonel stared at her sheepishly.

„Six of them are not fit for transport. They are Ascaris. We have to leave the seriously wounded here. The troops must get out of here. On the hill, we are an ideal target for enemy planes. The British will take care of the wounded. It's war. There's no other way."

„Where do you want me to go, Colonel? My farm may already have been occupied by the English. My children are in Nkoaranga with the missionaries."

„Go to your children. You are safe at the mission."

„Then I'll take the badly wounded with me! Give me an oxcart. I'll take them to the mission station. If you leave the wounded here, they will be prisoners of war!"

Colonel Paul von Lettow-Vorbeck looked at Margarete Trappe. He admired her fearlessness.

„Good, then take the black Askari with the lung shot with you. He still has a small chance of surviving. We should spare the others the long journey in the oxcart. They would die. I wish you good luck, Mrs. Trappe."

*

She dressed the wounded Said in civilian clothes and had him put on the ox cart. She tied Comet to the back of the cart. Then she drove off, homeward. The April sun was at its zenith when, after six hours of driving, she was arrested by an English military patrol and taken to Moshi. The small town on the western foothills of Mount Kilimanjaro, until three weeks ago a German district capital, had been taken by the British almost without a fight.

She knew the Major to whom she was presented at English headquarters. He was the man whose stallion had had a fight with hers on the open road in Arusha years ago, and with whom she had had a heated argument afterwards. Three times in the following years, she had seen him in Arusha and talked to him about horses. Each time they had concluded that they did not like each other. He was an officer who had left military service early, one who bred horses in Nairobi – and did not like the Germans.

„*What a surprise*," Major Brown said, grinning condescendingly at her. „*The smart little lady with the black stallion from Arusha!*"

She chose to ignore the triumphant undertone.

„I'm a little surprised, Major! I didn't know England wanted to win the war by making women prisoners of war on the way to see their children and stopping them from taking badly wounded civilians to the mission hospital."

The officer reacted angrily.

„Are we your enemies?“

„It makes no sense, Mrs. Trappe, to play the innocent lady. We know that you trailed a big cattle herd and at least fifty horses to Lettow-Vorbeck. You are guilty!“

„What do you mean by that – I am guilty?“ she got worked up. „Is there any law in England or any martial law claiming me, as a German farmer, to cede my cattle and horses to the enemy?“

„Are we your enemies?“

„Not my personal ones. I have absolutely nothing to do with this cursed war. But if I had waited for you to get to my farm, you would have confiscated all the cattle and horses, wouldn’t you?“

„That’s the way it is in war!“

„But they have been my animals up to now, my private property. And I simply decided to give them to Colonel von Lettow-Vorbeck. That can hardly be a punishable offence . . .“

She was about to continue when an older man entered the room. She could tell by his rank insignia that he was a General. The Major jumped up from his chair, saluted, and greeted him with a familiar „General Lane, this is Mrs. Trappe – Margarete Trappe.“ General Lane smiled at her and took a seat. She sensed that this was her chance.

„I want only one thing, Major: I want to get to my children, to my farm. And I want to get this poor fellow to the mission hospital. He’ll die otherwise. Unless your doctors take care of him. He’s a civilian.“

Major Brown squinted sheepishly at the General, who pretended not to listen.

„Well, now, I can only comply with your request if you surrender your weapons – and the horse. Consider it confiscated! It is the spoils of war!“

„What do you want? My hunting weapons? The horse?“

Margarete Trappe was beside herself with rage. She felt the Major’s arbitrariness.

„With all due respect, Major, I have the feeling that you are not quite familiar with the living conditions of a woman farmer in Africa. Am I supposed to take a wooden club to keep lions away from my farm and my children? Do you think I'm going to shoot English soldiers with a Mauser rifle or a Parabellum?"

Out of the corner of her eye, she saw the General grinning secretly to himself.

„And as for my horse, so far, no one but me in all of German East Africa has managed to ride that stallion. He hates men! None of your soldiers will stay in the saddle for more than thirty seconds, you can be sure of that! He's totally unsuitable for the troops. He'll probably end up at the butcher's. No, Major, you won't get my stallion. I'll shoot him first!"

The Major became visibly angry. He nervously moved his cap, which was lying on the desk, back and forth.

„That's enough . . ." he was about to assert his authority when the General stood up. He stopped next to the Major's desk and opened Margarete Trappe's ammunition box on the table. Astonished, he took out a coin. The rupee had a hole right in the middle. The General nodded, impressed. „Who was this marksman?"

„Me, General."

„From what distance?"

„Maybe fifty paces."

„With your Mauser carbine?"

„Yes."

General Lane reached into the box again, pulled out another half dozen rupees. All of them were riddled with holes.

„You did it?"

„Yes!"

„Nice shots! Very impressive, indeed!"

He scratched the back of his neck thoughtfully and held one of the perforated coins out to Major Brown.

„You should show these to our soldiers, Major. That's how German settlers shoot in Africa! Let's hope the German soldiers can't shoot as well."

Then he turned to Margarete Trappe: „Keep your weapons, Mrs. Trappe. And keep your beautiful horse!" In impeccable German, he added: „You can take the wounded man with you too. But promise me, as an officer of His Majesty the British King, but also as a father of three children and as a lover of noble horses, never again to do anything that could prolong this unfortunate war by even one minute. By that, I mean, Mrs. Trappe: go home to your children! Stay out of this idiotic war, which everyone claims they don't want and everyone also knows is absurd. It's enough if a megalomaniac German Colonel called Lettow-Vorbeck thinks he has to conduct world politics for the German Reich from Africa. Anyway, Mrs. Trappe: stay out of this war, will you? Will you give me your word on that, as a lady?"

She gave General Lane her word and soon after drove the oxcart towards Meru. Said, the Askari, was lying on the cart. He was asleep. The English military doctors had changed his bandages and given him painkilling medication. But they had also told her that he had little chance of surviving.

Her journey by oxcart through the steppe between Kilimanjaro and the Meru Mountains was an agony for her, marked by wistful memories. Ten years ago, she had ridden almost the same way to look for a new home on Meru. How happy she had been then! And how incredibly happy she had been during these years here in East Africa. All her childhood dreams had come true. Even more: she had built a beautiful farm, had three healthy children – and a man she loved: Anthimos.

Now, haggard from the hardships of the last few months, she drove this way again in a rickety oxcart. She had no eyes for the beauties of African nature around her. Fear dominated her thoughts. There was war in Europe and here in East Africa, too. What had become of her farm, she did not know. What would the future hold for her? In the back of the cart lay a half-dead African. In her pocket, she had a letter from the General allowing her to possess two weapons – a Mauser carbine and a Parabellum pistol – and her stallion Comet. She was now subject to English wartime laws. Twice a week, she had to report to the English military administration in Arusha and show the weapons and the horse.

In the afternoon of the next day, she approached the Meru. Her heart beat faster. Here were her children! Soon she would be able to hold Ursula, Ulrich, and Rolf in her arms again. The smiling faces of the three of them came to life before her eyes with every metre she came closer to the Meru. But Major Brown's face also appeared before her. Try as she might to block out his hateful gaze as she departed, she could not. She fervently hoped that she would never meet him again.

Ursula, Ulrich, and Rolf cried continuously with happiness for more than an hour after greeting their mother in front of the mission station in the early evening. The children sobbed heartrendingly and clung to her so tightly as if they feared their mother would leave them alone again. For the first time in years, Margarete was struck by the thought that she had put the children through too much. Sure, there was always Karimbe, the children's boy, Gillala – and Tine too. But the way the three of them were holding her now, she felt that it had not been right to have left the children alone for so long. „No," she sobbed late that evening, as she lay in a room with all three of them on a makeshift bed, and the children fell asleep with happy faces almost simultaneously in her arms, „no, I won't leave you alone again."

Said Nyamweya, the German officer's African shoeshine boy, died one day after their arrival at the mission station Nkoaranga. As a Christian and as a German soldier, he was buried in the mission's cemetery, below the church, near the edge of the forest. On the plain wooden cross, Margarete Trappe wrote: „Said, a peace-loving man from Tana River." Together with her children, she placed two blue-red banana blossoms next to the cross. She knew from his stories how much the Askari had loved these magnificent blossoms. Then she turned and looked down into the valley for a long time. Her children looked at her in wonder as she murmured, „Too bad! It's only the Maasai steppe you can see from up here. I would have liked him to be able to see Kilimanjaro from this place."

Shortly afterwards, she drove home with her children in an ox cart down the road and further up the mountain to Ngongongare.

*

The farm was in a terrible state. The fences of the Legurucki cattle boma had been torn down, goats, sheep, and chickens stolen. The Ngongongare cattle boma was also empty. Far and wide, none of their former farmworkers could be seen. Even as she approached, she saw makeshift huts of *Waarusha* – strange men with their wives and children instead. Clearly, they had believed that she would never return. Margarete ignored the illegal settlers and continued uphill in silence. Karimbe, the child boy, greeted her from a distance. He was standing on the terrace, wildly waving his arms in the air. His remarkably hearty laugh echoed down to her and the children, drowning out even the creaking of the oxcart. „Jambo, Mama! Jambo, Watoto,“ he cried out to them, heartbreakingly honest and happy.

„Karimbe, Karimbe – Habariako,“ Ursula screamed and sprang from the driving ox cart. In no time at all, she ran towards Karimbe. The children boy bent down and caught her with arms opened wide. His tears of joy were clearly visible at a distance. He approached the ox cart with Ursula on his arms. Ulrich and Rolf now also ran towards him, embraced his neck, and hugged him lovingly. Ursula gave him lots of kisses on the cheek.

„*Memsahib*, it is good to see you and the children back here on Ngongongare. What is this house without the children? It is a dead house.“

A little later came Gillala, who had formerly been in charge of the horses. The children greeted and hugged him too. Margarete was glad to see them. But she was too tired and too sad to talk to them any longer. Exhausted, she put the children to bed. Then she sat down in the kitchen and stared in bewilderment. It was only very late that she saw the two envelopes lying on the kitchen counter. The first letter was from the district office in Arusha. She glanced at the

date. The letter had been issued only a few days after she had driven
the herd away. Hastily she skimmed it:

*. . . as we have been informed by the English military administra-
tion, your husband, Lieutenant (ret.) Ulrich Trappe, has been trans-
ferred from Italy to an English prisoner-of-war camp in India. His
state of health was described as satisfactory . . .*

Her eyes fell on the second envelope. Dark premonitions came over
her. The seal of the British Empire adorned it. Hastily she tore open
the envelope. The letter was only a few days old. The contents, written in English, were difficult for her to understand. Word by word,
she tried to translate the text. But she couldn't quite manage it. Fran-
tically, she searched for a summary of the content. Margarete's gaze
lingered on the last paragraph:

*. . . therefore, we have to inform you . . . that all your assets depos-
ited with your bank in Arusha, as there are: savings books, cash,
jewellery, and securities . . ., are confiscated with immediate effect
and placed under the receivership of the military administration of
His Majesty the King of England . . .*

Her thoughts were racing. This letter was nothing more than an official expropriation. She would lose everything, absolutely everything: the farm, the cattle, her money, the savings – everything! She
was poor, the children and she were homeless. She was poorer than
ever before – and far away from Germany, far away from friends
who would help. Being poor in Africa as a white woman with three
children and no husband, it flashed through her mind, is cruel! Completely exhausted, she sank into bed around midnight. The last
thought she had before she fell asleep was that she would like to
take her own life. It was the first time in many years that she had
toyed with this thought again. Back then, when she had had to leave
her beloved paternal estate Petersdorf to move into the small flat in
Bahnhofstraße, everything had also seemed as hopeless to her as it

did now. She had stood on the bank of the Bober, had already made up her mind to throw herself in, but had not summoned up the courage to do so. Now she had the thought again, but this time she also had the courage. The hopelessness of her situation suffocated any desire to live in her. Everything that had given her life content was lost or threatened. The First World War was raging in Europe. She had not heard from her mother or her sisters for a very long time; German East Africa had turned into a battlefield; Anthimos was in an internment camp, Ulrich was a prisoner of war. Her property had been confiscated and the large herds of cattle and the magnificent broodmares, the reward for her hard work of the last few years and, as it were, the basis of her future, were also gone. It was only a matter of time before she would lose the farm, her home. The war, which she had wanted nothing to do with, had taken everything away from her. Why and for what should she still want to live?

Margarete heard three-year-old Rolf wailing in his sleep in the next room, heard Ursula, the eldest, talking to the little one and singing him back to sleep. At that moment, she knew she had to go on living.

For three days, she sat apathetically on the terrace or in the kitchen, staring ahead, hardly eating or drinking, unable to think a clear thought. Karimbe lovingly cared for the children, took them to the nearby stream, let them splash in the water there, kept them busy feeding the remaining pets, and encouraged them day after day to go on new, varied excursions into the surrounding area – just to keep them from seeing their mother's despair. In the evening, the three of them quickly fell asleep, completely exhausted. Only on the second evening had the youngest come to his mother, snuggled up to her with questioning eyes, and asked in a squeaky voice: „Mummy, are you so sad because Uncle Anthimos hasn't been around for so long?" For moments she had smiled, taken the little one by the hand, and sat with her children in the room until they had fallen asleep. Nevertheless, her will to live would not and would not return. Suddenly Kinai was standing in the yard. The Maasai was doing something she had never seen the Maasai do before. Something she would never have allowed him to do, would even have punished it as disrespect – in the past: he came up to her, hugged her, and said nothing at all for a long time, just held her like that. And she felt that something had happened with this embrace. Kinai had come to help her.

„*Jeyo*," he finally began to speak, „I don't like the English! They want to lock up the Maasai in the steppes at the foot of the Meru and the Ol Doinyo Le Engai into reserves, just as they have already done with our brothers on the other side of Kilimanjaro. They steal our cattle, the pride of every Maasai, so that their soldiers have meat to eat – while we starve. The laws of the English make a poacher out of any decent African who goes through the wilderness with a bow and arrow to shoot a gazelle. The English do not like Maasai with spears in their hands! A man with a spear is an enemy to them. They will soon forbid young men to kill lions with spears here too. But our young men must do this, *Jeyo*! That's the only way they can prove their courage, so that they can become *Moran*, real warriors. *Jeyo*, I don't like them, these English! Do they want to take everything away from you too?"

„Yes, they have already started!"

„Shall we fight them, *Jeyo*? Together . . . ?"

„What do you mean? Are you going to fight planes with your spear?"

„No, *Jeyo*. The *Bwana Ndofu kufa*, lord of the dead elephants, the one you always look at like you've been chewing too much Mira; he told us then that wisdom is a better weapon than the spear in the hand of the angry."

Suddenly she had to laugh. She laughed so loudly that Karimbe came running and stared at her in amazement. The children stood next to him and showed with shining eyes that they were happy to see their mother laughing again for the first time in a long period. All the tension of the last few months burst out of Margarete. Tears streamed down her face. The fact that she had obviously always looked at Anthimos the way one looked after consuming that stimulating Mira narcotic herb was incredibly funny to her. Margarete had always believed that no one had noticed anything about her love for Anthimos. Suddenly she felt a very deep, intimate affection for her African servants, especially Kinai. They knew everything, but they had kept silent. Perhaps because they did not like Ulrich at all. Anthimos, however, they appreciated, even worshipped. Actually, she thought, looking first at Kinai and then at Karimbe, these Africans, who are labelled „savages" by so many whites, are actually much more warm-hearted and honest in their feelings than I know from most of my German neighbours and friends. Yes, they are more honest in their feelings: They show and say it when they like a person. And they show it when they hate him.

There was no doubt Kinai hated the English. And he seemed to want her as an ally.

„You're not just saying that, Kinai? You have an idea, don't you?"

„Yes, *Jeyo*, I do! But we'll have to team up for that: you – and the best and bravest *Morani* of my Manyatta. You have wisdom and a rifle. And we Maasai are fearless! We have eyes and ears to see and hear things that you do not even know exist. If we join forces, *Jeyo*, we will come through these bad times well. And the English will not be able to catch us . . ."

What Kinai ole Chieni proposed that evening, Margarete Trappe could not have imagined even in her wildest dreams. She, who as a child had been familiarised by her father in the forests of Silesia with the strict rules and the code of honour of a Prussian huntsman and had submitted to the regulations of German hunting laws without contradiction, became a poacher.

Necessity made her ignore all hunting laws. It was not particularly difficult for her because English laws now applied. And she was not prepared to accept them. Destitute, deprived of all means of livelihood by the war, left to her own devices as a woman with three children, she suppressed all moral resentment and took the path of pragmatic illegality to ensure her survival.

While a bizarre military cat-and-mouse game was developing in German East Africa between the German troops under Colonel von

Lettow-Vorbeck and the English army under the command of General Smuts, Margarete Trappe, together with Kinai ole Chieni and three other Maasai, began to poach. The ban on hunting imposed by the English catapulted them into lawlessness. The once so honourable „White Huntress", known beyond the borders of German East Africa, became a poacher.

The Maasai tracked down the game, and she shot. Margarete did it ruthlessly; she wanted to survive. She shot elephants for ivory and killed rhinos, killed lions and leopards, and after only a few months, she could no longer count how many crocodiles she had killed for the leather. With the utmost secrecy, five of them set off for hunting grounds far away from Momella and Ngongongare, poaching at Lake Manyara, the Tarangire River, and in the southern foothills of the Ngorongoro Crater. They avoided human settlements, including those of African tribes. They hid the trophies until they were sold to their Arab and Indian middlemen in the Ngurdoto Crater, where Margarete had once killed Gurumico with Anthimos. It was a lucrative business. The rigorous hunting bans imposed by the English occupiers had caused black market prices for ivory, rhinos, and other trophies to skyrocket.

Hunting buffaloes in particular developed into a lively source of money. *Mbogu* or *Nyati*, as the buffalo is called in Swahili, was a sought-after object of exchange, especially among the Maasai in neighbouring British East Africa. Hunting buffalo was dangerous and an extremely risky undertaking without a rifle. Firearms of all kinds had been confiscated by the British. Margarete, however, not only possessed the carbine that General Lane had left her, officially confirmed. She also had Anthimos' heavy elephant rifle. Every buffalo killed was a big step towards survival: For a single rawhide, which Maasai warriors used to make shields, but which was also used to make containers and all kinds of utensils, the Maasai were prepared to pay up to forty goats. She then sold the goats officially on the market in Arusha – and let the English authorities live in the knowledge that she was earning her living quite legally with goat trade. But poaching in the African wilderness did not remain entirely without leaving traces.

*

Major Brown was furious. Two Sergeants of his troop stood frozen like pillars of salt in a guarded position in his office in the former German *boma* of Arusha. The officer paced up and down without giving the two soldiers a glance. Suddenly he shouted: *„Bloody hell! It can't be that a single German woman is fooling half the English army! It can't be! It must be possible to catch this smart lady from Ngongongare in the act, right, Sergeant Taylor?"*
The Major stared the addressed Sergeant in the eye.
„She's clever, Major, very clever," Sergeant Taylor was about to launch into an explanation of why he and the Special Branch of the British Army, which had been deployed for more than a year, had so far not succeeded in proving that it was Margarete Trappe who was behind the more than eighty elephants poached, fifty rhinos and the countless buffaloes and lions that had at least been officially reported. But the Major rudely interrupted what he was saying.
„She's clever – and we obviously only have idiots in the field! Or why does a task force of thirty English soldiers and half a dozen African trackers fail to convict this damned hag? Tell me, Sergeant, please, explain it to me! And as plausibly as possible. Because I don't want to have to explain to General Lane that a German settler is fucking with us, Sergeant! Because it's gonna cost me my ass, Sergeant! So, speak up!"
The Sergeant paced nervously.
„She knows the African bush like few other white men, Major. She rides like a man, shoots like a man, and thinks like a native poacher! And she obviously has several Maasai to help her poach – not to mention the black marketeers who peddle the captured trophies through channels we still don't know about. When she rides off the farm, she leaves no tracks after a certain point. She always takes some route through swamps or rides in rivers. Suddenly she disap-

pears. She is quite simply impossible to observe out there in the wilderness . . .“

„When you go hunting, Major,“ the second Sergeant stood by him, „like every other white man here in Africa, you pack boxes of utensils: clothes, provisions – all the things you need out there in the bush. Mrs. Trappe doesn't do that! She rides off as if she were going to Arusha to do some shopping. And then suddenly she's gone, disappeared without a trace.“

„Don't tell me such African fairy tales, Sergeant,“ the Major interrupted him. „This is a European woman: slim, fragile – and no African spirit! She's got to eat something, drink something, change her clothes when she's out in the wilderness for weeks on end – doesn't she?“

Sergeant Taylor finally saw his chance had come to justify the failures in the hunt for Margarete Trappe.

„No, Major. She doesn't have to.“

„This supposedly fragile, delicate, pretty woman, Major, digs a hollow in the ground for her hips at night by the campfire, a hollow for her shoulder – and lies down. Just like that, on the ground. Without a mosquito net! And, what makes the whole thing even crazier: Her horse, this Comet, stretches out next to her and lays his head on her belly while she sleeps . . .“

No sooner had Sergeant Taylor said what his African spies had reported to him than he knew he had made a mistake.

„You must be suffering from a particularly severe form of meningitis, Sergeant Taylor,“ Major Brown bellowed. His head was running red. His eyes sparkled angrily. „Well, well . . . ! So, the horse lays its little head in the lap of its dainty mistress at night by the campfire in the middle of the African wilderness. And then they both fall asleep peacefully, and the lions and leopards and all the other maneating animals of Africa also lie down peacefully in bed and let the only poaching white woman in Africa have a good night's sleep so that she can shoot some elephants again the next day! So, are you completely stupid, Sergeant Taylor, to even tell me such fantasies? Am I in a fool's house here?“

„It . . . it's the truth, Mr. Ma . . . Major! This woman is fearless – just like the Maasai," the Sergeant stammered, squinting at his comrade for help. It had been clear to him even before this conversation that the Major would react in this way. But everything he had just reported corresponded to what was spreading like wildfire in the huts of the Africans about this Margarete Trappe and what his spies had told him. Sometimes it was said that she rode hippos through raging waters; sometimes it was narrated that this *Jeyo* only had to look rhinos in the eye, and the monsters would retreat. Meanwhile, such stories were being told all over East Africa. He had long been convinced that most of them were true.

„You yourself, Major," he took advantage of a pause in his superior's thinking, „told me about a year ago that it is actually not possible even for an experienced marksman to pierce a coin exactly in the centre at fifty paces – and a dozen times at that! But you also said that Mrs. Trappe claimed to be able to do just that."

„What's that got to do with it now?" the Major hissed.

„Well, the fact is that we have found a total of fifty rhinos in the last twelve months, all of them, without exception, struck down by a very specific shot, Major. There's a crack shot at work . . ."

„What kind of shot is that?" the Major interrupted him. The Sergeant was glad not to be shouted at.

„None of the carcasses found show a leaf shot or a long-range shot. As I am sure you know, a rhinoceros first attacks with its head held high and at a stretched gallop. These primal beasts are as good as blind. They race off first and attack anything that moves. It is extremely difficult, almost impossible, to shoot them in the head from the front! Only when the attacking rhino is very close, does it lower its head so that it can spear the enemy with its horn. All the dead rhinos we found had a bullet hole above the head in the neck! So, the shooter must have always waited until the animal was about ten metres away. And then the shot had to be right. And absolutely precisely – fatally – fifty times in one year . . ."

Major Brown remained silent, embarrassed. He suddenly suspected that he had done his Sergeants an injustice.

„What actually happened to that spy, that Meru man you planted at the Trappe farm?“

„He refused to continue working for us after four weeks.“

„Why is that?“

„He says a spell is protecting *Jeyo*. And that spell caused him to discover three scorpions in his bed at Trappe Farm in one week.“

„You mean he's been exposed?“

„Yes. The few blacks who still work for Mrs. Trappe are as thick as thieves – and they're sticking by her. They haven't been able to get money or threats to say a word about her. They keep quiet!“

Major Brown paced up and down the room again. Concentrating, he thought aloud: „When this Mrs. Trappe sets off, i.e., goes hunting, she always rides her stallion, right?“

„Yes, she only has the one horse. And she has a permit for it – signed by General Lane himself. When she rides out, there are always four Maasai with her. They run as fast and have as much stamina as the horse! We can never keep up without being spotted. At some point, the five of them are gone, as if they had disappeared from the face of the earth. What they do then, we don't know. They know every square inch of the country for twenty miles.“

Major Brown looked up. Thoughtful as he spoke, it was evident from his words that he was very upset.

„It is unbelievable! Half the world is in a state of war. In East Africa, more than a hundred thousand Allied soldiers are trying to put down a German mini-army – and at the Meru, two detachments of English soldiers have had nothing to do for a year but to apprehend a single white poacher, the only poacher in Africa. Surely this cannot be true!“

The Major took a deep breath. „Sergeant Taylor, ride to the Trappe farm and tell this German to deliver her horse and Mauser carbine here tomorrow. And tell her she'll be imprisoned if she doesn't comply. Oh yes, one more thing: Tell her, Sergeant Taylor, that this is an order from Major Brown himself.“

*

She rode through Arusha like a lady. But she was dressed like a beggar. Self-confident, her head thrown proudly back, the reins casually in her right hand, Margarete sat bolt upright in the saddle. The Mauser carbine in her left hand and a cigarette in the corner of her mouth, her brown hat pulled down low over her face and her sunglasses, she trotted through the city.

The indigenous people were loitering in front of the *Dukas* and whispered, „*Jeyo.* " British soldiers were staring at her. They wondered why the white lady with the magnificent stallion was wearing grubby shorts, a torn shirt – and two different shoes.

The black stallion seemed to float over the road up to the former German *boma*. A strong north-easterly wind blew through the eucalyptus trees on both sides of the road below the *boma* and tangled the horse's magnificent mane. It flared its nostrils and rolled its eyes at the faint memory of the man standing there in front of the white fortress-like building. Major Brown was standing in front of the gate of the former German *boma*, pretending to be relaxed. But he wasn't. Sullenly, he stared at the white woman riding towards him. Her pride, her body language provoked him, but he also registered that she looked very bad. Her hair was cut short and stringy. Deep wrinkles and shadows under her eyes suggested that she slept little and was ill. Although she was deep brown, she looked sallow. He had learned weeks ago from mission doctors that Margarete Trappe suffered from very severe attacks of malaria. She was very thin, almost gaunt – emaciated. A pitiful person, he thought but quickly repressed this pang of pity. He did not like this woman, would have liked to put her behind bars. But General Lane, whom he had informed earlier in the day about his plans for the alleged German poacher, had come to a different decision. This annoyed him beyond measure. As soon as she had taken a seat in his office, he let Margarete Trappe know what he thought of her.

„Nice shoes you have on, madam. A unique combination, indeed: brown and black. The black goes well with the black horse . . ."

„Poverty leaves little room for style and etiquette, dear Major. But better to wear one's own shoes in two colours than to have to wear a uniform that stands for a system that puts a German mother and peaceable farmer on the begging stick!"

The Major failed to smile. „I'm sure you've also heard that poaching has increased drastically lately, haven't you?"

Snappishly, and alluding to the English army's futile attempts to turn in Colonel von Lettow-Vorbeck and the German troops, she replied, „Yes, that has not escaped me, Major. Obviously, the English army is not quite succeeding in establishing peace and order in this once so beautiful and peaceful country. Of course, if it takes one hundred thousand soldiers to catch a few German officers and their African porters, it's no wonder you can't get the poachers either."

Major Brown was inwardly seething with rage. But the General's directives forced him to keep his composure. He found it very difficult.

„Let's not fool ourselves, Mrs. Trappe. We have overwhelming evidence that four of your farm employees have been poaching in a virtually gang-like manner for many months. The leader of this criminal gang is a Maasai named Kinai ole Chieni . . ."

Margarete thought her heart would stop at the Major's first sentences. Panic overcame her. She felt very weak anyway. The severe malaria attacks she had been having regularly for almost a year were leaving their mark. The constant life in the wilderness during her illegal hunting trips had scarred her. She knew she was very skinny. The unhealthy and gruelling months out in the bush had taken their toll and drained the last reserves from her body. The two injuries to her leg and hip sustained in an elephant and a buffalo attack hurt and healed poorly. She was a physical wreck, but she had no choice. She had to poach, had to live in the wilderness for weeks to feed her family.

The English Major's words hit her like a punch in the stomach. She had expected everything. She had feared that she would be accused of poaching, that she would have to hand in her weapons. But she had not expected that all the poached elephants, buffaloes, and rhinos would now be blamed on her friends, the Maasai. Margarete struggled for breath and tried to appear relaxed.

„The Maasai don't have guns," she tried to argue logically.

The Major interrupted her rudely, „We are very tempted to arrest the four Maasai. With the evidence we have, they would either be locked up in a labour camp for life – or hanged straight away. We are at war, Mrs. Trappe. Martial law is in force in East Africa."

„If you lock up the Maasai, they will die," she pressed out helplessly. „Freedom means everything to them. In prison, they wither and die."

„We realise that. But we must also make sure that poaching stops immediately. Otherwise, the other blacks will think they too can poach with impunity."

„And what do you intend to do now? If you have evidence, as you claim, then I don't understand why you are summoning me here."

The Major suddenly looked very annoyed. She sensed that she had said something wrong. And she wondered why the Major hadn't just come to the farm to arrest the alleged poachers.

„Mrs. Trappe, let's not talk past each other," he began to speak with a noticeable accent. It seemed as if he had to restrain himself very much. „I tell you quite honestly, Mrs. Trappe, that I am firmly convinced that you, you personally, are instrumental in this poaching. However, for reasons I do not fully understand, General Lane, whom you met a year ago, may not agree with the consequences I have proposed. He has given me orders which I must, of necessity, obey."

Major Brown went to his desk, picked up a document, and skimmed it briefly. Margarete could see that the document bore the letterhead of the English military administration.

„You know English, Mrs. Trappe?"

„Not perfectly. But mostly enough to understand what a document says!" she replied, feeling her voice threaten to fail. With a shaky hand, she took the document. Hastily she skimmed the document. She did not understand exactly what was written there in complicated official English. Something about a life sentence. Panic-stricken, she looked at the Major.

„What is this about exactly? I don't think I understand . . ."

The Major took the letter from her hand. He took an unbearably long time before replying: „To put it in a few words, Mrs. Trappe, it is written here that because of your excellent knowledge of the country and nature and the services you have rendered in peacetime to the preservation of the wildlife in East Africa, you will henceforth have the honour of being Honorary Game Warden on behalf of the British Empire! Should you sign this letter, you are bound by your honour to do everything in your power in the future to protect the wildlife of East Africa and to help ensure its continued existence. You and your assistants, these Maasai, will, of course, be paid for this activity.“

The early afternoon ride from Arusha back to Ngongongare plunged Margarete Trappe into conflicting thoughts. Many questions tormented her. The fact that the English not only discouraged her from poaching by offering to make her an official Honorary Game Warden of the British Empire but at the same time made her an ally, she found tactically brilliant. It was the second time that General Lane had shown not only wisdom but also much humanity. And this although there was a war between Germany and England. All right, the pay arrangements Major Brown had suggested to her would guarantee little more than survival. In fact, her activities were rewarded on a success basis. Of all the trophies secured, she would receive from the military administration fifty percent of the going rate on the black market. That was a fair offer. And it would finally give her time again to take care of her children, who had been looked after almost exclusively by her sister Tine and Karimbe all these months.

What preoccupied her much more on the ride back to Ngongongare was the future of German East Africa – which no longer existed.

She herself no longer felt anything about the war in East Africa. The fighting was taking place far to the south of the country, more than a thousand kilometres from Arusha. The news situation was very complicated. British sources could only tell that Major General Lettow-Vorbeck and a small force of German soldiers and African Askaris were supposedly about to surrender. But she had heard that over and over again in recent years. Only from Africans, she got really reliable information. According to them, Lettow-Vorbeck had inflicted heavy losses on the British in the Kilwa and Lindi outback as late as spring 1917. However, it was also said that the German troops were now on the run into southern enemy territory, as far as British Rhodesia and Portuguese Mozambique, and consisted of only three hundred Germans and almost one thousand eight hundred African Askaris. The Allied forces, the Africans rumoured, numbered more than a hundred thousand soldiers.

The very scant news of the war in Europe that filtered through to East Africa only gave an idea of the horror that was taking place there. When she learned that Greece had declared war on Germany on June 29th of that year, her thoughts had been with Anthimos. Was he a soldier at the front? Was he fighting Germans? Was he even still alive? When would this madness finally stop?

Questions upon questions flashed through her mind until, after an hour's ride, she eventually saw the Tululusiek Rock near her farm. Finally, she would have more time for Ursula, Ulrich, and Rolf. At last, she had a glimmer of hope that the war would end soon, that everything would change for the better for them too. When the war was over, she would also be able to find out where Anthimos was. She had not received any sign of life from him for almost four years. Would he come back to East Africa, back home, to her, after the war?

From far away, she could hear her dogs barking and the children laughing. A giraffe with her baby crossed the path in front of her. It was a beautiful November day. The rainy season was over, and the nights were slowly getting warmer again. Hope sprouted in her. She fumbled for the English-language document in her shirt. It was a strange feeling to suddenly be working for the English. What had Major Brown said at parting? „Perhaps you should improve your English, Mrs. Trappe. It could be that in the future you will have to speak English instead of German in East Africa. If you really want to stay here on Kilimanjaro, that's what you should do, Mrs. Trappe: learn English.“

Chapter 14

The „Lion of Africa" had lost the war for German East Africa, but he was received like a victor. Tens of thousands of Berliners lined the streets from Lerther Bahnhof to the Brandenburg Gate in Berlin on this Sunday, March 2nd, 1919. Even the flat roof next to the Brandenburg Gate was crowded with onlookers. The entry of the East African fighters sent the people of the imperial capital into a frenzy of victory. „Three cheers," the masses hailed the heroes of the nation.

Moustachioed and rather grimlooking, imposingly wrapped in a black cape, Dr Heinrich Schnee, the last governor of German East Africa, rode at the head of the delegation on a white horse. Only a few steps behind him followed the proclaimed hero of the nation: Major General Paul von Lettow-Vorbeck. With sunglasses, his tropical hat turned up at the side and martial facial expressions, the „Lion of Africa" sat bolt upright in the saddle and occasionally looked behind, where Major General Wahle and Captain Looff, the former commander of the cruiser „Königsberg" sunk off the East African coast, followed.

„Three cheers," hailed the crowd. No one thought at that moment that the German Reich had plunged the world into a catastrophe with millions of dead. There was nothing to celebrate in this first post-war year, but the crowd cheered and threw flowers to the soldiers coming behind the mounted officers. On foot and far less impressive, there marched the pitiful remnant of the Schutztruppe that had fought battles in East Africa for more than four years, the purpose of which no one dared to doubt on this day of jubilation. Thirty officers, one hundred and twenty-five non-commissioned officers, and enlisted men – was all that had returned from Africa to the German homeland. On that day, no one spoke of the Askaris and porters, the nameless band of Africans who had carried this campaign on their black backs and thousands of whom had lost their lives. The daffodil-adorned tribune on Pariser Platz was overflowing with distinguished guests of honour. Representatives of the Reich and city governments, the army, and representatives of the colonial war associations crowded to see the legendary swashbucklers from Africa. Young men of the „Deutschnationaler Jugendbund" waved the German flag. Pickelhauben helmets, black top hats, and pith hats dominated the scene. War Minister Reinhard, Admiral Rogge, and Berlin's mayor, Dr Reicke, gave flaming speeches. Major General Paul von Lettow-Vorbeck visibly enjoyed being celebrated at home as the „moral victor" of the war in East Africa after a seemingly endless odyssey across Africa. He had not won this war for the colony, but he had created a myth – his own.

His gaze passed over the crowd in Pariser Platz. For moments, Paul von Lettow-Vorbeck remembered the final phase of the war, the gruelling marches of his soldiers across East Africa, worn down by malaria, diarrhoea, and injuries and suffering from deficiency symptoms. For years they had fought in guerrilla-style. Mostly they had been on the run from the Allied troops and the sobering truth. The truth was that this war for the colony had been unwinnable. His tactic of using the small army of Schutztruppen to tie down strong English formations and thus keep them away from the theatre of war in Europe had quickly turned out to be an illusion. The inherent mechanisms of the African bush war and the bloody game of catch-me with General Smuts had left little room for his geostrategic ambitions. He had only looked ahead to know where he could flee with his followers and where there was food to be captured.

But yes, there had been a sudden surge of hope when he had learned that in November 1917, the Zeppelin L59, loaded with weapons, ammunition, and urgently needed supplies, had taken off from Bulgaria for East Africa to supply his troops, which were cut off from the rest of the world. But whoever had given this order in Berlin: the airship had turned back over Kharthoum.

And so, he had continued to flee from the enemy. He, his one hundred and twenty-five non-commissioned officers, the one thousand one hundred and sixty-eight Askaris, and several hundred African women. They had marched as far as British Rhodesia, where news of what had happened back home reached him and where, on orders from Berlin, he had handed over his troops in Abercorn, Rhodesia, to the British General Edwards.

No, not he had surrendered! Germany had done it! Berlin had made that decision! He had not surrendered to the Allied superiority but had held the German flag high until the end, had brought back a piece of German soldiering untainted. It was regrettable that the colony of German East Africa had fallen, but its brief existence had nevertheless proved the German people's gift for colonisation. Those compatriots who had remained behind on Kilimanjaro, German farmers, and settlers, he was sure, would appreciate his heroic attempts to save German East Africa.

*

She screamed and sobbed, and her children did not know why. Karimbe was trembling. He was afraid because he had never seen her so desperate. Kinai ole Chieni was afraid of what was about to happen to *Jeyo*.

Margarete Trappe had not even had two years to believe that the end of the world war could also be the end of her period of suffering. For barely a year, she had been able to hunt poachers in the vastness of East Africa on behalf of the British Empire. And she had little time left to use the wages from her work as an Honourary Game Warden to build up a new herd of cattle, breed goats, and sheep and think of good broodmares. She and all the remaining settlers in the former German East Africa had celebrated the collapse of Germany, the armistice that amounted to a capitulation, the abdication of the emperor, and the proclamation of the Republic on November 9th, 1918 with a day-long festival of joy. Peace at last! It seemed that the German settlers would be allowed to remain in East Africa. The settlers' wives had dreamed of their husbands returning from the prisoner-of-war camps. Margarete even had hopes of starting a new, happy life here in East Africa with Anthimos, perhaps under English rule.

Reflection had then arisen at the end of January 1919, when the representatives of thirty-two states had met in Paris for a peace conference under the French Prime Minister Clemenceau's chairmanship. What, they had thought in faraway Africa, would the victorious powers impose on the German Reich in terms of punishment? Then, in mid-May 1919, the first details about the Treaty of Versailles leaked out to East Africa, and fear suddenly arose among the settlers on Kilimanjaro that Germany would lose all its overseas colonies. She had become afraid for the first time that she would have to give up Ngongongare, Legurucki, and Momella.

No sooner had the German Reich Ministers Müller and Bell signed the Treaty of Versailles on June 16th, which was initially brusquely rejected in Germany as a „peace dictate", than German East Africa had become a mandate territory of the League of Nations founded in June 1919. Tanganyika, as the former German East Africa was now called, fell under British administration. She had still greeted this news with jubilation because her relationship with the English was excellent by then.

However, the idea of all the statesmen who met in Versailles to ensure lasting peace for all mankind by establishing a community of nations and the decision of the victorious powers to blame Germany alone for the world war, were ultimately the end of her dream of a happy life on Kilimanjaro. With the Treaty of Versailles, Germany lost all its colonies – and Margarete became homeless. On the table in front of her was the deportation order! She had to leave Africa! Major Brown, escorted by some English soldiers, had delivered it personally. The letter was written in English. She understood English very well by now, but the Major summed up in a few words what she did not want to believe: „I deeply regret this development, Mrs. Trappe, believe me. But it is an order. I ask you to adhere strictly to it."

„Adhere to what?" she sobbed.

„You are ordered to leave your farm by the middle of September this year. You are only allowed to take your personal clothes and those of your children and dependents. Furthermore, you are al-

lowed to take five hundred rupees per adult and two hundred and fifty rupees for each child, or items of equal value."
Margarete Trappe stared at the officer. She wanted to speak, to ask, to shout, but she could not make a sound. The Major knew what this woman wanted to say and ask. The other German settlers to whom he had delivered this expulsion order had all asked the same thing.
„No, you can't sell anything that's on the farm . . ."
„But I have almost six hundred cattle!"
„No, nothing!"
„. . . three hundred sheep and goats . . ."
„Sorry, absolutely nothing!"
„Fifty horses? *My horse* – Comet?"
„*No, madam*. Everything is confiscated. I am truly sorry. As I said before, you have to leave your farm for good on September 15th . . ."

*

More than ten years ago, she had come to this country by ox cart. She had brought her three poisoned children to the mission at Nkoaranga with an ox cart. It also was with an ox cart that she had brought the severely injured black Askari Said Nyamweya to the mission hospital. Every time, dramatic events had forced her to climb on such a vehicle.
Today, too, such a cart stood next to their little house in the shade of the twelve cypress trees. They had planted one of these trees for each year in their paradise. A small troop of mounted English soldiers stood beside it. Major Brown was not with them. The soldiers looked very embarrassed.
Karimbe had run away early that morning. No, he had not gone away. He had run, raced down the valley past the children's little swimming pond without turning around once, then disappeared into the nearby woods. He hadn't wanted the children to see him crying. Margarete, however, had seen it.
The four other black farm workers stood beside the cart with the two oxen harnessed to it. They were crying without tears.

The few steps to the rickety oxcart with the few suitcases on the loading platform were the hardest of her life. The children sat between the suitcases. Tine kept their heads pressed against her. One of the English soldiers seemed to sense her thoughts, „You can have my horse, Mrs. Trappe . . .“

She smiled at him.

„Thank you, soldier! I rode Comet for twelve years. The best horse in all of East Africa! Now I'm fair game for a war I didn't want. I have lost everything that I hold dear and that gave my life meaning. Thank you! You are very kind. But on a day like today, I will certainly not ride any other horse.“

Just beyond a clearing with an idyllic lake on whose shores giraffes, zebras, antelopes, and gazelles grazed peacefully and which the Maasai call Serengeti Ndogo, stood Kinai ole Chieni. Like a bronze statue, he stood leaning on his spear on one leg, the other bent and pressed against his knee, next to a hill from which there is a magnificent view of the Maasai steppe. He was not alone. The boy next to him looked over at her very shyly. He was barely older than five and wrapped in a red cloth thrown over his shoulders. She had never seen him before. But she was aware that it was El Ngongongare, the son of Kinai ole Chieni.

 Margarete did not want to remember how she had taken this boy out of his mother's womb in an emergency operation. She found it hard to look at him now. She could not bring herself to do more than a fleeting glance out of the corner of her eye. „Kinai . . . Kinai! *Jambo*, Kinai . . .“ her children suddenly screamed at the back of the ox cart and waved at him. She wanted to smile at him too, but she couldn't.

The ox cart rattled past the two of them. Suddenly she felt the gaze of the Maasai and his son behind her. She felt their eyes following her and the children. It hurt her, tore at her soul. More than that. These looks killed something inside her.

„Mummy, where are we going?“ Ursula's question snapped her out of her despair. The ten-year-old babbled blithely, which made Margarete realise that she still hadn't understood that this trip would be a journey of no return. She had tried to explain to the elder why they had to leave Ngongongare. In vain. How could a child understand what even she as a mother did not understand to the last consequence?

„Are we going to visit grandma in Germany?“

„Yes, we're going to visit grandma.“

„When are we coming home again?“

„Home?“ muttered Margarete Trappe to herself, barely audibly. She found it very difficult not to cry. „Home? I don't know . . .“

Apathetically, she stared out at the vast Maasai steppe through which she had come here twelve years ago – on the same road. In an ox cart. But happily. Up here then, in the thick fog, the colobus monkeys had fled over her. Today there was better visibility. The sun was not shining, but she could make out the hill down in the valley where they had camped back then and where the Maasai had suddenly stood in front of them and called her „*Jeyo*“.

To the left of the path, the dense bushes were now thinning out. Between two mighty baobab trees, she squinted in the direction of Kilimanjaro. She did not dare to really look, for she was afraid that it would be the last time in her life that she would see it. But then she could not resist.

„Look,“ she tried to distract her children and pointed in the direction of the highest mountain in Africa. But the summit of Kilimandjaro was shrouded in dark clouds on this autumn day in 1919.

*

Corfu, November 15th, 1920

My dear Toute Sweet,

You know I am a very miserable letter writer. Still, I'm not particularly eager to put feelings and thoughts on paper that I don't know if I will have in a few years, and then people hold my written thoughts of yore against me.

During the last years, I sent so many letters from Greece to you and then spent months waiting for your reply. But as I never got any, I stopped writing as I felt that the letters did not reach you due to the war chaos. And I did not want to torture myself with flimsy hope anymore!

Yesterday I heard from a Greek friend who lives in Zanzibar and has good contacts with the English authorities there that you are in Germany with the children. I now sincerely hope that my letter with the few details I gave as an address will really reach you. I don't want to go on at length about everything that has happened or not happened in the last few years.

No, I don't want to, because I have been forcing myself to banish all gloomy thoughts from my life for some weeks now. I am succeeding quite well because I have hope, very concrete hope, of being able to return to Africa. Yes! Since, as a Greek, I have no problems with the new masters in East Africa, i.e., with the English, I am very sure that I will soon be able to go „home" again.

I have decided to go back to Africa. No, I will not hunt anymore! I never want to have to pick up a rifle again. At least not to shoot animals.

I just don't know if I will have the time to see all those wonderful, vast, and so magnificent landscapes of Africa again. Because strange things happen to my eyes. It is not age that makes my eyes tired. Nor was it the many terrible things I saw during the years of war. Three of my friends were killed in the war. The son of a friend lost both his arms. I think it would have been better for him to die too. He still has a very young wife, and I wonder how he will hold her in his arms and caress her, with these stumps . . .

No, all this is probably not the reason why my eyes increasingly refuse to obey me. Sometimes I wake up in the morning, and my eyes are very red, as if I had drunk too much gin (you know what I look like the next day!). I would have had reason to drink a lot, but I didn't do it in excess.

But I do worry a little about whether I can really make another long journey to all those places in East Africa that have given me such a fulfilled and beautiful life. This includes the many rivers and mountains and hills and animals that I have seen together with you. And that elephant graveyard, you know, I want to visit again. It's a really beautiful place for old elephants to die, isn't it?

Dear Toute Sweet, I really hope you get this letter and write me back very soon how you and the children are doing. I know that you had to give up your farm. Since the Germans have lost all their colonies, you will probably never be able to get your farm back. But I was wondering if I could try to buy your farm. As a Greek, that should be possible for me. That would be nice, wouldn't it?

Beloved Toute: Write back to me very quickly, will you? I will send you the address of my friend in Zanzibar. You can write to him there.

I embrace and caress you in my thoughts with all the gentleness that I am capable of with my shaky fingers, limping, and my eyes that are not so bad today.

Anthimos

*

The train journey had now lasted almost half a day. Outside the window, snowy winter landscapes flitted by. The countryside seemed oppressive on this foggy day. Nevertheless, she felt unspeakably happy. Again and again, Margarete Trappe reached for Anthimos' letter, read it, put it aside, stroked the envelope, closed her eyes, dreamed, drifted away into the past – and began to think of her future with every minute that brought her closer to Jena. She had not dared to think about the future for a long time. She had avoided thinking about the past. Her life was too dominated by the dreary present. Lost in thought, she leaned back and looked out the window of the moving train. The snow-covered birch trees and small frozen lakes united in her memories with the vastness of Africa, with the snow-covered Kilimanjaro, and with Anthimos' face to form a dream image. She could even recognise the scar on Anthimos' face. Smiling, she closed her eyes. She enjoyed this moment. It had been a long, long time since she had felt this good.

Cruel things had happened since she had left her farm more than a year ago. In Dar es Salam, where all the German settlers from East Africa had been locked up in an internment camp, she had had to wait with the children and with Tine for more than two months behind barbed wire fences for their ship to Europe. It had been the first time in her life that she thought she was going to die. A lot of things in her really died. First of all, hope.

She had had more than a dozen severe attacks of malaria in the camp. The fever, the high humidity on the coast, and the never-ending dull thoughts had worn her down so that she had weighed barely more than forty-five kilograms when a ship finally came, and they could all leave the unhealthy East African coast and the horrible internment camp.

Even though she had been afraid of what was in store for her and the children in Germany, she had been glad when the steamer had cast off and left the East African coast for the Suez Canal and from there on to Hamburg.

The train stopped in the middle of the track in front of a signal. She stood up and opened the window. Ice-cold air flowed towards her. Single snowflakes got caught in her hair. She estimated that they must be just past Chemnitz. The journey would not take more than an hour.

The anticipation of meeting the princess and the letter from Anthimos that had arrived shortly before made her euphoric. Suddenly all melancholy thoughts gave way to a wonderful lightness. Could it be that she was happy? Was that really possible? She was frightened of herself.

The day before yesterday, she had once again toyed with the thought of putting an end to her life. She had had such thoughts often in the past months. Not even thoughts of her three children had been able to curb these depressive phases. Yes, she had wanted to leave life. She was too tormented by life in the cruel confinement of her mother's flat in the Bahnhofstraße in Sagan. She suffered too much from the oppressive atmosphere in this country that had once been her home. Many people in Sagan had no work. Almost every family she knew had lost their father or a son in the war. Or their loved ones had returned from the front as cripples. Georg, the kind-hearted Georg who had wanted to marry her then, had also been killed on the Eastern Front.

Those were bad times. Everywhere. In Russia, she had heard, a devastating famine was killing hundreds of thousands of people. Tens of thousands of Volga Germans were said to have starved to death. Many of them came to Silesia as refugees, but people were suffering there too. It was a bad time for mercy. Germany was groaning under the consequences of the war – and under the incredibly high reparation payments that had been imposed on the German people at Versailles. She had read in the newspaper that Germany had to pay the unimaginable sum of two hundred and twenty-six billion gold marks to the victorious powers! But it also said that Germany could no longer make these payments due to the devaluation of money. The German currency was worth almost nothing. Many of her neighbours had long since switched to barter. The rupees she had been allowed to take with her from German East Africa were also worth nothing on the day of her arrival. She and her children had arrived poor in Sagan.

The train started up slowly. Margarete shook the snowflakes off her hair and closed the window. Her mirror image in the window made her wince. She looked pale and sick. Her hair hung straggly over her shoulders. Tine's Sunday blouse was too big for her; she had fixed it on her neck with a brooch. Her mother had borrowed her the brooch for the journey. The gilt-framed ivory miniature was an heirloom. „Take very well care of the brooch," her mother had told her, „it is extremely valuable and represents my gold reserve for bad times." She had almost burst into tears when her mother pronounced these words. Bad times! They were not to come; it was already bad times.

Outside, thick, fat flakes were now falling. The forests between Chemnitz and Jena were covered deep in snow. She dug an apple out of her handbag and bit into it. It tasted like coal. The taste of the wrinkled fruit reminded her of how her mother used to store apples in the coal cellar. And it reminded her of how, many years ago, when she was about twenty years old, she had hidden in that coal cellar for a long time on the day of Kaiser Wilhelm's birthday because she had been sad not to have a pretty dress to go to the ball at „Weißer Schwan" on Ludwigsplatz. Then, at the age of twenty-three, she had had a ball gown. It was only a borrowed one, but at least she had been able to go to the officers' ball together with Ulrich in the casino of Podbielski's 5th Regiment at Sagan. At that time, she had made the decision to marry Ulrich so that she could go to Africa. And back then, it really had been a wonderful emperor's birthday, with the torchlight procession through the city, with the magnificent military parade, with the balls at „Goldener Engel" and „Weißer Schwan". Yes, that had been a wonderful emperor's birthday. The ball gown, oh, how beautiful it had been! Now she no longer had a ball gown. She didn't even own a coat. Only a few years ago, she had dined in beautiful dresses with counts and princes on Ngongongare. Now she had none of that. And she would hardly have needed it again. For Kaiser Wilhelm II's sixty-second birthday was still only in the wistful memories of some Germans. It would have been his birthday two days ago, but there was no longer an emperor in Germany. He, who had always been so fond of saying, „One empire, one people, one God," and had long lived in the conceit, „Only one is master of the empire, I will tolerate no other," had abdicated, fled into exile in the Netherlands. Germany was now a republic. Not monarchists but socialists shaped political events.

One of those in Sagan who refused to accept this was Wilhelm Jahn. He lived in the house next door on Bahnhofstraße. The former dye shop owner and naval officer had become poor in the turmoil of the war. But he was a monarchist. The night before last, he had celebrated the emperor's birthday: alone, drunk. He had sung and bawled loudly all evening to the tune of „Heil dir im Siegerkranz":

„Herrscher im Preußenland,
Vater im Vaterland,
Voll Herrlichkeit!
Zu Gott in Himmelshöh'n
Gläubig wir aufwärts seh'n,
Herr, für Dein Wohlergeh'n
Beten wir heut.

Heil, Kaiser Wilhelm Dir!
Landes- und Meereszier
All sind wir Dein!
Dein, Herr, zu jeder Stund,
Und der Geschütze Mund
Tu es dem Weltmeer kund;
Donn're darein!"

„Ruler in Prussia,
Father in the Fatherland,
full of glory!
To God in heavenly heights
faithfully we look upwards,
Lord, for your prosperity
we pray today.

Hail, emperor William!
Land and sea ornament
we are all Thine!
Thine, Lord, at every hour,
and the cannon's mouth
make it known to the ocean;
thunder in it!"

The next morning, the police found Wilhelm Jahn. In his hopelessness, he had shot himself in the head. Strangely enough, his death

had triggered a reaction of defiance in her. Then had come the short letter from the princess and a few days later the letter from Anthimos. Suddenly the will to live awoke in her again. Yes, she wanted to live! She wanted to go to Anthimos, away from oppressive Germany – back to Africa. Back home. As quickly as possible, by any means necessary. But first, it was time to visit the princess. She hoped not to arrive too late in Jena.

*

The seventy-seven-year-old princess was not afraid of death. Full of kindness, she smiled at Margarete Trappe. „No, my dearest,“ she whispered, „it is not that I am going to die that worries me. My death was already predetermined at birth. I was brought up in this consciousness as a child at the court of my father, the venerable Sayyid Said bin Sultan of Oman and Zanzibar. No, I am not afraid of that. I am now seventy-seven years old. Whatever divine providence has predestined my existence on earth: I have been given much time.“
The old lady looked out of the window. The sun was shining, colouring the bone-chilling cold of this first day of February. It was a long time before she continued: „What worries me, my dear, is whether it will be God who calls me to Himself in kindness, or whether it will be Allah’s angry words that I will hear at my last breath.“
„You are a Christian! So are your children,“ Margarete Trappe tried to placate her friend. She did not succeed.
„As a good Muslim woman, I left Zanzibar in 1866. Out of love for a reverent Christian, I turned away from Allah. Now, as a bad Christian, I am about to die. It is a confusing feeling not knowing whose final judgement you will face.“
Emily Ruete, born Princess Sayyida Salme of Oman and Zanzibar, lived in a nice house outside Jena. The small flat she could call her own in her daughter Rosalie’s house was comfortably heated, and from the bedroom window, they both had a wonderful view of the city when they talked. For two days now, they had been sitting in

front of the flickering fireplace, talking about things they had always wanted to talk about. They had not seen each other for fourteen years, had only exchanged a few letters. But already with the first embrace on the day of her arrival, Margarete Trappe had felt again that feeling of spiritual kinship that had always connected her with the princess. She regretted only being able to stay until the next day, but she also noticed that the conversations were exhausting Emily.

Living far from her home in Zanzibar, and even more so the everlasting dream of being able to return home had left its mark on Emily. Her mind had remained young, but not her body. Her hair, still artfully parted and pinned back with a silver barrette, showed only a hint of black. Her eyes were small but full of kindness. She was not ill, not physically frail. She was just old and tired of life.

„Here, my dear," she spoke with strain, „I have made you a handwritten copy of a letter I wrote to the German emperor many years ago. Read it at your leisure some time. I think it will help you to go and find your own way. And this, this little book, I have also put aside for you. I want to give it to you. It is a wonderful book with many beautiful poems that have accompanied me through my life here in Germany and have given me a lot of comfort. It is by a woman called Annette von Droste-Hülshoff, a German poet whom I believe has been able to express both our pain, but also both our happiness, in such wonderful words as I don't think either of us will ever be able to do."

Emily Ruete reached for a book on the table beside her, leafed through it, and handed it to her friend.

„These are my favourite verses. It was the poem my husband, God rest his soul, read to me the day before he died in Hamburg."

Margarete Trappe took the leather-bound booklet and read quietly to herself:

Letzte Worte

Geliebte, wenn mein Geist geschieden,
So weint mir keine Träne nach;

Denn, wo ich weile, dort ist Frieden,
Dort leuchtet mir ein ew'ger Tag!

Wo aller Erdengram verschwunden,
Soll euer Bild mir nicht vergeh'n,
Und Linderung für eure Wunden,
Für euern Schmerz will ich erfleh'n.

Weht nächtlich seine Seraphsflügel
Der Friede übers Weltenreich,
So denkt nicht mehr an meinen Hügel,
Denn von den Sternen grüß' ich euch.

Last words

Beloved, when my spirit is parted,
Do not shed a tear for me;
For where I dwell, there is peace,
There shines an eternal day for me!

Where all earthly gramme is gone,
Your image shall not fade from my sight,
And I will invoke relief,
for your wounds, for your pain.

Nightly waves his seraphic wings
Peace over the kingdom of the world,
Think no more of my hill
For from the stars I salute you.

„It's beautiful! Anthimos would like it . . .“ Her voice trembled. She
had to take a deep breath. There it was again, that feeling that connected her to Emily. And there were also suddenly all those feelings
she had for Anthimos.

„Can you understand that I will try by any means possible to get back to Africa?"

The old lady smiled.

„Who else but me can understand it better, my dear! You love Africa. And you love this man. That is why you will have to go. Fate has taken me from Zanzibar to Germany. I followed love. Allah's punishment for that was cruel. Love for Africa led you to Kilimanjaro, where you found your true heart's love. You will, and you must return to Africa. I will be with you wherever I stay here on earth or in the realms of the Almighty. In thought and in heart. For I, too, once acted out of love. And I have never regretted it."

„But I'm afraid, Emily! Afraid that I will be too late. Anthimos has written some things in his letter that trouble me greatly. I know him as well as anyone can know him. He will never fully reveal himself. To no one! Many of his thoughts will always remain unspoken. He is like that."

„What are you afraid of?"

Margarete Trappe pulled the letter out of her handbag.

„He writes such strange things about the meaning of time! And especially about his eyes. I think he is very ill. And he knows it. And here . . ."

She flipped through the letter, skimming the pages looking for the relevant passage. Excitedly, she read aloud:

„. . . I just don't know if I will also have the time to see all these wonderful, vast and so magnificent landscapes of Africa again. Because strange things happen to my eyes . . . "

„He is getting old, dear Margarete. That's when the eyes get tired."

„Oh, if only it were! I think he has this strange disease. It's called bilharzia or something like that. I think the disease is carried by little worms or snails that live in the water in Africa, especially in still waters. It makes you go blind. Slowly, but inexorably. Anthimos took every opportunity to swim. He always ignored my warnings, saying that worms would take a very long time to eat up a Greek as handsome and tough as him. He was like that, Emily. He challenged life often. Always he took full risks. Anthimos never did anything half-heartedly.“

„You love him! That's why your fear is greater than the danger.“

„Oh, I don't know, dearest! How am I to explain it? His lines can only be interpreted if you know him; if you know how he thinks. Here, there is another such passage that worries me.“ Again, she leafed through the letter. Outside, the sun had set. The winter night settled over the land. In the room, it was almost dark. Only with difficulty could she still decipher Anthimos' handwriting. She read out:

„But I do worry a little about whether I can really make another long journey to all those places in East Africa that have given me such a fulfilled and beautiful life. This includes the many rivers and mountains and hills and animals that I have seen together with you. And that elephant graveyard, you know, I want to visit again. It's a really beautiful place for old elephants to die, isn't it?“

Margarete Trappe took a deep breath and looked questioningly at her friend.

„He means himself by that old elephant, Emily! Believe me, he's talking about himself.“

Emily Ruete took a match from the small silver pot beside the candlestick. The candlelight shrouded the room in a diffuse glow. Margarete could only discern the silhouette of her friend. Her contours stood out against the last light outside. For the first time, she saw how old Emily had become. Her facial wrinkles were as deep as the notches in the bark of old oak trees. Emily had turned her head away and was looking out of the window. The day was sinking into the snowy landscape on the horizon behind the town. The sky turned a steel blue.

Emily's breathing was heavy as she spoke with her eyes closed, „I am very tired now, my dear! Tomorrow, unfortunately, you will go back to Sagan. And you will go back to Africa. You know that. So do I. I have doubts whether we will ever see each other again. It is inevitable in both our lives that our destiny will be fulfilled somewhere between Africa and Germany. That doesn't bother me. Because in my thoughts, I am very often with you and with your dreams of love. Once, they were my dreams too".

Emily was still asleep when Margarete left the house the next morning and took a cab to the train station in Jena. The two days with the princess had made her very sad on the one hand but had also strengthened her plans. Yes, she would try everything imaginable to return to East Africa. The only question was how she could realise it. As a German citizen, she had no chance of returning to Tanganyika, the former German East Africa. She had no money, but the stories of the princess had given her an idea. A daring idea, yes, without question. But there was still a small chance.

Lost in thought, she took out the book of poems by Annette von Droste-Hülshoff and leafed through it. But she could not concentrate. The letter to the German emperor, Wilhelm I, which Emily had given her, lay folded up in the book. She opened it and skimmed the lines written in beautiful handwriting, dated June 14th, 1884. A smile flitted across her face. 1884! Two months after Emily had written the letter, she had been born. With every line she read in it, she drifted away from the present. It was a beautiful letter, so beautiful that she read individual passages silently to herself:

„. . . Your Excellency, in your characteristic kindness, may first allow me to preface the more legal, inheritance aspects of my following remarks with a few very personal lines. For just as day cannot exist without night, good cannot exist without evil, and passion cannot exist and be explained without pain, so my path of suffering cannot be understood without the knowledge of the power of love.
Love, as the wonderful yet sorrowful experience has taught me, is not an ideal, it is a longing. And it was precisely this longing that led me by the hand of my beloved from my distant homeland here to Germany and made me a subservient citizen of the German Reich and a professing Christian . . .“

Margarete Trappe swallowed with emotion. How sensitively and emotionally Emily wrote! She looked up and stared out of the window of the moving train at the Silesian forests just before Sagan. Back there, just a few kilometres away, was Petersdorf Manor, where she had been born. But Petersdorf was very far away from her. She had pushed it out of her memory. She had not been there once since her arrival in Sagan. She didn't want to sink into past dreams. She wanted to think of the future. Of Africa.

Again, she looked at the princess's letter, fixating on one word: „. . . obsessed . . .“ Are you obsessed, Margarete Trappe? What are you obsessed with? With Anthimos – or with Africa? Or both? What is it that draws you so irrepressibly away from Sagan – to Africa? Is it wise, after all you have experienced, to dream of Africa again now? Emily's dreams of returning to her homeland Zanzibar had been caught in the mills of world political turmoil – and crushed. She, too, had experienced something similar. What had Anthimos always said? „When elephants fight, it is the grass beneath them that suffers.“

But the war was over now. Anthimos would go back to Africa. And the princess had also encouraged her to do it: „Dearest friend, go – return to the Kilimanjaro!“ she had said the night before her return journey. But she had also added: „. . . when Africa's gods give you a smile, never forget that these Gods love to play with white souls.“

Afterword by the author

Originally, I wanted to present the melodramatic life story of Margarete Trappe, based on true events, as a documentary, i.e., as a non-fiction book. Out of consideration for still-living descendants, I finally wrote a novel biography, which became a bestseller in hardcover and paperback and was also sold very successfully through book clubs with partly different covers.

The German TV channel ZDF filmed the life story of Margarete Trappe as the two-part historical drama „Momella – Eine Farm in Afrika", starring Christine Neubauer, Horst Janson, and Frank Behnke. I was engaged as a consultant for the several months of filming in present-day Tanzania. The film is available on DVD.

For publishing reasons, it was not possible for me to write down the entire life story of Margarete Trappe. However, by popular request, I will outline the further course of „Jeyo's" life in the following. For „The White Huntress" returned to Africa. But her dream of living on her farm on Kilimanjaro ended dramatically.

Martha Margarete Trappe leaves Germany in 1922 together with her husband Ulrich, who had been released from internment in the meantime, and took up a position as farm manager on Woolsey Estate in South Africa at the invitation of the later Senator Malcomess. Her children stay with relatives in Sagan (Silesia) for safety reasons or to avoid further hardship. In order to be able to return to East Africa, she applies for English citizenship in South Africa, which is granted to her in 1924, after barely three years of exile. In 1927, she returns to East Africa with her husband Ulrich, who refuses to accept English citizenship.

Emily Ruete, born Princess Sayyida Salme of Oman and Zanzibar, dies in Jena on February 29th, 1924. A year earlier, the government of Zanzibar had granted her an annual pension of one hundred English pounds for the rest of her life – without recognising her hereditary claims to the Sultan of Zanzibar. She is buried in the family tomb at the Ohlsdorf cemetery in Hamburg. A handful of sand from Zanzibar, which she had taken with her when she fled her homeland, is placed in her urn. On her gravestone is written: „He is faithful in a deep sense who loves his homeland as you do." The Sultan's Palace in Zanzibar, where the princess grew up, the „House of Wonders", although declared a UNESCO World Heritage Site, is threatened by decay. A reconstructed room in the palace museum commemorates the princess. Very interesting information and pictures about this impressive woman can be found on the internet. The DVD documentary by Tinka Diaz, „The Princess of Zanzibar", is worth seeing.

Ngongongare, the Trappes' farm, is meanwhile bought by the English General Boyd Moss. Momella, the second farm of the Trappe family, is bought by the Greek Michael M. With their very last reserves, Margarete and Ulrich Trappe buy back Momella, but can only make a down payment.

The natives living in the Ruaha River region tell that in late summer 1924, a white man was seen entering the swamps but never returned. Since then, it is said, the „Lord of the Dead Elephants", as Anthimos was called, has watched over the ivory lying in the swamps there. No one has yet been able to recover the „White Gold of Africa". The grandson of Margarete Trappe's Greek lover still lives in Dar es Salam and owns one of Tanzania's most renowned big game hunting companies.

In 1927 Margarete Trappe gives birth to her fourth child, Rosi, in East Africa. When her daughter is born, several elephants stand around the newly built farmhouse for days. With the child's first cry, the elephants trumpet loudly. On this day, Margarete Trappe decides never to hunt elephants on her farm again. In the following years, several severe attacks of malaria cause Margarete Trappe to fall seriously ill and almost go blind. In 1928, she travels to Germany with her husband Ulrich, where they divorce in Sagan.

With a compensation payment of one hundred and fifteen thousand Reichsmark from the German Reich for her possessions in Africa lost after the First World War, Margarete Trappe returns to East Africa once again. Her excellent reputation as Africa's only white professional huntress again brings renowned and aristocratic hunting guests to her in Momella over the next few years. Among them is Prince Hubertus of Prussia, grandson of the exiled German emperor Wilhelm II. As early as 1934, Margarete Trappe is once again insolvent. She founds – unsuccessfully – a haulage company and digs for gold. With the rise of National Socialism in Germany, Margarete Trappe, being German by birth, is met with much suspicion by her English neighbours and friends in Tanganyika. The German farmers, in turn, shun her because she has an English passport. She is exposed to the harassment of the English authorities and is lonely.

With the outbreak of the Second World War, Margarete Trappe realises that accepting English citizenship – the only way for her to return to her farm in East Africa – was one of the most tragic mistakes of her life. Ruined once again and almost on her own, she begins to rebuild the farm. Supported by her ever-loyal African friends and farmworkers through the ages, she struggles for bare survival in Momella. Badly battered by the dramatic events, the once fun-loving, rigorous, and self-confident huntress becomes a quiet, peaceful nature and animal conservationist who refuses to ever shoot animals again.

On October 29th, 1940, Margarete Trappe is once again dispossessed and temporarily taken to an English internment camp. The turmoil of the Second World War tears her family apart. At the end of the war, she is expelled from the English mandate territory of Tanganyika on November 20th, 1946. She succeeds in reversing the expulsion. When she returns to her farm, all the cattle and goats have died of an animal disease. She is ruined again and ekes out a living by organising photo safaris.

In autumn 1956, the British Princess Margret, sister of the British Queen, visits Tanganyika. The absurd situation arises that the English princess is to award a British medal to all those African farmworkers who have worked for an English farm owner for more than thirty years. Margarete Trappe, a German by birth with an English passport, appears at this ceremony in Moschi with five Africans who have stood by her side as faithful and loyal workers and friends for more than thirty years.

On June 5th, 1957, Margarete Trappe, the „huntress who only learned to fear people", dies impoverished and lonely on her farm Momella. Already three days before her death, a herd of elephants moves onto the farm and stays there – a few steps away from her dying room. When Margarete Trappe fades away, the herd moves into the forest. The tribes living at Meru have since said that the Greek Anthimos, the deceased „Lord of the Dead Elephants", had sent these elephants to Margarete Trappe's farm to escort the soul of his beloved to the realm of eternalise peace – to him. Margarete Trappe is buried on Ngongongare, near her first small house in Africa. Gut Petersdorf near Sagan in Silesia, where she was born, is now abandoned to decay. The cemetery near the estate was flattened by Russian soldiers with tanks during the Second World War in order to „destroy everything German".

The heirs of Momella

Rolf Trappe takes over the Momella farm after his mother dies. But for him, too, the dream of an African paradise turns into a nightmare. Permanently insolvent, he is forced to pawn the farm. His attempt to capitalise on his mother's legendary reputation initially proves to be a clever move. In 1960, the American film company Paramount selects the Trappes' Momella farm as the base camp and filming location for the movie „Hatari". Through John Wayne, Elsa Martinelli, and Hardy Krüger, the Trappe farm becomes world-famous within a short time.

During the filming, the Prime Minister and later President, Julius Nyerere, comes to the farm. In a conversation with the German actor Hardy Krüger, he encourages him to use his world fame as an actor to „contribute to the building of an independent Tanganyika".

On March 4th, 1961, Rolf Trappe, Hardy Krüger, and Jim Mallory sign a contract providing for the future use of the „Momella Game Lodge" as a tourist domicile on the Kilimanjaro.

On December 9th, 1961, Tanganyika becomes independent. The following year, the people elect Julius Nyerere as their first president. Rolf Trappe and Hardy Krüger thus have an influential ally for their ambitious goals of a tourist paradise in East Africa. On November 19th, 1961, Momella is ceremoniously opened in the presence of distinguished guests from all over the world.

After a period of euphoria and a phase in which Momella becomes a world-famous African meeting place for the international jet set (the German film company Rialto shot the film „Unser Haus in Kamerun" here), Margarete Trappe's „African paradise" is caught up in its dark past. Rolf Trappe leaves the company because of money problems in a dispute with Hardy Krüger. Financial turbulence and legal disputes follow. German financiers bring about a short-term revival of the lodge. In the meantime, Hardy Krüger plans to supply all the hotels in East Africa with meat, milk, and cheese in the future by building huge freezers and large slaughterhouses. The plan fails with great financial losses.

In the sixties, the signs point to storm and change. The Tanzanian town of Ngare Nanyuki, where the men of *Ujamaa Kali* once planned resistance against German foreign rule and which was later razed to the ground by British troops as a „resistance nest" against the new white (British) colonial masters, develops into an ideological centre of the Tanzanian independence movement. A new black African elite, including the first Tanzanian president, Julius Nyerere, and many former missionary students of English and German colonial masters, lead the African states to independence. In Kenya, the Mau Mau fight against white settlers. In Tanzania, the first tendencies towards an „African socialism" become visible.

Rolf Trappe and his family, described by Hardy Krüger as the „Buddenbrooks of Africa", are more or less expropriated by the socialist government of Tanzania. Their land on Meru is declared a national park and, according to Hardy Krüger, „. . . sixty-three years after Margarete Trappe's arrival in East Africa, it again belongs to the elephants once and for all".

Margarete Trappe's small farmhouse on Ngongongare is still preserved and serves as a guest house for the Tanzanian national park authorities. The nearby three graves of Margarete Trappe, her son Rolf (deceased 1984), and her daughter Ursula (deceased 1999) are still there. Today, a lodge for tourist use stands on the Trappe family's farm Momella.

Halinka Trappe, Rolf's widow and thus Margarete Trappe's daughter-in-law, who was driven out of Poland under dramatic circumstances during the Second World War, once said to me in Arusha:

„Once I was a lady, now I am a beggar. My dreams of a life in the Garden of Eden Africa have become nightmares. Just like my mother-in-law Margarete's too . . .“ Halinka died on Christmas 2004.

About the author

Rolf Ackermann was born in Duisburg, Germany, on January 24th, 1952.

As a former undercover agent (employed as a civil servant) of the German intelligence service, specialized in international terrorism, he got deep insights into a world that remains closed to most of the people.

He published features and reports at nearly all renowned German newspapers (school radio), audio dramas at the German TV-station WDR, and books, especially historical novels at very prestigious publishing companies, as well in his name as under the pseudonym Manfred Morstein.

Rolf Ackermann is said to be an Africa expert and reported, especially from war and crisis regions. He lived ten years in Kenia and eight years in Namibia. His long-time stay in East Africa inspired him for his biographic novel „Die weiße Jägerin" (new title „Die weiße Jägerin von Afrika"). It is the story of the young German Margarete Trappe, who lived her dream of a farm in Africa in the last century. The German TV-station ZDF presented the extraordinary life story of this impressing woman as a docudrama in two parts „Momella – Eine Farm in Afrika". Rolf Ackermann was bound as a consultant for the production.

In 2007, he founded San Foundation, a private help organisation for KhoiSan („bushmen").

In 2016, he was chosen as „town clerk" in Otterndorf, a town in the North of Germany.

He died on July 15th, 2016 after a short but serious illness.

Paperbacks published by Belletris-Verlag:

The White Huntress of Africa
Rolf Ackermann
ISBN: 978-3-940808-24-0

Die weiße Jägerin von Afrika
Rolf Ackermann
ISBN: 978-3-940808-18-9

Das Sion-Dossier
Rolf Ackermann
ISBN: 978-3-940808-19-6

Engelsfeuer
Heinz Körner
ISBN: 978-3-940808-02-8

Kontakt-Auf-Name
Kristina Löffler
ISBN: 978-3-940808-04-2

Seraphine – Traum vom Licht
Marie Graßhoff
ISBN: 978-3-940808-07-3

Seraphine – Kristalle der Sonne
Marie Graßhoff
ISBN: 978-3-940808-10-3

Seraphine – Schatten des Glücks
Marie Graßhoff
ISBN: 978-3-940808-14-1

Ohne Umweg
Ursula Dossier
ISBN: 978-3-940808-03-5

Weiß steht mir gut
Ursula Dossier
ISBN: 978-3-940808-09-7

Unter dem Mantel des Schweigens
Luise Winrich
ISBN: 978-3-940808-13-4

Illegale Drogen
Mike Gawen
ISBN: 978-3-940808-08-0

Illegale Drogen bald legal?
Mike Gawen
ISBN: 978-3-940808-15-8

Niemandsland – Bis zur Selbstaufgabe
Tamara Pirschalawa
ISBN: 978-3-940808-21-9

No-man's-land – Right up to the surrender of identity
Tamara Pirschalawa
ISBN: 978-3-940808-17-2

Dark Side Of The Moon – Eine Jugend in Frankfurt
Tamara Pirschalawa
ISBN: 978-3-940808-11-0

Traumfänger – Die Vision des Julius Balthasar
Tamara Pirschalawa
ISBN: 978-3-940808-22-6

Eltern & Kind GmbH
Tamara Pirschalawa
ISBN: 978-3-940808-16-5

Gesichter der Gewalt
By various authors
ISBN: 978-3-940808-20-2

Hunderterblatt
Karl Pirschalawa
ISBN: 978-3-940808-23-3

Paperbacks published as e-books:

Gesichter der Gewalt
By various authors

Engelsfeuer
Heinz Körner

Kontakt-Auf-Name
Kristina Löffler

Unter dem Mantel des Schweigens
Luise Winrich

Niemandsland – Bis zur Selbstaufgabe
Tamara Pirschalawa

No-man's-land – Right up to the surrender of identity
Tamara Pirschalawa

Dark Side Of The Moon – Eine Jugend in Frankfurt
Tamara Pirschalawa

Traumfänger – Die Vision des Julius Balthasar
Tamara Pirschalawa

Eltern & Kind GmbH
Tamara Pirschalawa

Further E-Books:

Hunderterblatt
Karl Pirschalawa

Traumfell (From „Gesichter der Gewalt")
Heinz Körner and Alexandra Böhm

Der Graugetigerte (From „Gesichter der Gewalt")
Tamara Pirschalawa

Zwei Welten (From „Gesichter der Gewalt")
Tamara Pirschalawa

In einem anderen Land (From „Traumfänger")
Tamara Pirschalawa